# HEART OF SHERWOOD

## EDALE LANE

PAST AND PROLOGUE PRESS

## CONTENTS

| | |
|---|---|
| *Preface* | v |
| Chapter 1 | 1 |
| Chapter 2 | 10 |
| Chapter 3 | 25 |
| Chapter 4 | 38 |
| Chapter 5 | 48 |
| Chapter 6 | 59 |
| Chapter 7 | 69 |
| Chapter 8 | 84 |
| Chapter 9 | 95 |
| Chapter 10 | 107 |
| Chapter 11 | 117 |
| Chapter 12 | 130 |
| Chapter 13 | 140 |
| Chapter 14 | 150 |
| Chapter 15 | 163 |
| Chapter 16 | 174 |
| Chapter 17 | 185 |
| Chapter 18 | 192 |
| Chapter 19 | 201 |
| Chapter 20 | 218 |
| Chapter 21 | 233 |
| Chapter 22 | 244 |
| Chapter 23 | 260 |
| Chapter 24 | 270 |
| *Author's Notes* | 287 |
| *About the Author* | 291 |

Heart of Sherwood

By Edale Lane

Published by Past and Prologue Press

All rights reserved. No part of this book may be used or reproduced in any manner without written permission of the publisher, except for the purpose of reviews.

Edited by Nicole Field

Cover designed by Natasha Snow

This book is a work of fiction and all names, characters, places, and incidents are fictional or used fictitiously. Any resemblance to actual people, places, or events is coincidental.

Second Edition July 2019

Copyright © 2018 by Edale Lane

Printed in the United States of America

❦ Created with Vellum

# PREFACE

First and foremost I wish to thank my incomparable partner, Johanna White, for her help and encouragement in completing this novel. She devoted much time and effort to proof-reading and double-checking my research as well as making sure I did not give up before finishing.

Next I want to acknowledge my friend and horror writer Alexander Brown for inspiring me to start writing again after a ten year hiatus. Not only that, but he played an essential role in getting some of my short stories placed with publishers. Cheers to Alex!

Another important mention goes to my book club friends, the Ladies that Read of Vicksburg, Mississippi, and our leader Karen Nelson Sanders who has been faithful as a beta reader of all my recent manuscripts, ready with thoughtful comments, questions, and suggestions. It is very nice to have such a positive support group in my home town.

I am immeasurably grateful to Samantha Derr and the professional and gracious staff of Less Than Three Press for not only giving me a chance, but for believing in me and the quality of my writing. In conclusion, I must thank you the reader for likewise giving me a chance; may I never cease to bring you fresh, thought-provoking literary entertainment!

"Never doubt that a small group of thoughtful, committed citizens can change the world; indeed, it's the only thing that ever has."

~Margaret Mead

## CHAPTER 1

*Sherwood Forest, Nottinghamshire, July 1193*

Brown leather boots trod softly on the dirt path beneath a canopy of oaks and birches, skirted by verdant shrubs and lush ferns that overlaid the forest floor. A covey of quail were disturbed and scurried off cooing nervously to each other.

Dusky gray woolen trousers brushed the boots of the figure draped in a dark green cloak. The hood was pulled up around the sojourner's face while a bow and full quiver hung across the back and a short sword dangled in its sheath from a leather belt fastened around a rust-brown doublet. The cream sleeves of a linen tunic were also visible, but the tall, lean traveler's face remained hidden.

Sherwood Forest itself was timeless, a mix of primeval vegetation and fresh, new growth, inhabited by a myriad of animal life. It was a place of wonder, adventure, and danger. Rumors abounded of bandits that hid out in the woods as well as mystical tales of spirits and sprites. As with all the great forests of England, Sherwood was technically owned by the crown which with King Richard away meant his younger brother, Prince John Lackland. Those caught poaching in the forest faced severe penalties at the hands of Godfrey Giffard, the current Sheriff of Nottingham who, having found favor with the Prince, had power over the shire. However, the magnificence of nature that wove the forest together, leaf and vine, hart and fowl, had no inkling that their existence was merely for royal pleasure. They continued to thrive as if kings and princes were of no more consequence than a dung beetle.

The new human interloper was no stranger to Sherwood. Each step took Robyn farther from the home of her birth and further into the unknown. Her emotions churned like the North Sea in a violent storm, flowing into anger, then ebbing into grief. Nothing was as it should be and, for the first time in her life, she felt totally powerless. She did not care for that feeling. She was so immersed in her own thoughts she did not notice the mountain of a man who stood in the middle of the narrow bridge until she was almost atop him. She halted abruptly and stared up at him with curious chestnut eyes, careful that the hood concealed her face.

"Ah, a hearty traveler," he greeted jovially in a booming baritone voice, gripping a staff the breadth of a small tree in his left hand. Standing erect, he towered over her–despite her being a tall woman–with a frowzy tree-bark beard, tousled shoulder length dusky hair, deep-set hazel eyes, shoulders as broad as a door frame, and arms as thick as Yule logs. "I must ask that you pay the toll."

Robyn narrowed her eyes, contemplating the colossal older fellow. "What toll do you mean, sir?" Her voice was naturally deep and somewhat ambiguous to gender, but she altered her accent to sound more common and less high-bred. She knew he could not make out her features beyond the lack of a beard on her jaw because of the hood she wore. That and the men's clothing she donned would give the first impression of her being a young man. "Last I heard, this was a public road."

"Ah, well, yes, you see," he began, relaxing his stance, a glint of humor in his broad face. "It seems Prince John is taxing everyone nowadays. And, while I admit the tax I charge will not be adding to His Highness's coffers, it will help me and mine to have a better meal or two. So, out with it, lad. Let me see your coin."

Under different circumstances, Robyn may have been amused or felt compelled to donate to the unfortunate bandit, but he had caught her in a foul mood and quite lacking in resources. "I am sorry to disappoint, oh mighty man of the bridge, but I have nothing to donate to your supper. So if you will kindly step aside, I have places to be."

He bellowed a roaring laugh and declared, "What an impudent little insect! I must teach you a lesson. Have you a staff?"

Robyn held out her arms, dropping a bag filled with belongings she had hurriedly packed. "You can see I do not. While I do have bow and sword, I prefer not to kill anyone today."

The bridge master, clearly feeling not the least bit threatened, replied. "I see you are a man of honor who deserves a fair fight." He stepped away to pick up a more averaged size staff from the other side of the stream. Robyn removed her bow and quiver to achieve a better range of motion, but kept her hood up. "Here you go!" He tossed the wooden rod in Robyn's direction and she caught it. "First one in the drink loses."

She let her hands become accustomed to the feel of the staff, balanced it, spun it a few times, and then settled on a grip style. She gave him a satisfied nod, putting her shoulders back confidently.

"You have grit, lad–I like that." He held his staff in a relaxed stance and motioned for the traveler to attack first. Robyn opened with a standard thrust that her father had taught her to test the giant's mettle. He moved with remarkable speed for someone his size, handily blocking the move and taking a swing of his own.

She blocked his blow, but its power sent shock waves through her hands and arms. She had spared with her brother before, but he had struck with far less force than this Herculean adversary. Robyn took a step back to re-evaluate. Why hadn't she chosen a different approach to this problem? She could have given him the money, or simply shot him with her bow. She could have lowered her hood and revealed her identity, believing he may let a lady pass. But no. She'd thought she could play his game. Now she wasn't so certain.

Robyn adjusted her stance, feet shoulder width apart with her weight on her back foot. She feigned high and struck low giving him a good rap on the shin.

"Oi!" the burly man exclaimed in surprise. "The insect can bite."

He swung out at her chest high, but she hastily ducked and sent another jab, this time to his knee. Next he swiped at her low. Being light on her feet, she jumped the rod landing nimbly. They continued to knock their staffs together until, under a powerful blow, Robyn's snapped in two.

She looked first at the severed pieces in her hands then up at her opponent. This could not be good... or could it? Two weapons, meant she could block with one while attacking with the other. She pursued this strategy, spinning and jumping to avoid any possible bone-breaking blows while bruising his shins and forearms with her lighter strikes. He was bigger than her, but she was faster. Seeing him loom to one side, she took advantage, crouching to sweep his feet out from under him with both pieces of broken staff in unison.

His weight shook the wooden bridge when he fell. Utterly dumbfounded by this scrawny lad, he toppled over the edge through three feet of air to land with a splash in two feet of clear running stream.

Robyn bent over the side, her hands on her knees breathing heavily and asked, "Are you harmed?" The summer day was warm and the water was likely refreshing, so she wasn't overly concerned.

He sat up, spitting water and wiped a broad hand down his face, then peered up at her with rounded eyes. "What the blazes! How did you… who are…?" Then, if possible, his astonishment grew as he looked at her and really seemed to see her for the first time. "I know you–you're Lady Loxley! What the devil are you doing out here in the forest alone?"

Robyn had not noticed that in the course of the fight her hood had fallen down after all. Without it, her flowing acorn brown hair and feminine countenance were revealed. She quickly threw the hood back over her head and began to run from him.

"Wait!" he called after her. "I know your father; I am a friend, John Naylor."

Robyn skidded to a sudden halt and hesitated.

"My friends call me Little John," he added, though he still didn't advance on her.

She knew that name from her childhood. Lord knew she could use a friend, but was it safe to expose herself when the sheriff had ordered her arrest? With some misgivings, she slowly turned to face the wet man.

John stepped out of the brook leaning on his staff with the effort. "Milady, please forgive an old fool; I didn't know 'twas you."

Her head down and covered she quietly replied, "I am no longer the Lady of Loxley. I am merely Robyn."

"Nonsense," he said and motioned to a fallen tree trunk near the road. "Come, sit. Tell Little John what the problem is; perchance I can help."

The adrenaline from the fight had evaporated, and all that flowed through Robyn's veins was cold reality. She sat beside Little John on the log and lowered her hood. After a moment of silence, she raised misty eyes to his gentle, rough-hewn face.

"I recently received word that my father and brother Thomas, were killed fighting in the Holy Land. As proof, my father's sword was returned to me." She laid a hand on the sheath at her side and glanced down at it.

"Oh no," he uttered in honest sorrow. "Dear, sweet Maid Robyn." Despite being wet, unkempt, and having just tried to knock her upside the head with a tremendous quarterstaff, Little John wrapped a compassionate arm around her shoulders. He drew her to his strong chest like she was his own long, lost child. "This is grave news indeed. Please know I admired Lord Loxley, and that I feel your loss."

Regardless of all previously shed tears, Robyn felt the lump in her throat, the knot in her stomach, and the warm, moist trickle on her cheeks. She was almost glad of his next question, and the opportunity to change the subject.

"But, why are you alone in Sherwood dressed as a boy?"

She sniffled, wiped her eyes with the back of her sleeve and raised a defiant face that smoldered with barely bridled rage, the bite of which sounded in her voice. "The Sheriff of Nottingham paid me a visit no sooner than the envoy had left the manor. He claimed he was there to pay his condolences, and to see that I was well taken care of. You may know my mother and younger siblings died eight years ago from the pox and so now I am all alone. But then the law does not allow for a daughter to inherit her father's estate. Subsequently the Sheriff offered a 'solution' to my problem: according to the law, I could still inherit the land and title if I married. But with so few young lords available, who was possibly eligible enough to wed a woman of my station?"

John shook his head with a snort. "Let me guess."

"Right. Nottingham said he would be most agreeable to marry me and take over Loxley Manor–as if I could ever abide such a thing!" Robyn reverberated with fury. "When I told him I'd rather wed a donkey, he didn't take it so well. The next thing I know he has declared me a traitor to the crown and all my title and lands forfeit." She sighed, trying to release that wave of anger. "He was determined to have Loxley with or without me; so it was without me. The problem is, I am now wanted for treason. There is no way I will be judged fairly with Prince John's friend Giffard as my accuser." She lowered her head to the big man's shoulder releasing some of her tension. "I thought I'd run away, hide my identity, and maybe somehow I'd get by with it. 'Tis only my first day away from home, but already I am found out."

"Now there, do not fret child; Little John won't tell anyone. I'll protect you; in fact..." He made a dramatic pause, his vocal inflection rising to an optimistic tone. "I have an idea."

Robyn lifted her head, her eyes gazing up at him with suddenly renewed hope.

"You see, the Sheriff declared me an outlaw, too, and put a price on my head all because I tried to make sure there was enough food to feed my family. They are still safe on the FitzWalter lands, but all because I wouldn't give him and his damnable tax collectors every penny and bag of flour–" He stopped, shook his head and gave her shoulder a pat. "Well anyway, there's a small gang of us who have taken up residence in Sherwood. You could stay with us, at least until you figure out something that would better suit you."

Excitement flashed across her fair face. But she couldn't afford to get too excited. Not yet. "You must give me your oath." She straightened up, her enigmatic eyes pinning his with demand. "I want no one else to know who I am."

He looked puzzled and absently stroked his beard. "I don't understand. These boys would show you respect. If they didn't, I'd crack their heads."

"That isn't it. I'm not afraid of being assaulted; but I fear that anyone who aids me could face a hangman's noose. It is safer for everyone if they think I am a random boy who ran away from Sir Guy of Gisborne's cruelty or was spotted stealing bread or something. Please, if you honor my father as you say you do, keep my secret."

Little John exhaled with a nod. "Aye, sweet lass, if you are sure that's what you want; I'll do it for Lord Loxley, and for you."

\* \* \*

LITTLE JOHN HELPED PASS the time as they strolled along the dirt road by telling all about the forest and the band of men who had gathered around him.

"Deep in the heart of Sherwood," he said in his best story-telling voice, "stands the oldest tree in all of England. Huge, it is, an oak with branches reaching as far as you can see. That is where our camp is set, snug under her protection. We call her Grandma. 'Tis nothing but a tent village, but it's home - close enough to the stream for getting fresh water and far enough away to not flood when the rains come hard."

Robyn tried to listen, but stray thoughts continued to shoot into her mind like needling arrows, preoccupying her with memories and imaginings of what might have been if her father and Thomas had returned from the crusade and if the pox hadn't taken her mother and younger siblings.

"We are almost there now," she heard Little John say and giving her hood one more tug. She stood a bit straighter. "Good afternoon, fellows," he called.

Robyn smelled the smoke of the campfire and something that could have been rabbit stew coming from a large iron pot. Some of the men sat around the fire chatting and shooting dice while a few others meandered up to the group wearing curious expressions. They ranged in age from younger than herself to older than John Naylor, and they were all dirty and smelled of male sweat.

"Who's the whelp?" asked the eldest as he squinted up at them without rising.

"My friends, may I present a newcomer to our number. This is Robyn..." His face went blank as he stared out over his outlaw gang. He then glanced over at Robyn and thought quickly. "Hood. This is Robin Hood, of Nottinghamshire who, like all our present company, was unjustly outlawed by the Sheriff. Now he's a wee bit young and a little shy, so let's not all overwhelm him at once with questions, but I would like you to introduce yourselves. He's going to be staying with us a while. Alan?" He gestured toward a cheerful chap who stood about Robyn's height and held a mandolin in one hand. "Why don't you start?"

"Pleased to make your acquaintance," he chimed in a lyrical tone. "Alan A Dale at your service." He gave an elaborate bow that caused some of the others to chuckle. His sandy hair was short and choppy, and he had a wispy mustache and goatee, ruddy cheeks, and luminous forest green eyes that danced with laughter.

"Alan is a minstrel," Little John added for him. "Quite a skilled entertainer."

"Sadly, the Sheriff did not agree," Alan said. "He took a sudden and violent dislike to a song he overheard me performing." The others laughed, looking at each other as though they shared the inside story. "Would you care to hear it?"

"Another time, Alan," Little John replied waving him down. Beside the fun-loving Alan sat an even younger lad, this one in a red silk shirt with no beard at all and a sweep of black hair above intense indigo eyes like the depths of the sea in the midst of a tempest.

"I'm Will Scarlet," he offered in a friendly voice. "I promise not to pick your pocket if you'll return the favor." He crossed his heart in humorous gesture but the laughter never reached his eyes.

"Young Will here may look unassuming," Alan added with a jab to his friend's ribs, "but he is a dangerous fellow to cross."

"As skilled with a sword as he may be, that fat Friar in the back can fence circles around him," the eldest of the men added throwing a nod behind him.

"Who are you calling fat?" boomed a powerful voice. A middle aged man with his dusty brown hair ringed in a tonsure, wearing umber robes, turned with a mug of wine in one pudgy hand. His round cheeks were rosy beneath deep-set gray eyes. "Friar Tuck, lad, and I'll tell you this for free: keeping this bunch on the road to the Pearly Gates is a full time endeavor!" The clergyman was clean shaven, and did not appear to have missed many meals.

From beneath the shadow of her hood, Robyn spoke for the first time. "Why is a good friar outcast with thieves and knaves?"

"Because he is a good friar, boy," answered the same older man. He was thin as a twig with a protruding Adam's apple and scraggly gray whiskers. "I'm Gilbert Whitehand," he said with crotchety cantankerousness, "and Friar Tuck here is the finest swordsman in all of England. Why, he could beat that bloody Sheriff of Nottingham with one hand tied behind his back!"

"Oh, good sir, your words are too kind," Tuck answered with a laugh and gulped down his wine. After a proper burp, he continued. "Well, what was I to do? The soldiers accompanying Prince John's tax collectors were brutalizing my parishioners. Was I to just stand by and do nothing? I say there is a time for prayer and a time for action!" He raised his double chin and gave an approving nod.

"Unfortunately, he killed a few of those soldiers, which put him on the Sheriff's most wanted list, man of the cloth or not," Little John concluded.

"Gilbert Whitehand," Robyn mused admiringly. "I know that name. You are one of King Richard's men at arms."

"Yes, well, ancient history now," he said dismissively. "There seems to be no place for a knight loyal to Richard so long as he remains captive across the sea."

Friar Tuck took a step closer to the old man. "My friend Gilbert here came to my defense, spoke out against the Sheriff, and was rewarded for his years of service, and his valor in the Holy Land, by being thrown off his estate; his lands and title confiscated."

"Sounds familiar," Robyn muttered.

"What's that lad?" Gilbert asked. "Speak up." Then he tilted his head. "And how does a peasant boy know the members of King Richard's personal guard?"

Robyn shifted her weight thinking quickly. "I said the Sheriff is the real traitor to the crown. And you may be surprised at what a poor lad such as myself may know."

Little John looked out at them and threw a thumb at Robyn. "As much as I hate to admit this, young Robin is here because he knocked me off the bridge."

At Little John's words, the camp froze in place, not even a breath taken. All eyes turned incredulously to the beardless youth in the cloak and hood standing beside the best quarterstaff fighter in the shire.

Feeling more at ease, Robyn rattled off the names so far. "Good day to you Alan A Dale, Will Scarlet, Friar Tuck, and Gilbert Whitehand. Now for the rest of you before I lose my wits from smelling that rabbit stew!"

They all laughed, delighted, and continued the introductions. There was Much the Miller's son, who was a short man in his mid-thirties with curly honey hair and beard. David of Doncaster, the youngest, with long black hair covering the scars where the Sheriff had his ear cut off for stealing a loaf of bread, and Arthur Bland, a sturdy, ruddy fellow wanted for poaching deer in the forest. To her great relief, the rotund Tuck graciously handed her a bowl of stew and invited her to join them. Together, they were nine merry men. With Robyn, they were ten.

That night in the safety of the outlaw camp, Robyn pondered her situation. Nottingham might be sheriff of the shire, but he was not all powerful. He was under Prince John. But John was only a prince. Who really held the power?

# CHAPTER 2

*Windsor Castle, July 1193*

A few hours after sunup on the morning before St. Mary Magdalene's Feast Day, an unlikely rider on a gorgeous dapple gray palfrey returned to the stables inside King's Gate at Windsor. A scrappy stable hand jogged up to secure the horse and offered a hand to the equestrian. "Did you have a good ride, Your Highness?"

"Very refreshing!" sounded a robust, energetic female voice. The seventy-one year-old Eleanor, Duchess of Aquitaine, Countess of Poitou, Duchess of Normandy, Countess of Anjou and the Queen Mother of England was the most phenomenal woman of her time. As her riding boots touched the ground, her escort caught up.

Statuesque with a commanding air and still strikingly beautiful even in her golden years, Eleanor stood taller than the stable hand and a fair number of the nobles at court. With a gloved hand, she removed her riding bonnet to reveal shimmering silver hair with enough red left in the strands to hint at the fire they once held.

She handed the young man the reins, her intelligent dark eyes evaluating him even as she said, "I want you to rub down her legs with liniment oil; she felt a bit stiff this morning."

"Yes, Your Grace," he said with a bow and led the horse into the stables while the men at arms dismounted.

An ordinary looking, though weary, man in uniform approached the

Queen Mother. "Your Highness, why is it that you constantly make it so difficult for us to keep up with you? A guard should ride before you to make certs the path is safe."

She raised her chin and met his eyes, giving him an amused smile. "I have found it advantageous in my lifetime to always take the lead. But you are always welcome to try." She winked flirtatious at the man more than half her age and began a deliberate march toward the castle kitchens.

Two scullery maids with their hair tucked up under white caps were on the kitchen's back porch scrubbing pots when they saw her approaching dressed in her riding attire.

The younger of the maids commented to the other, "Don't you think the Queen is too old to be out riding? She could have a fall and be done for."

"Shhhhh," shushed the matronly, plumper maid. "Are you daft? Let her hear you suggest such a thing and you'll be on chamber pot duty for a month. No one tells Eleanor of Aquitaine that she is too old for anything!" She immediately lowered her head, stopped scrubbing and curtsied. "Good morrow, Your Highness."

"Good morrow, Your Highness," parroted the younger maid with a curtsey.

"It is a good morning!" Eleanor declared. "I shall be down to break my fast shortly. Is Mistress Baker about? I wish to discuss the menu for tomorrow's feast with her."

"I saw her in the pantry just a moment ago, Your Grace," the older maid replied.

"Thank you," Eleanor returned courteously. Then glancing at the younger maid's pot she pointed out, "You missed a spot," before striding through the door.

*** 

AFTER SEEKING her head cook and thoroughly instructing her on the menu, Eleanor, accompanied by two ladies-in-waiting, retired to her chamber in the royal residences of the castle on the north side of the Upper Ward to change into her day gown for breakfast. Once she was satisfied that her deep red gown with gold trim and flowing sleeves was properly arranged, she dismissed the girls and marched two doors down the passage to her son's room. The high oak door being closed, she knocked vigorously then waited for a count of five before turning the knob and throwing it open.

A disheveled, sleepy eyed man with strawberry blonde hair and beard sat up in annoyance until he saw the intimidating figure of his mother in the doorway. Two young women, one with long raven hair and the other in straw blonde curls, peeped up from the sheets on either side of him.

John's expression turned to an embarrassed scowl. "Mother, what cause have you to enter my private rooms?"

"Private?" she inquired raising an eyebrow. "It doesn't look very private to me. Really, John, it is clear you have no shame, but have you no discretion either?"

"Whatever you want of me, can it not wait until noon?" he moaned.

Eleanor lost patience with him. "No," she curtly retorted.

He motioned for the two young ladies to leave, and each wrapping a sheet around herself, they scurried off leaving John in his silk under garments and a blue woolen blanket. "You love to embarrass me," he complained, with heat in his voice. "Whatever complaint or report you have for me can wait."

"I think not, son." She entered the high ceilinged chamber and closed the door behind her. "Twenty and seven years a grown man, and still you behave like a child, fooling around with servants while you have produced no legitimate heir with your wife, Isabella. And, if that isn't bad enough, there are rumors at court you are carrying on affairs with married noble women!"

John raised his chin and flashed her his most charming smile. "Can I help it that women love me?"

She crossed the room to the side of his huge walnut bed and her arms folded with a look of disgust in the line of her mouth. "I doubt love has anything to do with it. Asides, how does one go about saying 'no' to the Prince? But that is not the reason I have come."

"What then, if not to instruct me in my husbandly duties?" He relaxed back into his pillows looking bored.

Eleanor said, "You should pay more attention to Isabella; you need an heir, a legitimate one. Your behavior is not just a humiliation to her; your affairs spit in the face of the Church and lower your esteem with the people."

"The Church, the people," he mocked. "What do I care about those? I am the prince and heir apparent behind my brother; I can do whatever I please."

"Just because one *can* do a thing, it does not follow that he *should* do that thing. Being king means far more than getting your way; it is about respect, strength of character, strength of will."

At that he sat up, green eyes flashing. "I have ambitions, Mother. I will be king one day, and I will have the power to lock you up like my father before me should you stand in my way."

Eleanor took a seat on the edge of the bed. "I feel that I have failed you. Because of my imprisonment, I missed being there for your formative years. Perhaps if I could have influenced you then, we wouldn't be going around about these things now. You must understand that I do want you to be king–when the time is right; when it is your turn. But that ill-advised ploy you and Phillip of France attempted with Henry Hohenstaufen, offering to pay him to keep Richard imprisoned–that is not the way to go about it! It was cowardly, underhanded, and unchivalrous, not to mention treasonous."

"And was it not treasonous when young Henry and my brothers, with your backing, stood in rebellion against my father?"

"We stood up to him face to face, militarily and politically, in a fair fight, which your father won. But we never conspired in secret with an enemy nation!"

John returned to his childish pout and laid back onto his pillows. "You know I am not a warrior like Richard. I cannot stand up to him in a fair fight and live."

She brushed a bare hand across his forehead and cradled his fuzzy cheek. "Then be patient, dear boy. Help me get Richard back. Show him your support now, and I will give you mine later. Your brother is many years your elder and you are sure to outlive him. You need more time to mature. Take on military training, listen to your tutors, grow in wisdom, make the political connections you will need with your nobles and foreign princes, go to your wife and produce children. I need you and your King needs you. Help me raise the ransom to bring him home and one day the power will be yours—when you are ready for it."

John's sullenness deepened. He wanted it now; he wanted it all now. He had been working on another plan… one that would take them all by surprise and prove he was strong and capable enough of a leader to take the throne. As he'd just said, he could not hope to challenge her or the

King outright. So instead he nodded and kissed her hand. "Undoubtedly you are right, Mother. I will assemble a team and ride out across the land. I will help you raise the money to bring my brother home from his captivity. Then, will I finally have your blessing?"

She smiled a proud and doting smile at him and kissed his cheek. "Son, you may not always have my approval, but know that you do always have my love."

\* \* \*

AFTER PARTAKING of the morning meal of manchet bread, cheese, and fruit, Eleanor sought out the leader of the castle's troupe of troubadours, a fancifully attired musician from her native Aquitaine, Alberic. His colorful costume of green and yellow paneled tunic belted over red tights added to the flair that was part of the troubadours' appeal.

"Alberic, has the new hurdy-gurdy I ordered arrived yet?" she asked.

"Yes, Your Grace," he replied with an obligatory bow. "Just yesterday, along with a musician to play it, Gilbert de Anjou. They say he is the best, and I had to bribe him with a teaching position to lure him away from his previous post. I trust Your Highness can find a post for him. You demanded only the best, so…"

"Do not fret; that is exactly what I asked for." Eleanor gazed toward a tapestry featuring William I and knights on horseback as she pondered. "The University at Oxford is expanding and I have long wanted it to include music among its courses. Compose a letter informing the institution that I wish this Gilbert de Anjou to be hired on as a professor of music. Since London is only a day's ride from the castle, it should not interfere with his obligations here."

"I shall see to it right away," he declared with a bow.

"Not so fast, Alberic." She held up a hand to stop him. "I wish to consult with you on the music selections for the feast tomorrow evening. Naturally, all selections should be in the Courtly Love style, consisting first of music for dining followed by tunes suitable for dancing." Eleanor produced a piece of paper from a small pouch tied to a cord around her waist. "I have taken the liberty to make a list of titles that I especially want to have played."

He took the list and glanced over it. "Excellent choices, Your Grace. Some of these will feature Gilbert on our new hurdy-gurdy."

"Precisely. As you see there is a mix of instrumentals and tunes with vocals. I am determined to bring culture to this island if it is the last thing I do!" Eleanor smiled at Alberic who beamed back, very pleased to be the lead musician in the court of the leading patron of the arts in all of England. He bowed once more and scurried off, list in hand, to prepare his troupe for the upcoming event.

As Eleanor continued down the stone walled corridor with its narrow cross-shaped arrow-slit windows, she happened upon William Marshall, the Earl of Pembroke.

"Good day, Your Highness," William said with a courteous smile, a sweep of his arm, and a deep bow. He wore a royal blue surcoat with white ermine trim. At forty-seven years of age, gray had crept into the brown of his beard and temples, but he was still as strong and fit as ever with eyes the deep bay of a destrier. The famed knight who had bested over 500 opponents in tournaments and never lost a bout was the living embodiment of chivalry, a code and conduct that Eleanor promoted. Because he had gained the respect of all the people, Richard had placed William, along with Eleanor, on the board of regents he left in charge of the kingdom while he was away.

"Good day, Sir William," she returned with a slight nod. "I have been meaning to speak with you on a matter of import. Have you a moment?"

"Certainly. How may I serve you?"

"This is about how you may serve your King. Perhaps you will escort me on a walk about the grounds," she suggested as they were passed by a young lord with an attractive blonde on his arm.

"'Tis a lovely day for a stroll," he agreed and held out his arm for her to take. Together they exited the castle and all of its prying eyes and ears.

Encompassing over thirteen acres, Windsor Castle was one of more than eighty bastions erected during the reign of William the Conqueror, and one of a group of strategic fortifications constructed around London. One day's ride from the city and each other, these castles held garrisons that could easily be reinforced and protect the capital. Most were originally motte and bailey style wooden structures, but many, including Windsor, boasted stone keeps. In fact it was William I who introduced stone castles to the British Isles.

Windsor was of particular import due to its commanding posture overlooking the River Thames, its location along a major overland road to London, and its proximity to the Saxon royal hunting grounds. Henry

II, Eleanor's late husband, had established his royal palace there and embarked on a fourteen year building project which included renovating the keep and replacing the old wooden palisade with formidable stone walls interspersed with towers and turrets. Henry had Bagshot heath brought in from quarries to the south supplemented with Bedfordshire stone from the north to complete a castle he intended to stand for a millennium. He constructed the massive King's Gate and two sets of royal residences–one for his family in the Upper Ward and another for important guests and courtiers in the Lower Ward. His finished work rivaled any of the great castles of Europe.

"I trust you and Isabella de Clare will join me for the feast tomorrow evening," Eleanor began as they leisurely passed various grounds workers.

"We would be most honored," William answered as he nodded toward her.

Once they were away from any others, Eleanor began. "Richard trusted you. Surely after that debacle between John and Longchamp, you know well John does not always support his brother."

"Indeed. Rest assured that my loyalty to King Richard is without question. I allowed myself to be caught up in the affair only because I failed to see John for who and what he is." Then William shook his head. "One day, I may need to pledge John my allegiance–a pledge I would indeed keep. But as long as the Lionheart lives, I am his man, and yours, Your Grace."

"I appreciate you, William. Not only what you stand for, which is far and above the standard for all who would call themselves knight, but for who you are; I am pleased to consider you my friend."

"As am I, Your Highness. I sense something troubles you," he perceived and gazed at her in question.

Eleanor sighed. "It is John, as one might guess. I suspect he is up to something."

"Truly?" William asked. "Again? And so soon after trying to pay Emperor Henry to keep Richard captive?"

"Oh, he was much too quick to agree to help me raise the remaining ransom," she explained in an exasperated tone. Her keen eyes scanned the castle yard to ensure they were still alone. "No, he is sneaky and underhanded and definitely up to no good. He is taking off to tour the country, supposedly to collect tax money himself, along with his new friend Sir Guy of Gisborne. What can you tell me about Sir Guy? He is much older than John; I don't see what they have in common."

William stroked his beard as they made a turn at the castle wall. "He is my age, Your Grace, and twenty years ago was a strong contender in the tournaments. He inherited his father's estate and has been profitable with it. However rumor has it that his success comes at the price of cruelty to his serfs. About fifteen years ago he was banned from competing in any sanctioned events because he was caught cheating. It seems he substituted his official ash lances for identically painted ones made from maple."

Eleanor furrowed her brow. "I don't understand."

"You see," he explained. "The tournament provides lances for all jousters that are the same size, weight, and hardness, fitted with blunt ends to protect competitors. Invariably there are accidents. Sometimes a knight is killed, but that is not the aim. The point is to knock a knight from his horse. Lances made of ash are flexible and splinter fairly easily, so if a strike is indirect, the lance will break and the rider remains in the saddle; only a direct hit will unseat him. But Gisborne was substituting his lances with ones made of maple, a much harder wood, which does not splinter. That allowed him a greater chance than other competitors to unseat his opponent with only a glancing blow. Subtle, but still cheating."

"So he wanted to win unfairly," she mused. "That is what he and John hold in common. My guess is that Gisborne has pledged his fealty to John seeking advancement and reward from my youngest as soon as they place him on Richard's throne." She shook her head and looked to William. "I truly wish, I could trust my son John to be loyal to the King and wait his turn for the crown, but I fear I cannot. He has undermined the authority Richard left with us at every turn. And now that we are charged with collecting this 100,000 marks from a country barely more than a century old, from Saxons who distrust us and Normans who cannot spare the funds, we must become taskmasters of a people we would rather inspire to greatness than crush with taxes. The truth is, Richard is a better king than John would be. My prayer is that my baby will one day grow into his role; he can be more than he is–I know he can be."

"Only if he wants to be, Milady."

Eleanor moved her gaze to the castle and nodded her own agreement. "I already have a few spies in London, Warwick, Cambridge, and another in Nottingham," she stated matter-of-factly. Then paused looking up into his honest eyes. "But I think a little insurance is in order."

"Your Grace?" the Earl questioned.

"There is someone I feel I can count on who may be able to elicit exactly the information we need. I will speak with her about it on the morrow."

"Her?" Surprise lit his expression.

Eleanor's mouth twisted into a knowing smile that strained to hold back laughter and she flashed dark eyes at her companion. "Why, Sir William, surely you know better than to under estimate the power of a capable woman."

* * *

MAID MARIAN FITZWALTER sat at the long elevated table at one end of the great hall along with the royal family and high nobles of the court. Her long, honey colored hair was divided into two braids interwoven with a blue ribbon and arranged in a fashionable chignon. The ribbon complemented the indigo trim of her otherwise azure, full-sleeved bliaut, accented by a silver necklace set with a sapphire stone. Her eyes were the pastel blue of robins' eggs set beneath delicate brows on either side of a straight nose. Her bowed lips and apple cheeks were subtly colored with strawberry rouge to set them ever so slightly apart from her alabaster skin.

Marian's seat was between Isabelle de Clare, who was near her age, and Sir Guy of Gisborne, who was considerably older and a recent widower. Also at the table were Queen Eleanor, Prince John and his wife Isabella, Sir William Marshall Earl of Pembroke, Sir Aubrey de Vere Earl of Oxford and his wife Agnes, Sir Henry FitzCount Earl of Cornwall and Bishop Richard Fitz Neal, the nation's treasurer. At the other tables were dozens of lesser lords and ladies who had been invited to the St. Mary of Magdalene

The hall was a spacious rectangular room with a high ceiling that served many purposes, including feasts. Several large picture windows faced out onto Eleanor's beautifully landscaped gardens letting in daytime light. The wall behind the dining tables had but tiny arrow slit windows bearing a long row of wall sconces for light and various tapestries for warmth and decoration. Across the expanse of floor, used for dancing, was a wide entry door beneath the minstrels' gallery where Alberic and his troubadours played a selection from Eleanor's list. In the center of the room was a tremendous hearth with a square stone chimney displaying the red and gold Plantagenet coat-of-arms, two facing rampant lions, and

Eleanor's Angevin single gold lion on a red shield with one paw raised. Because the summer evening was warm, the great fire was not lit. Instead, round candelabras hung from the ceiling, brightening the room.

Squires and servants in sharp, clean attire scurried forth from a side door leading from the kitchens bearing platters of delightful delicacies to satisfy both the eye and appetite. There was thick pottage served in bowls made of bread, a roasted peacock arranged with its feathers on a silver platter along with a swan that was similarly displayed, a roast boar with an apple in its mouth, platters of cheeses, bowls of fruit, plates piled high with aromatic pastries, and goblets of wine. Everything was as Eleanor had designed.

Marian was sampling a beef fritter with plum sauce when Sir Guy turned his attention to her. "'Twas such sad news about the Earl of Loxley and his son," he said between bites of sautéed eel.

Suddenly Marian went still. She no longer heard the music nor considered the food as she turned her full attention to Sir Guy. "What about them?" she asked with concern. "I haven't heard."

"Oh dear," he replied in feigned concern and washed his morsel down with some French wine. "Word has recently arrived from the crusade. I'm afraid they both were killed." Marian's fair face paled with shock. "I understand your family was friends with the Loxleys."

"Yes, yes," she uttered. "I grew up in a nearby manor and we visited each other regularly. This is such distressing news." Marian found herself no longer in a mood for celebration, but she wanted to find out more about what had happened. "Have you heard anything of Robyn, Sir Loxley's daughter?"

Isabella, William Marshall's young wife, replied, "She seems to have disappeared. No one really knows what happened to her."

Though less beautiful than Marian, the young brunette came from a vastly more wealthy family as her wardrobe and jewelry attested. The two had developed a quick friendship during the week of William and Isabella's visit to Windsor from Kilkenny Castle overlooking their substantial holdings in Ireland.

Marian's expression went blank as she stared at the green-eyed Isabella. "What do you mean nobody knows?"

"Sweet Marian, do not upset yourself so!" Isabella put down her food and laid a hand on Marian's arm. "I heard one rumor that she has gone to a nunnery."

"A nunnery?" Marian couldn't believe it. "Why wouldn't she still be at Loxley manor? Was she so distressed by her loss?"

"I am sure it was a considerable blow, especially after losing her mother and younger siblings," Sir Guy concluded. "But you realize that, as an unmarried woman, she had no claims to the estate." Both his wavy copper shoulder length hair and his trim pointed beard bore streaks of gray. His mid-section had bulged with age, but his weight was also considered a sign of wealth. He gazed at Marian through hungry hazel eyes. "You should take note, my dear. A maid of your age must think about marriage yourself."

"You know I must wait for my father's return from Germany," she repeated, as she had many times before over the past four years. "Verily, I cannot marry without my father's approval. Now that the ransom for King Richard has almost all been collected, I feel sure he will return home with the King quite soon. But about Robyn…"

Sir Guy sighed an impatient breath and added, "Actually, I heard she has run off to Scotland."

"Scotland!" Marian was more confounded than before. "I can't believe she would commit herself to a nunnery or leave the country without telling me." Now Marian was not sure which new turn of events hurt her heart the most.

"She has always been rather strange," Isabella noted in as compassionate of a tone as she could muster. "I suppose it can't be helped, what with her being a Saxon and all. Why, I don't think she has been back to court since the summer of her coming out."

"What does her lineage matter?" Marian asked in derision. "She has not been to court because she has been busy managing the Loxley lands alone while her male relatives were giving their lives to defend our Christian faith!"

Sir Guy had gone back to eating but managed to squeeze a nonchalant word in between bites. "That is what a steward is for. I have one myself."

"It takes more than one person to run an entire estate," Marian noted, adding quietly, "to do it properly, that is."

Sir Guy changed tactics. He set down his knife and cup and turned his full attention to the eligible and desirable beauty beside him, attempting to comfort Marian in her time of sorrow. "Maid Marian, I have already arranged a trip to Nottingham for tomorrow and I promise to personally look into Maid Robyn's whereabouts." He used his most sincere tone, softening his eyes as he placed a broad well-manicured hand over hers. "I will find out what has happened to her for you and send word immediately so you will not be so distraught."

Marian smiled at him in gratitude. "Thank you, Sir Guy."

She had her suspicions about Gisborne's motives, as she did about every unmarried man who called upon her, but she did not think of him the way he thought of her. She regarded Sir Guy like an uncle or grandfather, or other such masculine relative, but not as a husband. While he always displayed chivalric manners to her, she had heard from peasants and serfs on her own family's manor that he was cruel and heartless, not even properly mourning his own wife's passing. They said he was more concerned with profits than people, with promoting his own political success than in honor, and that he could not be trusted as far as one could pitch a millstone. And while she had a propensity to believe such stories, there was always a chance folks exaggerated. For here was Sir Guy displaying empathy for her feelings... or did he simply want under her skirts?

"Don't mention it," he answered with a kind looking smile and patted her hand. "Anything I can do for the beloved goddaughter of the King will be my pleasure."

\* \* \*

MARIAN COULD THINK of nothing all night save what had become of her childhood friend, even when dancing the galliard and roundel. She was an excellent dancer and, though her mood was dark and pensive, she was compelled by her station to join in the evening's activities. She danced with several partners including Sir Guy, but became distracted to the point of desperation. After a pavane, Marian excused herself to the garderobe, and feeling slightly more relieved set out to speak with the Queen As it happened, Eleanor had also been looking for her.

They found each other just outside the hall doorway from which music and laughter poured. "Your Highness," Marian greeted with a curtsey. "I must ask for your leave to return home as soon as Your Highness may grant it."

Eleanor, seeing her distress, took the young lady by the arm. "Come, Marian. Have you seen the hybrid rose I have been cultivating in the gardens? I call it the Plantageitaine Rose."

Marian was baffled by the abrupt change in subject, but went with Eleanor outside. The Queen was in a regal verdant gown with long swooping sleeves adorned with gold and a thin gold band around her forehead. The moon was high overhead, and the garden was also lit by torches, so maneuvering the grounds was easy.

"I love the gardens," Eleanor said with a dreamy look in her dark eyes and a sigh in her voice. "So peaceful and private." Once they were thirty or forty yards from the festivities Eleanor stopped in front of a bed of roses.

Marian looked at them and commented. "They are indeed lovely."

"Tell me, child; why do you suddenly wish to return home?"

Marian straightened but was still much shorter than Eleanor. "I must find out what has happened to my friend, Robyn of Loxley. They are saying her father and brother were killed, and that she has disappeared. I cannot have peace until I know what has happened to her."

Eleanor studied the maid's sincerity and then fondled one of the roses. "I grafted cuttings from a rose variety I brought with me from Aquitaine to a bush native to this land. I think the result is a stronger, more beautiful and fragrant sort." Then she looked to Marian. "There are those who say Normans are superior to Saxons, but I have learned a secret; like the roses, each has something to offer the other, and we are indeed stronger together."

"I fail to understand why so many hold ill opinions of our fellow Englishmen more than a hundred years after the war," Marian voiced, puzzled again by the Queen's change in subject. "It has been at least three generations, yet some want to judge others based on their ancestry from before our nation was even established."

Eleanor gave her a bemused glance. "Some people consider what they have in common with their neighbor, while others see only what is different. My dear, I fear I must confirm what you heard this evening: the latest casualty report listed the Earl and his son as killed in battle. I regret not knowing what has happened to the daughter, nor did I know anything was amiss. She is your friend?"

"Yes, Your Grace," Marian replied choking back the tears that had been threatening all evening.

"Tell me, what is the nature of your relationship with Sir Guy of Gisborne?"

The burgeoning tears stopped in their tracks and a confused expression emerged on Marian's face. "What? Sir Guy? I have no relationship with Sir Guy."

A twisted smile crossed Eleanor's mouth. "That is not what court gossip says. My dear Marian, do you not know when a man is wooing you?"

"But I told him that I cannot even consider courting anyone until my father returns home to give his consent."

"Merely ascertaining the truth of the matter," she said and led them on a farther stroll. "You are Richard's goddaughter because your father, Sir Robert FitzWalter, is my son's dearest, oldest and most loyal friend. Even now, he sits encamped outside Trifels Castle in Germany, waiting to escort Richard back home upon his release. Despite the urgings of members of our court and warnings by the Holy Roman Emperor, he refuses to leave without his King. That is the loyalty of your father. What about your loyalty, Maid Marian?"

"I do not understand. I am unconditionally loyal to the King, and will challenge anyone who would say otherwise. In fact, I am very much my father's daughter," she declared.

"I thought as much," Eleanor replied as she paused beside some white flowering shrubs. After a careful glance around she explained. "There are those in England, even at court, even in my own family, who are not so loyal. I believe Sir Guy is among them."

Marian registered the line of conversation and the tour around the gardens. The Queen's words rang true for her. "I do not intend to wed him, Your Grace, nor any man regardless of his wealth or title if he does not love King Richard as my father does."

"It is fortuitous that you wish to return home, though not for such a grievous reason, as I would ask it of you anyway. Sir Guy and Prince John are planning to leave for Nottingham Castle to plot some scheme with the Sheriff there—I am sure of it. Both your manor and Loxley are located in the vicinity, so you can take time with your family, check on Maid Robyn and keep an eye on Sir Guy. I am not suggesting you promise him anything, but as long as his attention is fixed upon you, you may find yourself privy to what may otherwise be considered private conversations. It is imperative we discover what John, Gisborne and the Sheriff are about."

"I see," Marian said. "As long as I am there, I will do whatever is necessary to secure the return of my King, and my father with him."

"It could be dangerous," Eleanor warned, "especially if they become suspicious of you. Can you play at courting Sir Guy while holding him at arm's length with the excuse of waiting on your father's consent?"

"I believe I can; I will surely do my best. But how will you and I communicate?"

Eleanor smiled at Marian and took both of her hands in a firm, warm grip. "I will send you back with a crate of pigeons that fly only to my loft. When you learn something of import, write a short note and secure it in the little case that ties to its leg. If I need to get word to you, I will send a personal courier." Marian nodded and gave Eleanor's hands a little squeeze. "I am sorry to hear about the Loxleys, and I hope you find your friend safe and well."

"Thank you," the young lady said and bowed her head.

Eleanor moved one hand to stroke Marian's cheek. "Thank *you*."

## CHAPTER 3

*Sherwood Forest, Nottinghamshire, August 1193*

"You'll never guess who I saw strollin' 'round Nottingham Castle this mornin'," Alan A Dale challenged the others as he rejoined the camp with a smile on his youthful face and a spring in his step.

Little John scowled disapprovingly. "I told you to stay out o' town lest you be recognized and caught. We won't be able to save you from a hanging now, lad."

"He can't help it," Will teased with a gleam in his own sparkling blue eyes. "Alan's got hisself a lady friend–that buxom young Liz what works at the tavern, right?"

Allen's cheeks flushed, and he winked a clover green eye at his comrade. "She's an energetic lass, high-spirited, and she calls me her Honey Sop," he said beaming and took a seat on the log beside Will and Robyn near the campfire under the protective branches of the ancient tree. "But I saw someone else in town today." All eyes turned to him. "Ah, come on now, somebody has to guess!"

"King Richard!" exclaimed Much as he joined the youngsters and Little John. "Oh, please let it be King Richard!" He folded his hands as in prayer as he fell to his knees.

"Sorry, Much, but not today," Alan said. Not waiting for guesses, he continued, "I saw that beauteous Maid Marian back home from court. She was just strollin' about shoppin' at the market and keepin' company with Sir Guy of Gisborne."

Robyn perked up at the news, raising her head to look Alan in the face. She had been with the outlaw gang for a fortnight and had constructed her own dwelling of sticks and canvas. She knew they laid wagers about why she always kept her hood raised. Some bet it was to hide a scar or disfigurement while others said it was to conceal her true age. Long odds were on her being someone famous. Fortunately, no one had entered the possibility she was female. She was pulling her weight with chores and had proven to them all to be a good hunter and a sure-shot with her bow. Robyn enjoyed the company and engaged in more conversation, but was ever cautious about revealing any personal information. Sometimes she overheard the lads whisper and stare in her direction, wondering why she visited the latrine at odd times and never removed her cloak despite the midday heat.

Robyn had concluded that it was becoming too difficult to keep hiding her identity, and thought the time might be close to leave, but now that Marian was back… well, that changed everything!

"Mmmmm," Will vocalized brightly. "That is one luscious woman! I'd love to sop her honey!"

"Bugger that, Will!" Robyn snapped, tensing with bridled anger. "You shouldn't talk that way about Maid Marian."

Will's mouth fell agape in shock, his blue eyes widening beneath his length of black hair while Alan rubbed a hand over his sandy facial fuzz and shook his head.

"I think Robyn is sweet on Maid Marian, boys," Alan declared.

Arthur Bland ambled up with two rabbits for the pot. "Then he's out o' luck," he said joining in. "People in town are saying she's courtin' Sir Guy, not that any o' us could even lace her shoes."

"What!" Robyn cried incensed. "That is a vicious rumor and I demand you take it back! Marian would never court that fat, old, pompous arse!" Will and Alan exchanged glances and snickered. Robyn's mouth pursed in irritation. "She is far too good for the likes of him."

"Aye, that she is," Little John agreed. "I for one am happy to see a kind, noble lady like herself back in these parts. Mayhap she will provide a civilizing effect on Sir Guy and the Sheriff."

Robyn squeezed her hands together and bounced her knee nervously, but nodded at Little John's words. "But she is NOT courting him," she added in a low, determined tone.

"Whatever you say, Robyn," Will allowed. "Alan, did you think to bring your mates any hum back from the tavern?"

Alan reached into the bag that hung from a strap over his shoulder, withdrew a dark tinted bottle, and grinned with pride.

Robyn sat oblivious to the strong spirits, brooding over the rumor of her dearest friend and a man she loathed. She tried to imagine them kissing, but the idea disgusted her too much and she closed her eyes.

*I need to go see her, talk to her, find out for myself what's going on*, she determined. With Marian frequenting the Queen's court and Robyn occupied managing her manor lands, they had not actually seen each other in... *Has it truly been years?* Robyn realized as she counted up the months and seasons. And while they had not been in each other's physical presence, not a day had passed that Robyn did not regard Maid Marian tenderly, remembering their childhood escapades, their vows of undying friendship, the laughter and the light Marian had brought into her life following the death of her mother and younger siblings. She doubted she would be the person she had grown into had it not been for Marian.

As through a fog, Robyn perceived voices approaching.

"And here we are," Friar Tuck announced. "The Heart of Sherwood Forest and Grandma Oak." Robyn turned curious brown eyes toward Tuck's voice to behold a group of about a dozen peasants and serfs, judging from their rags and frailty.

"What have we here?" Little John demanded as he marched over to meet the newcomers.

"I'm sorry, Little John," the Friar apologized as he leaned on his walking stick. "They were wandering in the woods, lost and starving. I couldn't just leave them there."

"Who are they and why are they wandering around in our forest?" the outlaw leader asked in a private aside to Tuck.

But the Friar spoke loudly in reply for all hear. "These good Christians come from Loxley and Nottingham. Those from Nottingham were sacked and blackballed by the Sheriff and, unable to find work, had begun a journey to the next shire in search of employment when they ran into these folks from Loxley. There, they banded together." Holding a hand to his mouth, he spoke to Little John in a hushed tone. "Remember the law of hospitality, Little John. We may be thieves, miscreants, and tax evaders, but we are also Christians; we cannot turn away people in need."

Despite the dissatisfied twist of his features, the outlaw leader nodded in reluctant agreement.

Robyn had risen, aroused from her personal musing when she caught the name 'Loxley'. She stood beside Little John, hood hiding her face, and looked out at the dozen refugees. She recognized some faces.

"Why leave Loxley estate?" she asked.

An emaciated man with short mud brown hair who appeared older than his thirty-five years replied. "After word of the good Earl's death, the Sheriff came and seized the manor. He brought harsh taskmasters and armed men. They increased our workload and rummaged through our homes to collect Prince John's new taxes. We couldn't even keep enough food to live on."

Robyn felt a jolt of remorse like an arrow to the heart as he spoke. She knew this man. His name was Isaac. She knew him to be a hard worker and a cheerful family man.

He continued. "Roger, here," he motioned to a somber looking fellow in his twenties with straw-colored hair and beard and a ruddy complexion. "The Sheriff overheard him saying that things were better while Maid Robyn was running the manor and the Sheriff…" Isaac stopped, sparing a sympathetic glance at Roger while he swallowed. "Sheriff Godfrey Giffard of Nottingham, soon to be named Earl of Loxley, cut out his tongue."

A shocked silence fell over the outlaw band for a moment before murmurings and the shaking of heads began. The knot grew tighter in Robyn's stomach and she feared she would be sick.

Then Isaac led a young girl recently passed puberty to the front of the desperate group of sunken-eyed souls. She stood to his shoulders with a scarf over strawberry-blonde hair and small, tender breasts just budding. "My daughter, Christina, is a sweet, pretty girl. Unfortunately, the Sheriff thought so as well. A few nights ago soldiers came to our cruck and took her. They said she had found favor with the Sheriff and would be well treated. At first Beatrice, my wife, and I thought mayhap he had chosen her to be a household servant, but when they returned her the next morning…" This time he was unable to stop the tears. The gaunt Isaac hugged his little girl.

Beatrice stepped forward. She was a slight woman in a patched dress with searching gray eyes and two small boys clinging to her. "I don't understand," she stated, looking from one of Little John's men to the next. "Why would Lady Loxley abandon us? Why would she leave us to that monster?"

Robyn closed her eyes, pressure bearing down on her chest like an iron anvil. She couldn't breathe. She couldn't think beyond, *What have I done?*

"Now Beatrice, we can't blame Maid Robyn," another woman in the party said patting the grieving mother's shoulder. "I was there; the Sheriff evicted her. He even declared her a traitor for opposing his takeover of Loxley. What could she have done?"

Beatrice sighed and shook her head, her shoulders slumping like those of one carrying a heavy burden. Isaac regained his composure and wrapped his other arm around his wife in comfort. "So Friar Tuck tells us you are the leader here," he said looking up at Little John's grizzly visage. He nodded. "Since we abandoned our duties to our manor and fled our obligations as serfs, we are now outlaws, too, and wish to join your gang."

John looked them over then turned to Robyn, but she was no longer standing beside him. "I am saddened to hear of your trials, and the Friar was right to bring you here. Alan, please see to our guests; I'll return anon," he said and strode across the camp.

* * *

ROBYN WAS in the privacy of a thicket she frequented when she wanted to be alone; there John stopped, stood, and waited. He heard a sniff before she gazed up at him through guilt-ridden eyes.

"I know these people," she began as streaks of tears ran down her cheeks. "Roger worked in our stables. He would sing to the horses to calm them. He possessed a lovely voice and mayhap have been a minstrel, had he not been born tied to the land." She paused a moment, wiping her face with the back of her sleeve. "And Christina, Isaac's daughter... I remember attending her christening. I remember Mother explaining to me what the priest was doing and what it meant. These are my people, Little John, and Beatrice was right; I abandoned them. I was so busy thinking of my own situation that I didn't even spare one thought for them!" Robyn's chest heaved and more tears poured down her cheeks.

"How were you to know? What could you have done?" Little John wrapped an arm around her shoulders in comfort.

"Marry the Sheriff," she said and sniffed again. "Then at least I might still hold some sway, still watch out for them. He wouldn't have raped Christina."

"Child, if the Sheriff's tastes run to young girls, marrying you would have only postponed his actions."

She wiped her face with both hands and steeled her voice. "Then I should have killed him. I had an opportunity; I should have jabbed a dagger into his excuse for a heart."

Little John sighed and enfolded her in his arms. "Robyn, you are no murderer. You could no more have done that than given yourself to him in bed."

"But now he is extending his cruelty to my people. I was responsible for them and I just ran away and left them to him! What's happened is my fault," she said immersed in guilt and buried her face into his shoulder.

"Is everything that happens in the world your fault?" he asked. "Is it your fault King Richard was captured? Is it your fault your father and brother were killed? Is it your fault that evil men carry out their intentions? I'm sorry, Robyn, but in truth you just aren't that important," he added with a laugh.

Robyn, catching the joke, tried to release some of the burden she had heaped on herself. A slight chuckle found its way out. By then her sobbing had ceased. It was time to take action. "Gramercy," she replied and looked up into his fatherly face. "But what shall I do now? I have to take care of them, John. They are my responsibility. There is only one person I can turn to for help, one person whom I fully trust."

"Maid Marian?"

Robyn nodded. "I need to visit her straight away, but shall return tomorrow. I will not abandon them again, nor you and the boys. Marian is very clever and I'm sure she will offer to lend her aid. I know you didn't count on having women and children in your camp, but if you can suffer them for one night–" Her glistening eyes pleaded with him. She knew that he'd likely be hesitant to do so. How would they take care of so many people, especially the women and children? But, if Marian could help out, maybe that would change things. Would Little John feel better about inviting them to stay in the camp in that instance?

"What choice do I have? Turn them out to starve? I trust you to return with a plan." He loosened his embrace and Robyn took a step back with a deep breath.

"Thank you; you are a good leader and an honorable man, John Naylor. Once I collect my bow and quiver I'll be off. Can you make an excuse to the others for me?"

He nodded, and she was away.

* * *

ROBYN ARRIVED at the FitzWalter manor in the cool, quiet of the predawn morning. A lark had just begun its song and the air was damp with fog as she moved with precision to a particular niche in the rough stone wall. Pushing a white rock aside, as she had done innumerable times before, she dropped to her knees and squeezed through the hole. After looking left and right, Robyn began her sprint across the yard toward a familiar tree adjacent to the house. A dog barked in the distance, but rather than the sound of alarm, it was like a greeting from an old friend; no one stirred. She passed a chicken coop with hens nestled wing to wing on their roost. They, too, sounded their greeting with subdued clucks coming from deep in their chests. Grabbing hold of the lower branches, Robyn climbed the Rowan ash like she did as a child. Then holding on for balance, she traversed onto the branch that led to Marian's window.

She was suddenly struck with a disconcerting prospect; *Is this still Marian's bedchamber? Has she changed quarters? But why would she? While possible, it is too late to think about that now,* she told herself and stepped over onto the windowsill. The shutters had been left open to invite in the summer air.

Robyn recalled the last time she had snuck through Marian's window. It had been their last escapade before heading off to be introduced at court. *How long ago was it?* she wondered. With a balance of stealth and caution, Robyn now placed a silent booted foot inside the window on the laths of the bedroom floor. After taking another step into the dark room, she was startled by the sharp edge of a thin steel blade pressed to her throat. Her first thought was, *Oh, no! She's changed rooms.* But then a familiar melodious tone touched her ears, even though it emanated from a seriously chilled voice.

"Do not move, thief. I will not hesitate to spill your blood."

Robyn relaxed at Marian's voice and the tension evaporated out into the night. "Glad to see you're still keeping that dagger under your pillow," sounded her amiable reply.

"Robyn!" Marian exclaimed in a hushed tone and hastily tossed the knife onto the bed. She stepped out from the shadow at the edge of the window and embraced her friend with unveiled enthusiasm. Robyn wrapped her arms around Marian, laying her cheek to rest against hers. "I was so worried!" Marian gushed. "No one knew what happened to you. They said you had gone to a nunnery, or some nonsense."

Robyn lingered a moment in silence, enjoying the warmth of their touch. It had been far too long! She breathed in the scent of Marian's hair and was keenly aware that only a thin linen nightshift swathed the fullness of her breasts, the curve of her hips, and the smoothness of her skin. "And I heard you were courting Sir Guy," she replied in a whisper, her mouth to Marian's ear.

"Rubbish!" Marian loosened her hold on Robyn and stepped back to look up into her face. Reluctantly, Robyn allowed her to pull to arm's length, but kept one hand on her shoulder and another at her waist. "Why are you in these rogue's clothing?"

Robyn sighed, trailing her fingers away from the warmth emanating beneath that linen gown. She lowered her hood, unfastened the cape, and placed bow, quiver, and all on the floor. "There is so much to tell," she began, "and I fear I have two favors to ask of you."

Marian led her farther into the room, the pale light of dawn catching her golden strands and dancing over them like sunlight on a lake at midday. Robyn drank in her honest beauty, her soul filled with contentment; but she also felt a stirring, deep within her core, recalling vivid dreams involving herself and Marian in this same bedchamber. She tried to push the images to a distance and focus on the matter at hand.

"I was so sorry to hear about Thomas and your father," Marian empathized. Her eyes relayed the depth of her feeling. "You must be devastated."

"Your father is well, I trust?"

"Yes, for now," Marian said. "We receive letters from his camp in Germany where he awaits the King's release."

Robyn nodded and smiled. "I am glad to hear it."

Marian continued to give Robyn puzzled looks and finally blurted out, "What have you done with your breasts?"

Robyn bubbled over with subdued laughter. She was pleased that Marian had noticed. "My favorite bed sheet," she explained. "I tore it into a long strip which I then bound snugly around them under my clothing.

At first I found it tight and uncomfortable, but it allows me to run and fight much more effectively. That combined with this doublet is sufficient for hiding my more feminine assets."

"I don't understand," Marian said. "Why are you pretending to be a boy?"

A somberness replaced her light visage. "Then you haven't heard the whole story. You are fortunate, Marian; your father lives and you've younger brothers who can inherit for you. I had no one, and when the Sheriff showed up with his proclamations of how I had no rights to Loxley and I could marry him or be thrown out; well the reply I gave is not suitable for polite company. He took such great offense as to declare me a traitor and an outlaw. I suppose I could have gone to a nunnery," she mused. "But the possibility never crossed my mind."

"But disguising yourself as a highwayman did?" Marian wondered aloud.

"It seemed to be the most expedient course of action. But now I have reached a turning point," she said in all sincerity, fixing her gaze onto Marian's eyes of passionate blue. "Either I fully embrace my new role, or I keep on running."

"What are you saying?" Marian tilted her head to one side and gazed back at her.

"I joined a band of outlaws in Sherwood Forest and I can make a go of it with them; however, they think I am a boy. Then yesterday other people arrived, those who have been treated unfairly by the Sheriff, who were tortured, and starved, and stolen from by him since he took over Loxley." There was smoldering heat in her voice–not the kind she wanted to share with Marian, but the kind that seethed with hatred toward the Sheriff. "I must take care of them," she stated with determination. "I must redeem my failure in running away and protect them now. But I need your help."

"Absolutely," Marian vowed, "anything you need."

Robyn took a step closer, into Marian's personal space, a space she had always been freely allowed to enter. "I want you to cut my hair, like a boy's. If I am to make this work, I must commit entirely to my new persona, Robin Hood. And I can't be wearing that bloody hood twenty-four hours a day." She drew her long, brown braid from her back over one shoulder where it dangled down to her waist. She couldn't help but gaze longingly at it. As much as she knew this was the right course—the only course—to take, she couldn't wholly shake the idea of it being further punishment. But she had to set those thoughts aside.

Marian had no such lead in to Robyn's decision to purposefully cut her hair. Her eyes popped wide as she looked at Robyn. "Not your beautiful hair! Are you sure cutting your hair alone will be enough to convince people?"

Her words did give Robyn pause, however. She lowered her head as she pondered. "I have thick brows, a strong chin, am tall and slender hipped, and they already think I'm a boy. Verily, people tend see what they expect to see."

"I suppose you are right," Marian consented and reached one hand to stroke the long, acorn brown braid. Her hand traveled the length from just below Robyn's chin past her shoulder, knuckles brushing over her bound breasts. Robyn felt a sudden tingle, a tightness, a longing. Then Marian said, "If this is what truly you want, I will do it. Come, sit here at the dressing table."

Dawn's radiance streamed through the window, casting the room in strong contrasts of light and shadow. Robyn took the seat while Marian withdrew a pair of shears from a drawer in the dressing table. "There's no going back from this," she warned. "It would take ten years for your hair to reach this length again."

"I'll be lucky to live ten years," Robyn replied with a resigned sigh. "I'll never have my life back. Everything that I've ever known was swept away in an instant. The question now is how to proceed. This is the best scheme I could devise."

Marian untied the leather cord at the base of Robyn's braid and wove her fingers through her hair loosening it. "And the second favor?"

"I need to feed the poor, the homeless, the refugees, those that have come to us for help. I confess that I do not know how to accomplish that," Robyn admitted. "If I still had my lands and family resources, then it would be no problem; as it stands, I am as penniless as they are."

With the braid loosed, Marian combed her fingers through Robyn's hair. For Robyn, it was an immensely pleasing sensation that drew away every bit of tension and apprehension leaving only calm serenity. Robyn relaxed her shoulders and leaned her head placidly into Marian's hands.

For a moment it was as if there was no one else in the world–no war, no sheriff, no loss. Just Robyn and Marian and whatever was between them. In that instant, Robyn reasoned she could let it all go. If she and

Marian ran away together and left everything behind, that would be fine by her. For just a twinkling, her world became everything she had hoped for.

"I can give you some money to buy food for them," Marian offered as she continued to massage her fingers through Robyn's silky strands, "but it would only be a temporary remedy." And there was reality smashing the dream. Robyn had stopped running; she'd determined to take a stand and do right by her people.

"Your charity is greatly appreciated, but I need your ideas," Robyn said, snapping back to the moment as Marian reached for the shears. "You always came up with the best schemes, the grandest pranks, and each one a greater success than the last."

Memories brought a smile to Marian that touched her eyes. "Yes, but you were the one bold enough to carry them all out."

"Only because I had faith that your plans would succeed and succeed they did."

"Remember the time you poured ink in the town bully's ale? It turned his teeth black for a month!" Marian bubbled over with laughter.

Robyn joined her lightness of spirit. "And the best part is he never learned who did it."

"Well, you shall have my donation," Marian confirmed. "Come to think of it, I know quite a few nobles and merchants in these parts with deep pockets who could easily contribute to the cause. Why, they could feed your refugees for months and not even miss the coin."

A look of dismay returned to Robyn's face. "Like I'll convince any of them to be charitable?"

"Well." Robyn recognized the tone of Marian's voice at once; it meant she had a devilishly clever plan in mind. Brightness gleamed in Marian's intelligent eyes and a grin tugged at the bow of her lips. The shears went about their cutting and a woman's crown of glory fell unceremoniously to the floor. "Your band of outlaws, some swords, and some bows may convince them to part with their purses."

And then the spark passed from Marian to Robyn. "Are you suggesting that we rob the rich to feed the poor?" She couldn't quite help the grin on her face as she said the words.

"It's not like they will miss any meals, and I'm sure you can make better use of their excess blunt than they could. But you had better hurry," she added seriously, snipping the last bits of Robyn's hair. "Prince John is traveling about, raising more taxes. Queen Eleanor has raised two-thirds of the ransom from her holdings on the continent, but without the remaining portion she cannot secure the King's release. So you will need to hit them before the tax man does."

"And Sir Guy?" Robyn asked, narrowing her brow. She raised her chin bringing her eyes to catch Marian's.

"Sir Guy has recently lost his wife and is in search for a replacement. He seems to believe that I will suffice, but I assure you I have no intentions of accepting a marriage proposal from him, or anyone for that matter, until my father returns home."

Robyn let out a sigh of relief, joy beaming in her eyes and her soul at the certainty she was right, that there was nothing to this rumor about Sir Guy.

Then Marian took her by the hand and led her to a large looking glass. She stood beside her, showing off the results of the haircut. Robyn was rightly impressed. "I even look like a boy to me!"

Marian laid her head on Robyn's shoulder reaching one arm around her waist gazing at their reflections. As Robyn peered into the mirror, she thought of what a lovely couple they made and how, if things were different, they could be together. She realized she yearned for that more than ever in her life, even as she inwardly quivered. Then Marian continued.

"But I must consider marriage. After all, I will turn twenty in December. Most maids of our age are already wed. People are already saying, 'Marian thinks she is too good for anyone, how vain she is, and no man meets her expectations'."

"Bollocks," Robyn uttered darkly, and like a mist, her dream disappeared. "With the likes of Giffard and Gisborne to choose from, a nunnery sounds like a fine idea."

"I doubt either of us would survive in a nunnery," she said as she continued to linger at Robyn's side staring at the two of them in the looking glass. "We both love our freedom too much for that. And what of you? You turned twenty-two in May."

*She remembered my birthday,* Robyn thought and smiled a little despite herself. "I think I have just laid that question to rest," she replied as she scrutinized the face, hair and dress of a pageboy in the mirror.

"I wish I had options," said Marian gravely and lowered her chin casting her eyes to the floor.

*Of course she has options,* thought Robyn. *She can do whatever she wants.*

Then, without letting her brain have time to register the words, she blurted out in a playful manner, "Well, you can always come live in the forest with me and the outlaws." She meant it to sound like a joke, but in her heart she longed for nothing more.

"Oh, Robyn." Marian let out a disappointed sigh. Her hands dropped to her side, and she stepped away, glancing around her room as she spoke. It was completely light by then. "I have responsibilities. I have my family and my station to consider." Marian avoided eye contact as she spoke.

Robyn turned from the looking glass, her head lowered in regret at her own lost family. In that instant, Marian turned to Robyn, stepped close, and reached a hand to caress her cheek. Gently, she guided Robyn's chin so that their eyes met.

"I am so sorry," she began with heartfelt tenderness. "I didn't think, I didn't mean…"

"Do not fret," Robyn replied. "I know what you meant." She lifted a hand up to stroke Marian's where it rested on her cheek. "Anyway, I am getting used to being alone now. Naturally you have obligations to your family. They expect to arrange a fine marriage for you with a young man from a noble house."

"No, Robyn," Marian corrected her. She interlaced her fingers with Robyn's, which were already becoming rough from manual labor. Then she peered through Robyn's eyes straight into her soul and stated with absolute authority, "You are not alone; you are never alone. You will always have me." Marian stretched up and kissed her cheek.

A moment passed between them, and Robyn wondered if Marian felt what she felt–the energy, the passion. The room was so silent Robyn could hear the pulsing of both their hearts. But before another word could pass between them, there came a frantic knock pounding at the door.

## CHAPTER 4

"Maid Marian, come quick!" sounded a high-pitched, frantic voice.

Hearing footsteps in the hallway, Marian made a shooing motion with her hand and placed a finger to her lips as Robyn backed herself against the wall behind the ingress.

Marian opened the oak door just a crack and peeked out at a squat middle-aged woman with a round face, bug-eyes, and a button nose wearing a servant's apron and cap who nervously rocked from one foot to the other, a handkerchief gripped between two clenched hands. "Whatever is the matter, Anna?"

"I knew you to be an early riser Mistress, so I came to your door first," she explained with a look of acute distress.

"Yes, well, what is it?"

"An emergency! The deputy is here with some soldiers to collect young Charles. They say he is to hang!" At that point she burst into tears, blubbering into the handkerchief she had wound so tightly in her hands, and Marian knew gleaning further information from the servant was futile.

"Go tell them I will be there straight away to sort things out," Marian instructed. "I just have to dress."

She then shut the door, latched it, and glanced at Robyn with concern.

"Honestly," she muttered while rummaging through her wardrobe for the first day dress she could find. She slipped it on over her nightshift without bothering with the under garments. "If the Sheriff wants to play these games, can't he at least wait until a decent hour of the morning to begin?"

"How can I help?" Robyn asked in a hushed voice. They both knew Robyn couldn't be found in Marian's rooms.

"I'll handle this," Marian replied as she pulled up her stockings and slipped feet into her shoes. "When they think they can come onto our estate and snatch one of our mere boys to hang without our knowledge or consent, they have gone too far. What is the point of being noble if you do not have rights?"

With a stern, impassive frown, Marian fastened a cord around her waist that held her coin pouch and a ring of keys. Normally the keeping of the keys fell to her mother, Lady FitzWalter as chatelaine, but with raising the younger children and worrying about her husband's safe return she had delegated that authority to Marian, saying it would help prepare her to be lady of her own manor someday.

"Stay in here and hide," she quietly commanded, pinning Robyn with her gaze. "If the deputy was to find out you were here, 'twould be more than Charles' neck on the line."

Robyn gave a silent nod and Marian scurried out the door where she met her mother and fourteen-year-old brother, Richard, who had been named after the King. Lady FitzWalter had tossed a surcoat on over her nightshift, her hair still tucked in its sleeping cap. Her eyes were dark and sunken, her lined face mirroring inward distress.

"They can't just come and take away one of our people, now can they?" she asked incredulously.

"It depends, Mother, on what they say he did and what proof or witnesses they have," Marian replied.

Richard, trying to display an air of authority, spoke up. "Charles is only twelve years old, a mere child; what could he have done that warrants this outrage? Asides, the Sheriff has no right. He goes too far!" With that, he raised his chin attempting to stand as tall as Marian and crossed his arms over his chest in defiance.

"Richard, stay here and look after Mother while I see what these men want and get rid of them."

His face, half man and half child, drew into a pout. "You cannot relegate me to the house."

"Oh, let your brother go out with you; he will lend credence to your words," their mother said. "But Richard, Marian should do the talking. She is more experienced at this kind of thing."

He nodded, satisfied at getting to save face, and jumped in front to lead the way.

* * *

INSIDE MARIAN'S BEDCHAMBER, Robyn slid to the floor where she wrapped her arms around her knees and lay her forehead on them, buried in thought. *How can I sit here while that vile Sheriff's men want to cart off a little boy to hang, for no good reason I am sure? But if I go and they discover my identity, then I will hang. Oh Lord, who am I?* she agonized.

Confused, frustrated, and lost, Robyn sat pondering her life and her future. Then, as if carried on a breeze, a still, calm voice spoke to her. It wasn't an audible sound, but more of a stirring from somewhere within her own soul. "Who do you *want* to be?"

*Who do I want to be?* She pondered the thought. *I've just committed to being Robin Hood; so then the real question becomes, who is Robin Hood?* She'd raised her head placing her chin on her pulled up knees and contemplated. *Not merely a thief or an outlaw... no. Robin Hood is brave and chivalrous, a crusader for justice who fights for the poor and down-trodden. He brings hope to the hopeless. Robin Hood is more than a person—he's an idea; the idea that we can be more than we are, that we can be better than we ever imagined, that we can rise out of our circumstances and accomplish something great. That is who I want to be.*

Again she perceived that inner voice speak with conviction to her soul. "So, what's stopping you?"

* * *

MARIAN AND RICHARD were met at the front door by a modest troop of serfs and servants who had gathered on the lawn. One, a distressed woman of thirty years with long, dark hair pulled back and covered with a green kerchief, was Charles' mother. Anna was huddled up beside her with a comforting arm wrapped around her waist and an angry scowl directed at the armed intruders.

FitzWalter Manor was a comfortable, if not grand, two story mansion constructed of cob and timber with stone chimneys and trim, and a shale shingled roof. From the front lawn, one could see the straw thatched roofs of the small serf village outside the manor's fence. Loaded stables and a cheerful garden were nestled in back of the house, with grain fields and pastures extending out from the dwellings in wide wedges. Beyond that looped the vast forest transected by only a few roads. One was the road from Nottingham with its spur that led to the estate.

Standing inside the open front gate, which had been closed for the night, were Deputy Edward Blanchard, two soldiers, and a squire holding the reins to four coursers. The deputy was an imposing figure of impressive stature and mature years. A frosted brown beard enveloped his square jaw and obscured his full cheeks while what hair was left on his nearly bald head was cropped short. He wore a black doublet over a white tunic with full sleeves and his onyx boots held a glossy shine. A sword hung at his waist and a bow and quiver were slung over his back. A soldier in chain mail wearing a steel helm with heavy nose guard stood on either side of him, each with his own strong blade. In two gloved hands, the soldier to the deputy's right gripped a gangly boy with wheat colored curls and a terrified face littered with freckles.

As she regarded the interlopers, Marian's blood ran hot, and righteous rage flashed in her eyes. But she understood it was not wise to act in a rash manner where the Sheriff's men were concerned.

After laying a hand on Richard's shoulder and fixing him with a glare of warning, she raised a pleasant, smiling face and strolled over toward the men as if they were invited guests. "Good morrow, Deputy Blanchard," she greeted. "So early for you to call on us."

"Good morrow, Maid Marian," he responded with a polite bow.

She continued walking until she was almost near enough to touch them before planting both feet in the grass. "I see you have apprehended one of my serfs' boys. I am sure we can resolve this matter forthwith. What damage has he done? I shall pay for it," she said coolly while reaching for her coin purse.

"No, Milady," Blanchard corrected with a stony, impassive expression, and continued in a detached tone. "There is a warrant for his arrest."

This announcement took Marian by surprise, but she suppressed her emotions. She had to appear aloof and nonchalant. The deputy withdrew a rolled parchment from his doublet and handed it to her. Marian hurriedly read it. "Poaching?" she gasped in astonishment. "This child? Pray tell, what creature has he allegedly killed?"

"He was seen hauling a dead boar through the forest," Blanchard explained.

Marian let out a laugh. "Am I supposed to believe this scrawny little urchin was carrying a beast that obviously weighed much more than he does? Did your witness see him kill the boar?"

"Not that I know of."

"Then how do you know he didn't just happen upon a dead animal and decide to take it home for dinner—provided he could physically do so?" she asked incredulously.

"But Milady, he should never have entered the forest," rebutted the deputy. "That is king's land, and it is prohibited."

"Now, now, you know children; they wander off," Marian continued in her most charming tone. Her gaze passed over the skinny child on its way back to the warrant. "I don't see a trial date," she said and returned it to Deputy Blanchard. He rolled it up without a glance and tucked it inside his vest. "I am certs there will not be enough evidence to convict him of poaching. Mayhap there is a lesser crime of trespassing in the forest he can be accused of."

"Begging your pardon, Maid Marian." Blanchard shifted uneasily, his voice becoming apologetic as he continued. "With all the money going to Prince John's new tax drive to pay the King's ransom, Sheriff Giffard has determined that holding trials for serfs and peasants is not a good use of Nottingham's resources. It would be a waste of time and money."

"Here, here," she scolded, finding it near impossible to hold back the fiery eruption building inside her. "This is one of my people you are attempting to condemn. He falls under my jurisdiction. I feel I must remind you that nobles have the right to carry out the discipline of their own serfs."

"Yes, Milady, that is frequently the case; but poaching on royal hunting grounds is a crime against the state and thus the Sheriff's domain." He held out his open palms in a gesture of humility as he explained, his hard features melting under the heat of her scrutiny.

A sudden dread rose from Marian's gut. *Surely he will listen to reason,* she thought, then tried a different approach. "Mayhap you are unaware I am King Richard's goddaughter; verily, I am in a position to speak for the King on this matter."

The deputy's slate gray eyes wavered from impassiveness and began to plead with her. "But the Sheriff says Prince John is acting in place of King

Richard while he is away, and because of a new rash of criminal activity, the Prince has granted Nottingham broad discretion to bring it to a halt. The Sheriff contends justice must be swift and harsh to deter future crimes, and that is why the boy has to hang."

"Hang!" Marian proclaimed in utter disbelief. "A day in the stocks or a caning is sufficient for this offense. What do you mean 'hang'?" The anger she had been holding under a thin veil of control burst forth. "Wait 'till Sir Guy hears of this! He will be most displeased indeed. And I shall send word to the other nobles that the Sheriff of Nottingham is now taking it upon himself to march his deputy and soldiers right onto anyone's estate, grab up any of their serfs that they so choose, charge them with false crimes having no substantial evidence against the accused, and haul them off for execution without a trial, all the while wanting to raise our taxes whilst depleting our work forces in this absurd show of power!" Heat radiated off her flushed face as if from a torch.

Marian knew that Giffard was clever and conniving enough to produce false witnesses and evidence if need be. Even through her anger, she could see the pain in the deputy's eyes. He was not the enemy, simply someone following orders. He lowered his head, and a sigh escaped his lips. "I do apologize, Maid Marian, for the intrusion onto your estate and for the duty of which I am required to perform. But your boy must return to Nottingham with us."

Richard could bear this insult no longer and rushed forward to his sister's side. He raised his chin with his most dignified air and proclaimed, "I, Master Richard FitzWalter, am in charge of this estate in the baron's absence, and I demand you stop browbeating my sister and release my serf so he can go back about his business."

Marian placed a hand on his arm and whispered in his ear, "Richard, it won't work. We must think of something else."

Richard's frightened eyes darted to Charles, a boy only two years his junior; a boy he had played with not so long ago; a boy who, despite their difference in station, Marian knew to be his friend. Then his gaze passed over the granite soldiers and raised to the deputy's daunting face. "Right, sister. We shall set forth at once to seek the aid of our neighbors. We will bring the council of nobles down upon Nottingham and see what they have to say about this usurpation of *our* authority!" With fists clinched at his sides, the youth stretched to his fullest height and tried to appear intimidating; but beside the colossal deputy, he only looked like a mouse.

Marian cast an inconsolable gaze over Charles. He looked so small and helpless and she desperately wanted to save him, but feared she could not. She took her brother's arm allowing him to escort her back to the house. Her eyes were drawn to the tear-streaked face of the boy's traumatized mother and she had to turn away. It was then she spied in her peripheral vision a cloaked and hooded figure striding around the side of the manor with a bow in one hand and an arrow in the other. Instantly her stomach leapt into her throat and she froze in her tracks. Terror seized her heart, squeezing it until every fiber of her being reverberated with its beats.

The tall, lean individual whose face was obscured by a dark green hood took several more steps then planted booted feet. A commanding voice rang out drawing all eyes. "Let that child go—*now!*"

* * *

Deputy Blanchard was surprised but not shaken by the stranger's demand. "And who might you be?" he asked crossing thick arms over his brawny chest and narrowing his bushy brows.

Realizing she was not ready to reveal a name Robyn creatively answered, "I am the Lord of Sherwood. The lad was on my land with my permission, and if you will be so kind as to instruct your guard to release him, no one need be harmed this day."

Blanchard, in no mood to be toyed with, uncrossed his arms and huffed out an impatient growl. "There is no 'Lord of Sherwood' save Prince John, and I do not take orders from highwaymen in hoods. Take him!" he ordered motioning to the two soldiers. The one on his right released Charles as they both pulled their swords and dashed toward the hooded stranger.

Marian appeared to stop breathing, her eyes wide in stunned disbelief, but Robyn easily notched the arrow in her bow, drew back and fired. The shaft spiraled through the air and hit its mark in the first man's shoulder, piercing his mail and spinning him around with the force and shock of impact. Before his knee struck the ground, she had drawn and shot a second arrow into the other man's thigh. He cried out as he stumbled, pain twisting his mouth.

No sooner had Robyn released the projectile, she drew a third, shifting her aim to the deputy. But in the few seconds that she spent focused on the advancing swordsmen, Blanchard had armed his own bow. The adversaries stood poised in an instant of mutually assured destruction, each assessing the other. She knew Edward Blanchard to be an excellent marksman since he had won many tournaments over the years. Without blinking, he let loose his arrow, and it raced straight toward its mark.

Robyn's keen focus perceived the deputy's intention at the first twitch of his firing fingers and released her shot almost simultaneously. She knew his aim had been to her heart and had adjusted hers to match. Her intent had not been to take a life, rather to save one; now it appeared she and the deputy would both die on Marian's front lawn.

Time stopped for Robyn as images flashed through her mind's eye, remembrances of her family around the hearth, Christmas pudding, and two carefree girls dancing over a field of spring clover. *I love you, Marian*–the words she never dared say.

One heartbeat passed without a breath and then the unimaginable happened. Robyn's arrow struck the deputy's in midair, and like straw in a breeze they both fell harmlessly to the earth. Robyn had automatically reached for her next shaft and she stood with weapon cocked, aimed, and ready while Blanchard's jaw dropped in stupefied amazement, an empty bow in his hand. His gray eyes widened to twice their normal size as he marveled at the impossible.

Charles seized the moment and ran to his mother who hugged him and shed more tears. Marian, as awestruck as the rest, breathed at last.

"Who?" Blanchard stammered, trying to fit words together. "Who are you?"

Robyn had no explanation for the fortune that had just befallen her, and took no time to search for it, but immediately replied with authority, "I am the shadow in the corner, the monster under your bed, the wolf in the woods, the noise behind you in the dark; I am your worst nightmare." She imagined Blanchard waited for the killing strike while she still could not believe the one in a million shot that saved them both. But Robyn held her stance. "Come on, lad," she called to Charles without diverting her eyes from the deputy. "I'm taking you to a safe place."

He looked at her with awe in his gaze and spoke with hope. "But what about Mum?"

"Bid her farewell or bring her along."

"Just let me collect my cloak," she answered. "We will go with you."

"Meet us by the back gate straight away," Robyn instructed. Then the tone of her voice shifted from command to near playful amusement. "Maid Marian, if you will be so kind as to give your purse to the boy."

\* \* \*

MARIAN FELT as astonished as everyone else. Her heart pounded like a race horse threatening to leap from her chest, and her face radiated with exultation that Robyn had been spared. She had not yet fully comprehended what just transpired; she was too filled with gratitude and relief that Charles was to be spared.

"I beg your pardon?" she asked with a blink, trying to regain her wits.

"Your coin pouch," Robyn repeated, her eyes trained on Blanchard who was frozen in place. "Toss it to the lad. I am robbing you, my dear. We will need means for our escape. Quick, now. My arm grows weary and we wouldn't want anything unfortunate to happen to the good deputy, would we?"

Suddenly her words clicked in Marian's befuddled brain, and she understood what Robyn was doing. In order to keep Marian safe, and hide her true identity, she wanted the deputy and his guards to think there was no connection between them and that she was not acting with Marian's knowledge or consent. *Asides,* Marian thought, *I told her I was planning to donate to her cause.*

"Why you scoundrel!" She tried to sound more outraged than amused, but she was just so damned happy Robyn wasn't hurt.

"Oh, Milady–you wound me with your words!" Robyn feigned insult, a smile tugging at the corner of her mouth.

Marian unfastened her coin purse and handed it to Charles who gave her an uncertain gaze. Facing away from Blanchard, she smiled at the boy. "All is well," she assured him. "You will be safe."

"Gramercy, Milady," he offered as he took the pouch. "An' thanks for tryin' to help me."

Marian nodded and then turned to track her eyes from Robyn to the deputy and back while Charles trotted over to Robyn's side.

"Squire," Robyn addressed in a deep, demanding voice. The young man jumped as one roused from sleep. "Unsaddle those horses."

"Huh?" he uttered in confusion. The two injured guards had regained their footing and stood gripping their wounds unsure what to do.

"Holding back this arrow is a tiring task indeed; I suggest you act with haste," Robyn replied.

"Do it!" Blanchard commanded, then explained as he kept his gaze fixed on his foe. "He wants time to make an escape, which he will not have if we simply mount our steeds and dash after him."

Robyn inclined a slight nod to the deputy in acknowledgement and the squire uncinched girths and lowered saddles to the ground as rapidly as he dared without spooking the chargers.

As soon as the squire's task was complete, Robyn prepared to depart. "Get your mother and meet me at the back gate," she instructed Charles, who nodded admiringly at his new hero and scampered off. "Deputy Blanchard, I know you will give a full report to the Sheriff and I pray he does not hold you responsible. Do not bother to try and make chase, as I know the forest like the back of my hand, and you need to see to your injured men. I feel sure we will meet again one day. Maid Marian, thank you for your hospitality and your gold. I bid you all adieu."

She kept her bow aimed as she took several backward steps, then lowered it, turned, and ran. She met Charles and his mother and together they disappeared into the woods.

# CHAPTER 5

*Sherwood Forest, later that day*

Robyn found comfort in the lush seclusion the dense forest offered as she escorted her charges back to camp. Popular wisdom was to always avoid the dark, mysterious forests of England. There were wolves and bandits and possibly banshees or evil spirits. But even as a child Robyn had treasured the beauty and serenity of the woods and saw no reason to fear them. She reassured Charles and his mother as they marched deeper and deeper into the heart of Sherwood.

As if trying to keep her mind off of the tales of woe regarding the wilds, the woman talked almost nonstop about her life at FitzWalter Manor, her son and her husband who had been declared an outlaw by the Sheriff. "No doubt he is the reason the Sheriff is so determined to punish my boy," she explained. "Two years and he has yet to find and apprehend my John."

Robyn could hear the pride in Alice's voice as in her mind she connected the dots. Joy surged through her soul at the imminent reunion. She smelled the camp a good half mile before they arrived. Smoke rose from the fire, something yummy was boiling in the kettle, and there was the faintest whiff from the latrine. Their sounds also echoed through the trees: Friar Tuck's booming laugh, Alan strumming his mandolin, swords clinking in practice—Tuck and Will, she imagined.

Young David of Doncaster was on watch, perched precariously high in a tree, when he spotted their approach. With the agility and speed of a squirrel, he scampered down to tell the camp. "Robin's back, and he's got more people with him," he reported excitedly. Struck with curiosity, the men gathered under Grandma Oak, near the fire and its iron cauldron simmering with stew.

"Papa!" rang out Charles in animated exuberance as he stampeded up to the bear of a man and leapt into Little John's arms. Overwhelmed with joy, Alice followed right behind him to embrace her husband. A stunned and elated father opened his embrace wide and enveloped them both.

"Surprise," Robyn said with playful amusement as she winked at Little John.

"Alice, Charles!" Little John kissed them both, then asked, "But why are you here?"

Robyn strolled past as they told him the story. She stopped in front of the gathering who smiled and whispered amongst themselves as they watched Little John with his family. *'Tis now or never*, she thought, and lowered her hood.

Expressions of disbelief abounded and Will leapt up from his seat, pointing with one hand as he pushed the black flow of hair from his big, round eyes with the other. "You!" he uttered in amazement. Robyn held her breath, hoping for the best. "Why you're-" Will hesitated.

Robyn bit her lower lip, unable to breathe while Will's expression mirrored the comprehension of what his eyes beheld.

"You're much younger than we thought you were," he managed to blurt out, to Robyn's great relief. "David, you aren't the baby anymore!"

"Robin," David chimed in, "you can't be more than fourteen! Not a single hair on your whole face—not even a wisp on your upper lip!"

Arthur Bland elbowed his way to the center of the group of lads holding out a hand. "I win the bet," he said with a wide grin.

"Maybe not such a baby," she answered wryly.

"You joshing us?" Alan joined in with the others, swinging his instrument over his back by its cord. "I'm surprised you've left your mother's breast," he teased, a twinkle in his green eyes.

Robyn laughed and shook her head, relieved with wildest delight that her identity remained secret. "Alright, fellows, so I've been hiding a baby face. Not everyone sprouts whiskers before they can climb trees!"

Just then Charles dashed up to Robyn's side, his countenance beaming and his eyes all aglow to tell the story.

"You should have seen Robin!" he exclaimed. "Why, he's got to be the best shot in all of England. He struck the deputy's arrow and knocked it clean out of the sky—it was amaaaaazing!"

The lads all stopped their laughing and eyed Robyn with newfound respect. "Truly, Robin? You hit a flying arrow with—an arrow?" Will asked, slack jawed.

"What is this?" Tuck inquired as he waddled to the front of the crowd, rubbing his ample belly. "I knew you were a fair shot with a bow, but Robin-"

"It was nothing," she said with a shrug, trying to downplay the near impossible feat. Then she turned her attention to Alan. "Think quick!" she called and tossed the pouch of coins at him.

Alan hurriedly brought up his hands and fumbled to make an awkward catch. Then, if possible, his eyes grew even wider upon feeling the weight of the purse.

"You seem to have an easy enough time getting in and out of town unseen," she said to Alan. "Now, run buy us all some food, will you? Be sure to bring back bread, mutton, cabbages, some vegetables and apples—lots of apples," Robyn added with a twinkle in her eye.

Alan's gaze moved from the bag of coins to Robyn's earthy eyes. "You, you trust me with all this blunt? You don't think I'll just run off with it?"

"You may have resorted to thievery to stay alive, Alan A Dale," she conceded, "but you are a good lad at heart. I have faith in you. You'll do the right thing."

Alan put his shoulders back and stood a little straighter. Then he swallowed and tucked the pouch into his tunic. "No one has e'er thought me more than a scroggling. You can count on me, Robin. I won't let me mates down. But," he added with a scratch to his head. "All that may be more than I can carry alone."

"I'll go with him," Will volunteered with a grin. "That way we'll be sure he don't run off."

"Could we add some wine to that list?" Tuck asked.

Robin laughed. "Without a doubt." She felt a large hand come to rest on her shoulder and crooked to peer at Little John.

His cheeks were flushed, his eyes moistened and his lips trembled. Then he grabbed her in a powerful embrace. "You saved my boy's life, Robin! How can I ever repay you?"

She briefly returned the hug and then squeaked out, "By letting me breathe, for starters."

Loosening his hold, he stepped back, an expression of awe and reverence on his face. "I am your man. Whatever you say, I will do. What you did today…" John was so choked up that he could no longer speak without releasing a flood of tears.

Robin placed a hand on his shoulder. "I did what was right, what had to be done. Don't pledge an oath to me, my friend, or I will take you up on it."

"I do pledge my oath," Little John declared.

Robyn nodded, then turned to the rest of the group. "There is more from whence this money came. For years we have been robbed, cheated, and mistreated by the nobles, rich merchants, and crooked sheriffs. I say it is time that we take back what should have been ours by rights, to feed ourselves and care for these unfortunates who have come to us, not because they committed grave crimes, but because grave crimes were committed against them. I do not propose that we enact any revenge, for vengeance is the Lord's. We must try not to harm anyone, save in self-defense, but I have some plans and strategies as to how we can rob the rich, not for selfish gain, but for equity alone. Can any amount of silver restore Roger's tongue? Can any number coins return Christina's honor? And Friar Tuck's pulpit or Gilbert's title and lands? No. But they owe us, and we will take back what is owed. Above that, what spoils we acquire will be distributed to the poor and needy of Nottingham and the surrounding villages. Who is with me?"

Robyn spoke with such charisma and confidence as to draw them all in. As one, the troop responded, "Me; I am!"

John nodded in approval. "Listen, my friends. Robin may be young, but he is clever and God above knows he can shoot a bow! I say we follow Robin Hood and bring back some hope to this land. The Sheriff will try to stop us, he surely will. But shall we live our lives cowering in fear, hiding from a ruthless tyrant?"

"No!" they shouted. "We are with you."

John gave Robyn's shoulder a little pat and leaned in to whisper in her ear. "You are a noble, you know, a natural leader; running away couldn't change that. You just exchanged Loxley for Sherwood." Then he scooped up Charles, slung him onto his shoulders, and reached out a hand to Alice who beamed at him with joy.

\* \* \*

AFTER ALAN and Will had gone off to town and while the others were still buzzing with excitement, Robyn noticed the elderly Gilbert had returned to his lean-to. She walked up quietly and stood, waiting to be acknowledged.

He sat on a stone whittling a shaft. Anon, he looked up at her. "So, you shot the deputy's arrow out of the sky?" he mused. "Did you know he was a tournament champion at archery?"

"Aye, but in all honesty, it was either the luckiest of all shots or the hand of Providence," Robyn explained in humility. "I am good, but not that good… and I need to be." She knelt on the ground in front of him and he stopped whittling to look her in the face. "Sir Gilbert Whitehand, will you teach me?"

He cocked his head to one side, deep-set brown eyes widening with astonishment. "I would expect a young buck like you to be so pleased with himself after scoring so, bragging and boasting, and yet you come to me and humble yourself seeking instruction. I don't know who you are, but you are not who everyone thinks you to be. Still, I find that I trust you, and I do not give my trust readily."

"Mayhap I am just not as young as I seem, or not as foolish as most youths," Robyn replied.

He nodded to her. "Very well; I will teach you."

"Gramercy," Robyn said with a twinkle in her eyes.

Gilbert rose to his feet and Robyn stood with him. "Let me see your bow." He held out a hand, and she gave it to him. He scrutinized it carefully, rubbing long fingers across the wood. Then he tested the string by pulling against it several times and frowned. "You should string this tighter, then you will have more thrust, more power, longer range and better accuracy."

Robyn sighed and lowered her head. "If I string it any tighter, I can't pull it back."

Gilbert raised his gaze to the lanky youth and nodded. "Well, you should see Little John about that, lad. He will know how to put muscle on your bones." He handed the bow back to Robyn. "It is nigh about dark now, son, but come back in the morning and we'll begin. If we're going to be taking on the Sheriff, I'll probably have to train the whole lot of you ruffians."

"Indeed," Robyn replied with a wink as she slipped the bow over her shoulder.

* * *

*Nottingham, same day*

Deputy Edward Blanchard rode with his shoulders slumped through Goose Gate into the Old Saxon part of Nottingham leading his two wounded deputies who warranted a few stares from curious townsfolk. He absolutely dreaded facing the Sheriff with the bad news of the boy's escape and the new bandit on the loose. His brows furrowed as he wondered if he would be dismissed from his post, lowered in rank, whipped or caned or worse for his incompetence.

While older and more experienced than Godfrey Giffard, he had not been born into as high of a house and held no illusions of one day being sheriff himself. No, Edward had risen as much as he had hoped and did not relish the thought of a downward spiral to foot-soldier, guard duty or the dungeon.

Midtown was busy at noon in the bustling wool city of 1,500 residents as the deputy's procession plodded through the Old Market Square packed with vendors and merchants hawking cloth and cutlery, religious icons and playing-cards, crocks and cocks, and every conceivable tool, weapon and trinket. Few of the buyers and sellers even noticed the four as soldiers from the castle, injured or otherwise, were an ordinary sight. But one could detect a distinct contrast as they winded their way up the thoroughfare onto the higher ground of the Norman district. The houses were a bit sturdier, the taverns more boisterous, the aroma of baking bread more sumptuous, and the chatter of the citizens was in French rather than the native tongue. While a wooden rampart surrounded all of Nottingham, there was also a clear division between the low-lying Saxon and plateaued Norman parts of town with the market lying squarely in between.

It seemed to Edward that everything in Nottingham blended into dull browns and grays save for the colorful stained glass of the church windows—St. Mary's in the Saxon district, and the larger St. Peter's Church in the Norman district. The sullen procession continued past bakers, brewers, carpenters, cobblers and blacksmiths until they neared the castle gates.

"Alfred," he addressed the young page who had stood with the horses. "See they get to the apothecary."

"Yes, milord," he dutifully replied. The two soldiers with pale and twisted faces seemed as though they may slip from their saddles to the ground at any moment. "This way," he motioned, and they turned down a side street.

Edward took a deep breath, released it, and continued up a ramp and through the imposing gatehouse guarded by pikemen and two huge, round towers.

Like Windsor, Nottingham Castle had first been built by William the Conqueror a century before and upgraded to a stone keep by King Henry. It held a commanding posture atop a natural promontory known as "Castle Rock" one hundred and thirty feet above the River Trent. The stronghold was of particular importance as it protected the bridge over the river on the road from York to London.

As he rode through the outer bailey, Edward shot a glance toward the middle bailey where the royal apartments had been constructed. He knew Prince John and Sir Guy were currently in residence. *Mayhap the presence of distinguished guests will soften the Sheriff's temper,* he thought. Once he entered the upper bailey where the Sheriff's office, great hall, court and dungeons were situated, he dismounted, handed his courser off to a stable boy, and strode into the lion's den.

\* \* \*

SHERIFF GODFREY GIFFARD, most commonly known by his title, 'Nottingham,' was in a gleeful mood as he sorted through the documents on his desk. He had just dipped his quill into the inkwell to sign an order of execution when Blanchard stepped in.

"My lord," he stated in somber greeting, tucking his head and appearing contrite.

Nottingham finished signing the parchment, returned the quill to its holder, sprinkled fine sand over the wet ink and blew gently upon it. Even seated it was apparent that he was a tall man with a powerful, lean physique. Clean and combed black hair fell to the top of his broad shoulders and his matching beard and mustache were neatly trimmed. When he looked up at Blanchard with eyes as opaque as a moonless night, his smile faded, replaced by an impatient sneer. "Where is my poacher? In the dungeon already?"

"No, my Lord Sheriff," he answered uneasily.

Godfrey cocked his head to one side, eying his deputy with suspicion. "Did you let that fair-faced Maid Marian dissuade you from arresting him?" He raised his chiseled chin and crossed his black sleeved arms over his deep blue silk surcoat.

"No sir. She did try, and had a few good points, if I may add," he started to over explain. "She threatened to appeal to Sir Guy, to call together a council of nobles to address you over reaching your authority, but..." One glance at the impatient expression on Nottingham's face halted his babble. "A bandit appeared and took him."

"What?" Anger bellowed through his voice, while confusion worked its way through his features.

"He was an amazing shot with a bow," the deputy continued. "He injured my two guards, both of whom I've sent to the apothecary."

The Sheriff's eyes turned cold and hard. "I do not see *your* injuries."

"I would've had the churl, but he struck my arrow in mid-flight." Blanchard lowered his shoulders and shifted his weight to one foot shaking his head in dismay. "I have never seen anything like it."

"What did this brigand want with *my* poacher?"

"He said the lad worked for him, that he was the 'Lord of Sherwood,' or some such nonsense. Anyway, he held me at point while the boy made his escape. Sheriff, give me a unit of the garrison and at first light we will be in Sherwood tracking him down."

"Hmmm." He furrowed his brow and squinted at his deputy. "Could this have been one of Marian's men, carrying out her orders? You say she fought with you over the boy."

"My lord, I would think not. Why, she was as surprised to see him as I. Asides, he robbed her of a heavy purse."

Godfrey let out an exasperated sigh. "So, then what did this boothaler look like? Did you get his name?"

Blanchard lowered his chin and shook his head. "He was wearing a hood; I couldn't inspect his face, but," he added quickly raising his weary gray eyes. "He was young, beardless I think, average height and slight of build."

"That's just sardin' grand!" Nottingham glared at his deputy with disgust as he slapped a palm on his desk. Rising to his feet, the daunting lawman bellowed, "So, what? We have a wanted poster drawn with the image of a hood and nail it all over town? No name, no description? And I want him caught—by God's bones, I want him dead or alive! Preferably alive so I can kill him."

In two strides the Sheriff was around his desk and pacing with clenched fists. Although Blanchard was a stout, sturdy soldier, he edged a step backward out of his superior's path.

Then Godfrey stopped and rubbed a hand down his bearded chin. He sighed and shook his head. "No," he stated emphatically. "I'll not be swerked. This is a day of celebration and I will not let so minor of an incident disrupt it. Tonight at dinner, Prince John will bestow upon me the official title Earl of Loxley, and no escaped boy or inconsequential thief is going to spoil my moment." He turned his shark's eyes onto the deputy. "Take a detachment of men in the morning, find this hooded archer, and bring him to me. Understood?"

"Yes, my lord; he shall be caught!" Edward vowed.

"See that he is," Godfrey replied, pinning him with an unyielding gaze. "You are dismissed."

Blanchard lowered his head and took a few steps backward before turning to exit the room.

\* \* \*

MAID MARIAN WAS AN EXPECTED guest at the Sheriff's dinner that night. She did her best to look especially appealing for the evening, attired in a deep maroon bliaut with gold trim and sleeve linings and a golden silk cord wrapped around her waist. Her matching golden strands were arranged in two long braids interwoven with maroon ribbons. A gold necklace accented her throat, and she hoped it would draw Sir Guy's eyes up from her cleavage. Her seat was between Gisborne and his freckle-faced, red haired, unmarried daughter who was a year older than Marian. She knew Sir Guy was incensed when he felt Faye had been shunned at court due to her plain appearance, but the real reason none of the young noblemen courted her was out of fear and distrust of her father.

*What am I doing sitting at table with these vipers celebrating Nottingham's final insult as he claims Robyn's rightful estate?* She couldn't help these thoughts crossing her mind. But knowing this was her best chance to hear important news and be of help to Robyn and Queen Eleanor did keep her nerves steady.

She put on a peerless smile and pushed down the bile that churned in her gut.

"Nottingham is honored to welcome Prince John, our presiding monarch, and by the grace of our Lord, my friend!" the Sheriff waxed eloquent as he raised his goblet and tilted it toward the Prince. The other lords and ladies and Bishop Stephen of Lincolnshire all lifted their glasses making such proclamations as, "to your health," "God bless," or "long life." Marian followed in the gesture. A server had already taste-tested the wine before pouring it, just to be on the safe side.

Most of the conversation revolved around how wonderful John, Guy and Godfrey were, how worthy of their titles and lands, and how they undoubtedly deserved larger fortunes. When Robyn's name was brought up, the Sheriff shrugged and said it was better that she ran off; that way he could claim her estate without being stuck with a headstrong wife.

Marian did not finish the perfectly prepared pheasant, or the delicate buttered truffles, or the flakey sweet pastry that remained half eaten on her plate.

After an hour of celebration, Sir Guy seemed to remember she was there. "Why my dear, you have barely touched your food," he commented in surprise. "Are you not well?"

"I am in good health, my lord," she replied. "I do not possess a large appetite, but everything is simply delicious." She shot him a dazzling smile. Marian granted the feast was delicious and under other circumstances she boasted a healthy appetite. Nonetheless this evening her stomach churned in painful knots.

*This is all so unfair,* she thought. *Never mind how unfair they are to commoners, they do not even treat nobility with respect if they don't cow to their whims.* Her thoughts turned to Robyn, out there in the wood somewhere masquerading as a boy with a band of outlaws, and a pang of loneliness struck her heart. She missed Robyn! She had been away from her for years, but after their reunion she found herself longing to be in the company of her best friend. She found she hated the Sheriff for keeping them apart.

Sir Guy patted her hand with his own, a spurious smile glued to his thin lips, and turned back to Nottingham. "What is this I hear of a new bandit lurking about in Sherwood?" he asked, retrieving his hand to pick up his drink.

Marian's ears perked up at once while she tried to appear dispassionate.

The Sheriff sighed and shook his head. "Nothing for you or the Prince to be concerned with," he said. "Just an insignificant ruffian who will soon be in my dungeon. In fact a whole detachment of the Nottingham guard will be marching into the forest on the morrow to hunt him down."

Prince John titled his head toward the Sheriff while he chewed. "You didn't mention an encounter with a bandit."

"Because it is of no consequence," Giffard assured him. "Just a young buck in a hood with a penchant for rescuing poachers. Likely another illegal hunter himself. We'll catch him too."

Sir Guy put down his wine goblet and covered Marian's hand in feigned protection. He raised his chin and spoke to Nottingham. "Sherwood is near Marian's estate. If there is a dangerous brigand about, I think she should move here to be better protected. He has already robbed her once, from what I hear."

"Really, milord, that is not necessary," Marian insisted. "I am confident the Sheriff's men will have him in custody in no time and feel perfectly safe at my manor."

"I must agree with Maid Marian, Guy," Nottingham concurred. "We'll have this Hood in irons before this time tomorrow."

"Aye," Guy fudged removing his hand from Marian's. "If you say so."

Marian managed to make it through the awarding of the title without gagging or running off to the garderobe. She was incensed by how Guy talked about her rather than to her, and all of them thought so little of Robyn or her, or any woman for that matter. She was glad Gifford didn't actually want to marry Robyn, but how awful it would have been if he had done so! For the moment Robyn was free, and she herself was not in any imminent danger from Gisborne; but despite the facts, anxiety wormed around her insides.

## CHAPTER 6

*Sherwood Forest, the next morning*

Deputy Edward Blanchard sat stoically in the saddle atop his black steed leading a troop of twelve men-at-arms down the ten foot wide dirt road eastward into Sherwood Forest. The early morning light filtered through the dense growth of trees, occasionally scoring a blinding ray between leaves and branches into his eyes.

He wore his black leather doublet with matching boots and gloves again, but had added a steel helm over his thin fuzz of hair. At his side were a short sword and dagger while his bow and quiver draped over his back. The soldiers wore matching uniforms of mail coifs and habergeons over padded gambesons with black woolen trousers and leather boots. The uniforms incorporated the red and yellow colors of the Nottingham crest in the form of waist length capes that identified the castle to which the guards were bound.

They all sat alert in their saddles, on bay, sorrel, and gray mounts, with swords sheathed, a secondary weapon in one hand, and the other guiding their reins. Riding two by two behind the deputy, the first set of four held halberds upright, their pole ends resting on a stirrup. The next set of four had crossbows with quivers of bolts, and the last quatrain steadied long pikes across their saddles lest the tips become tangled in low hanging branches.

Edward refused to admit to his men that he had no idea where in the massive wood to search for the outlaw; instead he kept a sharp eye out for any sign of him or the boy. *If they are even still in the forest,* he thought.

He felt like a blade would hang over his neck if he did not find this thief and the young poacher. Of course he had a heart and would prefer not to see the boy hang, but following the Sheriff's orders was his duty. Nottingham bore the moral responsibility for the execution, not him. Moreover, the lad had broken king's law by witness account, even if it was Prince John who currently claimed authority over the royal hunting ground.

*Maid Marian did have a point; how could a boy so small carry a large boar? Richard would not like this at all.* His sharp cool-gray eyes scanned left and right and he cocked his head to listen for sounds. All he heard were the morning songbirds, the rustle of squirrels scampering about, and the horses hooves plodding ever onward. *Richard isn't here, but Prince John and the Sheriff are; and what choice have I but to follow my orders? Still, I can't help but wonder about this new outlaw. Who is he? Why here and why now? What if...*

His musings were abruptly interrupted by an arrow whizzing so near his face that he felt the breeze from it. Eyes widening in shock, he lifted a hand and shouted, "Halt! To the ready!"

But before he could finish giving the order two large tree trunks fell to block the road in front and behind the caravan and a flurry of arrows rained down around them. The men at arms gripped their weapons tighter, drawing them to the ready as they held firm to their horses' reins and turned their heads searching for their enemies. But they saw none.

"Ghosts of Sherwood," whispered one, and fear wove its way through the ranks.

In an instant half a dozen men armed with swords, staffs, and bows emerged from hiding holes in the ground at their feet while a literal giant approached through a mist set ablaze with the bright streams of sunlight before them on the road.

In a lightning quick reflex, Edward slung his bow into his hands, loading an arrow. But before he could fire, his hands felt the jolt of his weapon being ripped away by a shot from nowhere. He was stunned! How could this be happening?

The giant spoke as he neared and Blanchard got a better look at him. "Good morrow, Deputy," he said politely. "And what occasion have you to enter our forest this fine morning?"

Edward raised his hand signaling his men to hold while he cocked his head at the specimen before him. Then recognition lit on his grizzled face. "John Naylor, is that you?"

"Aye," the big man replied as he stopped and stood arms akimbo. "It has taken you long enough to find me, and now I have an army of my own, so what will it be?"

"It is a fortunate day for you, indeed," Edward said with some relief. "We are not here for you. In fact, if you and your party will just slip away back into the woods, I'll forget I ever saw you."

"Not here for me?" Little John frowned and his voice rang with disappointment... or was that humor?

"No. The Sheriff has sent us here to find a new outlaw, a young hooded buck who absconded with a wanted poacher and robbed Maid Marian, so you and your band are of no interest to us this day. If you would please just step aside, no one need be hurt."

"You hear that, Robin?" Little John said in a boisterous tone. "You rate a whole troop of Nottingham guard, but nothing for paltry John Naylor. What is England coming to?"

Confusion showed on Edward's face until Robyn stepped out from behind a tree. "Deputy Blanchard, so we meet again." He turned his gaze to whom he believed to be a lanky lad and reached for his sword hilt.

Robyn raised her bow with notched arrow. "Let's not see if your sword is faster than my shot, for I assure you, good deputy, it is not."

"So you are Robin," he said returning his hand to rest on the pommel of his saddle. "Robin who?"

"Hood," she replied, taking sideways steps out into the road. "And the company of men I command in these woods is far larger than the one you brought. As you know from our previous encounter, I prefer not to kill, but do not think that I won't if it comes to that."

Their eyes met and Edward could not help but foster respect for this new outlaw leader. "Robin Hood of Sherwood," he stated in affirmation. "Mayhap the Sheriff will be satisfied if I bring him the poacher. You and I need not fight this day."

Robyn laughed and shook her head. "That is not going to happen. What *is* going to happen, is that you and your men will dismount, disarm yourselves and disrobe, then march unceremoniously back to Nottingham."

Edward's eyes widened, and he sat a little straighter in his saddle. "We shall do no such thing! That is absurd!"

"No, deputy, it is what will happen. Did you think I would not anticipate you were coming after me? I know the Sheriff's black heart and know it well. Did you think I would be unprepared? You come to me with a dozen men, but hiding in these trees I have two dozen trained archers, not to mention the six standing around you. We have caught you off-guard and cut off your routes of escape. If you want to go home alive, you will do as I say."

"You, a mere boy, claim to command so large a troop? My men are skilled fighters in armor and your rag-tag bunch are no match for us," the deputy explained.

"Mayhap, if all other conditions were equal, but as you see they are not," Robyn replied with confidence. "We have your men surrounded and outnumbered. If you make a move, you will all be dead before a one of you can draw blood on us. But out of the generosity of my heart, I will order my men to allow you to leave unharmed, if you but comply. I would require you to promise to never again come looking for us, but we both understand the Sheriff would never let you keep that promise."

*I pray he lets me keep my life after this!* Edward thought. A quick scan of the vicinity did not reveal those hiding in the forest. He knew arrows had flown in on them from various directions, but were there really two dozen? He had only this Hood's word on that. Unfortunately, it would seem the rogue was right; they may be able to kill a few of Robin's men, but they would never get out of the forest alive. He hung his head and sighed. "It would appear that you are an honorable bandit, Robin Hood, to only humiliate us when you could easily have killed us all. But you are correct about the Sheriff. I pray he will be as merciful as you. He will not relent."

Robyn raised her chin and relaxed the grip on her bow and arrow. "Neither will I," she stated, a promise that puzzled him.

*Could this be some personal plan of retaliation against Giffard? If so, then he must be someone whom the Sheriff has wronged, or whose loved one the Sheriff has killed. That narrows it down to... everyone in the county.* He slumped and lowered his head. "Men, do as he says. Dismount, lay down your weapons, and strip off your mail."

"And boots," Robyn added.

"And boots? But you are making us walk through the rough forest ground; we need our boots."

"The road is fairly smooth, and you may keep your stockings."

The deputy shook his head in resignation and climbed down from his courser. He looked up at the steed and stroked her nose. *I love this horse,* he thought. *We've been through a lot together.* The emotion caught him unaware, and he choked back a tear.

"These fellows won't hurt you, girl," he said looking into big round eyes. "I'll see you again soon."

\* \* \*

ROBYN STUDIED HER OPPONENT. *He cares for the lives of his men and he even cares for his horse. He isn't like the Sheriff, but that doesn't mean he isn't dangerous. Surely Nottingham won't kill him for this.* She frowned as she watched the soldiers pile their arms and remove their armor. Then she stepped over to Tuck, who held his sword on their captives, and whispered in his ear. He gave her a confused look and then pulled out a scrap of parchment and a thin cylinder of lead from a pouch on his belt. The Friar would sometimes scribble down poems and prayers and Robyn recalled he frequently carried his instruments with him. She scratched a note onto the parchment with the lead stylus and folded it once.

When the deputy and his soldiers stood in their braies and stocking feet, Robyn walked up to Blanchard and gave him the note. Tuck, Little John, and the others were already gathering the chainmail and weapons and packing them on the steeds to be led back to camp.

"When you return, give this to the Sheriff; I pray it will save you from a hanging, honorable deputy. Mayhap one day we will meet as allies rather than enemies, but make no mistake." Her eyes fixed on his as one holding great authority, and her voice was as dynamic as that of a general. "Nottingham can send whomever he wants, as many as he wants, as often as he wants, and he will never find me. I will always be ready for him and will give my utmost to put a stop to his treachery, cruelty, and treason. You may think you have no choice save to serve him; but in my experience there are always possibilities."

He lowered his gaze and gave a short nod. "Then it is war, for neither will he stop hunting you. The Sheriff is a prideful man, and this insult will cause his soul to burn like a crucible toward you. I pray we are never pitted against one another, Hood, but if we are, I will be a most dangerous opponent without a doubt. Thank you for the letter and for keeping your word."

Robyn nodded in understanding. "Blanchard, I always make a point of keeping my word. Now, all of you back to Nottingham, and stay out of Sherwood," she called with raised voice. "If you think we appear and disappear as spirits, just wait until you encounter the real ghosts of the forest!"

* * *

LITTLE JOHN, Friar Tuck, Arthur Bland, and David of Doncaster escorted the deputy and his troop to the forest's edge. Robyn, Much, Gilbert Whitehand, Will, and Alan led the chargers about a mile toward their camp and then stopped.

"Will, run ahead," Robyn instructed, "while we wait here with the horses. Find Roger, the farrier, and tell him to bring his tools for I have a most important task for him."

Will nodded, turned, and scampered nimbly through the underbrush. Gilbert leaned against a tree studying Robyn while Alan patted a bay mare. "Your plan was a brilliant success, Robin," he said in admiration. "I assume you did not intend to hit any of them, but your first shot toward the deputy almost grazed his cheek."

"See why I need the lessons?" she replied with a half laugh.

"And the villager who lost his tongue," he continued. "You have an important charge for him as well?"

"Indeed," she declared seriously. "These horses are shod with a Nottingham smith's shoes. They will be far too easy to track. I need him to remove them before we are anywhere near camp. In fact…" Her face lit with sudden inspiration. "Alan, Much, gather some vines, stones, and start sharpening some staff length branches. The Sheriff's men will follow the horses to this spot and I want to set up some traps to greet them." The men grinned at that and set about gathering the necessary elements.

"Are you sure you didn't fight in the Holy Land?" Gilbert suggested. "A youthful squire, by chance, or as a page for a knight?"

"On my oath, I've never left England," she replied. "My father and brother served, but I have no such experience."

"And yet you have the mind and bearing of a commander in the field.

You rally those under you and give them important tasks and vital duties, praising and building them up," he perceived in amazement.

"Roger has lost his tongue, Sir Gilbert, not his hands. We need his talents; and yes, I suppose you or I could pull horseshoes, but he needs to know that he can still be useful. If you are accusing me of being a good leader, then I thank you."

"But you will not tell me how you come by these skills, any of them." When she looked away without a reply, he simply nodded. "That is your right, I suppose. You are still wary, and that I can understand, as you have only been with us a few weeks. But already you are in charge. The funny thing is, it seems very natural for you, as if you have always been making plans and issuing orders."

She returned her gaze to him with a hint of trepidation. "You have many years' experience leading men in battle. Do you think I should defer to you? Would you make war on the Sheriff?"

Gilbert sighed and shook his head. "I will never again lead men to their deaths, and was content to live out my last years in obscurity in the forest. But now you are here inspiring us to rob from the rich and give to the poor, to stand up to Nottingham's injustices, and who knows what next–rescue the King? You think you have secrets? Suppose, as an act of trust, I tell you just one of mine."

"If you wish." Robyn stepped closer to Gilbert, and they sat together on a large stone.

"About two years ago our forces arrived and captured Acre after a siege, where we took 2,700 Muslim hostages. Many of them were women and children. Of course we killed soldiers whom we fought, but that is war, isn't it?" He lifted his eyes to Robyn's and then lowered them to the earth. "The King had requested a parlay with Saladin, but the sultan refused to meet with him unless a peace agreement had first been reached. Instead Saladin began a negotiation for the release of the prisoners. This dragged on without him meeting all of Richard's demands. Thinking the sultan was not serious about forging a treaty, that he delayed too much, Richard became impatient. He had the prisoners brought outside the city walls where Saladin and his men could see them and ordered them all to be decapitated. My sword was called upon to mete out this judgment, and I fear no amount of prayer and fasting will ever cleanse the act from my soul. Saladin sent in his cavalry to try to rescue them, but our archers and catapults held them back." He paused to run a hand down his haggard face. "The cries of Muslim women and children are not unlike our own. Their blood is just as red. Is not the infidel a human being, also created in the image of God?" he asked lifting his eyes to Robyn's face. "If not for God's grace, I could have been born in that land, raised to believe their teachings. Was it right to slaughter unarmed prisoners of war, elders, women, and children along with the Saracen?"

Robyn wanted to offer him comfort and solace but, in her role as a boy, an embrace or a kiss would be inappropriate. She was not familiar with this story, and fully understood why it wasn't being told. Decent Englishmen would have been appalled by the slaughter. "You followed the orders of your King," she said in grave resignation. "What else could you do?"

"Naturally, the sultan reacted by killing all Christian prisoners the Saracens held, and soon after that the surrender treaty was finalized and we moved on leaving Acre in the hands of the French. With the blood of Christians on his hands, King Richard was remorseful and regretted his rash decision, but it was too late. That was a sad day, Robin, one I wish to forget. But sometimes I see them in my sleep and hear their cries."

Robyn nodded, lowering her gaze lest she spy the tears welling in his eyes. She knew of his nightmares though no one spoke of them. "I suppose if you suffer the torment of purgatory in this life, you will be spared its cleansing in the next. Your soul is saved by Christ's own sacrifice, and I believe the very fact that you feel sorrow and compassion for your enemies is proof of that salvation."

"Thank God you have been spared the horrors of real war, Robin," he said. Then her teacher rose and walked away.

She sat for a moment, head bowed, hands clasped between her knees. Thank God, indeed. But her father and brother had not. What horrors had they witnessed, or participated in? She closed her eyes not wanting to imagine.

\* \* \*

NOTTINGHAM CASTLE, *later that day*

NO SOONER THAN he had dressed, Deputy Edward Blanchard once again stood in the Sheriff's office having failed to perform his duty. Foreboding consumed him as Giffard read the note aloud.

"*Dear Sheriff, do not fault your deputy and his guard, for should the devil himself have entered my domain, he would have been sent fleeing with his tail between his knees. You need not waste time pursuing me, for I shall take every opportunity to pursue you. Sincerely, Hood.*"

Giffard fisted the note into a wad, gripping so that his nails bit into the heel of his hand. Then he hurled it across the room. "Bloody hell!" His face was red with fury just as Edward had predicted. "But you got a good look at him this time?"

"Yes sir, milord. I don't draw well, but I can work with one what can. His name is Robin Hood and he's right put out with you for some reason. Never heard of anyone 'round these parts with that name, so I figure he's from another county."

"You arse sardin' twit!" Giffard bellowed. "He's a bloody outlaw! He can make up any name he wants to call himself. How do we know who the hell he is or where he came from?" Edward shrunk back, his face turning pale. "You say he was very young and beardless, yet he commanded a host of brigands. How is that possible? Was he noble? He can obviously read and write, which would suggest a noble or clergy background."

"His dress was quite common, as was that of his men."

"So he took your mounts, did he?" The Sheriff plotted as he paced the straw strewn wood planked floor. "We can track them to his hideout. I shall go myself this time, to personally oversee the mission and make sure nothing goes awry. You," he said pointing an accusatory finger into Edward's chest, "will stay here and post guards at every entrance to the town. If he is foolish enough to come after me, we will catch him like a rabbit in a snare. Go fetch our best tracker and two dozen of the castle guard. I will *not* have that churl humiliating me while Prince John is visiting, is that clear?"

"Yes, sir," the deputy replied snapping to attention. "Right away, sir." He darted out before Giffard could change his mind, eternally grateful that he retained all of his body parts.

* * *

That evening, a stone-faced Sheriff returned to Nottingham leading half of his two dozen guards, battered and bloody. The others had fled in terror from the ghosts of Sherwood Forest and he doubted they would ever return to the castle.

    Robyn's traps had been all too successful, both halting their advance through the wood and upholding local legends. The large owl swooping down at dusk with its eerie cry was simply added luck. As much as a weary Godfrey hated to admit it, it was time to enlist the aid and ideas of his two friends. They must stop this insolent insurrectionist before he began to infect the people.

* * *

A STARRY NIGHT blanketed Nottingham as a man's hands reached into a cage atop one of the castle's turrets to retrieve a pigeon. He strapped a tiny cylindrical case around its foot, slid in a rolled note, and tied it shut. Cautiously he surveyed his surroundings while standing motionless for a few moments. Satisfied he was alone, he released the bird into the sky and watched it fly away.

# CHAPTER 7

*Windsor Castle, two days later*

An ordinary looking middle-aged man rapped on the door to Queen Eleanor's chamber. "Is Your Highness awake?"

The tall door opened with a quick jolt in the gloved hand of the robust matriarch. "Indeed, Marceau; I have already had my morning ride and heartily broken fast. Now, what news have you for me?"

He bowed and handed her a tiny tube-shaped leather pouch. "It arrived during the night. No one has viewed its contents, I made certs of that."

"Good. Your station may not receive the honor of a knight or spy, but your work is of vital importance to the crown," she said and smiled at him.

"Gramercy, Your Highness," Marceau replied, pleased to have received the Queen's praise. He bowed and retreated to the hallway as Eleanor closed the door behind him.

She carried the small package to her writing desk, took a seat and removed the note. *New outlaw in Nottingham. Robin Hood. Highly skilled. Hates the Sheriff. Acts honorably. Commands dozens. Price on his head.*

"Interesting," she mused and paused to consider the possibilities. Then she took out a piece of paper, dipped her quill into the ink well, and composed a letter.

*M,*

*What do you know of the outlaw Hood? Try to discover more. Is he loyal to the King? Could we enlist him as an ally?*

*E.*

"There," she concluded. She sprinkled bits of fine sand across the ink to prevent it from running, then let it dry before blowing off the grains, folding it into an envelope and sealing it with wax and a commonplace seal she kept for use in just such covert circumstances. After tucking the letter away in a secret compartment of her desk, Eleanor strolled over, opened her door and peered out into the hallway. Upon spotting one of the stewards, she called him over.

"George," she began in an aloof tone. "I have grown dreadfully bored with these bed curtains and wish to commission a new set. Do find me that merchantess, Amee de Neville who has secured good merchandise for me in the past, and make haste." She raised her chin to conclude the command. *She is one of my most trusted agents and will raise no suspicion taking this letter to Marian.*

"Right away, Your Highness," George pledged with a cordial bow. He was thin as a reed, and almost as frail, but properly cultured with impeccable manners that suited Eleanor. "I was on my way to find you." She raised her brow and pursed her lips in annoyance, but the steward continued. "There is a prioress awaiting you at court. She arrived early and is very persistent to speak with you on a grave matter. I tried to pass her to one of the ministers, but she stubbornly vows that only the Queen will suffice. Shall I have her escorted out, Your Grace?"

Eleanor brought a hand to her chin. Now she was intrigued. "No, George; that will not be necessary. I will attend court this morning and see for myself what urgent matter has emboldened the prioress."

George stepped aside making way for the Queen with a chivalrous bow. "I will find our merchant and bring her to the castle."

"Very good." She graced him with a smile before proceeding down the corridor toward the courtroom.

Two attendants stood at the large double doors to the hall, the one on her left courteously opening the ingress for her. She nodded acknowledging him and promenaded into the official room. Very few courtiers were about at that hour, only two gentlemen playing chess at a corner table, a maid setting out flowers in their vases and an engaged couple making eyes at each other. In the center of the hall, standing near the throne, was a stout, buxom woman in an unadorned black robe with long, wide sleeves. The white draped wimple and black overveil completely covered her hair and her round, smooth cheeks did little to pinpoint an age. Eleanor decided that her visitor was neither young nor old, but somewhere suitably in-between.

When the prioress turned to the Queen Mother, relief lit her hazel eyes. "Your Highness," she uttered in a grateful tone, and bowed from the waist clasping her hands together in front of her. "Thank you ever so much for agreeing to see me."

Eleanor continued to scrutinize the clergywoman as she walked toward her. "My steward informed me that you were unmovable, so I had to see you for myself." She stopped upon reaching the Benedictine eying her with a curious gaze. "What is this matter of such great urgency?"

"I am Margery Dourant, second Prioress of Wallingwells Priory in the north of Nottinghamshire," she began with enthusiasm. "I have written to Your Highness twice before, but having received no reply, and what with unreliable couriers and highwaymen and the like, I presumed you never received my request."

A light of recognition sparked in the recesses of Eleanor's mind. The letters had arrived and she intended to respond, but had been so distracted by attempting to procure her son's release that nothing else registered.

"And so you have traveled all this way in person," the Queen noted. "This must be a matter of import. Prioress Dourant, you now have my attention."

A joyous smile radiated across Margery's face. "God bless you," she gushed and bowed again as she nervously fingered her silver cross. "As you know, the war has left many widows and orphans along with returning our brave Christian soldiers blind or lame, or maimed in some other fashion–even sickened in their minds and souls. And yet there are so few hospitals, and alms houses, to care for them. Nottinghamshire, in particular, is lacking facilities for the poor and indigent. Our Priory is small, Your Highness, and needing resources so that we may fulfill the Lord's work by building just such a house to care for our wounded crusaders and their widows and orphans who find themselves without food or shelter. I understand you to be a virtuous, good-hearted Christian woman, who is known as a great benefactor to the Church. We at Wallingwells are in need of your generosity now, more than ever." In an emotional outburst, she clasped the Queen's hand and dropped to her knees. "Please, Your Highness; help us."

Eleanor sighed and tugged upward on Margery's hands. "Stand up, Prioress." The words escaped through her teeth like a hiss. "'Virtuous' may have gone a bit far with the flattery, but you are correct that I patron the Holy Church. That fact established, I must inform you this is a bad time."

"This is a terrible time indeed!" she hastily agreed speaking with extreme passion. "For all my life local abbeys and priories could care for the poor in their areas alone, but because of the war the need has become too great. I have seen noble men reduced to pitiful beggars, common soldiers who fought in our Lord's Name, for Christ's glory and honor, carrying the Holy Cross with them into battle, return missing limbs or riddled with leprosy, brave men who shake and cry in the night from images that haunt their spirits. And the children! So many orphans, we cannot take them all in. Can you imagine turning away a child, a child whose father gave his life fighting for our banner, for our King?"

"Prioress," Eleanor interrupted. "I know well the horrors of war, and this one has lasted too long. I myself bear much of the misery of which you speak, which is why—while I agree with you wholeheartedly and would under any other circumstances gladly give you a hefty donation—all of our resources now must go to securing the release of King Richard. The royal family cannot spare the money you request at this time." Eleanor watched as Margery's fervor started to fade. "Have you not sent your petition to the Church, to Rome?"

"Indeed," she replied, her voice more somber. "And they gave me the same response. Resources are needed more elsewhere. Your Grace?" Margery turned haunted eyes up to meet Eleanor's. "Why was it necessary to send so many to die in a foreign land, fighting an enemy we have never seen for a reward we will never experience?"

"Vanity."

Margery tilted her head and inquired. "May I speak freely?"

Surprised, Eleanor's eyes widened. With a laugh she replied, "I thought you already were!"

Color rose in the Prioress's cheeks and she lowered her face. "Forgive me; I have never been in the presence of royalty before."

"There is nothing to forgive. What wish you?"

"I know that Your Grace will understand," Margery began. "The Church is like all other things; women are considered unimportant, less valuable, not capable, and even expendable. I truly admire you and can only imagine what it has taken for you to become the extraordinary and powerful person you are. The bishop could not be bothered with me. Of the three cardinals I wrote to, only one replied. But our work is important in the Lord's eyes and for the English people–your people. When King Richard's ransom is paid, and he has returned, will you remember my request?"

Eleanor recognized the struggle the Prioress grappled with; she had waged the same battle her whole life. She thought of her first marriage that had been political and how she managed an advantageous departure from it. She recalled the years spent locked in a tower because of the bitter disagreement between Henry and herself. How she had loved and hated that man! He had been her passion and her purgatory. But now her heart belonged to another man–her favored son, Richard. If anything should prevent his safe return, if John should seize the throne instead, she could find herself back in that tower, or worse. Even with her considerable authority, her power and influence, her wealth and property, all could be nil with one word from a man–John.

*I am getting too old to be locked up in towers*, she thought.

Eleanor met Margery's eyes and let out a slow breath. "You think, because I live in a castle, I do not recognize my people's plight, but that isn't true. I know all too well the shadow that has fallen over England, one that can only be dispelled by the return of the King. Once Richard is safely back, I promise to give consideration to your request to build an alms house in Nottinghamshire. I shan't forget you."

Once more relief washed over Margery's face. "Thank you, Your Highness," she cooed, and bowed to kiss her Queen's hand. "I already pray for you every day, but now I shall double my prayer time for you and the King. God bless you, my Queen; God bless you."

"Come now, Prioress Dourant," Eleanor said gaily. "Did you arrive with an escort?"

Big, round eyes looked out from that white, ivory face. "Two of the sisters and our driver are awaiting without."

"Bring them in. Your party shall take respite in the great hall before you journey back to Wallingwells. I am pleased to see that there are members of the clergy more focused on caring for God's people than filling their own mouths and furthering their political careers."

* * *

*Sherwood Forest, one week hence*

Robyn raised the heavy ax and slammed it down onto a length of thick branch, chopping it into manageable sized fire wood. In the summer heat, sweat poured from her brow which she wiped with her sleeve before repeating the aching motion. Some of the children pitching horseshoes nearby noticed her. Young Charles Naylor and Christina, Isaac's daughter from Loxley village, dashed over to see what she was doing.

"Why are you chopping the wood?" Charles asked, a confused wrinkle around his nose. "You are the leader. Here, I will do that for you," he eagerly offered.

Robyn lowered the ax and stomped the branch to finish the break. Smiling, she wiped sweat once more. "Thank you Charles, but let me ask you a question." He gazed up at her, enraptured and in awe, and nodded. "How do you think one best leads?"

He tilted his head and pursed his lips, concentration radiating from his features. Then he shrugged. "I always thought leaders just gave orders."

Robyn laughed and took a moment to sit on a fresh stump nearby. The two children gathered around her and it was Christina who spoke next. "Robin does more than just give orders, silly," she said shooting Charles a disapproving stare.

Robyn reached out a hand and mussed it through the boy's tawny hair. "By example, young man. The way to lead is by doing."

"Like when Lord FitzWalter rode off to the crusades with the King instead of sending a knight in his place, even though he is old," Charles offered in evidence.

"Precisely," Robyn smiled.

"But chopping wood is such an ordinary, unimportant task," Christina observed. "Wouldn't your time be better spent planning the next theft?"

"All activities are important," Robyn replied, "even yours. Here, I'll show you. Charles, you see that stack of logs I've chopped?" He nodded. "They are doing no good where they lie. Could you please carry them over to the wood stack near the fire for me?"

"Aye!" he said and scrambled to load as much of the tinder in his arms as he could manage. Christina giggled after him.

Once they were alone, Robyn spoke quietly to Christina. "I suspect his arms are as strong as mine." Surprise lit her youthful face. "'Tis true. That is why I must chop the wood, so that my arms and back become stronger. Sometimes it takes hard things to make us stronger, but we must never give up and never, never let anyone stop us from becoming everything that we can be. You see this ax head?" She lifted the tool to show it to the girl.

Christina nodded and shrugged. "It just looks like an ax head to me."

"To some people, you just look like a girl. Once this was part of a rock, buried deep in the earth, but someone dug it up and put it into a red-hot fire. The rock didn't like it, but in the fire all the iron melted and drained away from the rock and then it was poured into a mold. When it cooled, it was the shape of an ax head, but it was dull. The smith then scraped metal filings across this thin side over and over again, rasping away bits of iron. It probably didn't feel good, but it made the edge sharp so it could cut wood easily. Then it was fitted on its handle and became valuable to the people who use it. If it had stayed buried in the earth, the ore would have never known pain; it also would never do anything important."

Christina's eyes glimmered with understanding. "Things that hurt us can also make us stronger and more valuable, more useful."

"That's right," Robyn said, her eyes beaming compassionately at the damaged young woman before her. "You are not less than before; you are more. Don't ever, ever, think that you are less."

On impulse, Christina lurched forward and hugged Robyn, then whispered in her ear. "I know who you are, why your arms aren't strong, but don't worry; I won't tell anyone. They don't see like I do." Then composing herself, she sat back in her spot.

Robyn's eyes grew large with sudden fear, but the girl's gleaming expression eased her anxiety. "But how?"

"Shhh," she said putting a finger to her lips. "I don't just look at people; I see them. I see you, and you are a good leader. You always have been. No one else sees; they only see what they expect to, but they all know you are good. I don't know if they would follow you if they knew, so I will say nothing, not even to Mama and Papa. Even before, back at Loxley, you were always my hero."

Robyn's mouth fell agape in wonder at Christina's words and she found herself speechless with blush rising in her cheeks.

Christina smiled. "The ax story is a good one." Then she hopped up and strolled back to rejoin the children at play.

While Robyn remained in a state of disbelief that this child recognized her, Alan A Dale trotted up to her side. "The merchant wagon from York will be passing the east road through Sherwood tomorrow afternoon. It'll be the journey back to London after selling goods in the north, so will be loaded with coins, not merchandise. I hear the merchant in question puts his thumb on the scales and swindles the poor every chance he gets."

Robyn laughed and rose to slap Alan on the back. "Good work, mate. I'm leaving anon to select the perfect spot for an ambush."

"Not without me, you ain't!" Alan declared with a grin.

As the two started out of camp, they passed Friar Tuck hanging out his clean, wet blanket to dry in the sun.

"Good day, gents," he greeted. "Are we out for a stroll?"

"Stakin' out the east road for tomorrow's merchant," Alan replied. "Want to come?"

"Well," he stammered and rubbed his pudgy hands together.

"It would be helpful, Friar," Robyn added. "I've been meaning to ask you something, anyway."

"East road isn't too far, I don't suppose. Sure, I'll join you lads," he agreed, and they headed out into the forest. "What can I do for you, Robin?"

"You can teach me to handle a sword," she said. "Verily, I hear tell you are indeed one of the best swordsman in all of England and, well, we can't let all that fine knowledge stay locked up inside you, now can we?"

"I wouldn't say best," Tuck answered modestly. Then a worried furrow crossed his brow. "That Sheriff of Nottingham is damn dangerous with a blade, mind you Robin. He's killed many a man in a fair fight, more in ones not so fair. You aren't thinking of going up against him man to man, now are you?"

"Nothing like that," she assured him. "Not when I know I can best him with a bow. But I must be prepared for every contingency. Little John is helping me get strong, Gilbert is training me to be an even better shot, and so naturally, I turn to you for the blade. Don't worry, Alan; when I'm done with that, I'll be coming to you for music lessons," she said with a wink toward her cohort.

The men both laughed. Tuck asked, "Do you own a sword? Let's have a look at it."

She drew the steel from her scabbard and they paused while the Friar examined it. His mouth fell open in sudden astonishment. "Why, Robin, this is a crusader sword! I recognize the make, the quality, this cross in the hilt. Where ever did you get it?"

Robyn almost forgot to breathe. Why had she not thought about the uniqueness of her father's sword? "I found it," she offered as calmly as she could.

He shook his head. "No one 'finds' a sword like this, lad. God will forgive you if you stole it as long as you only use it in a righteous cause."

Robyn hung her head as if ashamed. "So I found it on a knight passed out drunk after he returned from the Holy Land. I figured he may not want it anymore, anyway." In her heart she asked forgiveness, not for theft but for lying... again.

Tuck returned her sword. "Well, you have a fine weapon. Let's see your grip."

Robyn held the sword the way her father had shown her, firmly, but not too tight.

Tuck nodded. "Yes, but turn your body sideways, like this," he demonstrated, "to present a slighter target, and keep your right foot out in front like so." Robyn mimicked his stance. "Good, good. We'll work more later," he said and commenced walking again. "We have a robbery to lay out, I believe."

"Yes, thank you," Robyn said.

"First, I shall teach you to fence," Tuck said and then grinned wide. "Then I shall teach you to fight."

"Are they not the same?" Alan asked.

"Indeed not!" Tuck bellowed with a hearty laugh. "Fencing has rules." Abruptly his tone darkened. "The Sheriff doesn't fence."

*  *  *

TUCK MADE sure Robyn and Alan could quote Psalm 1, Psalm 23 and several of the Confessions of St. Augustine before they arrived at the east road. Then they grew quiet as they walked up the dirt highway searching for a spot where the road was sunken below the surrounding earth and the trees were thick enough to conceal an ambush. They had discovered just such a stretch when they heard the rumble of a carriage and the clop of hooves ahead.

"You did say tomorrow, right Alan?" Robyn asked.

"Definitely tomorrow," he insisted.

"Back into the trees boys," Tuck said and waddled to squat behind a large shrub. They watched as an ornate white carriage pulled by a pair of sleek horses rolled into view. The driver wore fine clothes, and the carriage was adorned with gold trim. "It's a church carriage," Tuck whispered. "I wonder who's in there."

"Do you really want to find out?" Robyn whispered back.

"Yes, I do," Tuck said with resolve. "Wait here and I'll signal you."

The Friar seemed to defy physical law as he nimbly made his way down to the road to pretend he was just walking to Newark Greyfriars Abbey. As he suspected, the carriage stopped, and the door opened, but no one stepped out. Inside, Tuck spotted a middle aged bishop dressed in fine silks with a ring on every finger lounging on a cushion. Across from him sat two lads about Charles Naylor's age. They were not dressed so fine, and it was apparent they had not eaten so well as the bishop.

"Good day, Your Grace," Tuck said with an exaggerated bow. He could practically smell the money and corruption oozing from inside the coach. He smiled even as he seethed within. The humility of a lowly friar was well rehearsed by now. "I trust you and your charges are well."

"Indeed, Friar. On your way to Greyfriars?"

"Yes, Your Grace," he replied. "If you could be so kind, I would greatly appreciate your blessing, bishop?"

"Albrec, Bishop of Kirkstall," he replied in cool boredom. Without even casting his eyes toward Tuck, he held out a hand. "You may kiss my ring."

*Kiss his ring indeed! I want to kick his arse.* Tuck reined in his emotions for the moment while he leaned through the open door to kiss the bishop's ring. He made a closer observation of the man's wide nose, up-curled lip, flabby chin, and pinprick eyes. While his hands were fair and smooth, having never wielded a tool or been put to hard labor, there was a foul odor arising from his body, as if what he had eaten did not agree with him. Tuck suspected he ate too many cakes and indulged in too much imported wine.

"Are these lads new acolytes for the church?" he asked aloud.

The Bishop snorted. "They are orphans from the hospital at Leeds. I am taking them to a London workhouse where they can become useful members of society."

It sounded straightforward, though a bit out of the ordinary. Bishops, especially those who enjoyed their high station as much as Albrec obviously did, were not in the habit of personally transporting indigent children around the countryside. Something about the story was like ripe, sickening putrefaction in Tuck's nostrils. The boys appeared terrified, not grateful to be cared for, and the Bishop was much too smug. Tuck didn't like it at all.

"God's speed to you, Bishop Albrec," Tuck wished. Then he lunged forward, grabbed the Bishop by the front of his cincture, tugged him out of the coach, and threw him to the ground.

Robyn and Alan, who had been watching from the ridge above, turned to one another. "Do you think that's the sign?" Alan asked.

"I think that's the sign," Robyn answered, and they scrambled down the hill knocking the bewildered coachman to the ground and taking hold of the team's reins.

The furious Bishop yelled at Tuck. "You heretical fool! You'll be excommunicated for this. No, you'll be hung! Excommunicated then hung, never to be buried on sanctified ground. You will never enter the gates of Heaven for this outrage!"

Tuck had to punch him in the face just one time. "Save it for someone who believes that load of horse shit," he replied. "I know who the sinner is here. I can see it written on the boys' faces, the smell of fear pouring off them and that predatory look in your eyes. You call yourself a man of God?" Tuck exclaimed and then spit on the Bishop where he lay in the dirt.

Hearing the exchange, Robyn rounded the coach and reached a hand in for the boys. "Come on, now lads; you'll be safe with us." Hesitantly first one, then the other climbed down and huddled around Robyn, their heads just reaching her shoulders. She whispered into the first boy's ear. "Did he hurt you, do bad things to you?"

He looked away from Robyn, remaining silent, but the second boy nodded, tears spilling out of his eyes.

"All is well now," she assured them, hugging them to her side, her brown eyes hardening.

"His rings," she called to Tuck, "and that fine cross. And I'm sure he has a bag of gold somewhere."

Tuck nodded and began to tug at the bishops rings.

"You, you are no man of the cloth, but a common thief!" Albrec retorted with a sneer.

"Aye, bishop, I am a man of the cloth. And unlike you, who steal the very life from poor, innocent boys, I only take excess wealth from those who can well afford to do without it."

"No one is innocent," he sneered as Tuck snatched the jeweled cross from his chest.

"Least of all you," Tuck retorted with fervent contempt ringing in his voice.

They tied the bishop's hands behind him and hoisted him back into his carriage seat about the time his driver regained consciousness. "You know I will report this to the Sheriff at Nottingham," Albrec declared.

"Indeed," Robyn said. "It isn't like we aren't wanted men. Be sure to tell him this was the work of Robin Hood and his gang, will you? I'm sure he'll treat you to good wine and a meal for that detail."

"I shall tell him you kidnapped the boys," he continued in staunch defiance.

"Rescued, you mean," Tuck snarled. "Men like you, who put a stain on *my* church, who would punish others for your own sins, I just can't…"

Robyn touched a hand to Tuck's shoulder. She could feel the anger in him about to explode and feared he may do something he would regret. "Come now," she said softly. "God is his judge. You have two young souls to heal."

Tuck nodded and shot the Bishop one last glare before turning his back on the molester. After taking a few steps away Tuck shouted over his shoulder, "You hear that, bishop? God, who sees all and knows all; He is your judge!" And while the bishop's driver fumbled with his bindings, the three outlaws and the two liberated orphans disappeared into a thicket.

\* \* \*

Nottingham Castle, *the next evening*

A guard knocked at the door while the Sheriff and Sir Guy entertained an irate bishop in Nottingham Hall. Another guard opened it, exchanged several words, then walked up to the lords' table to deliver a message.

"My Lord Sheriff, a Henry Fulkerson, merchant of York, would like to come in to report a robbery today on the road through Sherwood."

Godfrey dropped his cutlery which clanged against his pewter plate as he stared wide-eyed at the guard.

"You see," Bishop Albrec said. "These bandits are a menace, one that you must deal with Sheriff, or soon no one will travel through your town. Word will get out and you will be a laughingstock."

Godfrey was grateful that Prince John had left the previous day so that he did not have to endure this humiliation in his royal presence. *I will have this dealt with before John returns again*, he assured himself. He fumed at the bishop's words, dropped so carelessly between the bites of venison he devoured. *Does the fool not think we have tried? One could more easily catch the wind!* He gritted his teeth and replied with a snarl. "Show the merchant into the hall forthwith."

Sir Guy gave a stern, disapproving look at the Bishop who continued to eat and drink oblivious to his offense. "I have complete confidence in Sheriff Gifford, Your Grace, as should you. You would also do well to not insult your host while you dine at his table."

"Oh, Sir Guy, no insult was intended," he replied and patted his mouth with a cloth.

Henry the merchant entered and bowed low before the Sheriff. "Lord Sheriff, they surrounded my wagon, and they took everything," he said, still looking a bit shaky from the experience. "It was my first robbery, you see? Well, not everything I suppose, as I still have the clothes on my back. And, well, they took the cart and gelding and all the money I made selling my wares in York."

"Hmm," Giffard mused as he sat back and stroked his black beard. "They took your wagon."

"Yes, my lord. Is that of import?"

"I don't know. What do you think, Guy? What would Hood want with a wagon?"

"I suppose he could haul around a greater amount of loot in a wagon than by just carrying it," Gisborne suggested.

"What is he planning to do with it all? And where is he hiding it?" As Godfrey began to shift his gaze toward Gisborne, he spotted a serving girl making too hasty of an exit from the hall. "Stop her!" he shouted pointing at the young maid.

The brunette servant stopped and turned, shaking even as she tried to stay calm. "Me, milord? What did I do?"

"What *did* you do?" he asked. "Come here girl, I won't bite." A guard escorted her to their table where she stood contritely, gaze to the floor, and curtsied. "Why in such a hurry to leave?"

"I, I," she stammered. "I wanted to make sure there was enough wine on the table for all our guests, milord."

"No, no," he said following a hunch. "You made no move to leave until I began to ask questions about Robin Hood, questions that mayhap you know the answers to."

"Me?" Shock and dismay seized her. "I am nobody; why should I know anythin'?"

"Because, my dear, you ran."

"My lord, why, I did no such thin'!" She began to shake and her voice trailed higher and higher.

Sir Guy used a soft, fatherly tone to put her at ease. "Child, no one is accusing you of wrong doing, but this Robin Hood has assaulted and robbed a Holy Bishop, kidnapped two innocent young boys and has now stolen this honest merchant's entire means of operating a business. He is a dangerous criminal and any rumor you may have heard in town or in the kitchens could be vital to our arresting him and saving those poor children from certain corruption. The Sheriff knows *you* have done nothing wrong; he merely wants you to tell us what you may have *heard*."

"Well." She bit her lower lip, then huffed out a breath. "It is doubtless untrue – you know how rumors go–but what people are sayin'…"

"Yes?" prodded the Sheriff.

"The word is out that he is givin' food and coins to the poor, milord."

Godfrey leaned back in his chair with an incredulous sigh and exchanged a glance with Gisborne.

"I haven't a clue what he'd want with a wagon, unless he has so much food and money to distribute that he needs somethin' like that to haul it all around, I suppose," the serving girl continued. "I haven't seen anythin' of the sort; it's just what folks is sayin', that's all."

"Thank you," Sir Guy said with a smile. "Now, see, that wasn't so bad, and no reason for you to run from your lord. I'm sure Hood has started this rumor himself so that he can pretend to be some kind of folk hero, when really he is nothing more than a petty thief. You have done well."

She sighed in relief. "Thank you, Lord Gisborne. I want to help."

"Well, don't just stand there; go fetch that extra wine," commanded the Sheriff.

"Steal all that money just to give it away?" repeated Henry. "That is witless!"

*Mad like a fox*, thought the Sheriff. *Who is this Hood and what is this insanity all about?* But he nodded in agreement with the merchant. "Witless indeed, and likely not true. A false trail he is laying to gain the support of local serfs is all." But he exchanged a knowing look with Gisborne.

"Do not worry, Fulkerson," Sir Guy said with confidence. "We will see to this brigand and his gang forthwith. Will you join us at table?"

He nodded. "That is most gracious of you, Sir. I would be honored."

Another plate was set and food trays passed to the new arrival. Nottingham wanted Robin more than ever, but if these rumors were true... a plan began to form in the dark recesses of his cunning mind. If he was distributing his spoils to the needy, then he could be caught outside of the forest in a place of Godfrey's own choosing. He leaned his mouth to Sir Guy's ear. "Find out for certs if this rumor is true. I want to know what peasants, what villages are receiving aide if it is so. Understood?"

Gisborne nodded in agreement. "I will send my best spies; we'll know soon enough."

*If you love the commoners, Hood, that is your weakness and will be your downfall. A carefully laid trap is all it will take to rid me of this thorn in my side.*

# CHAPTER 8

*Sherwood Forest, September 1193*

Robyn and Will Scarlet took shelter under Grandma Oak as a soft rain blanketed the camp. In the past few weeks the villagers who had taken refuge there had put themselves to work transforming mere blankets strung between trees into rough-hewn structures with sod roofs that may indeed survive the coming winter. Nearby, a corral had been erected for the horses and Roger tended to them daily without ever having been told. Gilbert oversaw the creation of a secret hideaway dug into the side of a hill whose entrance required pulling a lever disguised as a root. The cavern was large enough to store the wagon and stockpiles of food and loot. When summer had begun, Robyn could have never imagined how events and relationships would unfold. And the best part was, they were actually helping people. Having been given a purpose greater than securing their next meal, the outlaw band had changed as well, exhibiting a certain hope and pride that she had not recognized in them when first they met.

Her knowledge that the Sheriff was still looking for them, and was likely brewing a scheme of his own, was ever on her mind as she sat staring up into the nurturing branches of the mighty tree, watching droplets slide down the leaves and plop off into small puddles. *He tried once to nab us on our way to Nettleworth, therefore, he somehow discovered we were coming. I want our next drop off to be back at Loxley. Isaac says*

*Nottingham has taxed them so severely they haven't food stocks for the winter. But to sneak into the devil's own backyard...* Her resolve had not wavered, but the plan must be foolproof.

"You are old and wise," Robyn said to Grandma Oak. "What do you think about it?"

Will laughed. "It's a tree, Robyn. It can't think–much less hear or answer you."

"Oh, but she can still tell me things," Robyn asserted with a sly grin. "She didn't grow so large or live so long without having a secret, and I intend to find out what it is." She jumped up and began to examine the great oak more closely than ever before. *Christina said everyone looks, but she sees. I need to quit looking and start seeing.* She ran her fingers along the rough trunk as she circled the ancient hardwood, examining every bump and wrinkle, line and scar. Then she looked up. "Will, give me a boost."

He shook his head giving her a discerning look. "You aren't going daft, now are ye?" Still, he cupped his hands for her foot.

"No, not just yet. But she wants to tell me something." Robyn stepped off Will's shoulder onto a massive limb and began a slow, careful climb, analyzing its parts and its whole. Will stood beneath keeping watch. Then she shouted from somewhere high in the branches, "I've got it! I know the secret of this marvelous tree!"

"Good," Will replied, squinting up, shielding his eyes against the raindrops. "Now come down and take care about it."

A few minutes later Robyn dropped down beside him, landing in a crouch. She stood up tall, a broad grin across her smooth face. "Will, it's amazing! So simple and yet, so brilliant! Why did I not see it before?"

"What?" he asked in bewilderment?

Robyn grabbed his slender shoulder enthusiastically. "It's not just one tree! There are at least two, maybe three. Hundreds of years ago they sprouted up so close to each other that over time, as they grew, their trunks became intertwined into what appears to be one tree."

Confusion still marked his expression. "So?"

Robyn's face beamed with inspiration as she tried to help him understand. "One of us alone can only do so much, make so much of a mark. But two or three together are stronger, don't you see? Robin Hood will succeed, not because he is one man, but because he is all of us together!"

"We are all Robin Hood?"

"That's right!" she exclaimed. Instantly her thoughts turned to Marian.

She was never far from her heart, but Robyn recognized what lay at the core of her discovery—she was better, stronger, smarter, and more courageous with Marian than on her own. To accomplish what she set out to do that morning in Marian's chamber would require the two of them together.

"Well," Will shrugged. "More numbers, more strength; makes sense I suppose."

Robyn patted his upper arm and pulled up her hood. "I have to leave and won't return until the morrow. We still have time before our scheduled drop off at Loxley and I'll bet the Sheriff will try something." Will shook his head as she trotted off.

"John!" Robyn called as she jogged up to his hut. He peeked a furry face out from behind a hung blanket. "I'm going to visit a friend. Don't let anyone do anything or go anywhere while I'm away."

John nodded. "How about to the privy? Can we go there?" he asked followed by a snicker.

"Only if you post a guard," she tossed back lightly. She snatched up her bow and quiver, slipped them over her shoulder, and headed for the corral. Having acquired horses made travel much faster. Robyn had adopted the deputy's black charger and taken to calling her Crusader. Together they sped out of camp in the direction of Marian's manor.

* * *

MARIAN'S FAMILY was hosting Sir Guy and his daughter for dinner, and a servant was just clearing the table after the meal.

"Fay, would you care to see my embroidery room?" Lady FitzWalter asked the shy redhead.

"I would love to," the petite young maiden with a snowy face spotted with freckles and a long auburn braid replied amiably.

As the two rose to leave, Lady FitzWalter called to her oldest son, "Richard, can you please make sure that your little brother and sister mind Anne, and finish your lessons before you go to bed."

He made an impatient smirk and rolled his eyes with a groan. "Yes, Mother," he uttered in aggravation. Marian knew what their mother was about and shot her an icy glare of disapproval.

"We'll be back shortly, and mayhap James will favor us with a song or a tune on his lyre," she said with an encouraging wink, and escorted Maid Fay de Gisborne out of the hall.

Sir Guy looked all too pleased with the relative privacy they had been afforded. "Marian, I must say, your cook is extraordinary!" he complimented.

"Let me call her, and you can tell her yourself," she suggested.

"Oh, no, don't bother her," he said, his mouth down turned. She noted that his beard and mustache had been recently trimmed to keep their stylish shape and he smelled of rosewater and cloves. It was evident to her that he wanted to impress her with his gentility. She had no choice but to feign interest, without giving him too much encouragement. "So your mother embroiders; what are your pastimes? Do you dance or play music?"

"I know most of the court dances," she answered, "and I enjoy poetry and music. I attempted to learn the harp, but am not very accomplished."

"I recall how well you danced during the festival at Windsor," Gisborne complimented her with a smile. "You shone among the other ladies, so graceful and natural on the dance floor."

"Sir Guy," she said bashfully, lowering her gaze in modesty. "You give me too high a praise."

"Rubbish," he answered, raising his chin, his eyes flowing over her soft, well-endowed form.

"I understand you were a champion at tournaments not so long ago," Marian commented.

Gisborne straightened and attempted to suck in his gut roll. "Indeed," he replied proudly. Then changed tone when he continued, "Alas, I suffered a back injury and the physician said I should not joust again lest I become an invalid, so I was forced into early retirement, but not before winning my share of tournaments, and that's the truth!"

He laughed, and she smiled in return.

"I'm certs you were quite successful." Marian knew Gisborne had been banned from competing for cheating, but she wasn't going to mention that embarrassment. "In fact," she said with a tilt of her head, inspiration striking as she tried to steer conversation in a different direction. "I believe if you were in charge of finding the outlaw Robin Hood instead of the Sheriff, he would have been caught by now."

"I must say it took old Godfrey long enough to enlist my aide, but at last I think we have a plan that will work."

Her eyes flickered. "Is that so?" Then she dismissively played with her hand cloth and glanced about the room. "The rumor is that all the soldiers fear to trek into Sherwood Forest on account of the ghosts."

"Superstitions and old wives tales!" he retorted with a frown and turned in his chair toward her. "Commoners! There is just no way to endue them with rational thought! But we don't have to make them go in the forest if we can lure the bandit and his gang out." Guy sat back with a satisfied grin on his noble face.

Marian wanted to nudge him for more information without seeming too obvious. "But if he feels safe hiding in Sherwood, what could possibly entice him out? Why, if I were an outlaw and had found a good hiding spot, I would simply stay put and avoid capture."

"That is because you are wise, Maid Marian, and this churl is fraught with weaknesses."

"Weaknesses?" she inquired.

"Without a doubt," Guy answered with a nod. "Everyone has them, I suppose, but Godfrey and I have determined what this Hood's is, you see." Sir Guy looked up at a servant lad approaching. "Boy, I would like another piece of pie," he said casually and seemed to lose track of his conversation because he stopped talking.

*Can the man keep his mind on anything other than his appetites for even a few moments?* Marian thought in exasperation.

"Right away, milord," the lad replied and skipped off to the kitchen.

"Guy, you fox," Marian complimented him with a bat of her lashes. "I knew you would come up with a plan. This weakness, is it in his fighting skills, or his poor sense of direction, pray tell?"

"Oh, Marian, you truly do not understand these matters, do you, my flower?" Sir Guy laughed.

"Then I pray thee, Sir, educate me." This is why she had agreed to invite him to dinner. She needed to learn the Sheriff's plan so she could warn Robyn.

Gisborne sighed, his eyes lighting up at the plate of pie being placed before him. "Here you are, milord. Enjoy!" the boy said before scampering away.

Marian wanted to ask if the bandit enjoyed pastries too much, if that was his weakness, but she refrained. She knew her sharp tongue would do nothing but get her into trouble, so she must continue to feign ignorance.

After a few bites, Guy continued. "You see, milady, being a mere commoner himself, Robin Hood shares a sort of kinship with the poor. He thinks he can feed them and care for them and steal from us to put our hard earned coins into their slothful pockets. While I am certs he keeps the lion's share for himself, spies have told us he actually distributes handouts to manor serfs and village peasants. He *likes* them, you see?"

Marian's face turned to honest puzzlement. "No, Sir Guy; I am not certain that I do."

He beamed at her with the pride of one who had just solved some great mystery. "We use the poor as bait to draw him out. You know, rough them up, ask where his hideout is, hang a few. Once word gets to him—and I've no doubt it will—he shall come and try to rescue them. That is when we spring our trap. Brilliant, isn't it?"

Marian felt as though her heart had stopped beating for an instant. She sat frozen, trying to maintain her composure while every instinct in her being was to beat the nobleman senseless.

While it was true she had been raised in privilege and enjoyed her lifestyle because of the labors of her family's serfs, she was also a devout Christian woman who believed all people, rich and poor alike, were God's children and her brothers and sisters in Christ. Her parish priest taught that generosity toward the poor was a virtue. Her father never mistreated their serfs and made sure each one had food around a warm hearth. But Gisborne and the Sheriff planned to indiscriminately kill peasants who had done no wrong just to lure Robyn out to be captured. The plan was… evil. She could think of no other word.

Trying to mask the shock and rage she was holding back, she swallowed hard and forced a smile. "Brilliant indeed." Not knowing how she could stay in the room with him one moment longer, Marian was thankful to hear her mother and Gisborne's daughter returning.

"And that was the end of Marian's adventures in embroidery!" Her mother laughed and Fay followed her lead.

"Oh, Papa, you should see!" she squealed. "Lady FitzWalter is a true artist!"

"She is," Marian agreed, relieved by the distraction. "The hour is late, Sir Guy, and I still have things to which I must attend before I retire for the evening." Marian rose to join her mother at the end of the table. "We have so enjoyed your visit. You must come again soon."

"Well, yes, I suppose it is late," he reluctantly agreed frowning down at the half piece of pie that remained on its plate. "Nottingham is planning a feast for Michaelmas in little more than a fortnight. There will be dancing, and I would be enchanted if you could join me at the castle for the festival."

"I must consult my calendar," Marian said, then added. "I should love to come if there is no conflict. Good evening my lord, Maid Fay." Marian curtsied and strained to keep from running to the stairs.

"I will see you out," Lady FitzWalter offered with a genuine smile.

* * *

HIDDEN IN MARIAN'S ROOMS, Robyn heard her footsteps coming long before she opened the door. Robyn got to her feet and moved back before Marian walked into the shadowy room, closing the door and latching it.

"I thought you weren't courting Sir Guy," Robyn said with bemusement.

"Robyn!" Marian used years of practiced restraint to keep her excited voice to a hush. She turned to envelope Robyn in her arms.

Robyn reveled in her touch, eagerly returning the warm embrace. She breathed in Marian's perfumed scent, pressing a cheek to hers. This is where she had longed to be! This felt like home.

Marian loosened her hold so she could look into Robyn's face, her own blue eyes shining with glee. "What took you so long to come and see me?"

"I've been a little busy, what with all the robbing from the rich, giving to the poor and avoiding being killed by the Sheriff," she replied jovially. "I did want to come sooner, but-"

"Marian?" called Lady FitzWalter from the hallway. Marian groaned, and Robyn slid back into the blackness of the corner behind the door.

Marian undid the latch and opened just a crack. "Yes, Mother?"

Lady FitzWalter sighed, bestowing a soft, misty expression to her daughter. "I know Sir Guy is not your first choice; he is a bit older than you," she began.

"His daughter is older than me!" Marian declared.

"By only a year," she replied. "But he is an important lord with a large estate, and look at it this way–he likely doesn't have that many years left in him, and then you could inherit and find a husband of your own choosing."

Marian threw her eyes toward heaven and let out a grievous sigh.

"Mother, please understand two things; first, I invited Sir Guy and his daughter in order to be hospitable while they are visiting Nottingham, *not* because I wish to encourage an engagement. And second, I have made it perfectly clear that I will not accept a marriage proposal from anyone until Father returns, and that is simply the end of it."

Lady FitzWalter's shoulders slumped as she sighed. "I don't think you quite understand a woman's poor position in the world, child. If he decides he wants you and there is no one around to fight him over it, he can have you whether you consent or not. You have been at court for several years yet not chosen a suitor, and I know full well you have been approached by a number of them. You are a woman, Marian, and cannot afford to be too choosey. It is not like there are many options; truly, only two—marriage or the church."

Marian leaned her head against the doorframe, her countenance plummeting like a sinking stone. "Then mayhap it must be the church, but I've still a year or more to decide. I have not yet passed the age of eligibility. You don't know Gisborne like I do. He is not an honorable man."

"Honor has its place, but if you set your sights too high, you may miss out altogether. I don't want you to end up alone." She reached a hand to stroke Marian's face as compassion and understanding filled her eyes. "Your father is an honorable man, and he has given me a good life, but there have been hurdles to overcome. It has not been the marriage I hoped for in some ways, but at least I have not been alone. After all, he gave me four beautiful children."

"Mother." Marian took her hand and offered her a warm smile. "I will not be alone; do not worry about that. Now, go on to bed and I'll see you on the morrow."

"As you say; sleep tight, Bright Eyes." She smiled and slowly retreated.

"God keep you and have sweet dreams," Marian called after her and closed the door.

"You see," Marian stated as she lit the candle nearest the ingress. "I have no intentions toward Gisborne, save to gain information, and there is something important I learned tonight. Did you hear?"

Robyn shook her head. "I could only make out muffled sounds, not clear words."

Marian took her hand and led her to the side of her bed. She sniffed the air making an unpleasant expression.

"Yes, that's me," Robyn admitted disparagingly. "It was raining and I haven't bathed for some time."

Amused affection shone on Marian's face. "I would rather have your scent after living in the forest than the rose bath odor of that hideous man any day."

A smile tugged at the corner of Robyn's mouth as she studied Marian's expression. *What is going on behind those dazzling eyes of yours?* Robyn wondered, guarding her heart.

"Back to matters of greater import," Marian said, the timbre of her voice low and serious. "Guy and the Sheriff are planning a trap in which to snare you. They intend to harm villagers in an effort to draw you out since you have become a hero to the poor. Based on your generosity towards them, Nottingham deduced that you would not stand by unmoved while they are being brutalized."

"God's passion, I will not!" Robyn declared in an angry hush. "When? Which village? I can't let the lousy swine punish innocent people on account of me."

Marian bit her lower lip and her shoulders drooped. "He didn't say. I am inclined to think soon, but as to where…" Her voice trailed off in disappointment and she plopped down onto the bed.

Robyn stood beside her, face scrunched up in concentration. "Would it be a village or manor we have already donated to, or another? How would the Sheriff know?" She ran her fingers through her short crop of brown hair. "He would certs have spies. He would go to somewhere we have been."

Marian reached up a hand and tugged on Robyn's sleeve. "Sit," she requested. "We'll figure it out."

"Yes, yes," Robyn replied absently as she sat, still focused on the Sheriff's diabolical plot. But her thoughts and emotions stirred as she became keenly aware of Marian's arm slipping around her waist, drawing their bodies together. She looked into those soft, ardent eyes as if floating through a dream.

"You see, this is why I have to stay here–to keep up with what malevolent exploits the Sheriff is planning, so I can warn you and try to help in whatever small way possible. If I came to Sherwood with you, yes, we could be together, but I would be of little or no use to you or our cause there."

Robyn licked her lips, her mouth oddly dry. She felt as if she had tiny goldcrests fluttering around in her belly. She turned her eyes to her own dirty hands that rested in her lap. "I thought you were staying here because you need to find a husband." At once she was profoundly aware of Marian's warm presence and the affection emanating from her touch. She sensed the unexpected tenderness of a kiss placed on her cheek, a kiss that lingered heartfelt and moist on her skin.

Marian's fingers worked at trying to arrange Robyn's hair in some semblance of order while she smiled knowingly. Robyn turned a hesitant gaze to her lovely face, a question in her shimmering brown eyes.

"I have known for a long time how you feel about me," Marian began. "It is so clear. When you look at me, there is such love in your eyes that no one else has ever shown toward me. I was careful not to reveal the same sentiments to you, lest both our hearts be broken when one of us would have to marry. I have spent years suppressing my emotions, telling myself we can ever only be friends. That is part of why I stayed away at court so long; I thought I would meet a handsome nobleman and what I felt for you would fade." She intertwined her fingers with Robyn's and gave her hand a little squeeze. "It didn't. Still, I was determined to do my duty, to be what society demands, until you came back into my life. Robyn, when you did what you did: when you strode out onto the lawn and faced down the deputy and his guards risking your life to save one of my boys, and you made that miraculous shot striking his arrow from the sky, it was like a sign from God to me. I knew in that instant that I could never settle for anything, for anyone less. I do not pretend to know how to make it work; I only know that I want to spend my life with you, and no one else."

For an instant, Robyn couldn't breathe. She was sure her heart did not beat and time stood still. Was this not the moment she had dreamt of from her youth? Had she not planned eloquent words of love to proclaim? Had she not written poems to recite? But now that Marian was here beside her, holding her hand, speaking the proclamation of love that Robyn had longed to hear like a thirsty man in the desert longs for a cool drink, she was stunned speechless. She swallowed, remembered to breathe and gave Marian's hand a little squeeze as she eyed her with hopeful anticipation. Robyn was conscious of joyful tears welling spontaneously but was powerless to stop them. Trembling and heart pounding now, she felt the blood pulse through her limbs as if for the first time.

Then it happened. Marian brought her lips to Robyn's in a gentle kiss, cautious but without reservation. And Robyn kissed her back, slowly at first, still not able to register the experience as dream or reality.

When Marian leisurely pulled away to look into her eyes, Robyn found she could utter but a few words. "I love you; I have always loved you. Is this real? Are you really holding me, kissing me? Or is it my imagination?"

A vibrant smile widened across her face, lighting her eyes and she stroked a hand over Robyn's cheek. "Very real," she stated deliberately. Then her fathomless eyes darkened as she saw the brightness strike in Robyn's countenance. "And I love you, Robyn of Loxley, Robyn of the Hood. I would follow you to the ends of the earth and never care to look back."

"Marian." Robyn spoke her name like a prayer before returning her lips to their kiss. This time it was longer, deeper, more stoked with passion and need, an urgency that had been building in both of them for a long while. It was several minutes before the mundane demand for air pulled them apart. "I am not sure what to do," Robyn admitted shyly.

Marian tried to rein in a bemused smile. "Let's start with getting you out of those clothes and wrappings, and see where things go from there, shall we? I think we may be able to feel our way through it."

Robyn practically melted into a puddle right then and there. She loved Marian, and Marian loved her in return! *I could die tomorrow and be completely fulfilled!* "I cannot imagine that there has ever lived a woman who was more blissful than I am at this moment." The declaration simply spilled out of her mouth while her body tingled all over.

Marian replied, joy radiating on her fair face. "Care to test that theory?" And she began unbuttoning Robyn's shirt.

# CHAPTER 9

*Sherwood Forest, the next day*

"Today we shall try something more challenging," Gilbert Whitehand stated as he tied two sand-filled burlap bags to a tree branch, one a couple of feet behind the other.

Robyn held her bow at her side, more tightly strung than when she had begun her lessons, and tried to concentrate.

"This first bag," he said holding it steady about chest height, "is an innocent villager." He then set the sack in motion, swinging like a pendulum. Stepping back to the second bag, he continued. "This is one of the evil Sheriff's guards about to kill the villager." He gave it a shove such that its swing alternated with the first bag and then stepped aside. "Your task is to miss the villager and hit the guard."

"Aye," Robyn said with a nod. She snagged an arrow from her quiver, notched it on the string, and raised her bow into position. Eying the swinging sacks, she let loose her shaft which sailed past the first bag before narrowly missing the second and striking the trunk of the tree. She winced, lowering her weapon.

Gilbert let out a little laugh. "At least you didn't kill the peasant." He took a few steps and pushed the bags to restart their swings. "Do not fret; most people miss their initial try. However, I note your focus seems wanting this morn."

*Indeed,* Robyn thought. Her concentration was sorely lacking. Still basking in the glow of the evening before, she found it hard to think of anything but Marian… her sensually magic hands, sizzling cherry lips, and full, supple breasts all creamy with a sweet strawberry on top.

*No! You have to focus,* Robyn commanded herself as she drew another arrow. *There is too much at stake; you must get this right!* She closed her eyes and breathed deep, wiggling her neck and shoulders to limber up and tried to clear her mind.

"Try again," Gilbert encouraged.

This time Robyn took aim with deliberate purpose. She estimated the timing of the swinging bags then let go the shaft which glided straight into its mark.

"Now there's a fine shot!" Gilbert complimented while he retrieved the arrow. "Take twenty paces back and let's do that again."

"Twenty paces?" Robyn's eyes widened at the prospect.

"The farther away from which you can strike your target, the better, Robin; you know that." Gilbert pushed the sacks and called out as he stepped aside, "Remember to read the wind and adjust for the distance."

Robyn felt the breeze on her cheek as she took aim. She raised the tip of her shaft slightly, waited to count the timing, then let it soar straight past the first bag into the second. "Well done!" exclaimed Gilbert. "It seems you are ready for the next step."

"There's more?" she inquired as she lowered her weapon.

"Back up another ten paces and I will tell you," he instructed. While she was counting off the paces, Gilbert strung up a third sandbag about two feet behind the second. It bore a round dot the size of a man's palm splashed in its middle. "The first two bags are peasants; don't hit them. This last one is the Sheriff sneaking up to murder the peasants. You can't let that happen!"

"Three!" she exclaimed. "From fifty paces? Is that even possible?" She squinted and pointed. "And what is on that third bag?"

An amused grin crossed Gilbert's mouth. "That's his wretched black heart, your target."

She sighed with a shake of her head. "I'll try."

"No you won't!" he demanded. "That is likely to get innocent persons killed. When faced with this situation, you must succeed; otherwise, do not take the shot. Robin, you *will* strike the bull's-eye and miss the two bags before it."

"As you say," she answered with a nod and took aim. Gilbert set the three bags in motion alternately. Robyn pulled the fletching to her ear and sighted down the shaft. She took a slow breath feeling for the wind, raised the tip of her arrow adjusting for distance, and calculated the rhythm of the swinging targets. In her mind, the bow and bolt became extensions of her will, not tools or weapons, but more like a limb, a part of her own body. Anticipating where the positions of the sacks would be by the time her shot would reach them, she let go. The missile spiraled through the air, whistling past the first and second bags and plunged into the painted splotch on the third.

"Bugger me!" Gilbert allowed, trying not to look too amazed. "Right nice shooting, Robin. But, will all be so calm and quiet for you to concentrate during a battle? I think not! Hey Arthur, Much, Alan! Come lend us your aid!" The three approached, along with a few other curious onlookers.

"What can we do?" Alan asked, his sandy curls sticking out in all directions.

"I need you fellows to make lots of noise, like a fight is going on. And shove each other about, so you can mayhap distract this fledgling marksman," Gilbert explained while he readied the swinging bags for another round. "We'll see how sharp his focus is now!"

A grin tugged at the corner of Robyn's mouth. She understood this was the true test; she must strike her mark in the midst of a battle under uncontrolled circumstances. "Good plan, Whitehand," she said with a nod toward him.

While the lads started laying bets as to whether she could make the shot, Robyn drew upon an inner strength, blocking out everything and everyone save her bow and the swinging bags. The men made clanging noises and shouts and pushed each other around while Gilbert set the targets into action. But Robyn's focus was singular and intense, and when she loosed the arrow, it struck its mark every bit as expertly as it had before.

The clamor ceased, and the lads stared dumbfounded with amazement.

"I don't believe it!" Alan exclaimed and blinked his eyes twice just to be sure.

"And from this distance?" added Much.

Gilbert maneuvered his way down the path to where Robyn and the others stood. With a look of astonished pride, he said, "Son, I never made that shot in training, not with the distractions. You are the master now."

Robyn cast down her gaze and shook her head amidst all the exuberant praise her fellows lavished on her. Then lifting her eyes to his she replied, "Targets are one thing; actual people are another. You have seen true combat and so far I have only been in a few skirmishes, nothing that amounted to life and death. But that is coming."

"Yes," he said grimly. "I believe it is. Which is why, when the time comes, you cannot think of your enemies as people, only as targets. If you for an instant consider their life, loved ones, or any good thing, you will hesitate, a lack of action that will surely get you killed. They are targets, nothing more, for that is all you are to them. You may perform your penance before God anon, providing you live to do so."

Robyn nodded. "I understand."

Just then, a gaunt man in his late twenties with stringy black hair and beard came trotting up to the group panting and sweaty. They turned their attention to him as he stopped short, doubling over to lean his hands on his knees. Arthur Bland reached out to steady him.

"What is it, Aaron?" Robyn asked as she stepped toward him.

"The Sheriff and his men," he let out between gasps for air. "Millhaven."

She nodded. "Aye."

Upon Robyn's return to camp that morning, she had sent out scouts to ascertain which village Giffard would strike, but she hadn't thought it would be this soon.

"Everyone, come hither!" she called out. Recognizing the urgency in her voice, each man and woman stopped what they were doing and congregated around Robyn. "It is time to put our plan into action. The good people of Millhaven need our protection. The Sheriff and his men mean them great harm; they are planning to kill innocent villagers because they want to find me." She cast her gaze over each individual in the crowd. "I will *not* let that happen! And neither will you. We are all Robin Hood!"

"We are Robin Hood!" the assembly shouted back as one voice.

"Arm yourselves and make ready; we move out in ten minutes." She scanned the group for Will Scarlet and jogged over to him.

"Prithee, you and David of Doncaster go with Isaac to take that wagon load of supplies to Loxley."

Disappointment dampened Will's eyes. "I would rather be fighting at your side, watching your back. I am skilled with my swords."

"Aye," she replied placing a reassuring hand on his shoulder. She stepped in closer and spoke with a quiet imperative. "Will, this is very important. I need someone I can trust with this mission. This is our best–mayhap only–opportunity to get these supplies to Loxley. The Sheriff will likely have all his guards with him in attempt to capture me; but if some are left behind you can hold them off."

"Aye, but," her friend protested. "You'll be in great danger. I feel like you are just sending David and me off to do something safe because we are the youngest."

Robyn snickered. "I thought you said I was the youngest!"

Will shook his head with a bewildered expression. "I don't know what you are."

"I'm not keeping you safe. I need you to do this."

When Will raised his blue eyes to hers they were steeled with resignation. "I'll get it done."

"Gramercy, mate."

* * *

MILLHAVEN RESTED along a sharp bend in the River Trent northeast of Nottingham, not far below the southern expanse of Sherwood Forest. While the city of Nottingham boasted a number of wool pounding mills used in processing the material, Bedfordshire built stone cutting mills to accompany their quarries, and lumber mills were scattered about the woodlands, this peaceful hamlet sprang up around a grain mill, a prerequisite for almost any community. A stone flute had been constructed in the river bend to catch and divert a swift flowing current to turn the wooden paddles of the undershot wheel which rose higher than the mill's thatched roof. The steady slap, splash, and gurgle of the wheel's perpetual motion had become a constant white-noise that the residents barely noticed.

Inside, the barrel-chested balding miller wearing a tan apron over his natural tunic pulled a chain which opened a hopper filled with wheat. The flaxen kernels streamed down a slipper and fell out onto the massive lower millstone. He aimed the end of the trough so that the grain was evenly distributed while the heavy wheel of the upper millstone, driven by water power, rolled in a circular motion around the lower stone crushing the grain into fine flour. The miller used a hand brush to sweep any stray kernels back under the smashing weight of the big wheel and to direct the newly created flour into sloping grooves in the lower stone where gravity would pull it to pour into open, waiting sacks. The inviting aroma of fresh bread wafted from the next building where the miller's wife was busy baking.

A trio of women were gathered around a merchant's wagon parked near the well in the town center examining his wares. Opposite them stood the weaver's hut. A work area consisting of a pole and thatch structure over a packed dirt floor was open on its southern side for light and air. Under the roof, four horizontal looms were operated by the weaver, his mother, and two daughters. Each sat on a stool working foot pedals while aptly sliding a shuttle through a set of wool threads stretched taut at both ends. After passing the shuttle from side to side, they would slap the new thread tight with a hand paddle that was attached to the loom's frame - all done to the rhythmic pounding of the smithy's hammer from next door.

"Did you hear what Izzy did?" asked one daughter in typical gossip fashion while her hands worked the threads in the loom.

"Izzy is such a featherhead!" replied the other young woman. "She's a featherhead and a fizgig!"

The weaver gave his daughters a disapproving look, but his elderly mother with her ash hair pulled into a tight bun didn't appear to hear their chatter.

The smithy's hammer stopped abruptly, and the weavers perceived the thunder of many horse hooves cantering into their small village. Dust puffed up into clouds, chickens ran squawking in all directions followed by bleating goats, their little bells clanging around their necks. The muscular smithy looked up from the red-hot iron rod to witness the Sheriff of Nottingham, his deputy and twenty armed men pull their mounts to a halt. A young mother snatched up her toddler and hurried into her hovel. The miller closed the grain hopper and stepped outside to see what was happening.

A herald holding a rolled parchment in one fist rang a hand bell with the other. "Hear ye, hear ye!" he cried out in a clear, resounding voice. "The honorable Sheriff of Nottingham, Earl of Loxley, and honorary tax collector for Prince John demands all inhabitants of this hamlet listen to this proclamation."

He waited while timid peasants gathered in the town center. The smithy set down his metal and meandered over wearing a curious expression. The miller, spotted with flour, and his curly haired wife stood across from the weaver's family. A carpenter, a chandler, and several laborers, joined the assembly along with about a dozen women clinging nervously to their small children. Four soldiers came in from the north and east escorting yeoman farmers and sheep herders from the surrounding fields.

Once it appeared they had all arrived, Nottingham nodded and the herald continued. "Be it known that this outlaw," he said unfurling the rolled parchment to display the image of a hooded, clean-shaven man, "is wanted for thievery, treason, and sundry crimes against the Crown. Any person or persons who has knowledge of this outlaw, known as Robin Hood, is required to give account to the Sheriff. Any person or persons found to be harboring said criminal, or lending him or his gang aid, or who knows of his whereabouts and fails to report shall be punished most severely. And any person or persons who accept food, clothing, coins, or any other contraband from said criminal will be found guilty of receiving stolen property and punished most severely. This is the decree of our Honorable Sheriff."

The villagers exchanged glances with one another before returning their eyes to the herald and the Sheriff, but all remained silent.

Sheriff Godfrey Giffard gave a signal with his right hand and he, Deputy Blanchard, and half of the armed escort dismounted.

"What?" Nottingham questioned as he sauntered around the well occupying the town center. Most of the guards on foot surrounded the village cutting off every avenue of escape should any peasant decide to run while two stood beside the deputy to protect the Sheriff should the need arise. "No one has anything to say?" His sable mane which fell nigh his shoulders was animated by a breeze as he cast a menacing glare over the congregation.

The blacksmith, possessing a fearless reputation, spoke first in spite of the tension rising from his gut. "Milord, what can we tell you? I have never seen the outlaw Robin Hood, nor do I know who he is or where he stays. I only know that one morn, when I awoke, there was a bundle on the doorstep." His gaze left the Sheriff and passed over his neighbors as he gestured. "We each had a gift bag with food, blankets, a few coins and sundries, and after discussion we guessed they could have come from Hood. But if it was him, he came in the night and we had no knowledge of it."

"So, you admit to receiving stolen goods!" Blanchard seized the opportunity. "You must surrender them at once."

"We didn't know they were stolen," declared the Miller, a shadow of gloom falling over his formerly cheerful countenance.

Godfrey continued to meander his way around, scoping the layout of the village and skimming his gaze along the rooftops.

"Why did you not report these... gifts?" he asked still scanning the vicinity. "Even if they were legally obtained, ten percent belongs to the church, ten percent to me and another twenty to the crown." Then his onyx eyes spied the blacksmith's hammer lying on its anvil in his open-sided shop.

While various voices repeated what the smithy and miller had said, Nottingham picked up the mallet, testing its weight in his hand. As he strolled back into their midst, he motioned to the two guards flanking Blanchard and pointed to the brawny smith.

"Receiving stolen goods is no better than thievery," he stated nonchalantly.

The burley man's eyes widened and he tensed as the lackeys in black leather and chain mail led him to stand before the Sheriff beside the village well. "My lord," he said shakily, then swallowed. "On my oath, I didn't realize the lot was stolen, nor do I have any knowledge of Hood. I am an honest man, and would tell you if I had such knowledge."

Godfrey inclined his head. "Mayhap you would, but punishment must be meted out, examples made. Stretch out your right arm."

"Milord?" Sweat poured from his thick brow as his ale tinted eyes pleaded. He started to comply, but one of the soldiers grabbed his arm roughly and slammed it onto the stone wall of the well. "I will pay you every copper owed!"

Nottingham stroked his beard and again scanned the edges of the wood. "One punishment afforded to thieves is to lose a hand," he mused. "But since you didn't actually do the stealing yourself, I may show mercy." Just as the smith's muscles began to relax, Godfrey jerked up the cumbrous tool and slammed it down onto the stunned man's outstretched appendage.

When he cried out in pain, the two guards released him and he clutched the crushed extremity to his chest. His anguished face turned up to the Sheriff's aspect of stone. "My hand! Bloody hell! Oh, God's teeth, how am I to work, to feed my family?"

The Sheriff dismissed the peasant's cries. "Why do you need to labor? You have Robin Hood to feed you."

The brawny smith stumbled back to his family and chanced to glance down at his red swollen hand, its digits splayed unnaturally as pain throbbed like the clapper ringing in the colossal church bell at St. Mary's. A lanky lad in his early teens and a petite blond woman drew to his side to comfort him.

Godfrey shot him a slant of disdain. He loathed peasants. They were unlearned, uncouth, foul-smelling, dirty creatures who regularly required a lashing to be motivated in their work. Passing a haughty gaze over the lot of them reminded him that they also reproduced like rabbits. A lazy, worthless class of reprobates whose only purpose was to provide food and labor for their betters. And while he understood full well they could not be trusted, he supposed that this crowd may actually be telling the truth. But that was beside the point.

"Now that I have your attention," he stated, "I hope that the rest of you will be more forthcoming about the person and whereabouts of this outlaw." He strolled up to the weaver's family. "You appear more intelligent than that rubbish," he said tilting his head toward the blacksmith. "Tell me about Robin Hood."

The weaver stepped in front of his mother and two daughters protectively, his stature like a stick-bug alongside the tall, well-honed Sheriff. "My lord, John speaks the truth," he implored. "We have never seen nor spoken with this man; how could we hope to guess where to find him? How do we even know 'twas he who bore us the gifts?"

Nottingham taunted the frightened tradesman. "Ah, yes, mayhap it was brownies or fairies who brought the food, or yet elves or leprechauns who supplied the goods and coins." Then his visage darkened along with the tone in his voice. "Do you take me for a fool?"

"No, no, God in Heaven, no!" The weaver dropped to his knees in show of his submission. "But verily, I know nothing about Hood!"

A thought began twisting its way through his devilish mind as the Sheriff stared over the weaver's shoulder at the town elder who stood stooped behind him.

"Old woman," he called, causing the weaver to lurch to his feet with eyes narrowed. Nottingham gestured to her. "Come forth." She shuffled toward him with a puzzled expression. "Now, you are old and wise. Tell me about Robin Hood. When will he be coming around again? Who is he really? You don't want to see your son beaten do you? You owe no allegiance to a murdering rogue. Speak!"

She squinted her ice-blue eyes and cupped a hand to her ear. In a gravelly, cracked voice she uttered, "Eh? How's that?"

"My Lord Sheriff," the weaver blurted out. "My mother is an old woman and doesn't hear well. She doesn't know anything. I implore you to leave an elder be."

"Worthless bag of bones!" Without the slightest hesitation he backhanded the matron sending her tottering off balance to be caught and steadied by her granddaughters. Gasps of shock, fear and dismay sounded through the crowd. The weaver's eyes flashed with rage and he clenched fists at his sides, but consciously chose to keep them there.

"You think you can hold out on me?" the Sheriff shouted. "Tell me what I want to know or I will start hanging you paltry churls!" The gasps turned to cries of terror as they clung to one another, tears beginning to flow amid pleas for mercy. "Blore all you wish; it will do you no good. Deputy, you soldiers," he called motioning to them to come, and they proceeded forward. "Let's see," Nottingham mused, passing a raptor's gaze over his flock of prey. Then he pointed. "Him," he said, his finger aiming at the smith's son.

"Ward!" his distraught mother cried out as her boy was snatched from them. She clung to her injured husband whose face reddened to match his hand.

"My boy has done nothing wrong!" he declared.

"That one," Nottingham pronounced, paying the squealing vermin no heed as he selected a farmer. "Her," he smirked, denoting the miller's wife.

"Mummy, mummy!" wailed three stair-step children, tears bursting from their big, round eyes, while their father held them back.

"Not my wife!" the miller howled in disbelief. "She is only a woman and knows nothing of outlaws."

The Sheriff again refused to answer or acknowledge their pleas. "Over there," he said selecting the traveling merchant who stood by his cart.

The indifferent hands of guards dragged the prisoners into the hub. "But milord!" protested the trader. "I don't even live in this village. I received no assistance from the criminal!'

"Yes, well, you should have better discretion than to do business with those who harbor outlaws," he answered dispassionately. "An example must be set." Then the edge of his lips curled. "Deputy, bring me the old woman."

A puzzled look crossed Blanchard's square face. Hesitantly he walked over and extended a hand to the frail, aged female, and she went with him without protest.

"My lord!" cried the weaver in dismay. "What would you want with someone who is clearly no threat to anyone? Prithee, do not harm my mother! Take me instead, for whatever your purpose."

But the Sheriff ignored his supplications. Noticing the displeased expression worn by his deputy, he pulled him aside while the other guards secured the prisoners' hands behind their backs. Blanchard's face was drained of color and his eyes betrayed his displeasure. "Milord, the old woman?"

Nottingham's voice cut like cold steel. "They must understand that none of them, from the oldest to the youngest, is safe and then we use their fear to force them to hand over Hood."

"But-" Blanchard hesitated, then asked in a hushed tone, "Are you sure they know where to find him? What if they are telling the truth?"

The Sheriff straightened and crossed his arms over his chest, regarding his deputy as one might an insect. "Are you capable of carrying out your duties, or do you need to be replaced?" He furrowed his stark brows accusingly at Blanchard.

Blanchard snapped to attention. "My lord, I have sworn an oath to obey the responsibilities of my office and to follow the Sheriff's orders; I do not intend to break that oath. However, my lord cannot order me to enjoy it."

Nottingham snorted, turning down his nose on his subordinate. "I couldn't care less how you feel, as long as you do as I say." He stepped away from Blanchard to look over his hostages and beyond them. "There." He spoke in a strong voice as he pointed to a large oak with sprawling branches standing near the mill and the river which powered it. One of the guards retrieved a pack from his saddle and carried it over to the tree. Other guards started rummaging through hovels bringing out stools. The villagers watched in horror as the first guard pulled ropes already tied in nooses out of the bag and tossed their free ends over a big, horizontal branch one by one.

"No!" "For God's sake!" "Do not do this thing!" The helpless shouts rose through the gathering as people sobbed and pleaded.

*Why do they blubber so?* Godfrey wondered. *It isn't as if anyone important is going to die.*

Nottingham's keen eyes scanned the edges of the village and the tree line for any sign of Hood and the outlaws. *Maybe I underestimated Hood,* he thought. *Mayhap he doesn't really care about the peasants after all.* Upon spotting no trace of outlaw heroes rushing to the rescue, he shrugged. Hanging a few of these churls just to set an example would be alright by him.

The villagers watched helplessly as their loved ones were directed to stand on stools and had ropes secured around their necks.

The smith's son tried to be brave, and replied, "Do not cry, Mum," when she called out his name. The weaver's mother was having a hard time keeping her balance as she waited for death to take her, while the other three beseeched the Sheriff for mercy, but to no avail.

With all in place, Nottingham strode forward baring a grim expression. "Once more I ask you people of Millhaven, who is this outlaw Robin Hood and where is his lair?"

"My Lord Sheriff," the miller answered, his features twisted with pain to match the writhing in his gut as he looked upon his beloved wife, perhaps for the last time in this life. "Do you wish us to lie? Shall we invent a story to tell you? By God's bones, we know not this Hood, nor where to find him. Do you not think to save my wife, the mother of my children, I would not turn over a thief to the law? We cannot tell you what we do not know!"

Nottingham curled his lip in a contemptuous sneer. "So be it." His eyes passed over the gathering once more and beyond them. All was still and quiet. He returned his attention to the souls whose light he would crush this day in order to strike fear into the hearts of serfs and peasants all across the shire and gave a nod to the soldier in charge of the execution. Deputy Blanchard stood rigid between the prisoners and the people, his sword in its sheath and his bow and quiver over his broad shoulders.

The executioner approached the nearest victim. All at once a muffled *whish* cut through the air and the executioner stopped, slumping down to one knee as he cried out in pain. An arrow shot through his foot had pinned him to the ground.

## CHAPTER 10

*A* second arrow whizzed through the air, slicing the noose around the young lad's neck, all before Nottingham spotted Robyn sliding off a roof.

Her knees bent like coiled springs as her boots hit the ground, then she tucked and rolled coming up with the cocked bow making a shot to sever the rope threatening to strangle the old woman. The agile smithy's son who had wriggled his hands free of their bindings caught her before she could fall, easing her down from the wobbly stool.

"Get him!" Nottingham commanded in a shout as he drew his sword.

Just as the two nearest guards began to draw their weapons, Little John emerged from behind the merchant's cart. Raising his staff, he made a quick swing to the left and back to the right, striking each guard's helmet with enough force to send them careening into each other. Stunned, they crumpled to the ground with throbbing heads spinning and white lights flashing before their eyes.

Another volley of arrows came from around the side of the weaver's cottage where Gilbert and Arthur Bland stood. Gilbert's shaft cut through the rope fastened about the neck of the Miller's wife, and she scurried to join the youth and the elder as they ducked for cover. Arthur's arrow narrowly missed the advancing Sheriff, and he halted abruptly, glancing back toward Robyn's men.

"Over there!" he shouted, pointing at them.

Allen and Much engaged a pair of guards with their swords while

Little John took on two by himself, the reach of his staff and power of his blows giving him the advantage.

Robyn looped the bow over her shoulder as she rushed forward, pulling her crusader sword to cut the last captives free before turning to see Tuck, long sword at the ready, step between the looming Sheriff and herself.

"Well, if it isn't Friar Tuck!" Nottingham exclaimed with recognition. "I thought you had gone back to the monastery." He took up a fencing stance across from the corpulent clergyman and motioned to him with his tip.

"They wouldn't let me return," he replied with a clink of his metal against Nottingham's. "You saw to that. Tsk, tsk; trying to murder more innocent peasants, are you?"

Nottingham answered with an advance amid a flurry of strikes. "No one is innocent," he sneered again.

But Tuck was an expert swordsman and held his ground, matching blow for blow.

No sooner had Robyn freed the last hostage than a bolt sped past her close enough to tear the sleeve of her tunic. She spied Deputy Blanchard across the way notching another arrow. A quick roll and she was behind the large oak. She sheathed her father's sword and swung her bow into her hands. Quickly, she replayed the image of the deputy in her mind's eye, taking note of his surroundings. When she stepped around the trunk her aim was trained on a large sign hanging over the blacksmith's shop which she cut loose with her arrow, dropping it on the big man. It was not sufficient to knock him out, she noted, but he did appear dazed for the moment allowing her to move her attention elsewhere.

Her band was vastly outnumbered and, though they had the element of surprise, they would not be able to hold off this troop of soldiers for long. Arthur and Gilbert had wounded a few guards but were currently being closed in on by a gang of six. Much was bleeding from a wound and Alan was retreating as he stayed off blows from two larger men. She was going to have to end it now.

The Sheriff was thoroughly engaged in his duel with Tuck, allowing her the opportunity to make the necessary play. She took several stealthy, rapid steps coming up behind Nottingham with her bow cocked.

"Stop!" Robyn thundered with the weight of authority. Startled faces all turned toward her as she stood six feet from the Sheriff, her missile trained on his heart. "I am too far away for your sword to strike and too close for me to miss. And, Deputy," she addressed as she saw him start to draw his bowstring out of the corner of her eye. "Your lord will be dead before you can loose your arrow, so don't even think about it."

Giffard stared at her from coal-black eyes. "Hood," he said in spiteful acknowledgement. "You and your men are surrounded and outnumbered, with no hope of escape. You may as well surrender."

A smile of inevitable triumph tugged at the corner of Robyn's mouth, but she controlled it. *Not quite yet.* She spoke with a calm assurance that unnerved the Sheriff and terrified his guards. "Are you certain about that? It would appear that you are the one in need to surrender. Yes, we are surrounded and outnumbered, but your life is in imminent peril. Mayhap Blanchard's arrow will hit its mark, but you'll never know, because you will be dead. And perchance your soldiers could carry on without your leadership and finish us off, but you'll never know, because you will be dead. I see many possibilities before us in the next several minutes, but only one certainty; you will do exactly as I say, or you will die this day."

The Sheriff gritted his teeth, started to move a foot, and then stopped. His expressionless face concealed whatever thoughts he was having and he began to relax. "I thought you may make an appearance if I threatened enough peasants you claim to serve. But tell me, Hood, because I am quite curious: why go to all the trouble to plan and execute elaborate robberies, put your own life in danger, as well as those of your followers, and thereafter give away your hard earned spoils?"

"That is simple," she answered, her grip remaining strong and her eyes trained on his. "Because you, Prince John and your lackeys have been robbing and abusing the people ever since King Richard left for the Holy Land. It started small, but it grew, with your unfair taxes, harsh punishments, absurd laws, and detestable practices. You take what is not yours, and those who are not yours, for your own pleasure and sport. You hide behind your position not to protect, as chivalry would have, but to amass power unto yourselves. You stole Sir Whitehand's title and lands, as well as the one you now possess; you stole Tuck's standing in the Church and you would steal the very hopes and dreams of the citizens of this shire if left unchecked. I am merely giving back what rightfully belongs to the people."

Nottingham's' face remained impassive. "Would you kill me, Robin

Hood, champion of the people? Would you retain their esteem as a murderer?"

"Only if I must," was her penetrating reply. "Now, this will stop."

He gave a shrug and glanced around at his guards. They had lowered their weapons, all but Blanchard, and had the hapless look of sheep without a shepherd.

"What? What has to stop?" the Sheriff asked mildly.

Robin's words came as crisp and frigid as ice with the intensity of a North Sea storm. "You will *not* abuse, torture, punish, or kill random villagers because you want to get my attention, nor to lay a trap for me, nor because they were recipients of my generosity. I challenge you to find another way to play the game with me if you must persist. But mark my words well: I know where you live. I know where you lay your head at night, on that red silk pillow in a great, tight bed. I know ways in and out of the castle and in and out of your manor house that even the mice have not found, and it would take nothing for me to end you where you lay should you choose not to heed my warning."

She watched the widening of his eyes at her vow and saw him swallow the lump that had come to his throat, but he calmed and issued his own challenge. "Then why not you and I, one on one, man to man? I would fight you in a duel with the guarantee of your freedom should you best me," he said making a slight motion with the blade still in his hand.

"Now, now Sheriff," Robyn chided with a nod at his gesture. "Mayhap if the weapon of choice was a bow. I'll not be goaded into a sword fight which I would be certain to lose. Now, command your soldiers to mount their horses and ride out of this hamlet."

He frowned at her. "In that case what is to stop you from killing me, anyway?"

"The deputy may stay, with his arrow trained on me."

Nottingham groaned, his face twisting from obvious aggravation. "Guards," he called. "Mount up and ride back to the castle." For a moment they merely mumbled, looking around at each other, then he shouted, "Do it!" That started them moving, the injured and uninjured alike. Robyn's gang gathered together by the well, Allen helping Much who pressed a cloth to his shoulder.

Once the soldiers were away, Robyn said, "Little John, lads, back off to the wood with you."

Tuck raised his chin defiantly. "We'll do no such thing! What's to stop them from killing you once we are gone?"

"The Sheriff will get on his horse and ride away while the deputy and I keep each other in check. When Nottingham is out of sight, we shall both lower our bows and be on our way. Is it a bargain, Blanchard?"

He waited for Giffard to grant a nod, and then he replied. "On my word."

Little John protested. "Robyn, you can't trust him."

But she nodded with a diminutive smile. "Yes, John, I can. You see, we have been here before, only it was the deputy under my bow. I kept my word to him; he will keep his word to me."

Blanchard acknowledged her chivalry with a slight dip of his head.

"Now, my men, Sheriff, off with you. And Nottingham," she added ominously. "Do not take my oath lightly. I can and will kill you if you engage in this kind of terror tactic again."

He snorted and sheathed his sword before making his way to his steed. "This isn't over, Hood," he vowed without looking back. "You shall pay for this insult."

Little John and the others accepted the smiles and gratitude of the villagers as they walked toward the tree line while Robyn and the deputy held back their arrows. "By the by, Deputy, your horse is being well cared for in my camp."

A look that could only be interpreted as joy spread over his face. "That is good to know," he said.

With the Sheriff out of sight and her arm aching, Robyn nodded to him. "That's enough, now."

They lowered their bows simultaneously. The blacksmith's mother rushed to hug Robyn and thank her for saving her son, but the smithy's son had darker thoughts. He took careful steps behind the deputy gripping a raised pitchfork.

"No!" Robyn shouted, instantly taking aim and firing. The boy was stunned as the arrow landed in the tool's handle a few inches above his right hand. Blanchard snapped around to observe the youth lower the makeshift weapon in shame. "My word was given, lad, and I keep my word. See to your family and thank the Lord above for your life this day."

He dropped the pitchfork, nodded at her, and scuttled off.

The deputy inclined his head to her, then spoke in a voice that sounded of admiration. "Nottingham will try harder than ever to capture or kill you now."

"I expect no less." Robyn met his eyes and gave him a nod of respect. She then turned to acknowledge the grateful townspeople, clasping some hands and patting children's heads, before making way to the forest beyond.

\* \* \*

SHERWOOD FOREST, *later that day*

ROBYN PUSHED ASIDE A FADED, worn wool blanket from the doorway of Much's lean-to. Little John, his wife, Alan and Friar Tuck were already huddled around him.

"Let me see what you've done to yourself," Robyn said in an uplifting tone and the others parted to allow her through. She had to kneel as his bed was very low to the ground.

He had removed his ripped and blood-soaked shirt and she was able to observe the gash clearly. Alice, who sat on a three-legged stool at his head, dabbed the remaining blood from his shoulder.

"No need to make a fuss," Much said. "'Tis only a scratch." He grimaced in pain as Alice touched the spot with the cloth.

"Much, my man, I can see right through torn muscle to bone," Robyn replied. "It will have to be stitched. Alice?" Robyn turned her gaze to Little John's wife. "Do you have a thin needle and fine thread?"

Robyn saw the trepidation flash into her eyes. "I have some sewing implements, but I have never stitched skin before."

Robyn responded with a reassuring smile. "You will do well; just keep the stitches small and close together."

Alice rose, shaking her head. "I'll do the best I can."

"You know, I'd really rather not-" Much began to protest, but Robyn ignored him.

"Friar, please bring me a bottle of your strongest spirits," she requested, and he nodded and ducked out through the draped doorway.

"I'm sorry to be such a bother," Much said as he looked around at his friends.

"You're no bother," Alan dismissed with a wave of his hand. "Except when you are being annoying and insufferable, but not because of a little wound."

"I am most proud of you," Robyn praised catching his attention. "You were very brave today and gave more than you got, I'd wager."

A pleased grin crossed Much's lips and his hazel eyes sparkled. Tuck returned anon with a dark brown bottle, Alice and her sewing bag behind him.

"This will peal the bark off a walnut tree," the Friar said as he handed it to Robyn.

She winked at him and handed it to Much. "Drink now, to take the edge off the pain."

He smiled, nodded, and proceeded to do exactly that. Suddenly he lurched up and began to cough, his eyes watering and face turning red. The other men laughed and Much pushed the bottle back at Robyn. "Bleeding hell, Friar!" he managed between wheezing and another cough; then he settled on his pillows. "But it does go to work right fast, I admit."

Without warning, Robyn poured a stream of the alcohol into his gaping cut.

Much screamed and lurched again as the liquid fire burned him to the core. "Bleeding Christ! Are you trying to kill me? What in the blazes was that for?"

"Sorry, Much, but easier getting it over quick," Robyn said with a contrite expression. "Alcohol cleans better than water, even if it does hurt like hell."

A dizzy delirium swept over Much's face and he slurred, "I think I may not feel the stitching now."

Everyone smiled and Robyn nodded to Alice, then stepped back to give her more room. As she started the first tentative prick of the needle, Robyn turned to Tuck. "Did you learn to make a salve or poultice at the monastery?"

"Aye," he said, recollection stirring in his deep set gray eyes. "I think I can get together all the ingredients. I'll start making it right away," he affirmed and hurried out.

"Much, I know why you went and got hurt," Alan said jokingly. Much tried to focus on him through glazed eyes and blinked. A broad grin ran across Alan's scruffy face. "It's certs to impress Evelyn, that bellibone who joined us from Nottingham," he grinned. "Now if you can only get her to take care of you whilst you recover."

"Bite your tongue, Alan," he managed before his eyelids became too heavy, then added hopefully, "Do you think she may?"

The men laughed.

"Honestly," Alice chided them with a motherly scowl.

By the time Alice was done stitching, Tuck returned with a bowl of gooey green stuff. "I'll just apply this and we can bandage him up," he said. Robyn nodded and took her leave.

* * *

ROBYN WENT DOWN to the stream for solitude after the stress of the morning, thinking of what the Sheriff would be doing next, thus to be prepared. She was washing a cloth stuffed with wool about the length and breadth of her foot, buried deep in her thoughts when she heard a twig crack and spun around with a start.

Her heart leapt into her throat before settling back down in relief. "Will! You startled me. How did things go at Loxley?"

"Better than with you, it would seem," Will replied with honest concern in his voice. "Are you hurt?" he asked pointing to the blood in the water that had come from her rag.

"Oh, no, I'm fine; but Much was injured. We think he'll recover shortly and be back to giving everyone a hard time."

"What's that you are washing there?" The curious lad came over and sat beside her on the bank of the brook.

Robyn was ready for that question. "This is my sword cleaning cloth," she said as she squeezed the water out of it. "It's padded so that I don't cut myself while wiping blood off the sharp edge of the blade. Made it myself, see?" She held the pad in her left hand and swiped her right hand down the middle as if it was a blade.

Will's eyes widened and his face warmed. "You are so clever, Robin. You think of so many things that sometimes it boggles my mind."

"Nah," Robyn uttered, lowering her head in humility. "So the supplies were all handed out?"

"Aye. And you all saved the villagers?"

"For now, but the Sheriff will be after us more than ever. We'll have to get rid of the horses."

Will's blue eyes widened with surprise. "What? I like ridin' better than walkin'."

"I as well," she agreed. "But they make noise, they smell and are impossible to hide on short notice, so they must go–all but the one that pulls the wagon."

Will nodded and began to fiddle with a twig, his elbows resting on his knees. Then he asked, "Do you have any family?"

The unexpected question caught Robyn by surprise. "No," she said as emotionless as she could. "Not anymore. I did have mother, father, sister, brothers, but… now it's just me. How about you?"

"Me mum lives in Nottingham with Timm, my little brother. Our papa died a few years back. There was an accident. Anyway, the Sheriff didn't care. He refused to give us more time to raise money to pay our taxes. That's why I had to start pickin' pockets, and I was good at it," he said and raised his eyes to hers. "Until I got caught. That was about a year ago and I had to run off out here in the forest or be locked up and sold off."

Robyn's expression changed from benevolence to bewilderment. "What? What do you mean, sold off?"

"It's what the Sheriff does. He can keep but a few prisoners in that dungeon of his, so it's only for short term, you know, those that will be let go, those what have relatives to pay them out, or those to be executed. Anyone with a real sentence is sent to serve his years in the mines. I've never heard of a'body comin' back from there alive."

"But, but, that's slavery–that's illegal. No native born Englishman is ever to be made a slave."

"He says criminals lose their rights when they commit a crime," Will explained. "Anyway, I had to run off, but I always feel terrible, all the time, because I left me mum and brother and I'm not there to take care of them."

"Why didn't you say something sooner, Will?" Robyn's eyes were flooded with compassion and she reached a hand over to his shoulder. "It is no problem to give a bag of necessities to them whenever they need it. Alan is good at getting in and out of town without ever being recognized. You and I could as well if we go on a rainy day and keep our hoods up. Will, we can take care of your family."

For the first time that day he smiled at her. "Thank you. That means a lot." He dropped his twig and tilted his head at her as if he was thinking. "You may have lost your birth family, Robin, but you have a new family with us. I would be honored to be your brother if you'd have me."

Joy warmed her heart at his acceptance of her, odd that she was, lying imposter that she was, and she beamed at him. She lifted her hand from his shoulder and mussed his shaggy black hair. "You don't know what you're getting yourself into, mate! Any brother of mine is likely to be teased, have pranks pulled on him, and get blamed for all my mistakes." She sprang to her feet, feeling light once more. "Brother it is, then!"

## CHAPTER 11

*FitzWalter Manor, the next day*

"So, Bertram, prithee how does the harvest fare?" Marian approached her father's steward where he worked keeping the records in the manor study. Bertram looked up from his books, quill still in one hand, and ran the other through his smooth salt and pepper locks.

"The harvest should be quite good for this year, milady," he replied. "The weather has favored us. Howbeit, much of our income will undoubtedly go to taxes once again," he added in dismay.

"Never mind about that now," Marian instructed as she stood peering over his shoulder at the ledgers. "We must be sure to hold back a percentage more of the grain from market this year." He looked up at her questioningly. She smiled and laid a reassuring hand on his stooped shoulder. "I want to be certs there is enough to feed all our families this winter, and," she added with a wink, "we will only be taxed on the income we make at market, not on what we have hidden in our storehouses."

Bertram smiled and nodded at her. "I pray you are correct. The grain will keep, and what we do not use can be sold next year."

"Precisely."

They were interrupted by Anne, who peeked in through the open doorway. "Milady?" she inquired tentatively as to not disturb important manor business.

"Yes, Anne?" Marian lifted her gaze from the books to inquire.

"A cloth merchant from London has arrived to see you. Shall I show her in?"

Marian hesitated for a moment. She did not recall requesting a visit, but then coming from London... "Yes, invite her into the hall and I will join her there." Anne curtsied and scuttled off. "Let me know at once if anything is amiss, Bertram," she said but glanced back at the parchment with a frown. "Are we actually selling to that Cheney character? He is a killcow and a cheat. He overcharges his customers while undercutting his suppliers."

Bertram's jaw dropped with surprise. "Milady, I did not realize!"

She smirked at him. "He offered you a cut, didn't he?"

"On my oath, I am flabbergasted to learn of his trickery!" The older man's face paled in front of her eyes.

Mayhap he was telling the truth, or he just didn't want to be dismissed. Marian's father had hired him, so she would grant him the benefit of the doubt. However, this led her to wonder what the steward had been up to in her absence.

"Find a more honest buyer for our grain, or else I shall be forced to do it for you. And by the way, Bertram–if I must perform your duties in your stead, what need have I to keep you in the employment of this house?" She fixed him with a powerful, knowing gaze and he swallowed a lump from his throat.

"Yes, milady. I will find a more reputable buyer at once. Why, the scoundrel was trying to cheat us! He'll get a piece of my mind."

Marian let the matter go for now; her curiosity was peaked regarding her visitor, who did not turn out to be what she was expecting. Standing there with a large bag overflowing with cloth samples, was a striking woman very stylishly dressed.

"Maid Marian, how wonderful to finally meet you!" the caramel haired merchant greeted with a broad smile. "Queen Eleanor has told me so much about you."

*Eleanor sent her!* Marian's heart leapt into her throat with excitement. "You have me at a disadvantage, Madam-?"

"Amee de Neville, at your service. The Queen thought you may be in need of a new gown. Mayhap we would have more privacy in your chamber, for a measurement?"

"Certainly. This way," Marian said and began leading her up the stairs. "I am in need of a new gown indeed, as I have been invited to the

Michaelmas Feast in Nottingham." Upon entering her room, she closed and latched the door, then turned expectantly to Amee.

The envoy set down her bag, withdrew a sealed letter and handed it to Marian. "Am I to send a reply with you?" she asked as she carried the precious parcel to her dressing table.

"I shall be traveling on to York from here," Amee replied. "You have another medium for sending notes, have you not?"

"I do," Marian said. "Now, what cloth have you for me, and what news of the court?"

Amee smiled and tossed her bag onto Marian's bed. "Plenty of both!"

\* \* \*

AFTER AN HOUR of conversation and choosing a fabulous deep plum wool with white silk for the lining and trim, Amee bid Marian adieu and returned on her way. Marian opened her letter and read it with enthusiasm.

After a moment's contemplation, Marian took out pen and parchment to compose a brief reply. She tore the strip of writing and rolled it up into a small furl. Opening a drawer, she withdrew one of the tiny note cases that attach to the pigeon's leg and slipped the message in. Next she visited the aviary on the roof, tied the case securely to a bird, kissed it for luck and launched it into the air. The trained pigeon struck out home and Marian smiled.

*I hope Queen Eleanor agrees; I so want to tell Robyn. Oh, Robyn!* Marian's heart warmed and her face glowed simply thinking of the woman that she loved. She closed her eyes, remembering the previous night and knew in her soul that Robyn was safe; she wanted her safe in her arms, in her bed where she belonged... but that would have to wait.

\* \* \*

NOTTINGHAM, *two days hence.*

DEPUTY BLANCHARD KNOCKED on Sheriff Giffard's office door with marked hesitation. Godfrey had been in a foul mood since the incident at Millhaven and Edward had tried to avoid him.

"Come," the gruff voice called and Blanchard opened the door.

"My Lord Sheriff," he began as he escorted a dapper noble into the room. "Sir Giles, Earl of Pipewall, wishes an audience."

The elegant and indignant Earl made a sweeping motion with his crimson cloak before tossing it over his shoulder and proceeded in attempting to make himself look taller by raising his chin and eying the Sheriff over the crook of his lengthy nose. "Nottingham, something must be done about these bandits of yours!" he exclaimed in a prudish tenor.

Nottingham sighed with a shake of his head, deliberately rose to his feet and stepped around his desk so he could tower over the whining noble before he spoke in a manner which strained to remain civil. "Do tell."

Under the terrible gaze of the robust Sheriff, Sir Giles' airs diminished. "My escort and I were assailed by this young fellow in a hooded green cloak and his confederates on our way back to York. They roughed up my knights, scared my driver out of his wits and threatened us with bodily harm if we did not hand over all our coins and valuables. Now I have to return home for more silver before I can complete my business transaction and who's to say I won't be accosted and robbed again?"

The Sheriff narrowed his eyes and stroked his beard pensively. "Precisely where and when did this attack take place?"

"Shortly after noon, only a few hours ago, on the east road through Sherwood Forest."

"Mayhap if we move quickly enough, they can be tracked," Nottingham voiced and looked to Edward as if in silent command to gather a troop.

The deputy nodded, turning to exit the chamber, but simultaneously an irate merchant stormed in. "Sheriff, I have been robbed!" His colorful silks were sweaty and soiled, and his puffy cheeks were beet red.

Giffard's eyes grew wide and his mouth fell agape. "Where? When? Speak, man!"

Edward waited to hear this report before leaving to gather guards.

"On the west road from Mansfield, through Sherwood Forest," the merchant explained in a vexed voice. "Perhaps 'twas a little after noon; the sun was high overhead. I think it may have been the outlaw I saw on your wanted sign. He was youthful and slender, wearing that same hood. He had a bow and a gang of ruffians with him. They stole all my goods–all of them! What will I do with nothing to sell?"

"What say you? Around noon on the *west* road? Are you sure 'twas not the east road?"

The angry merchant scowled in annoyance. "I think I should know which road I traveled, Sheriff. Do you take me for a simpleton?"

"No, not at all," Nottingham replied as he paced, his ebony brows knitted together drawing furrows between them. "But even Hood cannot be in two places at the same time. What is he up to?"

Just as Giffard raised a hand and looked at Blanchard to issue new orders, a tax collector, small in stature and dressed in a drab tunic and dark leggings, scurried in, his big round eyes looking up frantically at the Sheriff. "My lord, I have been robbed! The tax money," he moaned. "Whatever shall I do? Prince John-"

Giffard breeched the distance between them in two long strides to interrupt. "What? You, too? Where, when?"

Edward could sense the Sheriff's temper rising as Giffard pulled at his own hair.

"I was traveling the central road, past Rutherford Abby, with four armed guards, about noon today," he explained, wringing his hands with worry. "It was a trap, a planned trap, I tell you! Before I knew it, my guards were roped and tied to trees. There must have been six, no eight or more, and the leader was a young slender fellow in a hood. They took the portion of tax money I had collected and was bringing here, to you, my Lord Sheriff. It's not my fault!" Edward watched as distress changed to dread on the tax collector's expression.

Giffard snapped around and paced to the nearest wall which he slammed with the palm of his hand. "Bloody hell!" he shouted as he turned toward the trio of victims. "The sardin' brigand can't be in three places at once!" He wiped a hand down his face which was damp with perspiration. "He has played a trick on us, the bastard, using doubles so we don't know which one was the real Robin Hood. This is your fault, Blanchard!" he bellowed, pointing an accusatory finger at him.

"Mine?" His eyes grew wide as a queasy, panic flooded his stomach, threatening to make him ill on the spot.

"Yes, yours!" The Sheriff strode toward him with the full authority of his office. Next he spoke in a softer, more dangerous tone. "You had an opportunity to kill him two days ago, after the others and I left and the two of you stood alone, and you didn't take it."

"But, my lord-"

"Don't give me that chivalry bollocks about keeping your word; I know all too well that you are a *man of honor!*" He spit out the words with such disdain it took the group aback. Upon hearing their gasps of disbelief, Giffard reigned in his rant, and sought a more reasonable tone of voice. As he eyed the nobleman, he explained, "In truth, there is a place for chivalry between honorable men of station but, when dealing with criminals, sometimes we must employ their own tactics against them. In a recent encounter with Hood, we were at a bit of a standoff, you see," he continued motioning to the merchant and tax collector in turn. "Blanchard was forced to give his word not to shoot the thief in exchange for my safe release. Well, what say you all? Should he not have in that instance broken his oath to rid us of that pestilence?"

The three exchanged tentative glances, none wishing to speak first. Being the highest in rank, Sir Giles ventured a word. "Chivalry and honor are of the greatest import to a civilized society." He hesitated glancing from the deputy to the Sheriff. "But there could be a place for trickery when it is absolutely necessary."

The merchant spoke next "If I were to be caught with faulty scales, 'twould be the end of me; therefore, I venture to always be honest."

The tax collector nodded and proceeded to add, "I have always found mercy to be the noblest of virtues, my Lord Sheriff. Our Lord Christ had mercy on us as we should have mercy on those among us who have endeavored to perform their duties faithfully."

Supplicant eyes looked up at Nottingham who only hmmphed in reply.

Edward lifted his chin, standing at attention, his gaze fixed on a spot in front of him. "Sheriff, I cannot repent keeping an oath, no matter to whom it was given. I am a man of my word. I will do my duty to help hunt down this outlaw and bring him to justice, but I cannot break my word for any man. If I have sinned against you, milord, that I deeply regret; but you cannot require me to sin against God."

Giffard sighed considering his deputy with a twisted look of disgust. "I'm only saying if it were not for your bloody sense of honor, we would be rid of Hood by now. No one is asking you to sin against God, man," he hissed between his teeth. Then he turned his attention back to the meager assembly. "Now that we have established the import of keeping one's word, you have my oath that this scoundrel shall be apprehended and your property returned. I am working on a plan that will rid us of Robin

Hood once and for all. But in the meantime, I will dispatch extra patrols in search of the bandits' lair. You men are dismissed."

With heads bowed as much from fear as respect, the robbery victims pivoted and a guard escorted them out. The deputy was following them when Giffard grabbed his shoulder from behind. Edward turned sad eyes to him. "My lord?" His voice was soft and apologetic while apprehension churned within him.

"Send patrols out on all three roads, in case they may pick up a trail. I like that you are honest; I mean, at least that way I know I can trust you as well. But damn it," he swore shaking his head. "Just this once, couldn't you have seen clear to bend your word?"

Edward lowered his gaze and sighed. "You gave me no such order, milord, and to tell the truth, the thought of betraying a pledge never crossed my mind."

Nottingham released his shoulder and offered him a curt nod. "Get those patrols out immediately."

"Aye, milord."

\* \* \*

EDWARD SPOKE with his patrol leaders, instructing them on the roads they were to search. "Take only those who are not afraid of the forest," he said. "We don't need more soldiers abandoning their posts to flee in fear of some imaginary ghosts. And if you find a viable trail, report back to me and we will follow it in force." The men nodded and left to assemble their troops.

He was walking through a breezeway along a castle wall facing the lower ward on the way to his quarters to try to settle his stomach, contemplating the predicament in which he found himself, when an arrow whizzed very near his head, struck the stone behind him, and bounced to the paving stones. Instantly, the deputy snapped to alert, pulling his bow from his back. He scanned the courtyard and lifted his eyes to the walls surrounding the castle grounds.

Edward expected to see Robin Hood, but he was nowhere. Then he looked down at the arrow seeing that it speared a note. Edward was not accomplished at reading and writing, but he could make out simple phrases. Upon examining the scrap of parchment, he concluded that someone was waiting for him at the castle's side gate.

*It could be a trap,* he thought. But that would be exceedingly foolish given the location and number of guards swarming the grounds, and Hood was no fool. Curiosity tugged at Blanchard until he decided he must go see who was there. With his bow in his left hand and his right on the pommel of his sword, he marched across the hardened ground to the side gate.

Inside the stone walls near that egress, the Sheriff's blacksmith was working at his forge and a vendor offered soup in a bread bowl to those passing by. People were coming and going as was common at that hour of the day, but there was no sign of the outlaw.

Edward purposefully strode through the open gate and looked to his left, his right, and straight down the street. No Hood. Out of the corner of his eye, something caught his attention and a familiar feeling washed over him. Edward turned and saw a big black mare tied to the hitching rail that ran along the castle wall at the gate. For a moment he stood in stunned silence, not believing what he saw.

"Maggie?" The courser raised her head cocking her ears toward him. She made a motion, raising her chin like a nod and whinnied, pawing one hoof at the ground. Unbridled joy surged through the brawny deputy, evidenced by the brightening of his face and eyes. He let go of his weapons and hurried to her, brushing a hand along her thick neck. "I, I don't believe it!" He glanced around again, searching but not seeing the honorable outlaw. She was well-groomed and well-fed, he concluded; then he raised a hoof to check it - clean and trimmed, exactly as he would have kept them.

Edward's sense of relief was so great it brought tears to his eyes. He stroked her nose and cheek, noting that even his saddle and bridle had been returned along with his horse. Suddenly memories of the day Maggie was born flooded back into his mind as if the eight years were but yesterday. His lovely young wife Margaret had stayed out in the stables all night to ensure that the foal's birth was smooth. Edward had found them the next morn lying together in the hay near the dam's feet.

"It's a precious black filly," she had beamed.

Edward had scooped Margaret up for a kiss. She doted on that baby its whole first week as they tossed about names to call it. Beautiful, sweet Margaret, who had loved him despite the difference in their ages, who lived to please him, who he so much did not deserve! Soon afterward she was there in her bed, burning up with fever, asking if he would check on the foal for her. Typhoid. *Why did it strike her and not me?* The priest came to give her last rites, and Edward held her hand as she left this mortal plain.

That is why he named the filly Maggie, and why she meant the world to him. He had not loved another woman since, had instead thrown himself into his work, increasing in rank and skill.

Wonder overwhelmed him; the Sheriff's enemy, a common thief, had not only taken such good care of his beloved companion, but he had returned her to him! Why? And how bad could Robin Hood actually be?

As he thought back over their past encounters, Edward realized that Hood hadn't killed anyone–merely made threats and stole from them. *And he gave it all to the poor?* But what was the deputy to do? Giffard intended to execute Hood for certs, and the odds were strong that eventually he would be caught. *Perhaps he will move on from Nottingham and seek his fortune in a different shire,* he hoped. But given what he knew of Hood that was unlikely. *Who are you, Robin Hood, and what are you about?*

Those were questions to which Edward feared he would never learn the answers. "Come, Maggie, let's get you back to your stable where you belong. I hear a big bucket of oats calling your name!"

No sooner than he had untied her and started for the gate, the deputy heard a commotion behind him. He turned to see a poor peasant in a worn, ripped cap, leading a fine bay gelding by a rope over its neck.

"That's right," he answered to someone in the crowd cheerfully. "Just found 'im wanderin' the road on the edge of the wood. If ya hurry, ya might find one fo' you'self."

In an instant it made perfect sense. *Hood is getting rid of the horses he stole! He must think they are a liability, or may give away his hiding place.*

"Excuse me." Edward spoke in a strong, authoritative voice. The peasant looked up, and his expression fell. "Thank you for finding one of our lost steeds. A while ago some of the garrison's horses got loose, and you, my fine fellow, have returned one of them."

Woe swept over the gaunt man's face like a shadow.

"Do not fear," he added pulling a few coins from his pouch. "There is a finder's reward for returning any of our missing coursers."

Life sparked back into the peasant's eyes as he traded his rope for the deputy's coppers. "God bless you, good deputy!"

"And if you find any others, there will be a reward for them as well," he added. Then a misty Edward Blanchard led both steeds through the castle gate.

* * *

ROBYN SMILED to herself before turning away to continue down the street with the modest ramble of a farmer. She didn't look a thing like her infamous alter ego wearing a tattered tan tunic over worn gray trousers wrapped in a mud-brown cloak and hood. Sheriff Giffard must be as mad as a hornet by now after the day's events, she reckoned.

The plan had been simple: Will Scarlet and David of Doncaster were both slender youths and, when dressed in attire similar to Robyn's and carrying bows, gave the illusion that the notorious outlaw was in three places at once. They had divvied up the gang members between them and collected a satisfying booty to be distributed among the poor. The attacks also made for a perfect distraction from the central task at hand, mostly carried out by the refugees of the camp which was to loose the horses at various corners of Sherwood. Robyn had only returned the one.

She glanced about her surroundings in the busy market square with a nostalgic tug at her heart. The streets and crowds and vendors appeared unchanged, but she was changed. No one noticed her at all, a fact dually comforting and disconcerting. She looked up at the artful stained glass windows of St. Peter's and felt compelled to cross herself as she passed. *How long has it been since I attended mass?* she wondered, but was consoled with the knowledge that Friar Tuck had seen to her spiritual needs as well as her sword training.

As she raised her gaze to the street before her, a familiar figure caught her eye. She knew every curve of that luscious body, every line of the exquisite face - Marian! Robyn's heart leapt into her throat at the sight of the woman she loved and who, by a miracle of fate, loved her in return. She simply could not allow this opportunity to see and hold her, if only for a moment, pass unrealized.

Robyn continued down the street toward where Marian stood examining scarves on a merchant's cart and then slipped inconspicuously into a side alley. When she had checked behind each building and found the corridor empty, she crept back up the narrow walkway near the busy street and cupping her hands to her mouth, made a bird call. She waited in expectation. When nothing happened, she repeated the sound. Soon a curious Marian peeked around the corner. Robyn lowered her hood, grinned, and scampered farther into the shadowed passageway and around another corner. Her anticipation grew as she heard Marian's footsteps follow.

As Marian rounded the bend into the blind alley behind the row of buildings, Robyn grabbed her and pulled her into an alcove at a random establishment's back door. When Marian's eyes met hers, they melted from alarmed to enraptured in an instant.

"Robyn!" she exclaimed in a low, breathy tone.

Robyn caressed her cheek, reveling in the husky sound of her own name from Marian's lips. She could wait no longer. Drawn like a roaring tide to the seashore, her mouth came down over Marian's, searing with urgent passion. Marian wrapped her arms around Robyn's neck and opened herself to the kiss, enticing her lover to delve even deeper. Robyn plunged in thirstily, driven by a longing deep in her core.

Presently, she drew back for breath and to gaze into Marian's eyes. "When I saw you here just now, I knew I had to hold you in my arms." She was glad Marian had remembered that old bird whistle signal from their childhood.

Marian ran fingers through Robyn's hair, beamed up at her and asked, "And what brings you to Nottingham? Overjoyed as I am to see you, I wonder if it is safe."

"I had business with the deputy."

Marian's eyes widened, and she took a step back. "Robyn, you didn't-"

A grin tugged at the corner of Robyn's mouth as her hands slid to Marian's waist. "No, I wasn't here to murder him, and why would you think such a thing of me?"

Marian rapped the back of Robyn's head and gave her a stern frown. "I was not going to say that. I was only afraid you might try to confront him."

"On his own grounds? Not bloody likely!" She leaned in and kissed Marian's forehead, stroking her back with one hand and tangling the fingers of her other in Marian's golden strands. "I was returning his horse. We had to be rid of the lot of them as they proved too difficult to conceal."

Marian nodded and sank into a tight embrace, rubbing her cheek along Robyn's. "That was very generous of you."

"Well, Blanchard seems to be an honorable enough fellow," Robyn observed as she closed her eyes and breathed in Marian's scent. "I think he is trapped by the Sheriff like everyone else."

"That has been my observation as well."

Robyn was thrilled as one of Marian's hands lowered to cup her hip.

"I will be attending the Michaelmas Feast at the castle in a week and shall try to gain more information as to what the Sheriff and Gisborne are plotting. Mayhap the Prince will be in attendance, and I can also uncover what he has been about."

Robyn opened her eyes and pinned Marian with them. "You be careful. I don't like you taking chances. What if they were to discover you are spying upon them?"

"Me be careful? What of you taking on an entire troop with a handful of outlaws?" Marian's voice was edged with desperate concern.

Robyn caressed Marian's shoulders. "You know I couldn't let Nottingham kill those people. All is well." She smiled and gently brushed her lips over her lover's. "Then I shall come visit you the night after the feast to see what you have discovered… or purely to enjoy your company."

"I will be very much looking forward to that!" Marian repeated the light kiss Robyn had just given her. Then she cocked her head displaying a perturbed expression.

"What?" Robyn asked innocently.

"It isn't fair, you know," Marian remarked. "You pop in to see me whenever tis convenient, or you make me wait weeks between visits, but I can't come to see you. I don't even know where to find you."

"My sweetling, it is much safer for you if you do not know where to find me," Robyn explained while keeping her body tight to Marian's. She could feel the ebb and flow of Marian's breathing against her own chest and brought her breath into rhythm with it.

"And what about that which is safer for you? Suppose I discover that the Sheriff is off to commit some heinous act, or that he has captured one of your friends, or his spies have discovered your hide out and he is on his way forthwith. How then can I use this information to warn you, or get a message to you, if I don't even know where the blazes you are?"

Robyn paused to consider Marian's point. "But I can't just bring you to the camp; what will everyone think?"

Marian smiled mischievously. "They will think that we are lovers, which is, by the way, quite true." Her blue eyes danced at Robyn, working their magic to try to soften her resolve.

"But Marian, your reputation," Robyn said. "Consorting with outlaws? What if word were to get out?"

Marian raised her chin. "You let me worry about my own reputation."

Robyn sighed in dismay. She now felt pinned between two rational points of view. "I will give it consideration, and that is the best I can promise at the moment. Marian…" She voiced the name with the sweet reverence of a prayer. "I do so love you; if anything were to happen-"

Marian placed a finger to Robyn's lips. "And you think I do not feel the same? We are both in this, Robyn. There is no turning back for either of us."

At once Robyn was consumed by the heat of Marian's kiss on her lips, endowed with the same searing fervor as before. She felt the moistening between her thighs as a reflexive response while burning need tugged her into a whirlpool of elation. Her heart pounded in her chest as she cradled Marian tightly to herself.

When at last they broke the kiss, Marian found her voice first. "You should go now; every moment you delay increases the chance of your being discovered." Her tone was lush and ragged, her eyes bearing the stormy intensity of sensual passion.

Robyn nodded in somber realization. "And every moment I tarry makes it all the more difficult for me to let you go. The night after the feast," she repeated. "I will be at your window."

She closed her mouth over Marian's once again in a last stolen drink to see her through the coming week. When she drew away, Robyn trotted down the obscure alleyway without looking back, afraid that if she did, she would be compelled to return to that warm embrace, as steel to a magnet. With great resolve, she pulled up her hood and disappeared into the city.

## CHAPTER 12

*Windsor Castle, September 22, 1193*

Eleanor sat at the head of the heavy oak table in Windsor's great hall wearing an elegant white and gold silk gown draped by a red mantle.

After greeting her assembled ministers, she spoke to the sergeant at arms. He quickly snapped to attention. "I want the hall cleared and you to stand guard at the door. We are not to be disturbed."

"Yes, Your Highness, at once." He clicked his heels together motioning to the servers.

Eleanor watched the guard and servants leave, waited for doors to close, and then turned her consideration to the assessors. "My lords, let us begin with a report of all ransom taxes gathered thus far. George, take dictation of everything said."

George, the secretary for this meeting, was seated on Eleanor's left. He nodded, spreading out parchment in front of him, and dipped his quill into an ink well.

"Bishop Fitz Neal?"

"The entire collected funds have been tucked away safely at St. Paul's in London, under lock and key and heavy guard," he told the gathering. Richard Fitz Neal of London served as the nation's treasurer and was clean shaven, with a neat gray tonsure, black bishop's robes, and baggy, azure eyes, deep set in a grandfatherly face. It was not unusual for members of the high clergy to hold political appointments. Fitz Neal had been chosen for his post based on both his skill with numbers and his honest character. "Both the Queen's and the Archbishop's seals are on the chests, and I have confidence of their security."

Hamlin de Warenne, Earl of Surrey, (formerly Hamelin de Anjou) hailed from Eleanor's holdings across the channel. He picked up a meat pie, then pinned Fitz Neal with a scrutinizing gaze. "It seems that all the attention drawn to the treasure would alert thieves who will likely try to steal it," he commented before taking a hearty bite.

"Yes, but-" Hubert Walter paused dramatically, a knowing sparkle in his eyes. He sat on George's other side. As the Chief Justiciar and Archbishop of Canterbury, he was the most high-ranking man in England outside the royal family. "Word just happened to leak out that a Holy Relic, recovered by our brave Christian warriors from the clutches of the infidels, is being held in the Cathedral under heavy guard, waiting to be revealed at Christmas midnight mass."

"Clever!" Hamlin exclaimed, as he munched down the mincemeat. He had left off his chain mail for the formal meeting, but still wore a rich mahogany doublet over his deep wine tunic, and as always, kept an arming sword at his side.

"Your Grace." Color rose in Eleanor's cheeks as a mischievous grin crossed her lips. "Surely the head of the Church in England did not tell a lie."

"Indeed I did not," Hubert answered, mirroring the expression. "I merely mentioned the possibility of the arrival of an important relic to one of the sisters and, when the guards began appearing, the rumor spread."

"We have been most careful with keeping the location of the silver chests secret," Fitz Neal assured them. He opened a small ledger book. "I have recorded each of your deposits here, but let us go over them to be certs there are no errors. Sir de Warenne, I show twelve thousand from Anjou." His eyes met Hamlin's who nodded while he washed down his last morsel with a draught from his goblet.

"That is after three rounds of collections," Hamlin explained. "I do believe every lord, merchant, and commoner in the land has been thoroughly relieved of their clinkers."

Eleanor's gaze settled on the hairy, robust Hamlin. She could not help but be reminded of her late husband whenever they were together. The illegitimate nature of his birth had barred him from succeeding to any throne, but he had been supportive of his half-brother. Eleanor had been pleased that Henry arranged an advantageous marriage for the young man granting him the title Earl of Surrey. This once knight, currently earl, was a better uncle to her Richard than John was a brother.

"Yes, I am sure," Fitz Neal muttered, "as with those in my district, which by the by has contributed nine thousand silver marks. Now, Lord Arundel, I have twelve thousand five hundred for you."

Arundel lifted a handkerchief to his mouth and coughed while he nodded. "Aquitaine has done her part," he said meeting the Queen's eyes. She inclined her head toward him in approval. She worried for this William whose health had been at issue for months. And yet rather than send an envoy, he had come in person to present her homeland's portion of the ransom. *Normans are a hearty lot,* she thought proudly, *even when they are ailing.*

"Indeed," the Bishop agreed. "Now for the London district; Sir Londonstone, it says here you brought in ten thousand marks."

The mayor stroked his beard with one hand while reaching for a wedge of cheese with the other. "That matches my records, Your Grace. I fear that many of the individual collectors hired may have diverted coins into their own corrupt pockets. I have not been able to personally supervise them all."

The Queen Mother was pleased with Henry Fitz-Ailwin's appointment as the capital's first mayor. In addition to being a capable administrator, he endeavored to instill a sense of chivalry, culture, and learning in the city as she had requested. He was also honest, a trait she greatly appreciated.

Fitz Neal nodded. "I suspect the same deceit regarding my collections as well."

"Leave it to a national crisis to bring out the grift in folks," William Marshall said with a sigh, shaking his head in disgust. He picked up a meat pie and bit off a large portion. Of all her advisors, ministers, and subjects, Eleanor loved him most. *If only he was unmarried, and I was twenty years younger,* she thought before reality sunk in. *Very well, thirty years younger.*

Hubert finished out the tally. "From the churches and monasteries of

England, I have acquired eight thousand, five hundred silver marks. Everyone was willing to cooperate, save Geoffrey the Bastard of York who refused, declaring that the diocese of York holds primacy in England rather than Canterbury; therefore, he owed me nothing. In truth, I never expected his cooperation."

"One must wonder," Marshall posed to the group, "if mayhap his loyalty and his blunt are pledged to Prince John. My brother Henry, who is Bishop of Exeter, speaks poorly of him."

"I have found Geoffrey foremost to serve his own purposes," Hubert replied, "and everyone else be damned. Still," he added with a shake of his head, "he insists that he opposes John's rebellion plans and remains loyal."

"Let us move on," Eleanor said. She didn't have time to spend squabbling over what the product of Henry's infidelity was doing to upset everybody around him. Richard had granted Geoffrey the prestigious position of Archbishop as his father had asked, giving him great power, and still his bastard brother held bitter resentment toward her son. He was ambitious, possessed of a tumultuous nature, and had a habit of excommunicating anyone who spoke against him. Eleanor dismissed him as one would an irritating fly.

"While we have approximately fifty-two thousand German marks worth of silver, etcetera, under guard at St. Paul's, my youngest son has yet to appear with the portion of ransom he had promised to obtain. The last letter I received from him was over a month ago when he reported all was well, and the coins were flowing in." She sighed, clasping her hands together on the table before her. "We cannot count on him to turn over any assets he acquires; furthermore, I fear he will use what he can gather against us."

"Have you any word from your spies, Your Grace?" Mayor Fitz Ailwin inquired.

"No specific details at this time," she replied. "Hubert, I am so deeply in your debt for the unenviable task you had in collecting state funds from Church coffers. And I can guarantee that your monarchs would not have asked it of you had there not been extreme circumstances. We will do our best to repay each bishopric and monastery in short order."

Hubert inclined his head. "I see it as a necessary evil and completely concur with your decision in the matter." He took a sip of his wine and listened as she continued.

"Thank you for your generous and ungrudging approval. In desperation, I have written to Pope Celestine III asking if there is more the Church will do."

"But Your Highness," Bishop Fitz Neal interjected. "Our Holy Father has already excommunicated both Leopold of Austria and the Holy Roman Emperor for blatant disobedience to his decree against kidnapping Christian rulers to hold for ransom. What further actions are within his power?"

Eleanor gave him an incredulous stare. "Surely you jest? He is the Pope! His resources are limitless, and it is quite clear to the rest of Europe that Leopold and Henry are not concerned in the least with the security of their eternal souls. Excommunication means nothing to monarchs who consider themselves above the Bishop of Rome."

"I beg your pardon, Queen Eleanor," Fitz Neal responded with a bowed head. "I understand this is a trial for you, even more so than the rest of us. But there is no precedent for a Pope to contribute financially from Rome's resources."

"As I recall, it is also unprecedented for a Christian king to kidnap another Christian king during a time of war with the Saracens," she duly noted. Eleanor then turned her attention back to the group at large. "Be that as it may, I have been in continual negotiations with Henry Hohenstaufen. I informed the 'emperor', as he likes to be called, that 100,000 marks of silver was an impossible amount. Why, that would equal more than twice the annual sum of all the money made by every person in England! What's more, we were already on the brink of financial ruin after spending nearly the entire national treasury on the crusades. I requested that he reduce his demands to seventy thousand marks–still an absurd demand, but more attainable. Therefore he has replied with a counter-proposal."

She opened the emperor's letter while taking a moment to wet her tongue from her goblet. Her ministers sat forward in their seats more attentively than before.

"He says he is sympathetic to our inability to raise the required funds in a timely manner and recognizes that we assuredly wish the return of our King, and so forth, but he must have assurances." Then finding the appropriate line, she read from the letter.

"*It will be acceptable to his Royal Highness to release Richard the Lionhearted upon delivery of seventy thousand silver marks along with two hundred noble* hostages to be held in our land until a complete amount of one hundred and fifty thousand in silver be paid."

"One hundred and fifty!" exclaimed Marshall. "That is another year's full income for the country!" The men shook their heads in dismay, each turning to comfort from the food or drink set before them.

"Longchamp will be given charge over the hostages while they are away, to ensure their wellbeing, and that no harm befalls them while we continue to raise money to bring them back home," the Queen continued.

"Longchamp!" Arundel's exclamation seemed more than Eleanor thought he could have mustered and, in fact, it was following by a coughing fit.

"Your Highness," Hubert addressed with concern in his voice. He gestured with his hand as he spoke. "Justiciar Longchamp's behavior is often unseemly and lacking discretion."

"Many of the nobles will be reluctant to entrust him with their sons for several years," Bishop Fitz Neal added. "He is somewhat undisciplined in his personal practices."

Hamlin sat back in his chair and crossed his arms over his broad chest, scowling. "Good God, my lords, just say it like it is! The man is a sodomite, and every court from here to the Holy Land knows it. They may tolerate him in France, as Phillip is more indulgent of that kind of thing, but-"

"That is enough, my lords!" Eleanor raised her voice and her chin as her authority quelled their complaints.

She remembered the talk when Richard was a younger man, and he and then Prince Phillip had been close–very close. Her son had confided in her that he loved the dauphin and did not wish to travel to England and be separated from him. She knew Richard well, but she likewise understood politics. There could have been no good end to this liaison. She worked behind the scenes to discourage the affair, urging her son to marry or at least to travel. Then Richard became entangled in the power struggle with his brothers against his father and spent less and less time with Phillip, who he then described as 'clinging like a choking vine.' So he severed the relationship, and that may be one reason King Phillip was now conspiring with John against him, for what lover wishes to be the jilted one? The subsequent reputation Richard earned as a fearsome warrior crushed any rumors from circulating in regard to his masculinity.

Still, Eleanor knew her son's heart and his inclinations, and that he had other lovers since. She was proud he had learned the lesson of discretion; sadly, Longchamp could honestly care less how he was perceived.

The men quieted, but retained their worried expressions even as Eleanor spoke with regret. "Longchamp is now an old man, and incapable of forcing anyone. No matter how distasteful you may find his personal habits, the justiciar is proficient in his responsibilities, and Richard has confidence in him. If the nobles will not entrust him with their sons, they can certs trust him with their daughters. Moreover, it will be my solemn undertaking to visit the noble houses, calling upon them to send a family member to stand in the King's place."

"As you say, Your Grace," Hamlin replied respectfully with a nod in her direction.

"So, if you accept the offer," Hubert began, "we still need to raise at minimum eighteen thousand more, in addition to money for the trip. We have been through three rounds of tax collections already. Can it be done this year, or must we wait for spring?"

Mayor Fitz Ailwin gave the expected answer. "That is contingent on what Prince John does with the funds he has been extracting in the north."

"Verily, it depends upon us getting possession of the tax money John has raised, whether by his relinquishment or not. I am anticipating a correspondence anytime now from one of my Nottingham spies regarding a new resource we may be able to employ in accomplishing that task. So, my lords, I have not given up hope on having the King returned to us by Christmas. Does anyone have a better solution than to tell Emperor Henry that we agree to his latest demands?"

The ministers exchanged glances, no one struck with a more inspired proposal. Then Hubert said, "Considering his current line of thought, Your Grace, if we ask him to lower the initial payment to fifty thousand, he will simply say we then owe him a hundred and twenty thousand more and four hundred noble hostages, which leaves us in no better position. But if we cannot raise the complete amount-"

"Then I will stall him with more negotiations while we do," she declared. "My lords, I wish to express my most sincere gratitude to you all for your tireless and thankless efforts in producing this incredible sum which you have brought for the freedom of my dear son." The words caught in her throat and, at that moment, Eleanor experienced a rare public burst of emotion. She was so practiced, so poised, so prepared for every eventuality that nothing ever escaped her control. But seeing the devotion of her ministers, and hoping finally to have her cherished son home in a matter of months, seized her heart and tugged. A tear crept into her voice and into the corner of her eye, one that she stubbornly fought back.

"It is our honor and privilege, Your Grace," Hamlin said warmly.

*So much like my Henry and my Richard*, she thought, and took comfort in his company.

* * *

AFTER THE MEETING DISBANDED, Eleanor invited Sir William Marshall alone to escort her on a walk around the grounds for a private conversation. "Must you truly depart for your estate in Ireland anon?" she asked, distressed by his decision.

"Your Highness, I should be there to oversee the harvest, and my wife is with child again. It is best for her to return home now before she gets too far along for travel."

"Congratulations!" she gushed. "That makes the fourth? You have been busy."

"Thank you, and you are correct; two sons and a daughter thus far," he answered with fatherly pride. "Asides, what need have you of me without the rest of the council? I am no financier."

She took his arm as they passed the gardens. "I know I cannot keep you for myself, William, but your presence brings with it strength, and England needs your strength now."

"Rest assured, if battle is required, I will be here in an instant to raise the standard," he pledged with sincerity.

Eleanor titled her head to gaze on him fondly. "All the more reason why I wish it to be you who should come along to guard my person as I visit noble families to query for hostages. You are the only man, living or dead, who has ever unseated my son Richard in tournament or in battle; who better to keep me safe?"

William lowered his head, a rosy color rising in his cheeks. Then he sighed. "I can do the next best thing. My nephew John, son of my oldest brother, is serving as squire to me. I have trained him and he excels in the fighting arts. He has also been introduced to the music and literature of courtly love, but could benefit from your excellent tutelage. Mayhap you will allow him to attend you in this endeavor."

She smiled in response. "That is an offer which I cannot refuse."

They were interrupted by the aviary keeper, Marceau. "Pardon me, Your Highness, my lord," he said as he bowed to each, "but you asked me to inform you at once when your next correspondence arrived."

"Yes, yes," Eleanor replied eagerly, releasing William's arm to stretch out her hand in anticipation of the note.

"This arrived just moments ago, and so I went in search of Your Highness." The Norman handed her the small case he had removed from the pigeon, then bowed and scurried off while Eleanor withdrew a small roll of parchment from the cylinder.

She began walking again and William fell in step. Her eyes lit with interest at the note and she passed it to her First Knight. "What do you make of this?"

He spoke in a low voice as he read the words aloud to her. "*Hood is loyal to Richard, skillful and works on England's behalf. Shall I bring him in? M.*" He wrinkled his brow and handed the paper back to Eleanor. "I take it this Hood is the resource you spoke of?"

"Yes," she said brightly, securing the message inside the locket that hung around her neck. "He is a bandit of sorts, has been giving that scheming Sheriff of Nottingham a right fitful time of it. It would seem he robs from the rich and gives to the poor. Why, it is almost chivalrous!"

"And so," William speculated as he watched autumn colored leaves dance in the breeze. "If John won't give us the money he has raised, perhaps Hood could steal it for us."

"Indeed." Her voice was practically gleeful in its enthusiasm while a speculative glimmer shone in her dark eyes. "But did you notice Marian's wording?"

William looked baffled. "What of it?"

"She speaks like she knows the man, and that part about 'shall I bring him in?' How could she do that unless she is already speaking with him? Curious, very curious indeed. Are you acquainted with any baron's son who goes by Robin or Robert or similar sounding names who is also an expert marksman?"

He stroked his beard thoughtfully, then shook his head. "Not that I am aware of, or that live near Nottingham, anyway. Do you think the Sherwood bandit is a nobleman?"

"I think he is someone Richard's goddaughter trusts and, because I trust her, I will proceed accordingly. The intelligence I have collected thus far confirms my suspicions. The Sheriff, Sir Guy, and John are plotting something, and they have been collecting money. Now to discover the exact nature of their scheme, and then we shall rely on Marian's chivalrous thief to get us that silver."

# CHAPTER 13

*Nottingham Castle, Michaelmas, September 29*

A line of fancily clad noble men and ladies filed out of Nottingham castle's chapel following the morning's Mass of St. Michael, which kicked off the day's festivities. Landlords looked forward to it as rent paying day. For farmers, it signaled the end of the harvest. For the faithful it honored all the angels, but especially the arch-angel who had cast Lucifer out of Heaven and down into the pit. Occurring just after the astral equinox, it was a day that marked the beginning of autumn. The wool garments and fur mantles worn by the nobility were indications of the cooler weather.

Marian walked beside Maid Fay de Gisborne and a few other young women as they made their way from the chapel to the great hall. "Mmmm, I can smell the goose roasting from here!" the excited, youthful Fay exclaimed.

Marian smiled. The girl deserved better than Sir Guy as a father, and she hoped she would end up with a worthier husband. Marian thought she looked quite fetching that day, in a pine green silk gown and ribbon woven through her auburn tresses.

"It will have stuffing, and a big, hot Michaelmas pie, just filled with blackberries. You can't pick blackberries after today, you know," she sagely instructed Marian. "So, they stuff them all into the pies!"

*Sir Guy will be happy,* Marian thought as they walked. *He is quite fond of pie as I recall.* "I am certain the cooks will spread us a marvelous feast," she said instead. Marian caught their reflections in a polished shield hanging between two tapestries on the stone wall of the hall. She was pleased with the plum bliaut with bell sleeves lined in white made from the fabric Amee de Neville had provided.

"Are you going to come out in the courtyard for the games?" Fay asked with exuberance.

Marian wanted to snoop around and try to listen in on conversations. She had spotted several newcomers at mass and Prince John was rumored to be in the castle. "Mayhap," she answered distractedly as she peered around the bend into the foyer outside the hall. *Ah, there is the Prince,* she noted, having not seen him in the chapel. He wore a small princely crown fitted into his feathery, ginger locks, along with numerous rings. His clothing was distinctive as well, being the only man with a white, furry mantle of arctic fox draped about an embroidered royal blue tunic. He was accompanied by the Sheriff, Sir Guy, that awful Archbishop of York, and three distinguished nobles and a bishop with whom she was not acquainted. *Barons, most likely,* she thought. Marian was struck with John's short stature as the sinewy Giffard towered over him.

Fay followed Marian's gaze. "Oh, Papa won't be joining us for the games," she said with a girlish giggle. "He has to meet with Prince John and the other lords."

"I see," Marian answered, trying to muster a smile for Fay.

"Papa says he looks very much forward to your upcoming marriage, and that I should not feel awkward having you as a step mother even though we are about the same age."

Masked fury erupted through Marian's veins at those words, but in an act of extreme self-control to refrain from any unbecoming response, she reined it in and took a moment to breathe. *Older,* she thought. *You are older than I, you twit, and yet one would think you had not completed your tutorage!*

But she calmly replied, "Fay, dear, we have not spoken of setting a marriage date. Truly, there is none to arrange such a contract until my father returns from Germany. Now, let us enjoy the festival and simply behave as friends." Her eyes left Fay to watch the nobles file into a room and close the door, leaving Deputy Blanchard standing guard. *Bloody hell! I'll not discover what they are about now. Mayhap later.*

\*\*\*

NOTTINGHAM CASTLE HAD no throne room as no king held court there; however, the Sheriff's office served somewhat the same purpose. This was where he would hear petitions, accusations and defenses, and mete out justice as he saw fit. It was also the chamber in which he held private meetings. Within, the stone walls were softened by armchair height wainscoting and scenic tapestries. The morning light streamed in through a glass pane window behind the Sheriff's desk while a few lanthorns (called such because the panes were designed of thin, transparent horn) illuminated the corners. Giffard ushered in his guests across a wool carpet of red and white, bearing the helm and passant lion of his family crest, to a table made of elm with decorative etchings around its edge.

After exchanging greetings, Godfrey announced, "And now my lords, I yield to Prince John who has important news for us all." Turning his attention to the youngest man at the table, the Sheriff and other nobles bowed their heads in deference to their Prince.

After taking a sip of mead from his goblet, Prince John raised his chin in the practiced air of royalty and summoned his most authoritative tone. "Thank you Godfrey, for the use of your castle and your loyal service. You all know our host, the Honorable Sheriff of Nottingham, Sir Guy of Gisborne, and my half-brother, Geoffrey, the Archbishop of York." They inclined their heads as each was introduced. John motioned to the corpulent man to his left. "His Grace, Bishop Albrec of Kirkstall has newly joined our association, as he was divinely inspired while in prayer one evening."

The Bishop raised his double chins, a look of self-importance consuming his countenance. "It is a pleasure to serve one as politically wise and foreseeing as His Highness, soon to be King John," he waxed eloquently.

The Prince motioned to his right. "My loyal barons, Sir Hugh Diggory of Derbyshire, Sir Raoul de Clarc of Cornwall, and Sir Lambelin Bondeville of Somerset."

"I hear your mother is lacking the full ransom for the Lionheart," said Sir Hugh with obvious glee. His wiry brown beard looked as though it had not been groomed in a decade, but his ample musculature was apparent through a fitted red tunic. "Years ago, when he was but an upstart and I but a squire, he dared to rebel against King Henry. I stood with my father for the King, and in course of the battle Richard dealt a blow to my leg that failed to heal properly. I must say, I never cared for him as a man or king."

"Indeed, he is but a reckless warmonger," Sir Lambelin, the fair-haired youngest of the barons agreed with a gruff frown and took a vicious bite out of an apple. Continuing as he chewed, "If he hadn't thrust us into that damnable crusade, my father would still be alive running our estate and I would be winning at tournaments."

"Undoubtedly we all have reasons to dislike the King," observed Sir Raoul, the distinguished and elegant elder of the cadre, his neat gray moustache and goatee trimmed around thin lips. "Personally, I find Prince John to be far more generous with his barons than his brother ever thought to be. He understands that Normans are the rightful noble class and has taken every opportunity to reward vassals loyal to him with Saxon land. His Highness," he said with a delicate motion of his hand toward John, "is also a man of shrewdness and cunning."

Prince John was plainly pleased by this merry praise. "So gentlemen, since we have a festival to attend, let me be brief. I collected over twenty thousand German marks worth of tax money here in the north which the people believe is going for my brother's ransom. However, the chests of silver will go to pay for a large army to supplement our ranks and allow us to take the throne before my mother can secure Richard's release. Even if he does return to these shores by Christmas, it will be too late. We shall be entrenched, commanding every major city, port, and castle. What, with most able-bodied fighting men still in route from the Holy Land, or camped outside Trifels Castle, there are few but old men and boys to oppose us. King Phillip remains our ally and has pledged financial and political support. He is standing ready to formally recognize me as the legitimate King of England."

"Twenty thousand?" Geoffrey raised his brows in surprise. "Impressive."

Sir Guy laughed. "Closer to thirty, I'd wager! You should know that if every shire worked over its citizens with tax collectors the way Godfrey and I have done in Nottinghamshire, the amount would be twice that!"

"Your contribution is significant," John noted before continuing. "While the Martinmas Fair is taking place six weeks hence, I'll be bringing the lot of the cache through Nottingham on its way to Dunwich, where we will meet the mercenary captain to pay for our army. I need you and your retainers to help guard the silver hoard and to lead the hired soldiers against whoever dare not pledge his allegiance to me."

Sir Hugh frowned, scratching his unmanageable beard. "Word has traveled to Derbyshire of a wily outlaw roaming these parts. Is there any truth to it?"

Prince John looked questioningly at the Sheriff. "I thought you assured me Hood would be taken care of?"

"Yes, My Liege, and he shall be," Godfrey answered with an air of confidence. "The trap I have set for him is foolproof. First, there is a secret vault below the pulpit in the chapel where we will secure your fortune. No one else knows of it, nor is it known great sums of money are arriving. Then there is the archery contest."

"Archery contest?" inquired Bishop Albrec.

"Aye." The Sheriff's dark eyes danced at his own cleverness. "Hood fancies himself to be the finest shot with a bow in all of England. He will not be able to resist coming to compete and prove it so, but we'll be ready for him. Even if he employs a guise, I'll have him."

"How is that?" Sir Lambelin asked.

Godfrey's smile gleamed at them. "My soldiers have orders to surround and arrest whoever wins. He'll be locked in irons and off to the gallows at last, and the Prince's money shall remain safe. In addition, there won't just be me and my soldiers–there will be all of you and yours."

Sir Raoul looked thoughtful as he munched on a pastry. "It could work. However, you must realize that we retain very few fighting men to contribute. I fear that is why our lord, Prince John, is in need of mercenaries. I can bring my two sons who have been in training along with one old knight and a handful of foot soldiers."

"Well, clearly I possess no soldiers to offer," Bishop Albrec said innocently, raising his pudgy palms. "But I can help in other ways."

"What say you, brother?" John asked, turning his gaze to Geoffrey. "Will the Archbishop of York finally replace Canterbury as head of the Church in England? You know I will do that for you the moment you place the crown on my head."

Geoffrey tilted his head in contemplation. "I do like the sound of that. But I also do not relish the wrath of the Lionheart if you were to fail. Allow me time to think on things, and I will give you my answer at the fair. Be assured I will not discuss the matter with a living soul and, if I do commit, you shall have the full backing of York and the resources I withheld from Hubert Walter."

John nodded to him. "Very well; I shall grant you the time you require. My lords, are the rest of you in agreement?"

They all replied with an enthusiastic "Aye!"

Sheriff Godfrey Giffard raised his goblet. "To our lord, Prince John: long live King John!"

The others moved in kind, saying, "Here, here!" and "To our next king!" Then they all drank in unison, pledging their fortunes and their futures to John Plantagenet.

* * *

AT MIDDAY, a bell rang announcing the beginning of the feast which would continue all afternoon and into the evening. It was not uncommon for the nobles to gorge themselves beyond comfort, be excused to the privy to retch it all up, and then return to repeat the process. Marian found the practice wasteful and revolting despite its social acceptance. There would be music and entertainment brought by jugglers, tumblers and fools, and later that night when all were drunk on wine, some young bucks would seek the chance to get lucky with an inebriated maiden. Marian's hope was that spirit loosened lips would spill some bit of information.

She and Fay sat at the Prince's long table with the barons and bishops. Sir Guy invariably wanted to be seen with the most beautiful and elegant unmarried female in Nottingham, therefore Marian was placed on his left side across from the Sheriff and in proximity to the others from the morning's meeting. Noticing the conspicuous absence of the young princess whom she met in Windsor, Marian asked, "Your Highness, may I inquire after the Lady Isabella? I note she is not with us this afternoon."

Prince John raised his chin and smiled pleasantly. "Her ladyship was unable to accompany me this time. I do so much traveling of late that it would be quite impossible for her to keep up. But I will tell Isabella you asked about her."

"Thank you, Your Highness," Marian replied with a slight bow of her head. "She is a charming princess and an asset to any occasion. Please let her know she was missed."

Gisborne was well mannered enough to provide introductions to the newcomers and Marian made careful note of their names, though she was certain his motivation was to show off the beauty he had acquired in an attempt to elevate his standing with the barons. She continued to act her part as his polite, enchanting, and witless companion until a question arose about their betrothal; there she drew the line. "No, Sir Raoul, we have certainly not spoken of marriage at this early juncture. However, I expect my father, Sir Robert who serves at His Highness King Richard's right hand, to return home by the New Year. Then Sir Guy may wish to approach my father on the matter, but until then I am, shall we say, fair game?" She giggled girlishly batting her eyes at Gisborne and biting back the stream of insults she wished to hurl at him.

His hazel eyes smiled at her as he patted her hand. "You see why I must court this lady? As I have always maintained, a doting daughter becomes a doting wife. I will be so pleased with that measure of devotion!" The others laughed and congratulated him as though Marian were nothing more than a faithful mongrel hound whose purpose was to reply, *yes, master,* and obediently do whatever she was told.

She forced a smile. "Indeed, I am devoted to my father, and resolve to be just as faithful to whomever I am wed."

"Sir Guy," Raoul advised pointing a bony finger at him, "you had better treat that lady like a queen–she is an undeniably rare find!"

"Treat her like a queen I shall!" he declared. "And that gives me an idea." An uncharacteristic spark of inspiration over more than food, drink, or fashion lit on his face. "Sheriff, I have a capital suggestion!"

With a leg of mutton in his hand, Giffard raised his eyes to his friend across the table. "Do tell." He continued chewing while Sir Guy expounded on his notion.

"At the archery contest to be held at the close of the annual Martinmas Fair in November, Maid Marian should award the grand prize, don't you think? It could be something memorable, such as a golden arrow laid upon a satin pillow, and she should sit with us at the judges' stand to present the winner's prize. Is it not a splendid idea?"

Giffard huffed. "Splendid for you; it creates an excuse for thousands of people to see you seated beside her ladyship. We won't even need a pri-" he started to say, but then stopped himself. Marian watched the change in Prince John's expression and felt the abrupt tension among the men.

"I think it is a marvelous idea, Sir Guy," John declared in approval. "My dear brother's goddaughter is truly the only person present worthy to award such a prize."

"Thank you, Your Highness," Gisborne answered smiling with a bow of his head. "It is fitting that she be there for the big event, especially given the way she herself was treated by the villain."

"Why, Sir Guy, whatever do you mean?" Prince John asked with strained civility. His green eyes hardened on the baron who suddenly choked and turned pale. "You know with all the security present at the fair, there is no way any thieves or outlaws will be making an appearance to threaten anyone's purse."

"Why yes, Your Highness is quite right," Sir Guy amended and raised a cloth to pat sweat from his brow.

John turned a charismatic grin toward Marian. "It would indeed be the cherry on top to have Maid Marian award a golden arrow to the winner of the tournament. You will do us the honor, will you not?"

Feigning that she had no idea that anything awkward had just transpired, Marian smiled and nodded. "Verily, Your Highness, it would be my honor!" Her face lit with radiance. While they all settled back into their relaxed poses secure in the knowledge their plot had not been compromised, they were oblivious to the fact that her gleam was not for being chosen to present some ridiculous prize, but rather because her keen mind had put all the pieces of their scheme together.

\* \* \*

LATER THAT EVENING, Marian made a point of dancing with each of the barons in an attempt to glean more information from them. She learned that Sir Raoul was a widower, Sir Hugh could not dance without stepping on her feet and Sir Lambelin had wandering hands which she was obliged to discretely dissuade. She feared, if Sir Guy knew what he was about, he may throw down a gauntlet. But to her dismay, and despite a large quantity of drink, none of them said anymore about the archery contest.

As evening closed in, Marian bade her farewells. "My lords, you have all been so kind and Lord Sheriff, your festival has been a great success. Why, when I finish writing my letters, all of London will be envious."

"Must you depart so soon?" Sir Guy asked, disappointment sagging on his middle-aged face.

"Milord, it is well after dark and my mother expects me home. Asides, my carriage driver is awaiting."

Sir Lambelin jeered. "Who cares about the fleak?" His words slurred, and he swayed a bit as his uninhibited eyes raked over her lustily.

Gisborne flashed in fury at the younger baron when he saw how he looked at Marian. "She said her mother needs her at home, you lout!" He clenched his teeth and at once took on the posture of the knight he once had been.

Sir Lambelin backed down, tottering off to find a more willing female.

"Thank you, Sir Guy," she offered allowing him to kiss her hand and escort her to her carriage. But while he rattled on with some mindless chatter, she was straining to hear what the guards in the courtyard were saying to each other. She only could catch bits and pieces.

"Twenty thousand? I heard it was thirty," one said as they passed by.

"That's a soddin' lot of blunt!" another exclaimed.

"Shhh," scolded a less drunk soldier. "Don't be a blob-tale!"

*Prince John's tax revenue, it must be,* Marian thought as Gisborne handed her up into her carriage. *But is it already in the castle, or coming later? And when?*

"Sir Guy, you have been a wonderful companion this day, performing impeccably in accordance to the dictates of courtly love," she poured on the compliment. She was certain she saw a blush rise in his ruddy cheeks... or was it just alcohol?

"I do try, milady," he replied with a smile. She hesitated for a moment. Was he drunk enough to grill about the archery contest and the Prince's tax money, or would she betray her true intent? *Better to err on the side of caution, mother always says. At least I know they are laying a trap for Robyn and I can warn her.* "May I call on you next week?"

"I bear many manorial duties following harvest, but perhaps in a fortnight."

"Until then." Sir Guy gave her a gallant bow and closed her carriage door. Marian breathed a sigh of relief as the wheels rattled through the gate. A languorous smile overtook her face as Marian turned her thoughts toward home and the smoky, succulent woman who would be waiting to meet her. Even as her mind was amused recalling their first attempt at love making–steeped in bashful uncertainty, then flame-broiled with raw desire–her body reacted with a tightening of her inner thighs and a pulling at her nipples. The anticipation was more arousing than she could have imagined!

* * *

NEARBY, a large, shadowy figure loomed at the back door to the castle stables, shrouded in a charcoal cloak, his face hidden by its deep hood. He was met by a young fellow in common garb with raucous dirt colored curls.

"Were you seen?" the hooded man asked in an uneasy baritone.

"I don't think so," his companion replied with a glance over his shoulder.

There was a moment of silence. Then the big man handed the other a small leather binder tied up tight. "You are the only one I can trust with this, little brother."

His curly haired confidant took the package and tucked it snuggly inside his tunic. With a grave nod he declared, "You can count on me."

The shrouded hulk placed a hefty hand on his brother's shoulder. "Make haste straightway for Windsor and do not stop. Speak to no one," his low voice warned. "The fate of England is now in your hands." The young man swallowed, his wide, guileless eyes betraying the burden thrust upon him. Speechless, he caught his brother in a manly embrace before making his retreat. "Godspeed," he voiced after the lad in a hushed farewell.

## CHAPTER 14

*Sherwood Forest*

Robyn sat on a log near the campfire whittling sticks into arrow shafts, anxiously trying to fill the day until she could strike out for Marian's. She proposed to arrive after dark–it was just simpler that way. *What has she discovered? What will she be wearing? Will she be as excited to see me as I am to see her?* A million thoughts poured through her head. Her musings were interrupted by a trio of small children running about giggling who plowed right into her. She immediately withdrew the knife so as not to hurt any of them by accident.

Christina ran up behind them. "No! Don't disturb Robin, you silly gooses!" She grabbed one tow-headed boy by the arm and blushed with an abashed grimace. "I'm so sorry."

"No bother at all," Robyn replied. Then she tilted her head toward Christina in curiosity. "What do you and the other youths do all day?"

"Oh, well, I usually chase after the little ones and try to keep them out of trouble," she said as she shoved the threesome away from the fire site, "and help Mum with chores. Charles likes to go fishing, mostly so that he can feel important when he brings home something to eat. The two quiet boys are starting to do more than just sit huddled in blankets. What do you do all day? Important things, for certs," she added, her bright eyes scanning the area for her younger charges. Robyn followed her gaze and spotted them peering around oak trunks at each other, laughing and throwing acorns.

Suddenly a thought dropped into Robyn's head like ripe fruit falling from a tree, and she sprang to her feet brimming with inspiration. "Thank you, Christina!" she said placing a hand on the youngster's shoulder. "You have given me a wonderful idea!"

"I have?" Her eyes shone with pride.

"Indeed. Now, see to your little brothers and you will learn of my inspiration shortly."

Christina flashed a wondrous grin and ran after the urchins.

Robyn's gaze swept over the camp until it rested upon Alan A Dale traipsing back from the privy. "Alan!" she called. "I need you a minute."

He perked up and quickened his pace. "Do you require someone handsome, talented, or brilliant, 'cause I'm your man," he said with a whimsical smile.

She returned it with a mischievous gleam. "I have a significant project that needs doing, and you are indeed just the man to accomplish it." She draped an arm over his shoulders and walked with him around the camp as she explained. "You see all these children?"

"Aye," he uttered with a hint of annoyance in his voice.

"It has been brought to my attention that they need something important to do just like everyone else. It also occurs to me that winter is coming. Therefore, we are going to strike two birds with one stone, and you my friend, will be in charge of the operation."

"Huh?" Alan stopped walking and gave her a puzzled look.

"I want you to organize the children to become nut gatherers. There are plenty of walnuts, hazelnuts, and sweet chestnuts in the forest that can help sustain us through the winter months, and the mitings need an activity of import. You may fashion the chore into something fun… have them pretend they are squirrels, or," her brown eyes flashed, "turn it into a game and the one who gathers the most nuts wins. Wait," she amended as thoughts continued to cascade through her mind. "Separate them into teams with the littlest ones divvied up so it will be fair. Come up with a prize, create rules, use your imagination. You'll be brilliant!"

Alan's green eyes widened like saucers. "Me? You want *me* to be in charge of children? Have you gone completely daft?"

Robyn only grinned at him, her expression twinkling with delight. "Are children too much for you to handle? Is the challenge too great?" She slid her arm from his shoulders, taking a step back to give him room to breathe.

"Nay, 'tisn't that," he answered frowning.

"The youngsters all love you," she said. "They think you are amusing. Asides, if you keep running off to the tavern to see that girl of yours, you'll soon be having wee mites of your own."

A look of utter horror consumed his features in an instant. "Shall not!"

Robyn laughed in spite of trying not to. "Alan, mate, has no one told you where babies come from yet?"

Alan's cheeks turned so red she could have sworn they had been rubbed with strawberries. "I know where they come from," he uttered in a flustered whisper. "I'm just not ready to be anyone's Papa."

"Which is all the more reason you need to practice. Come now; all will be well," Robyn assured him. "It will be an adventure."

\* \* \*

FITZWALTER MANOR, *that night*

MARIAN WALTZED INTO HER BEDROOM, latched the door behind her and lit a candle. Raising her chin with eyes closed, she took in a deep breath through her nose and smiled. "What is that unfamiliar odor that touches my senses?" she asked whimsically.

"It's called clean," came Robyn's sarcastic reply. Marian turned a languorous gaze to Robyn who stepped out of the corner shadow. She had already removed her cloak, doublet, trousers, and boots, and stood like a tall drink of water in leggings and tunic. The corners of Marian's mouth bowed up in a radiant smile. "I wanted to, you know, not smell like an old shoe for once, so I rose before dawn to bathe in the brook." She eased toward Marian and the bed.

Marian shivered as she tossed her own cloak onto the chair at her dressing table. "That must have been cold."

"Indeed," Robyn replied huskily, taking another step.

Marian shrugged, feigning indifference. "You could have waited until you arrived here and had a hot bath in my chamber."

Robyn's eyes twinkled as she held her burgeoning laughter at bay. "I

# HEART OF SHERWOOD

suppose it wouldn't hurt for you to scrub me down anyway; I might have missed a spot."

Marian stepped in, her voice now more tinted with desire than humor. "You may rest assured that I will not miss *the* spot." Their lips met, jolting Robyn to her core, transforming fantasy into a reality almost beyond belief. Her arms wrapped around Marian as she was overwhelmed with a sudden and intense need to touch her, to hold her closer than breath. Pressed together, she felt Marian's heart beat against her own chest. Presently, the two drew apart for necessity of air.

"You definitely found the spot," Robyn confirmed in a ragged voice. "My heart."

She sensed the intimacy of Marian's unguarded eyes caress her face before she tugged Robyn in for another lingering kiss. Then, tilting her head, she mused aloud, "How do you do it? How do you live with all those men day after day without them ever finding out?" She unfastened the cord at her waist and proceeded to wriggle out of her gown and drop it into a circle of cloth at her feet.

"It is not easy," Robyn began as she drank in Marian's shapely form beneath her thin chemise. "I have to find odd times to use the privy, only chance to bathe or change clothes in the middle of the night, pretend to shave my face from time to time and never appear shocked or embarrassed when they so easily relieve themselves wherever." She shook her head with a little laugh. "There's a young girl from Loxley who recognized me, but she is good at keeping secrets." Marian lifted Robyn's tunic over her head and then sucked in her breath, her blue eyes blazing while a blush rose in her cheeks. "I unwrapped already–have been waiting quite the while. I was beginning to wonder if you were coming at all."

"Rubbish! You knew I would be here." Marian regained her composure and raised her gaze to Robyn's face while she pulled off her own chemise.

"Oh, and your maid? She is nothing if not thorough in her duties. I was obliged to duck into the wardrobe and under the bed as she continued to move in and out all evening." It was Robyn's turn to flutter as she cast a mesmerized gaze over firm, ample breasts that beckoned to her like Eden's fruit.

Marian laughed warmly and stepped in to touch Robyn, languidly running a light stroke along her skin. Robyn's body responded at once, being seized in a tingling sensation. "But what do you do about the flowers? That has to be the hardest thing to hide."

"Ah, yes." She chuckled and sat on the bed to remove her leggings. "I have to find excuses to disappear from time to time, and my brother taught me to make this scent disguiser from animal musk for hunting. It stinks to blazes and back, but you can't smell anything else. And trousers are much better for holding a rag in place than any feminine contraption." She stopped talking long enough to notice Marian sitting at her side, both of them now completely nude. Heat washed over her with tremendous force. "Will Scarlet almost found me out a short while ago. Very sweet boy, loyal to a fault, but none too bright."

"What happened?"

"He crept up while I was washing my bloody cloth in the stream. I made up some story about it being a sword cleaning cloth and he was so impressed he wanted one too." They both laughed before demanding need for each other seized control. Their eyes locked on each other's; Robyn raised a tender hand to cup Marian's face. "I have scarcely thought of anything but this moment since last I saw you."

"Nor I," Marian echoed with a shameless sigh in her voice. The kiss took its time, patiently savoring every taste and sensation, a lingering and steady seduction. Robyn's hands, now rough and strong, made their way gently, exploring, stroking, giving and receiving elation at their fingertips. She reveled in the magic of Marian's smooth touch, which was surprisingly intuitive given her lack of experience. Falling back onto the bed, they melted into one another, as generous as they were demanding, whispering utterances of endearment and pledges of devotion. There were instances when Robyn had to bite her own lip or close hers over Marian's to keep from crying out as the waves of passion carried her to new and wondrous heights. And when they were sated and fully spent, they lay in each other's arms, drenched in the sweat of their pleasure, floating on a sea of bliss.

"Well," Robyn offered once she found her voice. "I was clean… for a little while." A musky aroma hung in the air. "You'll want to perfume the bed before your maid comes in the morning."

Marian, too drained to move, placed a kiss to Robyn's shoulder where her head rested. "You are so precious!"

"This is like nothing I could have ever imagined," Robyn said dreamily staring at the ceiling. "It was as if for a little while there is no one else, nothing else in the whole world but you and me. And we could fly–like eagles, Marian–fly like eagles."

"I know," Marian breathed in awe. "I felt it; I was there with you, Robyn. I have never been closer to anyone, nor do I ever care to be. This, you, are all that I ever want."

Robyn's thoughts were arrested at that declaration. She ever only wanted Marian, but... "When this is all over, if we aid in getting the King back and protecting his throne from Prince John, we will be given a reward of some sort, but I'm not certs if he can or would help us to stay together. I mean, what would we say? What could we ask for? I love you Marian, with all my heart. And I want nothing more than to spend my life with you, only you. But what if that isn't possible?"

Marian raised herself up on her elbow to peer down into Robyn's concerned expression. A familiar look of bemusement crept across her face. "That may not be as difficult as you think." Robyn's brow furrowed in confusion and her eyes gazed questioningly up into her partner's. "You are not the only one who keeps secrets, you know, or goes sneaking out of her room at night. I have learned a few things about my godfather that I wager few others are privy to."

"Oh, now you must tell me," Robyn allowed, her curiosity piqued.

"Well," Marian began, trying unsuccessfully to stifle a broad grin. She played her fingers across Robyn's belly as she relayed the story. "As you are aware, my father is a true and loyal vassal to King Richard, and among his closest friends. On occasions, the King would stay at our manor while traveling through the region. One night while I was spying about the house after I was supposed to be in bed, I peeked into the guest room to see what the King was about." She paused for dramatic effect.

"And??" Robyn insisted.

"Let us just say that you will find King Richard to be quite understanding of our situation, and he and my father are far more than mere friends."

Robyn's eyes grew wide and her mouth fell agape in amazement. "Your father–and the Lionheart? Really??"

Marian's melodic laugh warmed Robyn's soul. "Yes, really. I suppose that is why he is my godfather, and why the King has no children of his own."

"Forsooth!" Once the revelation had sunk in, another thought began to haunt Robyn and her jovial countenance quickly faded causing Marian to frown.

"What's wrong?"

Robyn was aware of Marian's soft caress on her breast, a sensation that warmed her soul, yet threatened to undo her. She swallowed and then turned her face to look Marian in the eyes. "But you would want children. If you stay with me, you will not be able to have children of your own and you will grow to resent me for it. I cannot give you what you need to be complete, and for that my heart breaks."

"Oh, Robyn, no," Marian immediately consoled moving her hand to stroke her cheek. "That is not so. One does not require a man to have children, not while England is filled with orphans in need of mothers. Do you think there not enough love in my heart to give it to a child born of another?"

"Never," Robyn affirmed. "You overflow with love and kindness, grace likened to a saint."

"Then understand that if at some point I become desirous of children, we can assuredly adopt and give love to those who have none."

In that moment tears welled in Robyn's eyes as an intensity of love, joy, and acceptance that she had never known consumed her such that she could not express. She tenderly cupped her hand around the back of Marian's neck and drew her in to a reverent kiss filled with emotion that knew no words. Silent gratitude hung in the air until Robyn said, "T'were I to die this night, t'would be as the most joyful and blessed person to have ever lived. Marian, I truly do not deserve you–but if you will have me, I shall do my best to see that you enjoy the life you desire."

"If?" Marian smiled playfully. "I have already had you twice, and I think I should want to keep you. And that reminds me…" she began her energy renewed.

"Ah, yes," Robyn said as she recalled the reason she had come to see Marian tonight–well, the other reason. "What did you learn at the feast?"

"Not as much as I had hoped, but something that will prove highly useful."

"Tell me all!"

"It seems the Sheriff is planning to trap you with an archery contest at the Martinmas Fair. He has determined you will not be able to resist showing off your skill in front of all of Nottinghamshire, and his guards will be ready to arrest you on the spot the moment you win. Oh, yes, and I get to present the winner's prize of a golden arrow."

"Say you do, do you? A golden arrow?" Robyn teased.

Marian nodded. "Resting on a silk pillow."

Robyn chuckled. "Better than a golden apple, I suppose." She gave Marian's breast a teasing squeeze and winked. Marian's mouth dropped and a little squeak spilled out before she teasingly slapped at Robyn's hand. "So the Sheriff is banking on my pride, is he? Then he will be sadly disappointed when I fail to enter the contest, for I have no vanity that needs tending."

Marian smiled broadly, dazzling eyes beaming into Robyn's. "Precisely." She brushed a light kiss across her lips. "And then there is the matter of Prince John's tax collections, somewhere upward of twenty thousand German marks."

"Whew," Robyn sighed. "That would go a long way toward the King's ransom."

"And you can be sure he has other plans for it, but that's the part I missed. Giffard, Gisborne, the Prince, a couple of bishops and three other barons met in private in the Sheriff's office. Then they kept exchanging knowing looks all day, and if any were conversing when I neared, they would suddenly stop or change the subject. I overheard some guards gossiping about it, but I have no idea if the cache is there now, or if not when it will be coming through Nottingham–if it is even coming through Nottingham. I also couldn't discover what they plan to use the money for. My first guess is bribing other nobles to join their little revolt and try to steal the crown."

"Hmm," Robyn considered. "He would require more than a Sheriff, four barons and two bishops to pull off a coup. He would bloody well need an army."

Marian bit her lip, looking like she wavered on the edge of a decision.

"What is it?" Robyn asked in concern.

"There is something I have wanted to tell you, but was sworn to secrecy. As things stand now, I think it perhaps best that I do; what's more, I have essentially invited you into a secret plot to foil a secret plot anyway."

Robyn gave her a flat look. "Quit babbling; what is it?"

Marian took in a deep breath and let it out. "Queen Eleanor has enlisted me as a spy against the Sheriff and Sir Guy, to find out what I can uncover about their scheming with Prince John."

"What?" Robyn uttered in shocked disbelief.

"That is why I initially said I had to stay in Nottingham and couldn't come to the forest with you."

"Marian, such a thing could be dangerous. If you are discovered-"

"Which I shan't be," Marian stated confidently. "Asides, is anyone truly safe with a power crazed sheriff and conniving prince lording over us?" She touched a hand to Robyn's cheek. "I am being careful; do not fear, my sweetling."

"Do not fear? By rights I fear for you engaging in spying, even when I thought you were only doing it on my behalf. And while this is true, I am at the same time so very proud of you." Robyn tugged her back into her arms and they held each other for a long moment.

"When we do find out where the cache is, I believe the Queen will ask you to steal it for her."

Robyn snickered. "You told her about me, did you?"

"Well, not everything. As far as she knows, you are simply a chivalrous bandit who robs the rich to give to the poor."

"I am indeed," she admitted with a satisfied smile. "And even that is an identity you gave me."

"I only made a suggestion; you created the identity. Do you recognize you are a hero to the people? They speak of Robin Hood in awe. You have given them hope."

"I do what I can, but I think it not enough."

"Robyn." Marian pulled away from her and sat up in bed, her back against the headboard. Robyn followed her lead, sitting up beside her.

"What now? Are there any more secrets for you to reveal tonight?"

"No, you have them all now," Marian vowed. "But there is one you have yet to reveal to me."

Robyn sighed in frustration. "It isn't safe."

"It is unsafe for me *not* to know where to find you. Suppose I need to warn you of something I have learned, some innocents the Sheriff plans to murder, or a new plot or trap he has set? What if I get a message from the Queen and I must to tell you where the silver is being hidden. It's not like I would come strolling into your secret camp merely for a social call."

Robyn glanced at Marian and grimaced. "It's not that I wish to keep you away," she said, then nodded. "But you are right; it is time. If you can get me a quill and parchment, I will draw you a map which you must-"

"Commit to memory and then burn," Marian concluded.

Robyn gave her a nod. "Precisely."

Marian smiled triumphantly and planted a jovial kiss on her lips.

Then Robyn caught her face between her hands and gazing into her eyes with unmasked honesty, said, "I cannot see what the future holds, nor can I guarantee you tomorrow. But what I do promise is that as long as I am alive... as long as there is breath in me or my heart beats in my chest, I will love you with all my soul, and mind, and strength, and I will protect you with everything that is within my power. I also promise that I will not shrink from danger or flee from my cause, for it is just. I shall do my best to fight and win and live for the next time I can hold you in my arms, but I cannot step down from the course that has been laid before me."

Marian's adoring gaze was clouded with concern. She took Robyn's hands in hers, her eyes glistening as she broadened her smile to compensate. "I would expect nothing less from the strong, chivalrous woman whom I love."

It started with a kiss that should have meant good evening and farewell... it ended after another hour of deep, thirsty passion, and a desire to fit a lifetime of love into one night—just in case.

*** * *** 

ROBYN WAS MAKING her way back to camp when dawn began to filter through the forest canopy. She felt like she was dancing on the wind, light as a goose down feather and luckier than a four-leaf clover. She replayed the whole evening in her mind, experiencing the ecstasy all over again. Even so, her well-honed senses were as alert as always when they picked up the sound of approaching horses. Snapping out of her revelry, Robyn climbed a sturdy tree to observe the road that lay a few dozen yards ahead.

A troop of soldiers rode up and halted at the fork in the path. A stout, older man issued orders. "I want a squad to branch out in each direction, both down the road and into the forest. If you detect any sign of the bandits, shoot off your smoke arrow and wait for us to all meet up. Do *not* try to apprehend them on your own. Now, let's make the Sheriff proud, lads!"

They dispersed into groups of four to begin their search.

Robyn smiled wryly. They were nowhere near her camp, and one of those squads was about to ride into a trap, courtesy of the 'ghosts' of Sherwood. *Guess I'll have to take the long way home.* Once they were out of earshot, she slid down from the tree and chose a different path.

About ten minutes later, she heard the shouts of alarm, clanking of metal, and shrieks of the chargers. *That will teach them to invade my forest uninvited!*

Robyn's new route took her past a saw mill but, before it even came into view, she discerned something was amiss. There was a woman's scream, shouting and crying and some loud banging noise. She notched her bow, proceeding as swiftly as she could with stealth. She followed the road but kept to the trees and within moments had the situation in sight. Two dirty, raggedy men were terrorizing the woodcutter and his wife. She frowned in confusion. *These aren't the Sheriff's guards. Mayhap they are ordinary thieves.* She crept in closer, shot at the ready.

The fellow in a wool cap had just finished tying the woodman to a post, a bloody gash on his head where he had been struck. The bearded man was making angry demands of the bony woman. "Look, wench, it's like this: tell us where to find the bandit Hood and no one gets hurt. Got it?"

She cried some more, twisting the hem of her apron between her hands fretfully. "I don't know!"

"But you sees him sometimes, right? Where does he go?"

Then the man in the cap spoke to her husband, who seemed dazed but conscious. "Now I know you doesn't want us to hurt your woman, but we're going to have to if'n you don't speak up."

Next the bearded man lifted a rod as if to strike the traumatized wife. She whimpered and raised her arms in a defensive posture just before her attacker cried out in pain, the rod tumbling to the ground. In stunned disbelief, he grabbed his injured hand, counting his fingers and swearing. An arrow protruded from the discarded wooden bar and he lifted panicked eyes to a tall, lean, hooded figure armed with a bow.

"So you are looking for Robin Hood?" she asked in her most intimidating voice. "You have found him." She pulled back a shaft and aimed it at the man's chest. "I am in the morning mist that rises with the sun; I am in the evening dew that settles over the grass; I am in Nottingham, Edwinstone and Rutherford Abby; I am in every meadow of the shire and behind every tree in the forest."

"Mercy!" he begged, dropping to his knees. "Have mercy, Lord of Sherwood, for surely my lord will not!"

The man in the cap left the woodcutter and raced to his cohort, diving to the dirt beside him, and yanking off his hat in a sign of respect.

Confused, Robyn proceeded with caution. "Who is your master, and why do you seek Robin Hood?"

"We're Gisborne's serfs," the bearded man replied.

Then the other picked up the story. "Now that the harvest is in, he sent us all out, two by two, to track down Rob- you. He wants to impress Prince John by bringing you in afore the Sheriff."

Robyn's mouth twisted as her jaw hardened in disgust.

"Please, milord, do not kill us!"

"I am not your lord," she replied impatiently.

"Would that you were!" declared the chap clutching his hat. "We don't want to hurt no one. Those was only threats. But see here, if we return with nothing, Gisborne will give us the lash, he will."

"Words did not bloody the mill owner's head, now did they?" Robyn watched them, weighing their story.

Then the man burst into tears, burying his face in his hands.

"Woman," Robyn called. She had moved off to untie her husband and place a wet rag to his head.

"Aye?" Frightened eyes turned to Robyn as the woman rose from the bench where the mill owner sat.

"What has happened here?" She briefly glanced at her but kept her eyes trained on the two kneeling assailants.

"They just came demanding we tell them where to find Robin Hood, only we didn't know."

"Gisborne sent you, did he?" Robyn demanded.

"Aye," the men replied in unison.

"Then I shall not send you back empty handed. You," she said pointing to the bearded man. "Pick up that arrow," and he scrambled to obey. "Gisborne knows my fletching. Tell him you found me, and deliver him this warning: if any of you serfs are punished, or any peasants of the shire harmed because he wants to find me–and I will know–then he *shall* find me... in his bed chamber standing over him as he sleeps, pressing a silk pillow into his face until all breath has left his lifeless body. Can you remember those words? I want him to tremble as he tries to sleep, facing his own mortality."

"I,I-" he stammered.

The other man nodded in assurance. "Aye, milord, word for word."

"Good," Robyn concluded as she relaxed and lowered her bow.

As the dirty serf replaced the cap on his head, he said, "I know that you are the people's champion, and one day you will come and free us from the cruel taskmaster what makes us do these things. I right knows you will come, one day."

The hope in the kneeling man's eyes touched a place inside Robyn that she had never imagined she had. "I can't promise that," she replied.

"Ah, I don't need you to take an oath," he said bashfully. "I only know that you will, just like you came for these good people and saved them."

*It was only chance,* she thought remorsefully. Robyn turned her eyes to the couple sitting a few feet away.

"Thank you," the woman bade her. "We understand the Sheriff and Lord Gisborne will hurt whoever they can to get to you, but we are not afraid. Your men brought us food and blankets after the tax collectors took everything. We cannot betray you, because we do not know where you stay, and that is a good thing. Let them do what they wish; this fellow is right. You'll free us from their injustice; maybe not today, but one day."

Robyn bowed her head in sincere humility. "I will do what good I can, for as many as I can, for as long as I can; on that, you have my oath." Then she turned back to Gisborne's serfs. "You will not fault me for standing here while I watch you leave."

"No, milord," replied the bearded man as he scrambled to his feet grasping Hood's arrow in his uninjured hand. "We're away to deliver the arrow and your message. Pray he don't cleave off an ear or a nose." Robyn watched them scamper down the road, a raw gnawing in the pit of her stomach as she envisioned the brutality the serfs had described. Then she checked on the woodcutter and said her goodbyes before continuing back to camp.

# CHAPTER 15

*Sherwood Forest, October 8, 1193*

The afternoon was gray with a blustery wind whooshing leaves along the damp forest floor. More than a week had passed since Michaelmas and autumn was in the air. A trio of fat, red squirrels were busily gathering nuts from beneath an oak, while a vast flock of swallows blanketed the sky gliding southward to places unknown. Even though Robyn was often fascinated by her observations of nature, this day she was enthralled in a different activity.

A crisp sound clapped amid the din of whistles, laughs, and cheers as Robyn sparred with Alan and Arthur armed with pine practice swords under the tutorage of Friar Tuck. "Put your hip into the thrust," bellowed Tuck. "Your arm still has no power."

"Come on, Robin, you handle a sword like a girl!" teased Will.

*If you only knew!* she thought. Tuck had been so pleased with her progress that he was starting her with two opponents at once, as it was a very likely scenario in actual combat. After parrying both of them, Alan to her left and Arthur to her right, she decided brains must triumph where brawn fell short. First she feinted toward Alan, then hit the dirt with a tuck and a roll into Arthur's stance, thrusting a foot into the back of his knee. Totally unprepared, he buckled, and she was up swiftly enough to utilize a two-handed grip to chop his sword clean out of his hand. Her bewildered, ruddy comrade landed with a thud, looking up at her disbelievingly. But Robyn didn't take time to return his gaze, for her focus turned to Alan, whose mouth hung open beneath wide eyes.

"That there is cheatin'!" Arthur declared.

"There is no such thing as cheating in battle, my lad," Tuck said sagely, a proud smile tugging at his thick lips.

Alan, taking advantage of the distraction, leapt forward in a lunge toward Robyn, but she was ready for him. Her parry was followed by a forceful riposte, and she remembered to throw her hip into her thrust.

"Ow!" Alan exclaimed as he stepped back to rub his bruised forearm from where her stick-sword had landed. His frown was of exaggerated insult, but his green eyes continued to sparkle at her playfully.

"Oops," she teased, but remained on guard.

"Now, Robin, I want you to execute that second intention we worked on," Tuck called.

With a nod, she opened her attack with a thrust which Alan focused on blocking, but that was her feint. When he raised his weapon to counter blow, she dropped to one knee beneath his swing, and steadying herself with her left hand on the ground, thrust her blunt wooden sword upward into Alan's abdomen, but not so forcefully as to hurt him.

Tuck applauded. "And that, my students, is what we in the fencing world call a passata sotto. Use it sparingly, for if it is a move your opponent suspects, you will be left at a disadvantage."

"Does this mean I am dead?" Alan asked in jest.

Robyn stood up and patted him down, peering into his face which was level with hers. "Nay; same annoying jester, alive as ever, and likely wanting for a pint about now."

"Amateurs," Will scoffed and flipped his head to throw back his sweep of black hair. "Hey Friar, when will he be ready to take *me* on?"

Friar Tuck angled his face toward Robyn. "What say you?"

"You going to double sword me?" she asked Will.

He grinned. "If you think you are deft enough."

"Aye," she motioned with a matching grin. "Give me your best!"

He picked up the wooden sword Arthur had dropped and Alan handed him the other. "Good luck, pal," he bade him with a pat on the back and stepped aside.

Will rolled his shoulders and spun the sticks to get a feel for them. "Much lighter than steel," he mentioned casually.

"Aye," Tuck agreed with a nod. "I have the lad practice with a true blade against dummies, but we don't want anyone getting hurt. Sparring is meant to be..." The Friar searched for the right word, "merriment."

In a blink, Will's manner transformed from carefree to resolute while more members of the band gathered to watch. Robyn welcomed the challenge, for everyone respected Will's skill. Friar Tuck had trained her well, but she deemed she could also learn something from her youthful friend. Were it ever to become necessary to face the Sheriff, she would need all the practice and training she could acquire.

Will led with his right foot, advancing with a series of beats using his right-hand sword. Robyn studied him prudently, then traded up from parrying his blows into a compound riposte. As she directed her own assault, Will brought his left-hand blade into play, alternating swords in an attempt to keep her off-balance. The intense fencing conversation continued for several minutes with neither gaining an advantage as they tested each other's skills. Robyn was in the midst of formulating a plan to get around Will's aggressive style when young David of Doncaster ran straight into the field of combat, his long dark hair trailing in the breeze.

"Robin, mates, you'll never guess who's comin' this way!" The high pitch of his exclamation almost matched the height of his astonished brows.

The two ceased sparring at once, turning their attention to the lad. "Who?" Tuck asked first, tensing with alarm.

David swallowed and pointed behind him. "Maid Marian! I was on lookout in a tree near the road when I sees her ridin' up, pretty as a spring mornin', but then she took a calculated turn off the path and started on in this direction. She'll be here anon!"

Tuck relaxed while Alan snickered. "I told you Robin was sweet on her."

Then Little John asked, "Robyn, did you tell her where to find us?"

She nodded and handed Tuck her practice sword as she moved in the direction David had pointed. "She must have important news. Stay here, everyone; I'll return soon," and she took off at a jog.

\* \* \*

MARIAN SPOTTED Robyn before coming into view of the camp. She pulled her grey palfrey to a halt and allowed a dirty, sweaty bandit to assist her down from the saddle. Before saying a word, she wrapped her tall, slender warrior in a warm embrace.

Robyn kissed her cheek and spoke in a hush. "What news, my love?"

"A letter from the Queen," she replied, and reluctantly drew back to look up into Robyn's face. "Everything we need to know," she said and withdrew the paper from a pocket in her blue surcoat. She handed the letter to Robyn who read its contents in silence. Marian watched Robyn's expression and recognized the instant it shifted from curiosity to calculation.

"How soon before you must go home?" she asked as she returned the note to Marian's gloved hand.

"Mother believes me to be visiting the abbey to pray for father's swift homecoming; she does not expect me back until tomorrow," she replied as she slipped the folded parchment into her pocket.

"Good!" Robyn said animatedly as she grabbed Marian's hands in hers. "I will need your help to formulate a plan. I suppose you'll be meeting the lads at last. Are you sure?"

"Very sure," Marian responded with a coy smile. "Is your... dwelling private?" She was positive she noted Robyn's pulse jump at the question and suppressed a laugh as the blush rose in her lover's cheeks.

"Little is private in the camp, but no one shares my tent, if that's what you mean. Fear not, my fair lady," she declared with humorous affection. "There is more than enough room for two."

They moved into the kiss in tandem before Marian took Robyn's arm, offering her the reins to lead her mount. With her other hand, she straightened her golden circlet and smoothed back the simple linen veil that covered her braided strands.

"I am not sure how much to tell the others, or how to convince them to join such a dangerous mission," Robyn offered.

"They look up to you, Robyn. They have chosen you as their leader and they will do whatever you ask of them," Marian assured her, pulling closer as they walked.

Robyn sighed and shook her head. "That is what I am afraid of. What if I get them all killed?"

"You won't," Marian stated. "What if you sit idly by and let Prince John steal the throne?"

"You know I shan't do that," she declared, turning her eyes to Marian. "But each man must decide for himself; I'll not insist that anyone come with me. I suppose I will be attending that archery contest after all."

The whole gang was still in the small clearing, buzzing with excitement and speculative in their murmuring, but they waned to a hush as Robyn and Marian returned. Robyn handed off the reins to Much, who was recovering well from his wound.

Charles bounded over to perform an elegant bow before Maid Marian, just as Alan had taught him. Alice hastened to catch up with him, placing her hands on the youth's shoulders to restrain him. She smiled and curtsied. "So good to see you, your ladyship. I pray all is well with you and your family."

"It is, gramercy, Alice." Marian smiled warmly and Robyn stepped aside to let them throng around her with their words of admiration and praise, for Maid Marian's far reaching reputation was as much for her great kindness, as her exceeding beauty. She received them with humility and warmth, touching hands, and patting the heads of little ones. Marian was truly amazed to see the number and variety of outcasts whom Robyn cared for and led. Among them she spotted men, women, and children, Saxon, Norman, and Jew, thief and honest worker, a former nobleman and a defrocked friar. Her heart leapt at their enthusiastic embrace of her, for they were all precious in her eyes, each and every one.

Before Marian had time to become too overwhelmed by their attention, Robyn climbed onto a large stone at the edge of the clearing and called, "Friends, Maid Marian, the incomparable goddaughter of our dear King Richard the Lionheart, has brought us important news this day." They quieted and began to gather around their leader, Robyn's inner core of Alan, Will, Tuck, Gilbert, and Little John at the fore, interest reading on their faces.

She exchanged glances with Marian, who gave her a reassuring nod. Having everyone's attention, Robyn continued. "Maid Marian has received a report from Queen Eleanor about a plot to overthrow our King." Scowls and murmurs stirred through the crowd of loyal Englishmen.

"I'll wager the Holy Cross itself, that Sheriff of Nottingham is involved," Friar Tuck roared, his face reddening.

Robyn's eyes met his and she nodded. "The Sheriff, Sir Guy of Gisborne, and Prince John have conspired with barons and bishops from several counties here in the north against our brave King. Furthermore, the taxes they have been stripping us all bare to collect, the money that is meant to pay King Richard's ransom–they have other plans for that hoard." More head shakes and angry outbursts followed.

"Bloody hell!" Will cried, crossing his arms over his chest. Robyn recalled how hard the tax collection had been on Will's mother and younger brother, and how they had taken food and provisions to their cottage in town.

"One of the Queen's most trusted spies, embedded in Nottingham Castle, overheard their foul betrayal," she continued in a strong, emotion-filled tone. "Prince John wills to use it to hire a mercenary army to seize the throne while good King Richard is still imprisoned in a foreign land."

"That's not right!" Little John's booming voice proclaimed as his bushy brows drew together over intense eyes.

"Indeed, it is the height of treachery," Robyn agreed. "But we now know a great secret - that this cache will be held in Nottingham Castle a month hence, during the Martinmas Fair, before Prince John carries it to the coast to pay his foreign army. Therefore, the question is: what are we to do?"

Robyn paused for a moment to glance around as members of the camp rubbed their heads and chins and muttered to one another. She took a deep breath and pressed on.

"Thus far, we have done much good for the people of our shire," she declared smiling, gesturing to her band of outlaws. "We have fed and clothed the poor with funds the rich could well afford to lose. We have provided safe haven for the oppressed," she said motioning to the refugees among them, "and we have taken care of each other. But now, laid before us, is the chance to do something bigger, a pursuit of great import for all of England. If we were to empty the Prince's coffers and take that money to the Queen where it belongs, we would be foiling their traitorous scheme and securing the remaining finances for our King's release all in one daring raid."

She paused for a moment, her eyes and tone growing more serious, as she spoke to them all straight from her heart.

"It could be that we were born for this, for this very place and moment in time, to accomplish this great thing. Good Friar," she said, turning her gaze to him with an outreached hand. "Is it not like our God to use a handful of misfit outcasts to save a nation?"

Tuck gave a pronounced nod and wiped a tear from his eye. "It is indeed like our God! For, as the scripture says, 'God hath chosen the weak things of the world to confound the things which are mighty.'"

Robyn's eyes lit intensely, but were masked in dread as she concluded. "See here, my friends. I cannot promise that if we do this, we will all get through it alive; I cannot even promise the attempt would succeed. I would not fault a one of you for bowing out, as is your right as free men to do. But who are we if we do not try?" After a labored breath, she perused the gathering and called in a clear, strong voice, "Who is with me?"

"I am!" her friends cried out, some in unison, others following in quick succession. Excitement buzzed as they turned to one another in camaraderie.

A sigh of relief at their support escaped Robyn's lips, and a smile tempered with solemnity crossed her face. "It is settled then; we shall save the kingdom for the Lionheart! Little John, Friar, and all the lads, we'll meet in the morning to prepare our plans, but for now let us show Maid Marian our hospitality."

\* \* \*

GILBERT WHITEHAND, who was a friend of Sir Robert FitzWalter and remembered Marian from her childhood, escorted the honored guest on a tour while Alice Naylor and Beatrice from Loxley prepared food, and Alan strummed lively minstrel tunes on his mandolin. Children ran about playing games and laughter filled the air. But amid it all, Robyn felt the weight of responsibility like a huge boulder on her shoulders.

After a while the meal was served and Marian took a seat beside Robyn, her countenance aglow. "I had no idea," she began in amazement. "I mean, I was aware that you had a camp in the forest and that others lived here with you, but Robyn, what you have done here is extraordinary."

Robyn humbly bowed her head. "I haven't really done anything. It was Little John and Friar Tuck and everyone together. I may have facilitated and organized a wee bit, but-"

She was interrupted by Marian placing an admiring kiss on her cheek. "Extraordinary."

"Thank you," she replied simply.

Just then Christina approached carrying a tin plate laden with pie.

"Your ladyship," she said respectfully. "I know you most likely had blackberry pie at the feast in Nottingham, but me Mum made this, and she makes the best blackberry pie in all the shire." She held out the plate offering it to Marian.

"Thank you," she answered with a delightful smile. "One can never have too much blackberry pie. Not even Prince John, Sir Guy, Sheriff Giffard, nay not even all the nobles of Nottingham have ever graced me with a feast such as this one." She took the pie plate and set it on the log between Robyn and herself. "I know I will enjoy it immensely."

The young maiden's smile lit her eyes and then she ran back to her family.

"Is that the girl from Loxley, the one you told me about?" Marian asked. Robyn nodded. "You have done especially well with her. She seems so… happy. They all do."

"I wager they would be happier in their homes with all of their loved ones gathered 'round," Robyn replied and then took a bite of roasted venison.

"Who shot the stag?" Marian asked between bites.

"I did," she mumbled and Marian elbowed her in the ribs. "But John dressed it out and someone else cooked it–did it right well, too," she added with a wink.

Then Marian spoke in a hush, saying, "You're going to miss this, when the King returns and everyone is pardoned. You will miss the excitement and adventure, even the danger."

Robyn considered all her friends enjoying good food and good company by the firelight. "I will miss them," she responded. "But I knew from the onset this was only a temporary pretense. I would be doing well to keep it up for a year; eventually every boy becomes a man, his smooth face rough with hair." Then she turned her gaze to Marian. "I shall not miss fleas, lice, a damp, leaky tent and I do so wish to grow my hair long again!"

Marian smiled coyly. "Despite her earlier surprise and concerns regarding Robyn cutting her hair, she had grown used to it now. "Whether your hair is long or short, you are still beautiful. But here you are more than special–you are a hero of legends come to life. How can you just go back-?"

"To being plain Robyn of Loxley?" she concluded.

"I don't mean it that way." Marian stopped eating and touched a hand to Robyn's arm.

Robyn's face took on a bitter-sweet quality. "I don't need songs to be sung and stories told about me. I only need you. After King Richard returns, providing I am still alive and breathing, I will simply embark on a new and even more exciting adventure with you."

Marian's eyes began to glisten as she held back tears of elation. She swallowed and blinked. "Then I shall endeavor to live up to your expectations."

\* \* \*

LATER THAT NIGHT, after the dessert, dancing, and each one attempting to surpass the other when it came to entertaining Maid Marian, she and Robyn were finally able to steal away to Robyn's tent leaving the young lads to mind the waning embers of the fire. Once the tent flap closed, the two drew together in a tight embrace. Marian initiated a kiss that was long, deep, and searing, longing to give into the ache that only Robyn could ease.

Slowly, Robyn pulled back, taking Marian's face between her palms and affectionately brushing her lips. "Now, I need parchment and a quill," she said, her mind overflowing with ideas as she searched about by candlelight. Marian expected this. A plan for securing the silver must be devised before anything else, even if it took all night. She cast her gaze about and saw no actual furniture. There were a few crates, some filled with contents and others overturned to act as short tables, and there was a straw heap with some blankets thrown over it to one end. She scrunched up her mouth. There was much to be said for adventure... but there was also much to be said for comfort. *Oh well,* she thought. *What did you expect?*

"Ah, hah!" Robyn announced in triumph. "Now, we must jot down ideas, then line them up in order, sketch out a map of the castle, and then rethink, add, plan for every contingency." Armed with quill, paper, and a piece of wood to place them on, Robyn plopped down onto what passed for her bed. Then she looked up at Marian who stared down at her speculatively.

"Fleas you say? Lice?"

"Not very many," Robyn replied with nonchalant candor. Then, as if suddenly remembering something, she leapt to her feet. "I'm sorry! Let me help you down here."

Marian took her hand, shook her head, and laughed at the absurdity of it all. "Now I know why we conduct our visits at my house." Robyn raised her brows and shot her a sheepish grin. "It is well, my Heart; I would forgo every comfort for an evening with you spent plotting the demise of that traitorous John Lackland and his cohorts."

She nestled up beside Robyn and they set to work.

* * *

Hours passed in a flash and the camp was fast asleep by the time the preliminary strategy was completed. "I am not altogether certain about your part in the scheme," Robyn said with a frown. "There is clear danger involved. What if-"

"Danger involving *my* part?" Marian questioned incredulously. "Scarcely a speck, whereas your role holds nothing but danger!"

"I know what I'm doing," Robyn replied.

"As do I, by God's teeth! I am taking that money to Queen Eleanor. Why, if a haircut and a tunic can pass you off as a boy, then black robes and a proper habit will of certs disguise me as a nun."

Robyn weighed Marian's comment. "You will have Tuck with you, and he is the finest swordsman I've ever encountered, though he insists Giffard could best him."

"And that is what has me worried the most," Marian confessed as she paused a moment to caress Robyn's cheek.

"Taking him on is not part of the plan," Robyn reiterated. "If it comes to that, I'll handle it."

"I know," Marian said softly. Robyn relaxed and lay back on the pillows, Marian following her. "It is an excellent strategy, and it just may work."

"It *will* work," Robyn corrected with confidence. She stroked Marian's long silky strands, reveling in the sensation. *I could drown in those lipid pools of blue, so easily be lost in pleasure.* How she wanted it! But responsibility roared at her like a powerful beast, and she returned her attention to the issue at hand. "Now then, let us go over it all again to see what possibilities we may have overlooked." She felt Marian deflate as a ruptured wine skin. "I am sorry, Sweetling, but as much as I love the lads, there is no brain in this camp as keen as yours."

"I am not certain of that," Marian replied modestly, "but I agree this is of the utmost import. I am indeed grateful that you wish to include me in your plans."

Robyn looked at her in surprise. "Assuredly I would include you! I value your input, or I would not have asked for it. Do not grow impatient, Sweetling; before the night is spent, I will take you on another flight to the stars." She smiled at the flush that rose in Marian's face and met it with a kiss. "And now, back to the plan from the beginning…"

## CHAPTER 16

*Sherwood Forest, the next day*

Wrapped in her cloak against the damp chill, Robyn sat crossed legged on the moist earth amid soggy brown leaves and tiny crawling insects. She was meticulously creating a replica of Nottingham Castle from rocks and sticks, even placing acorns to represent guards. Earlier that morning she had spoken with Friar Tuck, explaining what she wanted him to construct.

"Give me a few hours," he had speculated, "and I believe I can have one ready to test out at the meeting." Then she had reluctantly seen Marian on her way, vowing to visit her on All Hallows Eve.

With the day well underway, the outlaw crew began to gather around Robyn, eying her model with curiosity.

"Hey, I know what that there is," Alan proclaimed sporting a look of recognition. "It's the castle at Nottingham. I've been there before, but I don't recall that part, or that over there," he said pointing.

Will plopped down beside them and tugged his cloak tight around his shoulders. "How do you know what all is inside there?" he asked.

Robyn glanced to Little John who ambled over with Gilbert. The two older men chose a fallen log to sit on. Returning her gaze to Will, she replied, "Marian's spent a lot of time in the castle and was able to provide me with details." *Of course I've spent plenty of time there as well over the years, but they don't need to know that.* "Here is the main gate, and that is the side gate," she indicated. "The armory, stables, kitchens. This is the great hall and the Sheriff's office. Upstairs here are the living quarters and this building houses the guest lodgings. Soldiers' barracks are back here. There are always guards at these stations," she explained while touching spots on her representation. "But there will be so many strangers coming and going because of the fair, anyone who acts as though they belong should not be questioned."

"That rock with the cross in front," Much pointed out as David helped him to a seat in the growing circle. "Is that a church?"

"There's a chapel in the castle," Robyn explained as she added a few finishing touches.

Arthur chuckled. "I wouldn't suppose the Sheriff spends much time in there, then."

Robyn looked up, satisfied with her reproduction, and passed her gaze around the gathering. She smiled as she heard the booming laugh of Friar Tuck as he left the camp center, clomping through the undergrowth to their meeting spot. Alan glanced over his shoulder to see Tuck toting a wooden keg. "God bless you, Friar! You knew exactly what would spark up this crew of ne'er do wells!"

Tuck shook his head, an amused twinkle in his eyes as he slung the barrel down and sat on it. "Why Alan, 'tis not even midday! Let us save a bit of mead for after supper." With a wide grin, he winked at Robyn and she nodded to him in return.

"Now, on with the plan. From November 11th to 19th, Nottingham will be hosting the annual Martinmas Fair, which culminates with the Sheriff's archery contest on the tournament field over here." She motioned to a spot northwest of the castle.

Little John frowned, scratching his beard. "I would be suspicious; he knows how good you are. It could be a trap."

"Certs it is a trap," Robyn agreed, "which is why I shall be competing in it."

"Huh?" Will offered her a puzzled expression.

"Marian overheard all the plans to catch Robin Hood at the contest, so I am well prepared. This works to our advantage though. Giffard will have most of the soldiers close to the tournament field, ready to surround me as soon as I fire the winning shot. That means there will be only a few left at the castle to guard the tax money."

"Ah," sighed Much. "And they don't think anyone knows about the hoard of silver bein' there."

"Precisely," Robyn agreed. "The Queen's spy said that the Sheriff plans to hide it in a secret vault in the dais, beneath the pulpit. Supposedly no one knows it is there." She looked over to Gilbert who was scrutinizing her image of the layout. "Whitehand, you have been inside that chapel, have you not?"

"Aye, numerous times," he replied. "But I have never been on the platform itself."

"Still, you are a learned man, and perhaps have come across switches that uncover hidden passages and such."

He nodded. "One castle I served in early in my career had a secret room where extra weapons were stored and the women could be hidden in case of attack. There was a torch holder that when pulled would slide open a panel in the wall."

"Good," she said with encouragement. "The lever will be somewhere that it is not noticed, mayhap appearing to be a mundane thing, or concealed out of sight, but it should be near the lectern. You will go in the guise of a priest and take young David with you to be your acolyte. Many clergymen from all around will be coming and going, so no one ought question you. It will be your task to discover the trigger and open that hide-away."

He nodded. "I will find it."

"I have confidence in you," Robyn assured him. "Now, Little John, you need to lead the others in securing the tax money once Gilbert has found it. Remember the castle guard uniforms, the mail and helmets and such we took from that patrol a while back?"

"Aye," he replied as inspiration passed from her eyes to his. "We'll be dressed as guards so no one will think twice about us!"

"That's right." She indicated an entry in the castle's perimeter. "This is where you enter. It is the gate facing in the direction of the tournament field. If anyone asks, just say the Sheriff sent you down to reinforce the castle."

Little John nodded, but David asked, "Why do I have to be Whitehand's aide or some such instead of one of the guards?"

Robyn had thought David much too young to pass as a soldier and had wanted to keep him safe, but she replied earnestly, "Gilbert must focus on finding the hidden lever and revealing the vault; he needs someone capable, with sharp eyes to watch his back and to come to his assist if discovered. You'll look very unassuming in clergy robes; no one would suspect what a good fighter you truly are."

Satisfied, he nodded. "I will watch out for him; you can count on me."

She smiled. "I knew I could. Now, once Gilbert has found it, he will send you out to get the others. Everyone will fill sacks with coins and treasure then hide them inside the mail shirts. You cannot shove too much in at once, or people may wonder why so many fat guards, so it could take you several trips in and out. You'll need to be as casual and inconspicuous as possible as you walk with your hidden stashes over near the front gate here," she pointed, "where Friar Tuck shall be waiting with a mead wagon. Friar, I presume your seat is a sample barrel?"

"Aye," he answered with a grin and pushed himself up with hands on his thighs. Then he showed them all the vessel. "I believe this is what you asked for—an ordinary looking mead barrel." He twisted open the tap and honey liquid began to flow.

"Hey! Don't waste that!" Alan shouted, his eyes widening.

Tuck laughed as he closed the knob tight. "Don't worry, my man, there isn't much in there—just enough to convince anyone that mead is all it holds. But look here." A pudgy finger pushed an almost invisible latch in between two of the oak planks and the cask opened in half. "The top swings up and inside there's a box in which to hide the silver. Once filled, it should be about the same weight as a barrel full of drink. These will be mixed in with full mead barrels on the cart. And one thing always needed at a festival is more spirits, am I right?"

"Well, I'll be!" Will's blue eyes shone with amazement. "That is genius!"

"Let us hope so," Robyn said. "When all the cache has been moved into the wagon, Tuck will ride off to Windsor. Maid Marian plans to accompany him disguised as a nun as she insists on taking the ransom to Queen Eleanor personally. There are any number of things that can go wrong. Allow me lead you through some of those possibilities and how to respond."

Tuck resituated himself atop his special barrel while the others watched and listened intently. Their confidence grew as Robyn spelled out what action to pursue if inquiries as to their presence arose, or if Gilbert was interrupted, or if guards were already posted in the chapel. In that last case, she instructed them to create a disturbance requiring them to rush out, such as a fight or fire.

"What about you?" Little John eventually asked. "What will you be doing?"

"Trying to keep the Sheriff and Prince John's attention on the archery tournament. I shall wear a false guise or they would recognize me right away. I shall stay in the competition long enough to make it interesting, but I'll miss before the final round. They will be confounded when it is Deputy Blanchard, a baron, or one of their knights who makes the winning shot. They are likely to detain everybody and interrogate us individually. However, if all has gone well at the castle and I get the signal that you have the stash, I'll simply disappear. If it is taking you longer, then I'll find a tactic to keep their attention focused on the contestants. I shall meet you all back here at the camp once I know Friar Tuck and Marian are safely on their way. Now, I am open to suggestions for improvements to the proposal, or any questions you may have."

They continued to discuss the plan and all the "what ifs" until time for the noon meal when Alice approached as a woman possessing great authority. "Men, I understand your meeting here is life and death for England, but soup and bread are hot. Whatever else you have to do will need wait until everyone has had their fill. I can feel a chill in the air, and 'tis a cold night on the way. Up, up, come on with you now," she instructed. No one dared disobey.

* * *

NOTTINGHAM CASTLE, *later the same day*

GODFREY GIFFARD SPORTED a cheerful disposition that evening as he laved and then changed clothes for dinner. While Prince John had gone to see about the secure transport of his fortune, the barons loyal to him remained in residence at Nottingham. Godfrey had been dividing his time between the castle and his new manor at Loxley, but with guests to entertain, he was now residing solely at the castle. They had enjoyed an invigorating day of hawking and he had scored the most kills.

The Sheriff chose a bright, sun-gold tunic and pulled it on over clean black leggings. He smiled as he thought about his prize falcon, Ra, named after the Egyptian god of the sky. He contemplated its blue-black head and beak, yellow accents, its keen eyes and strong talons, majestic wings and commanding scream. It was powerful, graceful, and lethal–a lot like himself. He mused that it was second in the sky only to the eagle, and that Prince John was like the eagle, and he the falcon. He smiled while fastening the toggles of his sleeveless burgundy doublet over the tunic as thoughts of taking his rightful place at the right hand of the new king flowed fluidly through his imagination.

Godfrey then turned to the large looking glass to groom his onyx locks. Choosing an ivory comb, he dipped it into a jar containing a mixture of aloe vera and wine, guaranteed to encourage a thick growth of hair and prevent its loss, and ran it through his mane, placing each strand precisely where he wished it to lie. It had been a good day, and now he would continue to impress his guests with the entertainment he had hired for the evening.

An unexpected knock at his chamber door caused his face to scrunch into a frown, and Godfrey turned his gaze from the mirror. "Who's there?" he bellowed in sudden irritation.

"Milord, it is I, Deputy Blanchard," the deep voice replied. "My apologies for the interruption, but a soldier has delivered word to me that I believe you will wish to hear."

Two lengthy strides brought Godfrey to the door which he cracked and scowled out. "Can it not wait until the morrow?"

"It could, milord, but it will please you, so I thought–"

"Very well, man, out with it!" he huffed as he stepped into the corridor and closed the chamber door behind him.

Blanchard produced a disheveled young fellow in a guard's uniform. His uncertain eyes darted to the Sheriff, the floor, the walls, and back nervously as he shifted his weight from one foot to the other. "Simon, tell the Sheriff what you told me."

Simon took a deep breath and began. "Pardon me for disturbing you, milord, but I had to tell somebody."

Giffard shot him an annoyed glare. "Tell somebody what?"

"Um, I recognized one of the outlaws in Robin Hood's gang; I mean, I know him, or knew him," he stammered. "Anyway, I am positive of his identity, and I thought, well, the Sheriff ought to know. Mayhap knowing who one of his friends is will help to capture the head brigand who's been causing all the trouble."

Godfrey's face lit with triumph, all hint of irritation vanished, as he stepped closer and draped a friendly arm around the lowly guard's shoulders. "Tell me, Simon; tell me all about him."

* * *

Nottingham three nights later

Deep in the bowels of Ye Olde Trip to Jerusalem, a popular tavern nestled at the base of Castle Rock, the Sheriff and his man-at-arms met with a figure shrouded in a dark cloak. They had secured one of the most private drinking rooms which was little more than a dim, windowless cave, designed for privacy. A guard posted at the entry ensured they would not be disturbed.

Godfrey raised his chin, eying the specimen before him with a bearing of superiority. "I am pleased that you received word so quickly and were of the disposition to meet with me."

The outlaw who sat across from him shook with fearful fury. "You have me mum, you bloody bastard! She hasn't done anything wrong. If you lay one hand on her, I swear-"

"Yes, yes, you'll do all sorts of terrible things to me," he interrupted without the slightest hint of concern. "But the fact remains, if you truly wish her to be released unharmed, you will tell me what I want to know. As of this moment, she is the guest of my dungeon; her status could change at any time. The charges against her are quite severe, I am afraid, and while no one enjoys the execution of a woman-"

"You can't!" he lashed out, shoving up from his chair. "She is innocent!"

Emory, Giffard's man-at-arms, placed a forceful hand on the man's shoulder and pressed his trembling form back down into his seat.

"Innocent?" Godfrey questioned in an amused tone. "She raised an outlaw for a son. Now, how innocent can she be?"

"Leave her out of this, you-"

The middle-aged Emory gave the man's shoulder a squeeze and he bit back the insult that was sure to follow.

"Prithee, Sheriff, do what you will to me, but let my mother go. She is a good Christian who is without vice or guile. Surely a man of the law would not falsely imprison or do harm to a blameless woman?"

"That all depends on you," Godfrey stated, his ebony eyes turning to ice. "Where is Robin Hood's camp?" Godfrey could feel the anguish ooze from the quivering lump of humanity across from him. He looked severely into those sunken, hollow eyes and smiled. "Where will I find him and the other outlaws?"

"I, I," he stammered. The man placed his palms on the table, apparently in a vain attempt to steady himself. After inhaling and releasing a long breath, he was able to put the words together. "I can't tell you that."

The Sheriff looked up at his underling and started to rise. "Evidently the churl cares nothing for the woman that bore him. We'll just have to make an example of her."

"No!" the man cried as he reached for Giffard's hand. "You don't understand!" Godfrey lowered his icy stare to the bony fingers gripping his wrist and the pitiful outlaw released him in a contrite manner. "I can't tell you," he continued, "because the location changes."

Intrigued, the Sheriff reclaimed his seat.

"Hood moves the camp at varying times with no advance notice. We may be in the same place a week or a day, and then he says, 'strike camp, we are going here, or there,' and we leave no trace behind. He's clever, Robin is. He'll have us bury the fire pit, rake the ground, scatter leaves." The captive emitted a nervous chuckle. "Why, by the time I return today, they could've up and left."

Godfrey rubbed his beard in contemplation. "That fits with the whole 'ghosts of Sherwood' charade and the traps, as well as why we have been unsuccessful at finding them."

Emory nodded in agreement. "Along with robberies occurring on roads through all areas of the forest."

"Then tell me, where would I find Hood on a given day? Certainly there is some forward plan of what hamlet he will visit, or what robbery he has plotted."

"We aren't told every detail," he said in a disappointed tenor. "Sometimes he just says, 'come on lads, we are off to here or there.' Honestly, I am not that important in the scheme of it."

The Sheriff sat back in his chair and crossed his arms over his chest. "It seems you are of little use. Perhaps we will schedule a double execution."

"No, milord, please!" he begged mournfully. "There are things I can tell you, useful things, things that are worth my mother's freedom!"

"Such as?" he inquired with a tilt of his head.

"The archery contest; Hood knows it is a trap."

"Ah," Godfrey huffed out as he uncrossed his arms and sat forward. "I suppose a fox like Hood would have figured that out. It is of no consequence, however. I will find another way to snare him. I wonder," he mused. "Would he show up to save you from the ax and your mum from the noose?"

"But Lord Sheriff, I am being forthright with you!"

"Mayhap, but what you have to offer… simply is not enough. Emory, bring him. I think it is time our guest reunited with his long lost mother in the gaol."

* * *

AMID PLEAS and dragging of feet, the guard and man-at-arms managed to transport the protesting outlaw through dark streets, up the hill, and into the castle. The procession then traveled down creaky wooden steps into the dismal dungeon below the stone keep. The first thing to hit the thief was the rank odor of suffering: unwashed bodies, oozing sores, urine, waste, and decay. Straw strewn about the dirt floor had likely not been replaced in weeks. Smoke drifted through the fetid air as torches on wall sconces and a smoldering fire provided the only light. He could hear murmurings and moans from prisoners as they rounded a bend and a circle of iron barred cells came into view. Frantically, his eyes searched the room until he heard a woman's gasp. "Mother?" he called in desperation as a mangy black rat scurried into a corner.

A slender woman with a long braid of ebony hair brushed by a few silver highlights rushed to her cage door, gripping the bars as she looked out. "Son!" wailed a distraught voice that cracked at the sight of him. "You should not have come; you should have stayed safe!" Dark circles hung below pleading eyes marring her otherwise attractive face.

"I had to, I must try…"

"I will give you one last chance," the Sheriff interrupted, "before forcing you to watch your mother tortured. Tell me something useful, or I am done with you!"

The woman straightened, lifting her head high. "Do not speak a word, you hear me? Not a word."

Giffard turned to the dungeon keeper, a thick-bodied, middle-aged, bare-armed man with a close-cut fuzz of hair. "Have you a hot iron?"

"Aye," he nodded, and pulled a poker from the fire.

"Wait!" the woman's son shouted and began to cry.

"Yes?"

Will Scarlet knew he had tried to mislead, tried to protect his friends, but this was his mother. What was he to do? He couldn't stand by and let her be brutalized. In some part of his soul he feared their fates were sealed regardless, but maybe–just maybe–if he gave the Sheriff something he wanted, not the whole truth, not every detail, but enough to convince him... he lowered his head and resolutely said, "He knows about the twenty thousand marks."

In an instant the Sheriff's demeanor changed. He snapped to attention. "Gaoler, give the woman a drink of water. Outlaw, you come with me." Giffard dismissed Emory and the guard, closing and latching the door behind them. "Now, we don't want outside ears hearing what you have to say, but it had better be worth my time."

Still shaking, he said in a low voice, "Hood knows about the Prince's tax money. He knows about the plot to take the throne before Richard's ransom is paid, and he knows it will be here, in the castle, during the Martinmas Fair."

Will watched the Sheriff's eyes go wide and his mouth drop in astonishment. "That is impossible! No one knows; only the Prince's closest supporters."

The cloaked man shrugged. "Mayhap a servant or a guard overheard your plans. I cannot say. Hood received a message. I know not from whom. The note told about the cache and the plot and he says to us, 'Let's save the King,' and everyone hollers, 'Save the King!'"

Still appearing shocked and shaken, the Sheriff turned his gaze to his prisoner. "So I have a spy. Whoever it is, he or she will be discovered and punished ever so severely. But now, I must know, what are Hood's plans? How does he determine to save Richard?"

"Well, milord," he began feeling more confident with such a huge bargaining tool at his disposal. "He hasn't finished hashing out the details, you see. Hood and his closest mates are trying to sort something out. So far they are aiming to think of a way to steal the money, but they haven't worked it through yet." He studied the Sheriff's intent, brooding face, and then offered, "If you could give your word to let me mum go free, unharmed, I could discover the plan and then tell you. That would be worth it, wouldn't it?"

"Indeed, that would be valuable," Giffard agreed. "You must ascertain every aspect, the day and time they intend to strike, how they think to gain the silver, then–and only then–will the wench which brought you into this world be spared. If anything differs a hair from what you tell me, she dies."

"But you need to promise, on your oath before God, that if I bring you the full plan, and everything goes as I report, that you will let her go," Will declared in earnest supplication.

A twisted smile tugged at the corner of the Sheriff's mouth. "Am I not a nobleman? Cannot my word be trusted? I pledge this, thief–if your word is true, then mine shall be as well. If your information leads to the capture or death of that accursed Robin Hood, you and your mother will be safe. Now, bring me particulars of this scheme quickly, lest I begin to believe you have played false with me and your blessed mother to save your own skin."

"I'll return in a week with all that I can learn, and if the strategy is not complete or if it changes, I'll come again to tell you more after that." He thought he could buy time that way. If he could string the Sheriff along, feeding him just enough truth to be convincing, but not enough to endanger his friends… it was so thin a line as to be non-existent.

Will cursed himself. He wished to die, but he had to save his mum. What would any man do in his stead? He would never betray Maid Marian, never tell of her involvement! He could never give up the location of their camp, exposing them all; thankfully, Nottingham believed the story about that. But what could he do? Should he tell Robin? Could the gang rescue his mother, or would an attempt merely get her killed? His heart was rent, his soul twisted, and he was released to deceive the very mates whom he loved. He could see no other course.

# CHAPTER 17

*Worcestershire, October 16, 1193*

Queen Eleanor was seated on a velvet cushion in her carriage across from her escort and student, John Marshall, Sir William's nephew. They had spent the last several weeks traveling from castle to manorial estate throughout southern England to call upon the noble families to do their part in volunteering hostages for security against the king's ransom. They were greeted with hospitality and respect at each household as they compiled a list of names. Eleanor found the task physically and emotionally draining, but to see the optimism in her expression and hear the power in her voice, one would never know.

Eleanor had been instructing Squire John in lessons on chivalry and courtly love when feeling a difference in the surface of the road, she looked through the carriage window to spy a quaint village of half-timbered cottages with creeper-clad walls and thatched roofs. There were picturesque gardens, what had not been taken by the frost, and St. Mary's church with its distinctive herringbone pattern stonework. They took a turn south and proceeded up Bredon Hill where Elmley Castle lay in a sea of meadows. Originally an earthworks and wooden castle, like scores of others throughout England, its stone enhancements had been added during Henry's reign.

"I have heard my father speak well of the Beauchamps," John stated. "Certs they will not disregard their honorable duty."

Eleanor turned to him with her most charming smile. "Let us do our best to convince them."

* * *

BARON WILLIAM DE BEAUCHAMP, along with his wife and two legitimate sons were seated at the lord's table on cushioned chairs with plates of food and cups of wine placed in front of them. Several knights sat at a table taking their noonday meal while a domestic swept old straw into neat piles which he would remove before scattering the fresh.

But Eleanor's keen eyes were drawn to a stalwart young man who rested alone by the hearth drinking from a tankard. His dress was finer than the underlings yet not so rich as the baron's sons. Curls of flame sprang from his head with a matching wisp of a mustache clothing his upper lip. His attention was on her, aware hers was on him, but he did not stir or speak.

"Milord, your hospitality is exceptional and most appreciated," Eleanor said after a short while of small talk. "But I am sure you know by now the purpose of my visit today."

"Indeed, we are aware of the situation," the elderly Beauchamp acknowledged. "My family is most loyal to England and the crown, as evidenced by the Welsh barons and rouge highwaymen I have turned away in my time as baron.

"We are most grateful for your faithful service," she replied. "But in this critical hour it is not your military that I require, but rather a volunteer from the noble house of Beauchamp to travel to Germany on behalf of his King."

Walter, who had been silent during the meal snapped his eyes to his father with resolve. "I have only recently taken a wife, and must stay with her until a healthy son is born. I am heir to the title and estate and cannot risk my life on some knight's errand with no successor of my own. It would be foolhardy and irresponsible."

William turned his gaze away from Walter hopefully toward Geoffrey.

"Don't look at me!" the young man exclaimed. "I've not yet completed my tutelage. Furthermore, I am to compete in the spring tournaments. How am I ever to become a knight of renown if I miss my first two years of competitions? All of my peers will be ahead of me and I will never catch up. You promised I would not be required to go, Father. Now, make Walter do his duty."

"You cannot speak to Father that way!" Walter declared in a raised voice. "You are the youngest, the one with no title, no wife, no responsibility."

"I have too got responsibility, Walt. And I grow weary of your ordering me about!"

"Boys, enough!" The baron eyed them each with icy darts cold enough to snuff out their heated debate. "My apologies, Your Highness," he said in a softer tone, raising his palms as if in surrender. "This has been the argument in my household for the past fortnight. But do not be troubled or think less of us. The Beauchamp family shall fulfill our obligations to king and country." Eying his sons, he continued sternly. "You two boys forget that I am still lord of this castle and father over you, and as long as you wish to gain money or land or live under my roof and protection, you will do as I decide–not as you bloody well please. Is that understood?"

His sons scowled, Walter crossing his arms and Geoffrey kicking the table leg. They both drooped their heads while tension hung in the room.

It was then that Eleanor once again became aware of the quiet red haired fellow by the fire. He abruptly stood with the bearing of an aristocrat and the physique of a warrior. "I'll go."

All attention spun to the young man as he casually sauntered across the hall toward them. "It would appear that Lord Beauchamp's legitimate sons have far more important things to do than rescue their King from his captivity, while I, on the contrary, have nothing to lose and everything to gain by the venture."

Eleanor liked him straightaway.

"Uh," the baron stammered and wiped his face with a wrinkled hand. "My apologies for not introducing my other son, Aylwin. His mother…"

"I'm the embarrassing bastard of the family," Aylwin acknowledged good-naturedly. "My mother died when I was twelve and when Father discovered I was being shuffled off to a monastery, he feared his unfortunate secret would get out." In courtly fashion, he bowed before Eleanor. "Your Highness, I am your humble servant."

"Aylwin, that is not why I brought you here," Beauchamp stated in an embarrassed hush. "Is that truly what you thought all these years?"

A bit of the smugness faded from the young man's ruddy face. "Why else? You never acknowledged me before that day and still have not given me your name."

The baron swallowed, old pain returning to his haggard aspect. "Your mother," he began, then glanced to his wife who stood in the background with her arms wrapped around herself. "I spoke with her about bringing you to live in the castle to be raised with your brothers, numerous times, but she would not hear of it. You were all she had, and somehow she needed you more. She would say, 'Will, you have two other sons while Aylwin is my world.' I felt it would have been cruel to take you from her. But when I learned she had passed... I was not so worried about my pride or reputation as you imagine. Many barons, even earls, counts, and kings father children outside their marriage; it is a common occurrence though not one of which to boast. I may have caused problems for myself through mistakes along the way, but you son—you are no mistake, nor do I think of you as such."

Aylwin lowered his head, blazing tresses falling across his eyebrows. "Then why did you never acknowledge me outside this household? Why have you not given me your name?"

"You are not stealing my inheritance!" Walter shouted as he leapt to his feet. "Aylwin, you may be first born, but you are nothing but a Scot's bastard. You will never be baron of this estate!"

"Walter!" A sharp and sudden sound came from Jeanne's lips. She stepped to her fair son and pleaded, "Please sit; let your father handle this." He huffed and scowled, but sat at his mother's request.

Aylwin straightened and shot Walter a disdainful glare. "I've no ambition of taking your title or birthright and if you ever paid any attention to me, you would know that." Then he dropped to one knee beside the Queen's chair so that his head was lower than hers. "Your Highness, I am a blood member of the noble Beauchamp clan and, if my father will testify to that in writing, I can uphold my family's honor as well as perform my duty to my King by traveling with you across the sea, a pledge against the ransom to release your son. My brother is correct in saying this castle will never be mine; let me prove myself to you, even as long ago another noble's son with no inheritance of his own did." He and John exchanged a look, for he was referring to Sir William Marshall.

Eleanor turned her face to Beauchamp, eyes lit with expectancy. "What say you, sir? Shall this young man represent your family to the King?"

"Yes, send him," young Geoffrey concurred. "He is always wanting to be part of this family, so let him fulfill this duty and prove that he is worthy of your name."

Beauchamp's tension eased, and a smile crept into his eyes. "Aylwin Duffy de Beauchamp," he stated, "is the, until now undeclared, seed of my loins. However, today I am proud to call him son, and honored that he has volunteered himself to take the place of our beloved King Richard." Then he looked from Eleanor to Aylwin and placed a hand on his shoulder. "Under the law, Walter is first born, the son of my lawful wife. But it was never my intent to cause you to feel any less my son."

Aylwin's eyes glistened as he rose and clasped forearms with his father. "Thank you," he said simply. "I will make you proud."

To the side, two youthful blond men frowned with narrowed brows in obvious jealousy, but Queen Eleanor's countenance bore a knowing and grateful smile.

*　*　*

NOTTINGHAM CASTLE, *October 20, 1193*

SHERIFF GODFREY GIFFARD was silent and brooding as he sat at table in his great hall. Although he had not spoken a word to them, he eyed the barons seated nearby with suspicion. He spied for signs in their demeanor, the quirk of their smiles, the tone of their voices, but could not be certain who among his peers was the Queen Mother's informant.

The pompous, corpulent Bishop Albrec of Kirkstall stuffed his face with pheasant and pudding. *He is doubtless guilty of gluttony,* Giffard thought as he studied the clergyman. *And I have heard rumors of his affinity for young boys–a good thing I have none.* He took a solemn bite from his hand-sized loaf of white bread. *But when he arrived after being attacked by the bandits, he seemed honestly afraid and offended. Unless he is a most excellent actor...*

Laughter roared from the other end of the table, rousing the Sheriff from his thoughts. "Hugh, tell us another!" implored Lambelin, Baron of Somerset as the nobles exchanged jokes.

"Indeed, I'd wager Lord le Clerc has tucked away in his mind the cleverest of jokes," Hugh suggested in anticipation. He gulped heartily from his goblet and then urged him on, saying, "Or is Cornwall void of levity?"

"Very well," the silver-haired Raoul consented. "As it would so happen, I knew an old Bishop who had lost some of his teeth, and complained of others being so loose that he was afraid they would soon fall out. 'Never fear,' said one of his friends, 'they won't fall.' 'And why not?' inquired the Bishop. His friend replied, 'Because my testicles have been hanging loose for the last forty years, as if they were going to fall off, and yet, there they are still.'"

The Sheriff shook his head and tried not to laugh, but the thought of the old man's family jewels hanging low and shriveled compelled a reluctant smirk. Then he eyed the Baron of Cornwall considering him while the others guffawed and downed more wine. *Of the lot, I'd wager him to be the most intelligent and with the least grievance against Richard. Could he be the one?*

As the Sheriff sat scratching his chin, Sir Guy spoke to him with concern. "Are you well, Godfrey? You seem melancholy this eve."

"'Tis nothing, Guy; my stomach is but a bit unsettled; that is all." He forced a friendly expression as he raised his eyes to Gisborne. *You are the only one I am certain of, my old friend,* he thought. He was about to excuse himself to retire when the evening's entertainment arrived.

"My Lord Sheriff," a long pole of a man in colorful silks and floppy hat addressed him while three other men and four women in similar costume filed in behind him. The men all held instruments while the women in neck-plunging gowns and fog-thin veils had empty hands and bare feet. "We are pleased to perform song and dance for you this evening," he said with an elaborate bow. Then he clapped his hands and each member of the ensemble took their place. They opened with a jig, the men playing the lute, viol, recorder, and tambourine in three-four time, as the women proceeded to skip, leap, and spin about the open floor.

Godfrey's mind was transported far from thoughts of espionage as his passions were stirred by the movement and melody, carried away by the sumptuous bodies of women writhing energetically before them. He would have any of them tonight– that was certain. But which one? The slender raven haired beauty, or the curvy golden-tressed delight? No, perhaps the brunette whose leaps and pirouettes caused his heart and groin to pound in tempo to the music… or the petite girl with ginger curls. He could see the sparkle in their eyes and the veils hid little of their exquisite faces. *Maybe 'twas but a servant or guard who alerted the Queen,* he thought. *I can always start torturing confessions out of them tomorrow.*

# CHAPTER 18

*Sherwood Forest, All-Saints Day 1193*

Robyn jogged along through the woodland at a moderate clip early that morning, having vowed to be back to camp in time for Friar Tuck's celebratory mass for the special Holy Day. There were a passel of holy days, it seemed, filling practically the entire calendar, one for this saint and that saint, and now all the saints who didn't have their own individual festival.

But then again, peasants and serfs worked six days a week and often went without food. Winter brought rain and mud and bone-chilling cold, and between sickness and wars, life was precariously uncertain. She supposed it was fitting for the Church to create occasions for feasting and celebrating; it was a welcome reprieve from what for many was an otherwise dull existence. But not for Robyn. Her soul was filled with love and purpose, and after a night with Marian she felt as though she floated on air. Elation flowed through her like a crystal clear river and she was very much glad to be alive. She finally understood the Song of Solomon. Yes, the priests taught it was an allegory of God's love for us and ours for him, but the profusion of flowery 'lips like honey', 'ravishing of my heart', and 'longing to be together' took on a new, tangible meaning since she had experienced the power of those emotions.

Dawn was just filtering in through the cloudy gloom and skeletal limbs of naked hardwoods. *It always takes longer to get light in the mornings counting down to the winter solstice,* she thought, *and gets dark so early. Too much dark, and too hard to keep time.* But she wouldn't be late.

As Robyn neared the camp, she came upon Alan skipping his way in from the direction of Nottingham. "And where have you been, pray tell?" she asked as he stepped in pace beside her.

"You know where I've been," he replied, with the same dreamy look in his eyes that hers held. "You aren't the only one what goes runnin' off to see his sweetheart."

She gave him a sideways glance and grinned. "And do you have honorable intentions toward your maiden fair?"

"You can bet your last shilling," he pronounced. "Liz is the apple of my eye, she is, and when we all get pardoned, I plan to make her an honest woman, I do."

Robyn smiled. "I am proud of you Alan, and happy for you as well."

"What about you and Marian?" he asked.

"That may be a bit more complicated," she answered, all levity vanishing from her voice.

"Aye, what with her being an important noble lady and all," he sighed. "I'm sorry; didn't mean to-"

"Fret not, Alan. What will be, will be. Today, I feel I am the luckiest bloke in the world." She raised her chin with renewed joy.

As they approached the camp, people were bustling about, some dealing with the morning meal and others helping Tuck with preparations for the mass. Little John was sitting on a stump with three walnuts in his massive hand. He gave them a squeeze and Robyn heard them crack.

She shook her head. "It amazes me the things you can do."

"Oh, that is nothing," Little John answered jovially. "All it takes is a big hand with strong fingers. But what you two did, sending the youngsters on a nut gathering expedition–a stroke of genius! Now I'll have something to nibble on for the whole winter."

As Robyn scanned the camp, she noticed Much sitting alone in dirty clothes, his face neither shaved nor washed. "What's wrong with Much?" she asked, her features drawing up in concern. "He hasn't been himself of late."

"Aye," Little John agreed as he popped a walnut into his waiting mouth.

"It's on account of Evelyn," Alan explained. "Pretty little gal who came with a family from Gisborne's manor. He is sweet on her, but she is promised to a craftsman in Nottingham. Her family wants a better life for her–can't blame them–and she is quite awestruck with her betrothed. I hate to admit it, but just between us, Much isn't that handsome."

"Not everyone is blessed with your fair face and abundant charm," Little John commented.

Robyn tilted her head toward Alan. "I didn't know we had acquired serfs from Gisborne's estate."

Little John laughed. ". We have new folks from all over. Last week, when we robbed Baron Thomas of Acker's place, we rescued two men and a woman he had locked in hanging cages to let starve." He shook his head. "There's just no reasoning the things humans to do each other."

"Where was I?" she asked, disturbed that she allowed herself to become so unaware.

"You, Will and Gilbert were holding up a merchant convey on their way to York," he said matter-of-factly. "The rest of us hit Acker–part of your being in several places at once ploy."

"That's right." Robyn rested a hand on John's broad shoulder while her eyes stayed on her melancholy friend. *He's right. I need to pay more attention to those under my charge. But the mission... the mission comes first.* "Gramercy, mates. Sometimes I get so busy planning ways to out-think the Sheriff that I forget to mind our own."

Just then David of Doncaster, acting as Friar Tuck's altar boy for the occasion, began to ring a bell calling the company to gather for the All Saints Day mass. Young and old, they gathered around and stood as was customary even inside a church building.

Friar Tuck, still wearing his everyday robe of mud-brown, lifted his hands and smiled out at his congregation. "The Lord be with you," he greeted.

"And also with you," they all replied as one, and the service was underway.

They went through the liturgy in a call and response with Tuck quoting his parts and the people replying in words and phrases they had all memorized since their childhoods. There was the *Kyrie Eleison*, followed by the *Gloria,* and then onto the prayers.

"For the Holy Catholic Church, for Celestine III our Pope, our bishop, and for all bishops, priests, and deacons, we pray to the Lord," the Friar spoke before the kneeling assembly.

"Lord hear our prayer," came their response.

After an extensive list of petitions, the people all stood and recited the Nicene Creed, the *Sanctus* and the Lord's Prayer. Neither Friar Tuck nor the congregation attempted to sing, but rather chanted their parts on a variety of practiced pitches. Scripture readings from the Old and New Testament as well as the Psalms were scattered amongst the participatory portions of the mass. When the time came for the Eucharist to be given, Tuck blessed the wine and the bread, and everyone filed into a long line to walk forward and partake.

Robyn began to ponder the sacrament. The general interpretation was that the bread and wine were mysteriously transformed into the literal body and blood of Christ. *The true miracle is that an all-knowing and holy God would even wish to save a wicked and perverse humanity.* She contemplated the intensity of the love and dedication she held toward Marian, whom she would kill or die for without hesitation. She was aware that the Church would frown upon their relationship, but more on the basis that it conflicted with societal norms than for any spiritual reason. It was not a high priority of the Church, as evidenced by the sheer number of priests and bishops with similar inclinations. As Robyn recalled, in earlier periods the Church had not disapproved at all. She remembered the story of saints Sergius and Baccus, a male Christian couple who refused to sacrifice to Roman gods and were martyred for it, and Ireland's St. Brigid and her soul mate, Darlughdach. She had read about the great devotion David and Jonathan, and Ruth and Naomi had to one another. It had even been rumored that both a ninth century pope and an Egyptian pharaoh had been women living in the guise of men, as she was now. Robyn didn't pretend that she would ever be looked upon as a saint; she just loved Marian, and nothing could convince her that was wrong.

*But loving her is easy,* she thought. *Marian is kind, and generous, and good; most people are none of those things. And yet...*

"The body of Christ," Friar Tuck said as he tore off a small bit of bread from the loaf.

"Amen," she uttered and opened her mouth to receive the sacrament.

"The blood of Christ."

She sipped from the cup in Tuck's hands and repeated, "Amen," before proceeding back to her original spot. *It doesn't taste any different,* she thought as her contemplations continued. But she did feel something–a quickening in her spirit. Some may call it a religious experience. Robyn was suddenly and acutely aware of how great and powerful God's love must truly be, that He would allow His only son to die for such wretched and worthless souls as mankind had thus far produced.

* * *

IN THE MIDDLE of the night, when all had been sleeping for hours, Robyn made her way to the privy as was her custom. In one hand she carried a pail of water and a cloth for washing, and in the other a lanthorn, for the starless sky was like a blanket of coal dust hanging ominously over the earth. Upon returning to her abode, she heard a startled cry and a clamor coming from Gilbert Whitehand's tent. Rushing over, she threw open the flap and held her lanthorn high as she peered inside. "Is something amiss?"

Gilbert, who had even alarmed himself with his night terror, lifted a hand to shield his eyes from the light. "Nay, Robin, all is well. No need for you to fret."

She relaxed her stance as her anxiety subsided. "The war again?"

He shook his head and wiped sweat from his brow, despite the cold of the evening. "Not directly." Then with his vision adjusting to the brightness, he looked straight at her. "A man should not outlive his children."

Robyn squatted to the ground to be on eye-level with the former knight. "I'm sorry; I didn't know."

"What are you doing out at this hour anyway?" he inquired.

She chuckled. "When nature calls…"

He waved her in. "No reason to let in the chill. Come."

Robyn crept inside, allowed the flap to fall behind her, and sat cross-legged, waiting for Gilbert to talk about his children. Instead, he voiced a new fear. "What if I cannot do it? What if I can't find the hidey-hole, or can't solve how to operate the mechanism that reveals it? This whole plan hinges on me being able to accomplish a task that I have not done before."

Robyn's voice resounded with confidence. "You will. I know that you can do this and shall not fail."

Propping himself up on his elbow in the make-shift bed, Gilbert shook his head. "How can you have such faith in an old man?"

"My faith is not in you, friend, but in the One who brought us together," she explained. "I believe it is God's will for King Richard to return to England. To do so, that sum of silver must go to his release, not to some mercenary army the Prince would use to usurp the throne."

"And why are you so certain of this?" His deep-set brown eyes gazed into hers.

"I am aware that the Lionheart has made mistakes, and he has plenty of blood on his hands. None of us is righteous, not a single one. But he wants to do good," she stated plainly. "His brother John–not so much."

"You speak as if you know the King," Gilbert noted.

Robyn thought of the several occasions upon which they had met: once at Marian's manor, another time in London, at Windsor in the spring of her coming out, and when she bade her father and brother farewell as the army set sail for the Holy Land. He would not remember her, she supposed; but she remembered him.

"Marian knows him," she said. "He is her godfather." Gilbert nodded, satisfied with the response. "That does not mean I lack confidence in you as well, master archer," she continued. "For both my skill and wisdom have greatly increased under your tutelage. You are very able indeed."

He expelled a short laugh. "I had a good student with whom to work."

Robyn smiled and pushed up to her feet. "I shall let you get back to sleep now, and I will do the same. I know I am many times your younger, but if you ever need someone to talk with... about anything..."

Gilbert's eyes glistened. "You are a fine lad, Robin, one whom I am proud to call friend."

She nodded and bowed her way out of the tent, re-invading the abyssal night.

\* \* \*

NOTTINGHAM CASTLE, *a few days later*

LATE ON A FROSTY EVENING, the cloaked figure stood nervously in shadow just within the castle's back gate. Thin trails of smoke meandered out of chimneys and drifted toward the stars as he blew into his cupped hands shifting his weight from foot to foot.

Emory was making his final rounds when he spied the fellow looking dreadfully out of place.

"You there," he called in a stern voice. "Who are you and what are you about?"

A hooded head bobbed up with a fearful gaze peering out. "I have news for the Sheriff," Will Scarlet said in a hush and he took a step back as if he were trying to fade into the stone wall and become part of it.

Emory stepped closer, his right hand resting on the hilt of his sword. As his eyes caught a better look at the man, he relaxed. "It is you," he said. "The Sheriff is expecting you. This way," he motioned, extending an arm in the direction of the hulking keep.

The man-at-arms escorted his charge into Giffard's office, appointed a guard to stand watch over him, and left. Will's heart beat so fiercely that he feared it would break his chest. His breathing came quick, and he began to sweat. *This is it,* he thought, *the moment I damn my soul to hell. But what choice have I?*

He wasn't sure if it felt more like an eternity or the blink of an eye, but the door opened and in strode the self-assured specimen with his polished black boots and matching doublet, broad shoulders draped with a fur mantle, and cold opaque eyes that were comparable to staring into a bottomless well. Upon being grasped by their icy glare, he looked away, lowering his head, and shuddered.

"I was beginning to wonder if you had decided to let your dear mother be hanged to save your own skin," the Sheriff uttered with a venomous hiss.

Will shook his head. "N-no, milord. Never," he uttered. "I now have enough information to bring to you about Hood's plan, but first…" Tentatively he ventured to raise his chin. After taking a deep breath he steeled his body and attempted a commanding tone of voice. "I must know that me mum is still safe and well."

An amused smile tugged at the corners of the Sheriff's mouth. "Emory," he beckoned without removing his eyes from the spy. "Show him to the woman." Then with a hand he dismissed the other guard and began to make himself comfortable while the man-at-arms took the informant on a short trip to the dungeon.

It was as dismal as he had remembered, and his spirit fell into gloom as they descended the spiral stairs. "Mum?" he called into the dingy cave-like cellar, where humans were being stored like out of season tools.

Will heard a gasp and then saw feminine fingers clasp a set of bars. "Why?" she asked. "I told you not to return, to stay away."

He rushed to her, covering her hands with his. "You know I could not," he answered, emotion flooding his voice. "All will be well, you'll see. I will get you out of here."

"But son," she pleaded. "You cannot betray Robin Hood and your mates. Is my life worth all of theirs?"

He leaned his troubled brow against the bars and uttered in a hush so reticent that he was certain no one else heard. "Fear not; I'll find a way." Then he spoke aloud. "I cannot let him kill you, I simply cannot."

"Come now," instructed Emory. "You see, your mother is unharmed."

"I am so sorry," Will said, his voice cracking as he tried to hold back sobs. "I never meant for you to be hurt; I only ran away to protect you and Timm."

"It is not your fault I am here, and don't be blamin' yourself," she scolded. "Be brave, son; don't tell him what he wants to know."

Tears running down his dirty cheeks, her son replied, "I have to. I love you, Mum."

As Will was being pulled away, she replied, "I love you more."

\* \* \*

WHEN EMORY RETURNED the distraught man to Giffard's office, he was summarily dismissed and the door closed. The Sheriff began to deliberately stalk around the chamber like a predator considering his prey. "Details, outlaw," he demanded coolly, "and they better be exact."

*You have no choice*, Will thought in self-loathing despair. "Hood will be at the archery contest just as you suspected he would."

"Surely he won't simply stroll up in his trademark green hood," Giffard sneered.

The comment sent a noticeable jolt through him. "I-I have no idea. I suppose he may conceal himself, but he didn't say. If so, none of us has seen it."

The Sheriff stroked the sooty hair on his chin in consideration. "He can hardly make himself shorter or thinner, but perhaps a bit thicker... and since his face is smooth, he may appear in a beard. Go on with it."

"So, while Hood is hoping all eyes will be looking for him at the contest, the rest of the gang is to go to the castle to steal the loot."

Giffard stopped and cast a sarcastic glare at Will. "Too obvious. I said details, you brainless churl. Do you think I would believe they shall attempt to attack the castle because I am at the tournament field?"

"No," he groaned, "not *attack* the castle. They will be dressed as guards so they can move about without being noticed." He watched as the Sheriff's face lit with understanding.

"A few months ago a patrol came walking back wearing nothing but their breeches," he mused. "But where will they be searching? Do they know where the treasure is hidden?"

Will hesitated for a moment, glancing about the room nervously. "In here," he replied. "Where else? Hood thinks you would lock something so valuable away here in your office, in the heart of the keep."

Giffard smiled, his ebony eyes glinting with delight. "You have done well, my little mouse," he said slapping the outlaw on the back. "If everything plays out as you have reported, your mother shall be released the moment they are captured. Otherwise..."

The outlaw swallowed a gulp, dread welling up inside him like a geyser ready to erupt. He nodded gravely.

The Sheriff gave him a slight shake then opened the door. "Do not fear," he added. "I only want to capture Hood and protect Prince John's assets; once that has been accomplished, there is no reason to keep the woman locked up. All will be well."

Will lowered his head and turned away to trudge through the empty streets of town. All the way back to the lair, he startled at every owl's hoot, every tree branch swaying in the breeze. Several times he rushed to crouch behind a bush watching for some unknown danger. He couldn't shake the feeling that he was being followed, and proceeded to spend an hour marching about in circles. But despite all his apprehensions, his careful thief's eyes never caught sight of anyone. *It must be my own guilty conscience,* he thought. Sometime in the night Will arrived home at his bed, exhausted but unable to claim the release of sleep.

# CHAPTER 19

*FitzWalter Manor, November 19, 1193*

Robyn lay on crisp, linen sheets amid fluffy, down pillows entwined with Marian, whose silky skin pressed warm against her own. *I could in contentment lie like this forever,* she thought. *'Tis bliss.* She drew in a languid breath, reveling in the ecstasy of their night spent together, the rest of the world being a far off and inconsequential kingdom. She could even imagine hearing the music of Heaven weaving its celestial melodies and angelic harmonies through her mind...until the moment was shattered by that damnable bird's song. With a sigh, she began to stir. "It is time."

Without lifting her head from Robyn's shoulder, Marian protested, "'Tis but midnight." She hugged Robyn closer and slid a leg between her thighs as if to pin her to the bed.

"If only 'twere so," she replied with a humorless laugh. "But that was the morning lark. The sun will rise anon and then it begins."

"Let us wait for the cock to crow," Marian suggested and began to place enticing kisses along Robyn's neck.

Robyn responded by combing her fingers through Marian's long, luxurious strands of gold. "I have displayed nothing but confidence in front of my men," she commented.

"As is right for you to do," her lover agreed between kisses.

"Ah, but inwardly I am not so certain," she admitted. "Sometimes I feel that I am not even in control of my own life; it is like I am an arrow shot from the bow of fate, spiraling through the air with no means by which to plot my own course or determine my own destination."

Marian pushed herself up, her full mane cascading over her shoulder, to gaze down at Robyn in the palest of moonlight. "So if fate is the bow and you are the arrow, what am I?"

Robyn's eyes brightened as they latched onto Marian's. "You, Marian, are the target," she declared, lifting a hand to caress her fair face, "the only goal I seek."

In an instant, Marian's mouth captured hers possessively, and Robyn eagerly drank from the well of honey that was offered her. If it was to be her last day on earth, this was the best way to begin it!

When Marian pulled away, she spoke with authoritative resonance. "You shall not fear and you shall not waver, because I know if there is anyone in the world who can succeed in this endeavor, it is you, Robyn. You have no reason to lack confidence, but if you do, take this assurance to heart–I believe in you, and am without doubt."

Her words brought a smile to Robyn's face. "You are my strength."

"Among other things," Marian teased and the morning lark called once more. Rolling over, she lit a candle, rose, and pulled on her night shift which had at some point been discarded into a heap on the floor. "I suppose it is time to create your false appearance."

Robyn watched as she crossed to her wardrobe, opened the doors and withdrew curious apparel.

"These were what my father used to wear around the manor when he didn't wish his good clothes to be soiled," she said as she laid out a faded reddish tunic, russet trousers, and a smoke gray mantle on the bed at Robyn's feet.

Robyn sat up wide-eyed, the sheet falling away from her breast. "They are much too large for me!"

Marian's mouth quirked into a half smile. "You shall wear them over your regular clothing, and we can stuff a pillow or two in where needed." Then she produced two wedge shaped items just smaller than her palms about two inches at the high end. "These we will place in your boots to make you appear taller," she explained. While Robyn scanned her costume with interest, Marian moved to her vanity table, opened the top drawer, and withdrew a pair of sheers and a long brunette braid. "I made a wheat paste and thickened it up with resin so it should work well to affix your new beard and mustache."

Robyn's mouth dropped in utter astonishment. "Is that my hair? You saved it!"

Marian stroked the braided strand reverently. "Certainly," she replied. "You don't think I would toss it away with the rubbish, do you? Every now and then I lay it on my pillow at night, so that I can touch a part of you, and feel like you are here."

Robyn's heart swelled, but she insisted there would be no tears this morning. "You never cease to amaze me," she confessed in wonderment. She slid from the bed and began putting on her own garments.

"It will take some creativity on my part to continue amazing you for the next forty years or so," Marian chirped with coy light dancing in her eyes.

*I am indeed the most fortunate woman in the world!* Robyn thought. *Prithee, God, let this day go well.*

\* \* \*

THE TOURNAMENT GROUNDS *outside Nottingham Castle*

SHERIFF GIFFARD, wearing his best silks over a thick leather jerkin for protection, stood near the nobles' stands which overlooked the tournament field an hour before the event was to begin. A razor sharp broadsword hung in its scabbard from his belt. A scattering of spectators had begun to trickle in while his watchful eyes passed over the scene. It was a perfect sunny day on which to conclude the festival, and a boon to catching thieves, finally to be rid of their annoyance. Sirs Raoul de Clar and Hugh Diggory were milling about chatting with some of the other barons before claiming their preferential cushioned seats under the covered canopy set up with a royal seat for Prince John, who would of course be the last to arrive as a signal for the contest to commence. Sir Guy, his daughter, and Maid Marian were winding their way through the crowd, politely wishing all a good morrow, when Sir Lambelin Bondeville and Deputy Blanchard, outfitted for the competition, stepped up to Giffard.

"Sheriff," addressed the smiling sandy haired Lambelin. "I fear I shall spoil your premise for identifying Hood as the winner of this tournament for, on top of my extraordinary skill, I am feeling quite lucky today."

Godfrey snorted, crossing his arms as he regarded the Baron of Somerset. "Is that so?" he inquired dubiously. "What have you to offer, Deputy?"

"Milord, I suspect our honored guest Sir Lambelin had a bit too much to drink last eve, as clearly I am favored to win this day," he returned with a rare smile. "But you can be assured I shall keep all my wits about myself when spying out the other contestants, as one of them is no doubt the outlaw we seek."

"I know you will, Blanchard," Godfrey answered with less chill than before. "Sir Lambelin, I wish you nothing but success," he added with a curt nod. Then he spotted his man at arms, Emory, and waved him over.

"Yes, milord?" The sturdy veteran reported to the Sheriff with a snap to attention.

"Gather half of the guards, take them back to the castle, and give them the instructions of which we spoke, making certs a dozen of your best are waiting in my office. And no one dressed as a soldier is to be allowed in without the password, is that clear?"

"Aye," Emory answered and strode off to gather guards.

Bondeville and Blanchard looked puzzled, and the deputy inquired, "Sheriff, what is this about? I thought the plan was to trap Hood here at the tournament, yet you send away half the guard?"

The imposing Sheriff stared down Lambelin with a hard gaze. "I'll just go get ready for my big win today," he responded and excused himself from the two lawmen.

Once they were alone, Godfrey stated, "There is a traitor in our midst, and the fewer who know of it the better. It may well be him," he said as his eyes trailed Lambelin walking away. "Alas, I have not been able to ascertain who it is, but someone has been singing to the Queen. I also found out Hood's whole gang will be at the castle to steal Prince John's hoard, but you need not concern yourself with that; it is covered. Your part is what it has always been–discover which of the other contestants is the outlaw and capture him."

Blanchard nodded. "That I shall do, have no doubt."

Sheriff Giffard slapped his deputy on the back and grinned. "And I don't even mind if you further humiliate him by proving you are the better archer first!"

A broad grin crossed the deputy's face. "I should enjoy that very much."

* * *

ROBYN WALKED along the path from castle to tournament field without drawing a single glance from the merrymakers. She appeared to be a tall, stout man with a full beard and mustache on his way to compete with dozens of others, both noble and commoner, in the open archery contest. A bow and quiver rested on his shoulders and he ambled with a limp, his left leg stiff, no doubt, from a mill injury, or mayhap from being kicked by a horse. In fact, Robyn had locked that knee to keep it taut as her sword hung hidden inside the leg of her outer set of trousers.

She paid close attention to every detail, knowing that at any moment she may have to fight or flee. Food carts were set up along the way offering a variety of sumptuous smelling dishes at a reasonable price. There were jugglers and fortune tellers, with a troupe performing a mystery play to one side of the path and a minstrel playing his mandolin and singing a popular Goliard song on the other. She switched her attention as she heard a great commotion and stepped around a vendor's cart to investigate. There was a lodge-pole planted firmly in the ground and chained to it by a ring and collar was a black bear being taunted by youths with sticks and barking dogs. While bear-baiting was a common distraction at fairs, Robyn found it cruel and pointless. Nonetheless, there stood a dozen fellows cheering and laying bets while the dogs darted in and out trying to nip the beast with their teeth without being mauled in the process. She shook her head and turned away.

A jester in colorful patchwork silks, a hat with jingling bells on his head, hopped in front of her. "Are you a man or a mouse?" he asked whimsically. "And where would I find the privy house?" Then just as randomly, he skipped away. She passed a group of masked and costumed mummers and a pardoner calling fair goers to receive forgiveness, for a small fee, before at last arriving at the check in station for archery contestants.

"Name," the scribe pronounced in a bored monotone without even glancing up from his ledger.

"William Smith," she replied using a common name.

"We have two William Smith's entered; which are you?"

"From Lincolnshire," she added in a husky, deep voice.

"Ah, here," he said and spared her a glance. He shoved the binder toward her and held out a quill. "Make your mark." It was not an insult considering that most Englishmen, even the nobility, were illiterate. Robyn drew an "X" where the scribe pointed. "Very well," he grunted as he retrieved paper and quill. "See the other participants over there?" He pointed at a group of fellows with bows and arrows standing together. "Go wait with them and you'll get your chance."

"Gramercy," she replied and ambled stiff-legged over to the others. Men of all ages, sizes, and walks of life had gathered for a shot to win the prize of a golden arrow to be awarded by the beauteous Maid Marian. For nobles it meant bragging rights and for commoners, food for the whole winter. She recognized a few of the contestants—Deputy Blanchard, and some local barons. Amid the tall and short, young and old, noble and common, she blended unremarkably.

* * *

DOWNHILL FROM THE FESTIVITIES, the castle overlooking the River Trent was quiet and void of celebrators, if not overstocked with armed guards. An old priest and his youthful acolyte strolled up to the main gate.

The stalwart soldier on duty stopped them.

"Who goes there?" he asked in an irritated tone as he stretched to peer up at the cheering horde only three hundred yards away. In disappointment, he returned his gaze to the clergymen.

The younger guard at the other side of the entrance barely glanced at them as he leaned on his pike and kicked at the dirt.

"I am Father Gilbert and this is David, a ward of my abbey," he answered with a cheerful smile. "I was invited to perform the noonday mass and we are here to make preparations."

The disgruntled sentinel sighed and waved a gloved hand. "Go on, then." He dismissed the frail looking cleric and his youthful counterpart, never suspecting how lethal both could be.

Gilbert was grateful to Friar Tuck's brothers of the cloth who had given him the robes for priest and acolyte. They had also graciously supplied a full nun's garb which lay hidden in the brush behind a certain Scots Pine. He noted that there were more guards than he had expected to see, but pushed down any inclination to panic; this was not his first mission.

When they reached the chapel, a sleepy, scruffy lad in mail that hung too large over his shoulders offered a polite bow and opened the door for them. Gilbert breathed a sigh of relief when he looked around to find them alone inside.

"David, you look about for the bread and wine while I arrange the Bible and candles on the altar."

He gave Gilbert a questioning gaze, but Whitehand just made a shooing motion at him while he began to examine every inch of the dais.

A few minutes passed and the guards at the gate swore when another cheer rang out from the crowd up the hill. "Shite duty, that's what we gets," the one with week old stubble on his chin complained.

"Aye, and I ain't never got to watch a proper archery contest in my life," added the younger of the two. "Ain't fair, I says."

While they grumbled over their unfavorable task, a party of men in soldier's attire approached the gate. A handsome, green eyed chap in the front of the group announced, "Sheriff Giffard sent us down here to reinforce the castle."

"What's the password?" muttered the stubbled elder guard with an obvious lack of enthusiasm.

Suddenly Alan A Dale's face went blank and a hint of panic ran through him. "Password?" he inquired, acting as though he knew it, but it had just slipped his mind.

"Aye, password. Old Emory says everyone's got to say the password."

"Oh, that password!" Alan announced in triumph, still clueless. Behind him, Little John gripped his sword hilt, ready to fight if necessary. Will, Arthur, Much, along with Isaac, Roger, and Fawkes, refugees who had volunteered and trained for this mission, stood motionless waiting to ascertain if the charismatic Alan could talk their way in. "Fear not, my fine fellow; the Sheriff told us right before we started down here. Now let me see... truly isn't fair, is it? Us having to sit around this empty castle whilst all the excitement is happenin' up on the hill? A cryin' shame, it is."

Just then a real soldier sped right through their ranks and skidded to a halt beside Alan. "Whew, I thought I was late. Had to, you know, spend a little longer in the privy than I had planned. Glad I caught up to the rest of you."

"Password," repeated the guard impatiently.

"Falconer," said the actual guard.

"That's right," Alan agreed. "'Tis falconer," and he added a confident nod.

"Very well, come on in. Geez, how many more guards does this empty castle need?"

"You're tellin' me," Alan exclaimed with a shake of his head as they all proceeded through the gate.

After they had taken a few steps, the late soldier considered Alan. "Do I know you?"

"Oh, we're new," he answered smoothly.

"That explains it. My group's off to guard the Sheriff's office; what about you fellows?"

"We were told to watch the chapel," Alan said. "Guess he wants this place really guarded well in case that Robin Hood shows up."

"Indeed! Good morrow." The soldier waved and trotted off toward the keep while Alan and his comrades sauntered over to stand around outside the chantry.

*  *  *

WILL SCARLET TOOK a few steps away from the others and leaned in shadow against the chapel's outer stone wall with his arms crossed over his chest keeping his head bowed. He wasn't sure which he was more terrified of: his mother being killed, being killed himself, or his friends finding out what he had done. He was convinced all three would transpire this day.

His brooding darkened to the point he was unaware of anything or anyone around him, trapped in a labyrinth of misery. He hoped that his tightrope act would work. He had told the Sheriff enough to satisfy him and buy time for his mum, but changed or omitted key facts. Would having the soldiers guard the wrong room be sufficient to save his friends? But, if they left the castle without his mother, she would be as good as dead.

Why hadn't he just told Robin what was going on? The longer he had waited, the guiltier of betrayal he had become until it was impossible to tell the gang. *My only chance is to make haste for the dungeon once the fighting begins,* he thought. *Free Mum, get her to safety, and then rush back to die with my mates.* It was a dismal prospect, but the best outcome for which he could pray.

He felt as if the very stones of the chapel burned his spine with righteous fire, paving the way to purgatory for his ignoble actions. He turned deeper into himself, wrestling with his own soul. *They could all die, King Richard lose his crown; Queen Eleanor and Maid Marian banished or locked away, and Robin? The friend I had called a brother? He would face a public execution, likely a drawn out and painful one, all because of me. There is no hope, no hope for my soul! I could tell Little John... I could tell him now, not that I had spilled the plan, but that I overheard the guards talking... that somehow they found out we would be here. I could warn them and we could get out safely... but then what about me mum?*

Will shivered despite the pleasant day, his eyes fixed on a spot in the dirt.

It took Much three times speaking to him and a shake of his shoulders before Will noticed he was no longer alone. "Wake up, Will!" he insisted. "We have to keep alert."

"Aye," he snapped with a nod while sweat streamed down his face.

"Don't worry, mate," Much tried to assure him. "All is well."

Nervously, Will lifted his eyes and nodded again to his friend. But all was not well, and he bloody well knew it. If ever there was a time to act, to warn the others, this was it. But no, it was too late now. "I'll be fine," was all he said before closing dull blue eyes from which the light had already been extinguished.

* * *

MAID MARIAN, attired in a fashionable back-laced, fitted gown of deep autumn blue wool with narrow sleeves flaring out dramatically at cuffs that plunged almost to the platform and encompassed by a double wrapped belt, sat on a cushioned chair between Sir Guy and Maid Faye. In proper modesty, her sunny strands were gathered up in looped braids and all but covered by her white fine-linen coif. On her lap rested a pale blue silk pillow bearing the prize golden arrow. Marian's eyes lit when she spotted Robyn walking forward with the other archers for the first round. She was quite proud of how her work turned out; even Robyn had exclaimed that she did not recognize herself. Anyone who had ever caught a glimpse of the outlaw Hood would never suspect this stocky bearded chap with the halt.

"Ah, look, Maid Marian," Guy said pointing to a contestant in noble dress. "There is my old friend Roland de Lacy, second son of the Baron of Leeds. He and I used to ride the circuit, competing in all the tournaments. While he excelled in archery, I always bested him with the sword." Guy seemed to swell with pride, raising his red-bearded chin as he waved out toward Roland. Marian wondered just how many championships Sir Guy had actually won in the past, and if any were attained honestly. "That's the thing about shooting a bow," he continued, having failed to catch his supposed friend's attention. "Age does not figure so much as it does in swords and the joust."

Marian studied the distinguished looking marksman wearing a thin moustache and goatee on an otherwise smooth face as he stepped up to the line. He bore good posture and a more robust stature than the baron seated to her left. "Do you favor Roland to win?" she asked, trying to seem interested in her would be courtier.

Sir Guy's belly jiggled with a short laugh. "Nay. I fear his eye is not as sharp as it once was, but he should fare well. I laid my wager on Sir Lambelin. You remember him from our dinner with Prince John at Michaelmas," he said sweeping his gaze over her.

"Ah, yes, the handsome young baron who had too much to drink, if I recall." Guy's face darkened at her use of the word 'handsome' to describe one he immediately realized could be a rival for her hand.

He snapped his attention back to the field as the opening shots were fired toward painted bulls-eyes. "Then again, Deputy Blanchard is a fine shot as well; and there is Robin Hood, should he actually dare appear."

"That is the plan, is it not?"

"Indeed." The competitors were divided in half as those whose shots landed on or nearest the center moved to the next round where the targets would be placed farther away, while those whose arrows strayed were directed to the rear. Then Guy turned a warm smile toward Marian. "My dearest, I have been thinking… there is nothing to be gained by waiting upon your father's return for us to wed. I have all confidence that he would not object to our union as both of our houses hold high reputation. We know not how long it could take to raise the ransom, how many times that greedy Emperor Henry will increase the amount, or even if he has any intention of releasing the King at all. If your father chooses to remain in Germany awaiting his release…" Guy trailed off, shaking his head sadly.

Marian shot him an irritated glance. "My father is loyal to King

Richard. He will wait and bring the Lionheart back to England. Then upon his return, the King shall reward all who remained faithful in his absence." *Unlike,* she added to herself, *those of you who plot with the Prince to steal his throne.*

Guy sighed and placed a hand over hers, an expression of deep concern on his face. "It is such a shame that our valiant King Richard did not simply appoint his brother John ruler by proxy while he is detained instead of a committee of regents. Our country needs a strong, decisive monarch to keep us safe and vibrant, not a bickering circle of old men and a woman whose heart is burdened with worry for her son. Would it be so bad if John were king?"

A cold shiver ran down Marian's spine. Though she knew he held them, this was the first time Sir Guy had voiced his opinions on the matter. That meant he was confident something would happen soon. *He must be thinking of the tax money paying the mercenaries to support Prince John as he usurps the crown. But he doesn't know we are about to bear that money straight to Queen Eleanor and across the sea. His cockiness could lead him to make a critical mistake.*

She waved a hand dismissively and giggled, playing the role of clueless female. "Certs John may be king one day if His Highness cannot manage to take to his wife long enough to secure an heir; but verily our Richard will return soon. We should not worry about such heavy things on this last day of Martinmas. Let us be light and gay, Sir Guy. My father shall come home and you may speak with him about acquiring my hand in marriage."

*When hell freezes over.*

\* \* \*

REFRACTED sunbeams spilled in from the clerestory, a set of three massive stained-glass windows arched around the wall constructed with large stones that encircled the rostrum, easing Gilbert's task as he ran dexterous fingers over the walnut pulpit and beneath the green silk drape which signified common time on the liturgical calendar. Nothing. The ornately carved pulpit with Norman reliefs hid no secret levers. He stepped to the communion table, which held the center focus of the platform, and examined every edge and corner, moving meticulously to the less flashy lectern at the other end. *I wish I knew what to look for.* Gilbert glanced up to see David playing with the flames of the candles lit at St. Mary's station.

"Stop that," he scowled. The lad gave him an innocent shrug, but left the tapers alone.

Then Gilbert focused his attention along the wall behind the altar. On either side of the set of large windows was affixed an iron sconce. *That's odd,* Gilbert thought. The sconces were designed to hold torches but sat empty. *Only beeswax is used in churches,* he considered, *not messy, smoke producing torches that would soot up the place.* The observation that they did not belong drew him in enthusiastically. He tugged on the one behind him, but nothing happened. Then he scooted over to the one behind the pulpit. When he pulled it there was first a click followed by a scraping sound. Turning, he watched as the walnut podium slid forward revealing a hole that had been hidden underneath. Something shiny glittered in the sunlight.

Hearing the sound, David ran over and joined his elder as they peered into the hollowed out space. An automatic light shone on their countenances as they beheld bag upon bag of riches. *We found it! It is really here!* It was almost too good to be true, but while David oohed and aahed in amazement, Gilbert knew their mission was far from over.

"Go give Alan the signal," he directed. "And try to hide some of that glow on your face."

"Aye," he said straightening, but had to take one more peek. "That there is more gold and silver than I thought was in the whole world."

"'Tis enough to buy a kingdom," Gilbert affirmed. "And that is precisely what it was collected to do. Run on, now."

The youth scampered to the chapel door, composing himself before he stepped through. He raked his gaze over his friends who stood about trying to seem like castle guards until it came to rest on Alan. When he cleared his throat to get his attention, all of their eyes turned to him. Unable to contain a joyous grin, he gave the signal by making the sign of the cross, then re-closed the door.

Alan could feel the energy in the air radiating from his comrades as he dealt with his own overload of emotion. This was big–so big and life changing... or life ending; that remained to be seen. Per the plan, he pulled an apple out of his pouch and strolled as nonchalantly as he could muster toward the castle wall bordering Nottingham town. He took a bite and looked around as he took unhurried steps. The two guards at the gate appeared as bored and disgruntled as ever. A handful of soldiers were patrolling the grounds, and he was aware that an undisclosed number of others were inside the keep. Once he reached a specific spot along the wall, Alan leaned up against it and took another nibble of the fruit. He peered to the left and right; satisfied that no one was watching, he tossed the half eaten fruit over his shoulder and over the rampart.

\* \* \*

FRIAR TUCK SAT on the driver's seat of a small wagon loaded with kegs waiting anxiously for the sign. Knowing it could take quite a while to discover the hoard did not make the wait any easier. "Good morrow, Friar!" greeted a jovial commoner in a throng of others making their way to the fairgrounds.

"God bless," he returned with a wave. It was not long until he heard a distant cheer on the breeze and surmised that the tournament had begun. He began to recite silent prayers with one hand cradling the reins and his other holding to the small cross that hung over his heart.

After some span of time between moments and hours, his meditation was interrupted when the sturdy dun draught cob lurched forward. Snapping to attention, Tuck scanned empty streets as all were enjoying the fair. His gaze fell to the horse itself.

Forgetting his command to stand, the horse stretched out his neck, adorned by a dark mane falling to both sides of his distinctive dun backline stripe, and strained against the reins with velvety lips reaching toward the ground in front of him. Tuck gave the cart horse some slack, and he took one step ahead to obtain his prize–the treat of a half-eaten apple!

"Well bless my soul!" Tuck let out in glee. "Saints be praised!" He beamed as the gelding rolled the fruit into his mouth and munched down upon it. He slapped the reins across his back. "Up now," he called with glee. "To the castle gate we go!"

Still chewing, the cob complied by pulling onward in an ambling walk.

"Good morrow to my fine friends," Tuck greeted upon reaching Nottingham Castle's main entrance.

The two guards on duty perked up at the sight of the kegs in his wagon. The older man hesitated before replying, "The festival is up the hill, Friar," and the younger one's hopeful expression began to fade.

"Ah, but that is why I am here instead!" he exclaimed, with a genuine grin. Then the pretense began. "The Sheriff may have banished you all to sentinel duty, but the ever benevolent Prince John does not wish you to miss out on all the merriment. He asked me to bring over these barrels of mead as a token of his appreciation for all that you do. The Prince wants you to know that you have not been forgotten."

"Then come right on in, blessed Friar!" the elder guard commanded with enthusiasm. "Warin, go fetch the others," he instructed the younger man, "while I help the good Friar."

"Aye!" he exclaimed in delight and he dashed across the courtyard. "Hey fellows!" he called waving to Little John and Arthur who stood just outside the chapel door. "The mead wagon is here for us. Come, have a draught." Then he scurried through a doorway into the keep.

\* \* \*

No sooner than young David had given the signal, Little John and all the band save Alan began to meander toward the chapel. It took great restraint to act nonchalant and unenthused as the big man forced slow steps and a bland expression, but nothing could slow his racing heartbeat. With Robyn off at the tournament, he was in charge. To be fair, he had led the outlaw gang before Robyn joined them, but they had never embarked on an undertaking so bold. He glanced around and caught sight of Alan tossing the apple as he spanned the threshold into the sanctuary. Out of habit, he crossed himself as he entered.

"Quick, over here," Gilbert called in a hushed tone while gesturing with one hand. Little John hastened to the platform, the others right behind him. "Here," the old archer in priest robes said as he shoved a heavy sack laden with coins into his hands. "Put these under your mail in the pouches the women sewed into your tunics. Quickly, now," he admonished while he and David lifted out bag after bag and the outlaws stowed away the treasure.

"Won't someone notice?" asked Much as he looked down at himself. "I appear fatter than when I came in here."

"Their attention is on the mead," John assured him.

"That's right," Alan chimed in as he was the last through the chapel door. "It's not like there are fair maidens out yonder sizin' you up for a husband."

Much lifted his brows at Alan's joke then acknowledged John with a nod. "All will be well, Much; just follow my lead," John said. "Not all at once, and half of you go around the other side like you've been patrolin'." At that moment he noticed Will standing apart, his chin dragging toward the floor. "Will?" The boy's head popped up, his eyes raising to meet Little John's. "Ready?"

He sighed, then nodded. "As I'll ever be."

"Now let's do this, just as we practiced and we are all home free." With that last encouragement, the big man led the way. He and Arthur were the first ones to amble out to the inner path around from the chapel door toward the front gate.

"Hey fellows!" called a diminutive guard as he waved to them. "The mead wagon is here for us. Come, have a draught."

"Don't mind if I do," Little John answered. "Gramercy, mate!" Then he watched the man scurry through a doorway into the keep.

"Good morrow, brave and loyal soldiers of the castle," Tuck greeted jovially. "Come, have refreshment compliments of His Highness Prince John."

"Just what I need to wet my whistle," Little John replied as he sauntered over to the cart, careful not to shift his hidden coinage about. However, the beauty of this plan allowed for any jingling sounds to be explained away by the natural clink of the chain mail. John beamed with appreciation for Robyn's genius. Everything had been carefully calculated, rehearsed, and adjusted as needed. Robyn had even insisted that they wear the mail twelve hours a day for a fortnight leading up to the heist so that each member of the team would look and feel comfortable under its weight.

Catching the senior gate guard's attention, Little John lifted a tankard, now filled with sweet amber liquid. "A toast, my good man, to the Prince—may God bless his soul!"

The guard, who had been the first to fill a cup, raised his and met gazes with the brawny giant. "To His Royal Highness—long life to him!" Then they both threw back their heads and downed a hearty quantity of fermented honey. What the sentry was totally unaware of was the scrawny black haired urchin, no longer in acolyte robes, who just slipped beneath the wagon while his mug was upturned.

Then Friar Tuck took his turn to engage the guard in conversation, recounting some exciting tale and asking for a story in return. Meanwhile

Little John, followed by each of the others, inconspicuously slid treasure bags out from under their mail over-shirts and into David's waiting hands. He stacked them behind a wheel without creating a sound.

"Thank you, kind Friar," Will said handing Tuck his empty tankard. "But we must be getting back on duty now."

"There is plenty if you need another round," Tuck answered smiling.

While the others filed out following Will, Little John once again engaged the guard's attention. "Who do you think will win the archery contest?"

He looked over the man's shoulder toward the tournament field where another cheer arose. The guard followed his gaze and began to speculate while Tuck lifted coin bags and placed them into the hollowed out side of the barrels. He had just secured the last one by the time the gate guard turned back around.

"Aye," Little John agreed with the soldier. "But if I had been allowed, I swear by all that is holy, I would have trounced all comers with the mace."

The guard laughed heartily, relaxed and warmed by his drink. "Indeed you would have!"

Little John gave him a friendly pat on the shoulder and started back on the way to the chapel passing a group of six castle soldiers eagerly striding toward the mead. *That worked well*, he told himself. *But it will require many trips to empty the cache. We may have to do something with that gate guard lest he become too suspicious. Yet if I bash him over the head and take his place, the others who all saw him there may think something amiss.* He scratched his head as he was bumped by Much who went rushing past him.

"What?" he inquired of the others.

"Says he must run to the privy this very moment," Arthur replied.

"Nerves," Gilbert confirmed. "Here, fill your pouch," he said and handed Little John another bag of silver.

"That's it!" he declared in triumph. Then he explained to the puzzled faces before him. "That gate guard will wonder why we keep coming back, and if we get rid of him the other soldiers will be alarmed–unless one of us takes his place temporarily while he visits the privy. With all that mead, certs he shall have to go."

"That will at least give us enough time to unload another batch," Arthur confirmed. "You have talked to him the most. Why not take a lap around the grounds then volunteer to watch the gate while he takes a piss?"

"I think it will work," John concurred, "but we should wait until that group of guards leaves."

* * *

Sheriff Giffard leaned forward in his seat stroking his beard, intense dark eyes bearing down on the contest below. The remaining eight contestants let loose their shots and the judges made their decisions.

The herald announced in a loud voice, "Advancing to the semi-final round are Sir Lambelin Bondeville, Baron of Somerset..." but he was interrupted by cheers and applause. The Herald waited for the crowd to quiet, then continued. "Sir Roland de Lacy of Leeds." More clapping ensued. "Peter the woodcutter of Kirton, Nottinghamshire." A huge ovation erupted from the commoner's section. "And Deputy Edward Blanchard, of Nottingham Castle." Shouts and approbation rose into the air from all over the fairgrounds as the disappointed quartet who did not advance trudged to the back.

"Something is wrong," Godfrey noted in a low, ominous tone. "Something is very, very wrong."

# CHAPTER 20

𝒫rince's John's ginger brows knit together as he turned toward the Sheriff. "Whatever do you mean?"

"I recognize three of those men and the fourth, this Peter the woodsman or whoever, could not possibly be Robin Hood."

"Are you certain?" asked Sir Guy. "We know the outlaw is adept at deception."

"Look at him!" Godfrey bellowed, his temper rising to the surface. "He is too short. Hood is almost my height, which means he is taller than Sir Lambelin, and see there," he said pointing. "The peasant barely reaches his shoulder. I dare say Maid Marian has a greater stature than he. Age and weight be damned, that is the one thing the scoundrel cannot alter."

"So," Prince John began as he tilted his head. "What does that do to your plan of catching Hood? If he is not a top contender as you supposed he would be—"

Godfrey's face flushed red with anger and he forgot his manners by interrupting the Prince. "Then he must be amongst those who were eliminated." Fury rose to a boil as the Sheriff leapt to his feet. "I know he is here; he has to be here! God's teeth, he is the best shot I've ever seen or heard of, yet he did not advance!"

"Calm yourself, Godfrey," Gisborne said in a soothing tone. "Mayhap he took ill."

"No!" he thundered again. "He is here, by the saints, I know it!" He hastily scanned the tournament field checking where guards were positioned and where the eliminated contestants stood off to the side. "We must seize all the archers while I examine each and every one." Giffard could feel himself shaking and recognized the rise in his voice that was paramount to panic. *Rein it in,* he told himself. *Control...* He took a deep breath and placed a hand on the railing to steady himself.

"But," Sir Guy peered up at him sheepishly. "The contest? It isn't over… Marian has to award the prize to the winner."

Godfrey passed a lethal glare over Gisborne before bowing his head to Prince John. "Sire, what say you? Shall we give the churl a chance to escape so that Sir Guy may attempt to court a maiden who shall never accept his proposal, or do we act now?"

Prince John met the Sheriff's gaze, knowing full well what was at stake. "Have your soldiers move in. The people came to see something spectacular and, if your outlaw is in the mix, they will not be disappointed."

Sir Guy pouted, but Godfrey's eyes shone like polished onyx as he nodded. Turning to face the field he shouted, "Halt the contest! Guards, surround those archers," he commanded pointing to the assembly of eliminated contestants. "Arrest them all!" He dashed from the platform, down a short span of stairs, and paced toward them with determination.

* * *

Sir Lambelin lifted wide eyes to Deputy Blanchard. "What is the meaning of this? I was about to win!"

Edward groaned and spared only a few words for the baron. "It means Hood is playing games with us."

He brushed past Lambelin and took swift strides toward the other participants. Most seemed confused and stood around docilely with their hands raised while pike wielding soldiers encircled them, however a few panicked and endeavored to run. A young man in fine clothes tried to climb into the stands, but was thwarted when a strapping guard grabbed his leg and pulled him down. An older fellow in more modest attire dashed in the direction of the forest, but he, too, was caught. A third, who appeared to be no more than a beggar, bolted wide-eyed and pale faced right into Blanchard, who seized him in one big hand.

"You there," he scowled peering at the scrawny runt. "Why are you running?"

The peasant wilted before him, his terrified visage turning up into the mighty deputy's stern expression. "I don't want to die!" he wailed as his knees failed him. Edward had to tighten his muscles just to hold the man on his feet.

"Who said anyone was going to kill you?" *This is not Hood,* he determined as he held the slight fellow like a rag doll. *He is lanky, yes, but not this scrawny, and his youthful face bore none of this fellow's marks and wrinkles.*

"But, but, the Sheriff ordered us arrested! I didn't do anything wrong!"

"Then you have nothing to fear. For God's sake, man–try to stand under your own power, will you? I have to find the outlaw; he is the one the Sheriff wants, not you." The pitiful specimen dropped to his knees the instant Edward released him. *Now where did he go?*

The keen eyed deputy was disturbed by the fact that Hood had evaded his detection throughout the morning. *I should have spotted him on the tournament field,* he thought in frustration. *Could it be he did not compete?* But Giffard had been convinced he would. *Mayhap that was part of the plan young Will Scarlet relayed to the Sheriff. Or did the informant lie?*

Blanchard studied the huddle of archers who stood surrounded by guards. *Too tall, too short, too old, too ugly,* he thought as he scanned the collection. *Wait!* He suddenly noticed that one of the men was missing. *Where is that stout fellow with the brown beard and faded red tunic?* He sped around the circle peering in and pushed a guard aside to get a better look. Then he caught sight of Sheriff Giffard marching toward them with a granite jaw and searing eyes. He lowered his head and ducked away. *I've got to be the one who finds Hood.*

Edward scanned the curious crowd, the vendors and entertainers, and even the other soldiers in his quest to find this aberration who had eluded him. Stepping away from the tournament field, he spotted a faint color under a bush off to the side. He rushed over and snatched up a worn red tunic. Under it lay a crumbled pair of russet trousers, an old gray mantle, and a couple of small pillows. *Clever thief!* he thought as he dropped the garment. *So who or what do you look like now? And to where did you disappear?*

"Deputy, here!" sounded a loud shout. Edward looked up to see a guard chasing a slender archer dressed in the same shirt and jerkin he had seen Hood wear before. The sprinter appeared to sport only half a beard and was tugging at that as he ran.

"After him!" Giffard commanded, and the troop of soldiers abandoned the rounded up contestants to chase Robin Hood.

Edward struck out in a line parallel to his quarry attempting to keep stride, but it soon became apparent that the agile youth, absent the heavy armor of those chasing him, had the advantage. The fugitive dashed nimbly between carts and horses, jugglers and minstrels, and managed to avoid knocking down an off-balance, overweight priest as he hugged a corner and started in another direction. *Does he intend to simply lead a chase?* Edward wondered. *He could have remained hidden and safe.*

Rounding the same corner, Edward stopped for a moment, leaned over holding his knees, and tried to catch his breath. It was then he witnessed the expertise he had anticipated all morning. Hood, far out ahead of the pursuing guards, drew his bow. The deputy followed his trajectory as the arrow sped toward the pole to which a very large and very angry black bear was chained. That first shot bounced off ineffectually. He watched in expectancy as the fugitive scampered a few yards closer and knelt to the ground to get a better angle. This time the shaft flew true, hit the ring knocking it off its hook and freed the ferocious beast.

Blanchard smiled at the skill, shaking his head in disbelief. The outlaw disappeared into the thicket as fair goers screamed in terror and stampeded in all directions. The ursine monstrosity would have possibly posed no threat had it not been worked into a frenzy by the tormenting it had endured from the baiting. It didn't seem sure which direction it should go, lunging left and right in anxious confusion. It charged a few steps forward and swatted away one of the dogs whose growl transformed into a yelp. Next Edward swore he heard a whistle of sorts coming from the forest edge. Guards were closing in on the desperate creature and it was struck in the shoulder by an arrow. It howled in pain, swinging its head and paws with tortured fury. Suddenly, it twisted its gaze to the brush where Hood had vanished, fell to all fours, and bolted, the soldiers dashing after it.

*Well, I'll be buggered!* Edward thought in amazement. *That lad certs knows how to cause a distraction. But I must find him anon.* Having regained his breath, the deputy took off running in the direction the outlaw had gone.

* * *

WILL SCARLET WAS BEGINNING to feel hopeful. They were collecting the remainder of the treasure and so far had been able to get it all securely stowed in Tuck's wagon without incident. *Mayhap this will work after all,* he ventured to think.

"There," Gilbert declared as he handed Will the final bag. "That's the last of it." The lads exchanged glances with expectant glee while Gilbert pushed the iron sconce back into place. The pulpit slid into position, and everything appeared as it had before.

"I'll go first," Alan volunteered. "Then you," he said to Will who nodded. He stood inside the door and made a slow count to twenty before stepping through. Alan was halfway across the courtyard as Will spied left and right taking measure. There seemed to be more soldiers milling around than earlier. The whole troop was looking up toward the fairgrounds and Will thought he heard a loud commotion, but his heart was beating so hard and fast that he couldn't be sure. *Alright, this is it,* he thought and stepped out.

At the same time a warrior wearing a veteran's sash exited the side door of the keep and bumped into him. "Pardon me," Will said keeping his head down.

"Watch where you are going," he bellowed in a gruff tone. "Hey, what were you doing in the chapel?" A strong grip seized his upper arm and spun him around.

"Only praying, sir."

Emory's mouth dropped and his eyes widened in recognition. "I know you!" he declared jerking up Will's chin with his other hand. "You're Will Scarlet, the Sheriff's little spy!"

Instantly Will converted into flight or fight mode, only not being able to choose, initiated both. He stomped the top of the man-at-arms' foot with the heel of his boot, twisted out of his grasp, and started to run.

"Guards!" Emory bellowed. "To the chapel! They are here!"

A wide-eyed soldier spun around drawing his sword, but as he scanned the courtyard, he saw no intruders. "Where?" he snapped out as his gaze darted to his commander.

"That one," Emory said pointing to Will, "and more as well. They are wearing our own mail and colors, so suspect anyone you do not know personally."

Will had only taken a couple of steps, but his thoughts had been racing. *What am I going to do? Why am I running? Mum! I must get to the dungeon and rescue her. But... I can't leave the others behind! This is my doing. These extra guards would not be here had I not... no, I will not run away!*

In a flash the lean young man ripped his blade from its sheath and spun to show these enemies his mettle.

"Long live King Richard!" he shouted at the top of his lungs and charged the startled guard who was drawing his sword. The phrase had been selected as a verbal alarm if anyone was caught or found out during the robbery. Emory's man barely raised his steel in time to ward off the formidable strike, but Will bore down on him advancing with a balestra and a chop knocking the blade from his hands. The unprepared guard fled back into the castle shouting for more soldiers to lend aid. Will promptly scooped up the fallen arming sword without breaking his stride.

He raised his gaze to Little John, who had just exited the chapel leaving Emory between them. Emory drew his broadsword and took a careful sidestep toward the keep door, an adjustment that situated the outlaws to his left and right rather than in front of and behind him.

"So, Scarlet, you brought your friends to the party, did you?" The sturdy man-at-arms shot his eyes from one to the other. "I'll wager the little rat didn't tell you, did he?" A grin spread from between his whiskers as Emory employed the divide-and-conquer tactic.

Alan turned and froze, a confused expression on his face, but Little John pinned Will with an offended glare. Reaching for the arming sword dangling from his belt, he stormed, "What is he talking about? How does he know your name?"

Arthur, Much, Roger, Isaac, and Fawkes filed out behind Little John at the same moment that a dozen soldiers fell into line with Emory.

Will saw the flash of pleasure in the commander's wink when he said, "Because he's been telling the Sheriff all about your plans to steal from him and we are here to stop you!"

That instant, those words, the look on his best friend Alan's face, the fury erupting in Little John–that had been Will's worst nightmare, the only thing worse than watching his mother tortured and killed before his eyes. He had always known, from the night he had been told Nottingham had his mum in the dungeon and he better show up to meet with him or else; he had known that one or both of those fears would come to pass and there was nothing he could do to stop it. Guilt tore at his soul, but sorry would not save his friends; only his swords could do that.

"You treacherous bastard!" he yelled at Emory in rage and charged.

Will's rash act of heroism took Emory by surprise and had it not been for several of the soldiers rushing forward he would have been cut in half. Will fought wildly like a berserker, spinning and striking out of reflex and instinct. He thought he saw Sir Guy and Maid Marian out of the corner of his eye, but he had to focus all of his attention and emotion on taking out as many of their enemies as possible to buy time for his comrades, and hopefully save their lives in the process.

\* \* \*

ROBYN LIT through the forest edge, not straying too far from the crowd yet remaining just out of sight. She wanted the soldiers to chase her; as long as she had them occupied, her men had more time to get the ransom money out of Nottingham castle. The idea of freeing the bear to create a commotion had popped into her mind the minute she saw it there that morning; moreover, she favored saving it from needless torment. That is also why she whistled for the beast to follow her, since it clearly had no clue which direction to take.

Robyn stopped for a moment and tried to pull off more of the hair which Marian had so securely glued to her face. *I hope it isn't permanent,* she thought as she rubbed at it. Then she listened and discerned voices and tromping boots.

"I think he went this way," said an excited, medium pitched voice.

"No, I'm sure it is that way," contradicted a booming baritone.

Robyn grinned. *I hope things are going this well with the others.* Observant of her surroundings, her acute gaze came to rest on a rock a little larger than an apple. Like a cat, she took silent steps, scooped it up, and hurled it several dozen yards away.

"There!" shouted a third voice, and all the boot tromping thundered off after the stone. Robyn, however, began to weave her way back toward the fair grounds.

As she neared the flustered crowd, she noticed a blacksmith shop with a stable along the side of the road. *That will do well,* she thought. *I shall climb up in the loft and have a look around.* Slowly, and calmly she slipped through the barn door so as not to disturb the horses. One raised its head in anticipation, but lowered it in boredom once it had determined she was not bringing food.

The other swatted a fly with its tail. Surveying her surroundings, she spotted the two animals along with four other empty stalls, and a large haystack in one corner. She had just noticed the ladder when she heard a creak. Her eyes snapped toward the sound and grew wide as she froze in utter disbelief. Right in front of her stood the hulking figure of Deputy Edward Blanchard.

Stirred but not shaken, she straightened her shoulders and raised her chin high while deliberately drawing her father's crusader sword. "I have no quarrel with you, Deputy. Stand aside for I have no desire to kill you." Her breathing came fast, and she felt a lump in her throat; she had not wished a fight with Blanchard, but if she must, she would win–there was no other option.

Blanchard pulled a long broadsword with his left hand and smiled. Curious. It was not a wicked smile, or a 'Now I've got you' smile. It seemed... friendly.

Robyn was hesitant, but took up her stance with fortitude. Then he answered, "Hurry, Hood, for there is no time to waste. Your men have walked into a trap at the castle. Giffard kidnapped young Will Scarlet's mother and coerced him into revealing your plans. They need you now if it is not already too late."

Robyn stopped stock still no sooner than her sword met his. "Why are you telling me this?"

With his blade pressed against hers, he took a step closer and spoke in a near whisper. "Because I am Queen Eleanor's man," he divulged with honest slate-gray eyes confirming his words.

"Truly?" Robin's heart leapt along with her spirits. She was cautious, but wanted to believe him.

"On my oath," he swore and lowered his weapon. "It was I who listened in on a meeting and discovered the plot which was revealed to you. Make haste; the mission must not fail."

Robyn was flooded with conflicting emotions like so many trickling streams rushing downhill after a thunderstorm. "I knew there was a reason I liked you," she admitted in relief and started to sheathe her sword.

"Wait, please, one thing," he said soberly. "You must give me a wound, or else the Sheriff will fault me for letting you escape."

She swallowed and gave him an understanding nod, then marched right up to his imposing frame. Laying the edge of her sword against his thigh, she reached behind his neck and pulled his head down until their foreheads met.

"God bless you, Deputy Blanchard; God bless you." As she released him, she stepped back dragging her blade deep enough to draw a flow of blood, but not so deep to sever an artery. "Sorry about this." She cocked her fist and struck him with a powerful left cross, throwing her whole body into the swing.

He swayed a little, allowing his head to fall lax under the blow. "Impressive," he declared, "for such a pup as you! Now, go save your men and the King." Still reeling from the emotional impact of Blanchard's revelations, Robyn raced past him fast enough to leave a breeze in her wake, out the front door of the stable, and on toward Nottingham Castle

\* \* \*

FRIAR TUCK'S heart leapt into his throat when he saw the fight start. He couldn't make out their words, but it was apparent something had gone terribly wrong. Next came the hardest part of all, the inevitability he had most fervently prayed against. He stood with his feet planted and a sweaty hand itching for his sword.

Every instinct he possessed screamed at him to plunge into the fray, and with every fiber of his being he wished that he could; but he had taken an oath. On more than one occasion Robin had pulled him aside to reiterate the importance, the vital necessity that he carry out his role to the letter.

"Friar," he had said with a reassuring arm draped over his shoulders in a tone both impassioned and dangerous. "Yours is the most important part to play of all. Should our lads be found out, should a battle arise, you *must* stand firm and you must *not* join in."

"But Robin," he had argued, "that is nonsense! I am the most skilled swordsman of you all, I dare say one of the best in England, and you expect me to do nothing to defend our friends?"

"You have two duties, and two alone," he had reiterated. "You *must* make sure the silver gets to Queen Eleanor, no matter what. If Little John, or Will, or I am killed, or even if we all die, it matters not–only that the ransom goes to free our King. For if that sum does not get to Windsor, everything else was for naught. Therefore, you *must not* react as to reveal your true intentions. You are the friendly friar who has brought drink to the castle guard and that is all. You may be appalled by the fighting, or frightened, or retreat into prayer, but you cannot in any way let on that you are in league with the bandits. Do you understand?"

"Aye," he had said. The plan was sensible; what Robin said was wise and true, but that made it no easier to obey.

"Your second charge is every bit as imperative as the first–protect Maid Marian." He would never forget the feeling that shot through his body at the intensity in Robin's gaze. "Get the silver to the Queen and keep Marian safe. Nothing is as paramount as those two. Nothing else matters. Do you understand?" he'd asked a second time. The vibrations in the young leader's voice reverberated through his heart even now. He knew it was what he had to do; he had no idea it would be this hard. "Swear it, Friar; I know your shepherd's heart. You must give your oath, on the Sacred Head of our Lord Jesus."

"On my oath," he had promised. "I will see the treasure and the lady safely to Windsor."

He looked on now, feeling more helpless than ever before as Will cut into a troop with no regard for his own life. Little John, who was not comfortable with a sword, slammed a big fist into the closest guard's jaw, rendering him a crumpled heap in the dirt. But before his body hit the ground, John snatched the pole-ax from his hands. He tossed the blade aside and began to spin the new weapon like a quarter staff, a confident smile overtaking his face. He used it with skill and precision as he littered the ground with soldiers. To their credit, Much, Arthur, and the others seemed to be holding their own against the trained fighting men. Gilbert covered his comrades with his bow, trying to stay out of sword-strike distance.

Tuck swallowed and gripped the side of the mead cart to occupy his hands. "What is this?" shouted the gate guard who was taken aback by the sight of castle guards attacking each other, and he sprinted toward the skirmish. That gave David an opportunity to roll out from under the wagon and retrieve the sword hidden amongst the barrels.

"Take care, lad," Tuck ordered him in a hush. The youth flashed him a smile and dashed into the mix.

In the confusion, some of the Nottingham guard ended up engaging Sir Hugh Diggory's soldiers who had been sent to reinforce the castle, because they did not know who they were. Alan worked to steer the battle closer to the mead wagon so they could unload the last of the coins.

Once he was in reach, Alan used the cart as a bit of cover to stand behind while warding off the blows from his attacker. He performed a lunge strike forcing his opponent to step back, then ducked behind the back of the wagon having just enough time to drop the bag of loot. Then he sprang up and danced off leaving his foe to give chase.

Tuck lifted his hands and began to pray at full volume as he shuffled toward the discarded money sack. "Saints preserve us!" he cried, then bent over, picked up the silver, and seeing that nobody was watching him, stowed it away in one of the trick barrels.

Following Alan's lead, the others took turns repeating the tactic until the whole cache was safely under Friar Tuck's purview. Then, as if there was not enough chaos, Tuck heard frantic shouts and shrill screams as a stampede of spectators ran down the hill from the fairgrounds toward the castle. Some of them spilled though the gate until they noticed the raging combat. One man was sliced by a stray sword strike before the converging mob abruptly changed course to escape back out into the street. *What is that about?* the flabbergasted Friar wondered. *Pardon me, Lord, but what the hell is happening?*

As Tuck stood holding tight to the reins of the disconcerted cart horse, another squad of armed men clad in mail rushed past the frantic citizens into the castle yard. They halted, staring at what must have appeared like a clash between guards, as all the combatants were dressed alike. One looked at him and asked, "What is this? Which ones are the outlaws?"

He held his hands palms up. "I haven't a clue! I was minding my wagon when all of a sudden one of them shouted at another and they broke out into this chaotic brawl."

"You had better get to safety, Friar," the soldier said in a tone more resembling an order than a suggestion. "We ran down here chasing after that arch-bandit, Robin Hood. He is on the loose, and it is no telling what he will do."

Friar Tuck clutched the cross at his chest and raised his eyes toward the sky, praying, "Heaven help us!" Then he replied to the soldier, "As you say."

He loathed to leave his friends to wage battle without him but, in agonizing regret, he understood that he must. All the money had been secured and the longer he tarried, the greater the chance it would be discovered. To this point, the Sheriff didn't even know the fortune was missing. He led the sturdy gelding pulling the wagon to the gate where the newly arrived warriors awaited studying the situation before plunging in and killing one of their own by mistake.

"Take care, good protectors of Nottingham," he admonished them. "I pray no one dies this day." And he did.

It was with a heavy heart and extreme effort that he climbed onto the seat and drove away. He felt like he was leaving a part of himself behind those walls. Robin's words and the penetrating resonance in his youthful voice compelled him.

"The mission is what matters. Above all else, no matter what—get the silver and Marian to the Queen."

Given no other choice, Friar Tuck steeled his emotions and rumbled down the street to the designated place to meet 'Sister' Marian.

\* \* \*

As ROBYN DASHED out of the blacksmith's stable onto the street, she saw Tuck driving a heavy mead wagon away from the castle gate. *Yes!* She gleamed in triumph. *They must have succeeded!* But her joy swiftly melted into distress as she detected the sounds of battle. She slowed her pace, weaving through the confusion in the thoroughfare.

"We were attacked by a bear!" one woman shrieked.

"Soldiers were arresting the archery contestants," declared another.

"The castle guards have gone mad!" announced a commoner as he held a blood-soaked cloth to his forearm. "They are trying to kill each other and cut me in the process. Bloody crazed, I tell you!"

*Not what I wanted to hear,* she thought as she slipped unnoticed through the crowd. Upon seeing a group of four of the soldiers whom she had been leading on a grand chase standing just inside the gate, she decided to go around to the side and slip in there instead. She meandered through the energized populace who continued to add more amazing details to their stories with each retelling.

She snickered and had to cover her mouth when she overheard one woman say, "And then I saw Robin Hood himself, tall and rugged as a mountain, leap into the sky and vanish like a fog into thin air!"

Once around the corner and off the main street, the crowd thinned out to only a small trickle making their way to or from the Ye Olde Trip to Jerusalem tavern at the bottom of the hill. Notching her bow, she crept through a side entrance and took inventory of the situation.

A good dozen of the guards lay moaning or unconscious on the ground while a few others simply swung a sword at whoever was near them. Scanning the mayhem, she laid eyes on each of her men. David, Much, and Arthur each fought beside one of the refugee volunteers as to lend them support while Little John and Alan, both bloodied, aggressively battled back two soldiers each.

All of a sudden one of the Sheriff's men approached Alan from behind brandishing a long handled pike. She tried to take aim, but Alan stood in her trajectory. In an instant, the spear-wielding enemy was struck in the back, dropped his weapon, and fell to his knees. She raised her gaze beyond the fray and spotted Gilbert, bow still in hand from having made the shot.

Away from the others and surrounded by Emory and three guards, she witnessed Will battling with everything he had. Blood ran from his head and left arm, but he continued to swing two swords. He needed her help the most. She got several shots off, wounding a couple of Will's attackers before Emory spun about to spy where the arrows had originated.

"Get him!" he shouted pointing at Robyn. Two large assailants rushed forward with weapons raised. She pulled two arrows and fired them at once.

Fortuitously, the guards were close enough together that each received a hit, but only one was halted by the strike. The larger of the two simply ripped the arrow from his upper arm and kept advancing. She then tossed her bow over her shoulder, drew her sword, side-stepped the stampeding hulk, and cut a slice across his back as he passed her. She scarcely noticed his yelp of pain amid the din of clanking steel and shouts of intimidation. Forward motion propelled him into the castle wall and he finally stopped, leaning against the stones for support. Again she started toward Will in time to see Emory's sword penetrate deep into his gut.

"Will!" she screamed in anguish as she charged. Emory had just withdrawn his blade when she struck him from behind. It was a disarming and disabling blow, but not a killing one. He crumbled to one knee in shock and looked over his shoulder at her. In anger and grief, she kicked him in the face and he tumbled back into the dirt, the sword falling from his hand.

She met two other soldiers who had been engaged trying to kill her friend and wasted no time with fancy fencing. She feinted toward the one on her left, then spun to her right, at the last moment striking the man's sword arm with such power as to break the bone. He grasped his dangling hand as he ran away in pain. Before the other guard had even registered what had happened, Robyn kicked his knee with her left foot and heard the crack. Regaining her balance, she brought her sword down against him. He lifted his weapon in both hands to block as he was in no position to fight back balancing on his only remaining good leg. The ferocity of her strike on the flat of his blade was enough to break it just as it had broken his comrade's forearm. Left with no means to defend himself, he limped away.

After a quick glance showed that there we no other conscious foes near at the moment, Robyn dropped to her knees at her friend's side.

"Will." She spoke his name with such tender compassion as she clasped her left hand in his. She sheathed her sword and pressed her right hand to his wound in hopes to slow the massive crimson flow.

He groaned in pain as tears mingled with blood ran down his face. "I'm sorry, Robin, I'm so sorry!"

"Don't worry about that, Will. Blanchard told me the Sheriff had your mum; it isn't your fault. Sure, I wish you had told me—we could have rescued her."

"I was afraid," he answered and then coughed a red spray. "I didn't know what to do, Robin," he said then paused to let out a tormented cry with his eyes squeezed shut.

"I'm here, Will; we're going to get you out of here. Everything will be alright." Pain gripped her heart as she knew that wasn't true. This wound was too severe, and the blood poured out too fast. She wished with her whole soul that he could be saved. *If we take him to a surgeon*, she thought, but no. She had grown to love Will Scarlet like a brother. Why hadn't he just told her? She shook her head as tears started in her own eyes. "Just hang on."

"Marian," he said as color drained from his once rosy cheeks.

"What about her?" Robyn squeezed his hand when she saw his eyes try to close.

He coughed again and winced in pain before continuing. "You have to save her. Sir Guy. He was draggin' her to the chapel shouting about how he wasn't goin' to wait any longer, and she was goin' to be his one way or another."

"Bloody hell!" Robyn toughened her emotions with new resolve.

"Robin," Will said as he gripped her hand with his last ounce of strength. "I'm beyond forgiveness, I know, but please…" He tried to fix his eyes on hers. "Save me mum. Save Marian, then save me mum."

Robyn's heart melted at his plea. "Of course you are forgiven; you're my brother, remember? Now don't worry; I'll get your mother out, safe and sound, you hear me? I'll free her." A faint smile crossed his red lips as he struggled to take a breath. Then she cradled his cheeks with her hands soaked in his blood and kissed his forehead. "You be alive when I get back, you hear?"

His eyes closed, a look of serenity calming his battered features. "I love you."

"No farewells, Will Scarlet," she demanded, then added. "I love you, too."

Robyn gently released him, set her jaw, and took off toward the chapel at a dead run.

## CHAPTER 21

"I'm not so certain about this, Sir Guy," Bishop Albrec said hesitantly as he stood before Gisborne and Marian at the altar. He clung to his prayer book with a very uneasy expression. "The lady does not appear willing, milord."

"I am not willing at all!" Marian spewed while her captor held tight to the end of the rope secured around her wrists. "See how he has bound me and dragged me in here?" Her face flushed with the same indignation that sounded in her voice.

"Your Grace," Sir Guy explained innocently. "An arrangement has been made. The lady forgets herself. She is merely having second thoughts."

Robyn didn't have time to watch the whole sordid scene play out; she needed to get Marian, Will's mother, and her men out of there before the Sheriff arrived. No one had noticed her stealthy entrance, so the arrow seemed to fly from nowhere taking them all by surprise. It pinned the bishop's miter to the wall behind him as his mouth fell open in a gasp.

His eyes popped wide, and he dropped his book. Raising his hands and stumbling back, he cried, "Don't shoot; I am a man of the cloth!"

Sir Guy and Marian turned at once to spy Robyn approaching as she slung her bow over one shoulder. "I know exactly who you are," she retorted in a low dangerous tone.

Gisborne pressed in front of Marian and announced, "Maid Marian is mine, and you cannot have her! There is nothing here for you, Hood."

She cocked her head, staring at him with piercing eyes as she halted a few strides away. "Marian is neither yours nor mine, Gisborne. She is her own person with a right to choose for herself."

As Sir Guy started to go for his sword, Marian yanked the rope from his hands and scurried toward Robyn.

"Thank Heavens you are here!" she exclaimed. Robyn pulled a dagger from its sheath in the small of her back and efficiently sliced Marian's bindings with its honed blade. Marian threw her arms around Robyn in greeting and kissed her cheek.

Gisborne froze with his pudgy hand on the hilt of his sword, a thoroughly confused expression emerging on his face, while Albrec inched his way toward the side door.

"What is this?" Sir Guy asked in a tone that expressed his offense. "Maid Marian, assuredly you are not in league with this bandit!"

She started to reply, but Robyn broke in, preventing Marian from saying something that could come back to harm her. "That is none of your concern, Gisborne," she stated. Replacing the dagger and laying hold to her own sword, she took a step away from Marian and looked her in the eyes. "You need to get to safety; I'll teach this oaf a lesson in manners."

"I am not leaving without you," Marian declared, holding her ground.

Robyn rolled her eyes and sighed.

With indignant ire glaring in his typically dull expression, Sir Guy jerked a shiny, unmarked blade from its scabbard and shouted, "I shall be the one teaching you a lesson, you insolent cur!"

Marian took a step back as Robyn crossed swords with her older, heavier opponent.

After trading a few blows, Gisborne continued. "You may be fine with a bow, but I was a tournament champion with lance and sword. You are a fool to challenge me."

His words rang hollow as she out maneuvered him at every turn. Sweat poured from Gisborne's brow and his movements were labored. Scarcely a minute passed before Robyn disarmed him and knocked him to the floor where he landed with a dull thud.

"Don't kill him!" Marian's voice beseeched her. "He is not of much import."

Gazing down into Guy's face, Robyn saw a little boy who bragged to cover his insecurities and looked like he had just lost his last friend instead of the cruel, arrogant conspirator that she knew the adult to be. She placed one foot on either side of his girth, scooped up a fist full of his tunic and spoke in a low, ominous growl. "If you ever touch Maid Marian again, I will end you." Then she slammed his head back onto the pine lath in a way she was sure to get her point across with a lump and a roaring headache. For good measure, she picked up his sword and in a smooth, fluid motion, lodged it into the floorboards inches from his right ear.

Sprinting the short distance to where Marian stood, she took both of her hands and the two locked gazes. "Will is dying, and I must save his mother from the dungeon. You know what you have to do."

She saw the instant grief glisten in Marian's eyes at the news about her friend. She gave Robyn's hands a squeeze. "Yes. God be with you, and I will see you soon." They parted ways after the briefest of kisses, Marian toward the castle gate and Robyn into the keep.

She met no resistance inside the stronghold as all the guards were battling in the courtyard, but the foul jailer stood in her way upon descending into the bowels of the fortress. He only grunted and yanked out the two arrows she put in him as a discouragement. When he flexed the bulging biceps of his bare arms and sneered at her with a mouth half void of teeth, she became impatient and struck him with a wrought iron candle holder which did the trick. Replete with emotion, she released all the prisoners and led them out.

The attractive brunette, although glad to have been freed, permeated with dread for her son. She thought not about her own safety as she ran through the mayhem to fall on her knees beside his motionless body and weep. Robyn dodged swinging swords to get to Little John.

"We're leaving," she announced. "Come, I need you to carry Will."

Little John frowned at her and crashed the pike in his hands over his attacker's head. "He is a traitor! Do you know what he did?"

"I do," came her somber reply. "He tried to save his mum from the Sheriff the only way he knew how. Did he not fight bravely at your side this day?"

He cast his gaze toward where Will's body lay covered in blood with his grieving mother beside him. He sighed, a tinge of guilt clouding his eyes. "Giffard had his mother? Blazes, why didn't he just say so?" Little John jabbed the blunt end of his weapon into the gut of a guard who was approaching from the left. "Woe's sake, he got hisself killed." The big man shook his head.

"I'll cover you," she said as she armed her bow. Then she shouted, "Hey lads, time to go!"

Little John lifted Will's limp body into his arms as effortlessly as he would have a child while the woman followed close behind. Gilbert joined Robyn near the side gate where they both laid down arrows for their friends' escape. Concern rose in Robyn as she saw Arthur and Isaac on either side of Roger hauling him through the sea of castle guards. Once clear of the exit, they all turned and ran for the forest edge, scattering and disappearing like leaves in the wind.

* * *

Sheriff Giffard, accompanied by his personal bodyguards, strode down the dirt road toward Nottingham Castle. He had been in process of examining each of the archers when all hell had broken loose. Spectators began dashing about in sundry directions, frantically screaming when the great taunted bear broke free. Soldiers had been dispatched to kill it and restore order, but they had not returned. Deputy Blanchard was nowhere to be found and Godfrey had determined that none of these contestants was his arch-enemy.

While the Prince and other barons watched from their seats on the platform in anticipation, he had seen Sir Guy stomp away with a protesting Maid Marian and a baffled Bishop Albrec in tow. With the event now totally disrupted and no hope of being restored, he concluded he had best check on the castle.

*This has been a miserable failure,* he bemoaned, grinding his teeth. But if the forty-thousand marks was safe, they were no worse for the misadventure.

He stopped short at the main gate as he spied the grounds littered with wounded guards and confounded combatants. "Why swing your sword at me, Hugo!" shouted one. "We have served together for years." He batted his fellow's blade aside.

"Begging your pardon," he replied and blinked his eyes. "In your helm and mail, you look just like the bandit I fought a moment ago."

In a quick scan of the yard, Godfrey caught a glimpse of two bowmen at the side entrance letting loose a last arrow each before turning to dash out of sight. "After them!" he commanded in a booming voice. Abruptly, all the remaining guards stopped still and turned their heads toward the Sheriff.

"You fools!" he bellowed in fury. "Chase down those archers. One of them is Robin Hood!"

In an instant, they obeyed, and all who could walk spilled through the gate into the street.

"You men, come with me," Gifford instructed his cadre of personal guards, and they raced to the chapel. A maid peered out of a castle door and Godfrey barked at her. "Get help for these wounded, you feeble-minded wench!" Then he shoved open the chapel doors.

His procession followed him in but waited near the rear as he rushed to the dais, pulled the trigger sconce, and watched as the pulpit slid back.

"Sardin' shite, it can't be!" Panic seized his heart like a vice and he began to tremble.

"My lord," inquired a soldier. "Is something amiss?"

"No, no, all is well," he replied in haste then pushed the lever to close the secret hole. "Stand guard on this chapel and let no one enter," he demanded.

"Yes, sir!" The bodyguards snapped to attention as their lord passed them.

Dread consumed him as Godfrey ran into his office and locked the door, then leaned against it as he tried to breathe. It was like endeavoring to draw air through a wet blanket as his heartbeat pulsed through his whole body. *My life is over! Prince John will have my head for this–literally!* He reached inside himself with granite resolve to calm the terror and focus that energy in a more constructive direction. *If we can catch him and get it back before the Prince discovers it is missing...*

A knock rapped at his door. "Sheriff Giffard, are you there?" He recognized that deep voice.

Once more commanding self-control, Godfrey turned the latch. "Deputy," he replied as he let him in and then re-locked the office behind them. "Please tell me you caught that sardin' swine."

But the look of dismay on the deputy's face said it all. "'Twas he what released the bear and started the confusion. We were all chasing after him through the woods. I did catch up to him once and we fought. God's teeth, Sheriff!" Blanchard declared in total disbelief. "He is skilled with a sword! Who would have known it? But after wounding me the little miscreant ran off, and with my hurt leg," he motioned toward the obvious tear in his blood-soaked trousers, "I couldn't keep up. Even now the castle guard is in pursuit."

All previous horror that had built up in Godfrey's emotions turned to silent rage. Every bit in command of this familiar sensation, he stared at Blanchard with lethal onyx eyes. "You," he began in a deliberate manner. "You mean to tell me that you fought with Hood, but he bested you with a sword and got away?" Pulses of dangerous wrath radiated from the sheriff's body as he took a step toward his deputy. "You stand here telling me this instead of pursuing him to the ends of the earth?"

"Milord, I will go back out at once," he replied. "I assumed you would want to be informed…" he trailed off, lowering his head which sported a painful looking black eye.

"Do you know what that churl did, Blanchard? Do you?" The Sheriff's words cut like a razor. "He absconded with Prince John's fortune." He stepped into the deputy's personal space forcing him to take a step back in turn.

"We shall retrieve it at once!" he declared.

Godfrey tilted his head considering this assistant who had served him for years. How could he have been so incompetent? Then reality melted away and his world became surreal. Nothing mattered anymore; this was the end of all things.

"Prince John will kill me for this, but be assured, Blanchard—I will not go down alone." Instantly the knife from his belt was in his hand and he was plunging it into the heart of the burly man before him. Blanchard's eyes went wide in shock while thick, warm blood poured over Godfrey's hand. "You shall not fail me again."

When he withdrew the blade, the deputy crumpled to the floor in a pool of crimson.

Godfrey peered down at him in curiosity. "You don't look so big now," he sneered as the last life drained from the one who had been his second in command. He reached down and ripped a piece of cloth from Blanchard's tunic which he used to wipe his hand and blade. *No, I will not go down alone. I will take as many outlaw-lovers and useless baggage with me as I can.*

Another knock sounded at his door. "Godfrey, quick!" The frantic cry was from his friend Guy.

Godfrey sighed. "I cannot force Maid Marian to marry you and we have bigger problems." He opened the door a crack and peered out at Sir Guy through dead eyes.

"Let me in!" he insisted. "I have to tell you what happened." Godfrey stepped aside, closing the door as soon as Gisborne cleared the threshold. "Oh good heavens!" he exclaimed upon seeing the deputy's body on the floor.

"He shan't fail me again," he replied coldly. "Said Robin Hood beat him in a sword fight."

"Oh dear, my friend, I fear he told the truth," Gisborne said in dismay. "On my oath, he is a fine swordsman; he even bested me! He took off with Maid Marian," he avowed, then stopped to rub his chin. "But, Godfrey, I think she wanted to go with him. It appears that she knew him and mayhap has been working with him all along. Impossible as it seems, she may have been our spy."

"Bloody sardin' hell!" Godfrey ran a hand down his face as dread raised its vicious head. "They got the silver–all of it."

"God's teeth!" Sir Guy's visage turned as pale as a weathered tombstone.

"You should be safe; perhaps you could grovel and make a larger donation to His Highness. But I would suggest a hasty retreat to your estate until the Prince has time to calm down and regroup."

"What about you?" Gisborne asked in genuine concern.

"My only chance is to be off this island before he knows there is no money to hire the mercenaries." They nodded to one another and clasped hands. "Godspeed, old friend."

"Saints protect you, Godfrey."

\* \* \*

THE RENDEZVOUS at the outlaw camp that afternoon was bittersweet. It was difficult for anyone to feel joy over their success given the price they had paid. By the time Arthur and Isaac had carried Roger to safety, he had succumbed to his wounds. They laid him on a blanket next to Will. Alan hugged his friend's mother close as he struggled not to break down himself.

"Someone should say something," Much suggested. "Shouldn't someone say something?"

"Friar Tuck isn't here," David answered as he sat on a log breaking twigs.

Little John and Robyn exchanged glances and nodded to each other before Robyn stepped towards their peaceful bodies.

"We all loved Will Scarlet," she began. "He could be moody and he could be gay; he could be pig-headed, but he was, by God, the most loyal friend." She swallowed the lump in her throat. "It may appear that he betrayed our plans to the Sheriff, but think about it—was anyone guarding the chapel?" The lads looked from one to the other while she paused. "No. And did they arrest Friar Tuck and confiscate the wagon with which we planned to haul the loot? No. And do you know why?" They exchanged gazes again before turning their eyes to Robyn. "Because he didn't betray us at all. Gifford threw his innocent mother into the dungeon and threatened to kill her unless he revealed our plans. He told him something, alright; he told the Sheriff enough to make him believe he was telling the truth. But whatever he gave up, it wasn't our actual plan. Will's heart was as pure as a virgin snowfall. And when the fighting broke out, did he run away?" Little John and Alan dropped their chins. "No. He was in the thick of it, battling with all he had to protect his friends. Tell me, what would any of us have done in his place?" She passed her gaze over each of them. "Would not any of us do whatever was necessary to save our mothers?"

"He should have told us," Little John grumbled. "We could have helped. He didn't have to go it alone."

"I agree," Robyn said. "But Will felt a special burden of responsibility. When his father died, being the older son, the charge over his family fell to him. And what did he do? End up on the Sheriff's wanted list, branded an outlaw. He carried the guilt that he wasn't there to provide for his mother and brother. I think that is what drove him to feel the need to do this himself. But for whatever his shortcomings, Will Scarlet gave his very best to us today and every day."

She stopped to sniff and wipe her nose as she could no longer hold back the tide of her sorrow.

"Today we won, England won, because of the sacrifices of our friends. Most of you did not know Roger the farrier well, but I had the privilege to have known him. He was not one of us, but came to us after Giffard stole Loxley from its rightful heir and cut out his tongue for saying so much. He was a kind and gentle soul who loved his King." *And his mistress*, she thought. "Roger did not have to volunteer to go with us today, but rather he chose to, even though he was not trained to fight as the rest of us. He did that to stand up for every man, woman, and child that the Sheriff or Prince John or one of their lackeys had harmed. He wanted to count, to strike a blow against injustice. And, I think he believed that he had nothing to lose."

Robyn took a breath and looked down at their fallen comrades.

"They are heroes of England, and when we receive our pardons, I will ask King Richard that their names be cleared as well."

The others nodded and verbalized their agreement. Then Gilbert asked, "Where shall we lay them to rest?"

Will's mother spoke. "I will bury my son in the churchyard of St Mary of the Purification, in Blidworth. It is where his father and I were wed and where he was baptized as an infant. Will you help me?"

They all agreed wholeheartedly. Then Robyn said, "Roger should be buried at Loxley, for it was his home. But as long as Giffard holds the estate that cannot be."

"I think he would like to rest here in Sherwood," Isaac suggested. "He was at home here too."

Robyn nodded. Then Alan, wiping at his eyes, said, "Will was my very best friend. I'm not sure what to do without him." Will's mother, still at his side, hugged him while they both shed tears and mourned his loss.

\* \* \*

THAT EVENING, Robyn patrolled the perimeter of their camp by the light of a half-moon peering from behind mist-like clouds. She had feared the Sheriff or Prince John may have employed a skilled tracker to find them, but thus far it seemed that had not been the case.

Now she remained too stirred up by the success and losses of the day to sleep anyway. Then she heard the sound of tromping footsteps approaching and crouched behind a shrub readying her bow.

"Alan, what are you doing out here?" She rose, putting away her weapon upon recognizing him. He smelled of drink and still looked sad.

"Oh, Robin!" he exclaimed as he drew to a halt. "Don't be jumpin' out from behind a bush at a fellow. I had to go in to see my Liz."

Robyn gave him an incredulous stare and began to speak.

"Now, before you go chastisin' me," he said raising his palms as if in surrender, "it turns out 'twas a good thing I did."

"Alan, I can't believe you were foolish enough to go into town tonight of all times!"

"See, there you go chastisin' me without even lettin' me tell you what I heard," he replied with impatience in his tone.

"Very well; what is so important?" Although upset that he had taken such a risk when everyone was looking for them, she also understood. *I wish I could have spent the evening with my girl.*

"So, I went to the tavern to see Liz and whilst I was waitin' for her to get off work, these two soldiers were down in their cups and goin' on about what they did this afternoon. Sheriff Giffard was so mad we stole the Prince's money and that he didn't catch you, he had to take out his anger on someone. So, remember that village we rescued a couple months back, Millhaven?"

Robyn nodded, an uneasiness weaseling its way into her gut.

Alan swallowed, his eyes starting to mist up again. "He took a group of men and burned it to the ground. The ones that was drinkin' said he ordered them to kill every man, woman and child, and even the livestock. They said, 'Even the livestock?' And they were feelin' guilt and shame over following the orders, but askin' each other, 'What were we to do?'"

It felt like someone had struck a dagger into her chest and slashed her heart to shreds. Robyn bent over covering her face and praying that she would not be sick right then and there. She expelled a guttural utterance of pain that had no words.

"I'm sorry to tell ye, but I knew you'd want to know. And I'm sorry for leaving camp, but I just had to... I needed Liz. I needed to know she was safe. You understand?" Alan took a step closer and reached out to steady Robyn.

Her mouth went dry and her eyes moist, but she managed to hold herself together. *That's on me! He killed all those people because of me—what I did, because he couldn't find me. Oh God, what have I done?*

She was shaking when she sensed Allen's comforting hand on her shoulder. *No,* another voice spoke inside her head. *It was Godfrey Giffard; he killed them because he is a bloody ruthless bastard. He wants you to feel guilty and to use this to draw you out.*

"Robin, are you alright?" Alan asked with genuine concern.

She nodded and straightened, rising with a grave intensity in her eyes. She turned around the guilt and grief and focused all her emotions on her enemy. What they had done was right and necessary. That tax money was collected from people to free King Richard and the treacherous John had used it for his own purposes. It had to go to the Queen; there was simply no question about it. And Giffard? "First Will and Roger, and now the entire hamlet of Millhaven," she said in a dark, determined tone. "There is something I must do."

"I'll come with you," he volunteered.

"Nay; I need you to stay here and watch over the camp. Keep vigil in case any of us was followed and sound the alarm if soldiers arrive. This is personal."

Her eyes bore into his with such grim purpose that he withdrew his hand, concern showing in his expression. With a nod, she struck out past him into the woods. "Where are you goin'?"

Robyn half turned around to meet his gaze. "To do something I should have done a long time ago."

# CHAPTER 22

*Loxley Manor, very late that night*

Godfrey Giffard hastily packed a leather shoulder bag that rested on the bed of the lord's chamber of his recently acquired manor. The furnishings had all been selected and placed there by the late Earl, as Godfrey had not had time to remodel and make the space his own. Since his flight would be swift and secret, he would employ no wagon or retainers to carry trunks, so most of his belongings must be left behind. As he stuffed some documents into a side pocket, he considered, *I have relations in Normandy... but Richard rules there as well. Mayhap I shall go to the Danes. I have always admired the Danes.* He knew the expeditious way in which Prince John dealt with those who crossed or failed him; thus, he had set guards all about the house and grounds with instructions to watch for and intercept assassins who might come for him. Nonetheless, he hoped His Highness would not be so quick to think to look at Loxley estate.

He selected a few of his favorite tunics and stowed them into the main body of the satchel over the trousers he had already placed there. The money pouch on his belt bulged where he had crammed every coin he could fit into it. *Just room for a few personal items.* His eyes scanned the candle-lit chamber as he reflected, *I shall never see this place again; I shall never see England again.* But he consoled himself with the knowledge that his skill and experience would make opportunities for him in whichever land he settled. His finest steed was saddled and ready in the yard below, so as soon as he was finished packing—

*Whoosh, thunk!*

Alarmed, Godfrey's head snapped up and his mouth gaped at the arrow that jutted from the wall opposite the bedchamber window. He straightened and tore his broadsword from its scabbard as he spun to face the opening. There, shrouded in his forest green cloak and hood, stood the lean figure of his arch-nemeses, Robin Hood.

"Guards!" he bellowed as his obsidian eyes flashed with fury.

"Now, now, Sheriff," the interloper chided in a tone that was far too intrepid. "Certainly you do not think that I left anyone conscious downstairs who may interrupt our personal duel, do you?"

"So much for your sense of fair play, coming to murder me with an arrow to my back," he growled.

Hood's mouth turned in a humorless half-smile as he slung the bow over his shoulder and drew a battle-worn sword. "If I was aiming for you, be assured I would not have missed."

"Then you are a fool, for I shall cut you to ribbons!"

Filled with rage, Godfrey charged toward the window, but the nimble thief sidestepped him with ease. Then, in the open area of the large chamber, the combat began. Settling himself deep into his stance, Godfrey reined in his emotions. *Don't be thrown off by his wiles; you have a chance now! The fool came to you and now you can finish him and retrieve the silver.*

Calmed by renewed hope, he opened his assault with a thrust, but the archer parried his strikes and followed up with a perfectly executed riposte. As they danced about the room, matching blow for blow, the Sheriff became increasingly aware that his foe did possess skill after all.

The outlaw must have read the expression on his face, for he began to taunt him. "You were not expecting me to match you with a blade, were you? Didn't Blanchard and Gisborne tell you of our bouts?"

"Aye, but you are no match for me," he declared and launched into a feint designed to trick Hood into leaving him an opening to strike; unfortunately, the churl was not fooled. He then had to back-step while Hood advanced with seriously vicious slashes. He warded them off, but not without receiving a small cut on his sword arm. All at once it came to him. "You are being tutored by that bloody Friar Tuck!"

Another smile appeared on that youthful, beardless face. "Indeed. He is a most excellent teacher."

"Take heed, Hood–I am a better one!" he spat out and lunged forward drawing blood from the outlaw's upper arm, but was unable to deal a serious injury. "Now we are even; however, know that you shall not leave this room alive. I will enact my revenge!" A sharp exchange followed, causing sparks to fly from their steel.

Hood rounded, keeping his back away from walls. Godfrey noticed a change in his attacker's expression at his words. It darkened menacingly. "You should not have killed the innocent people of Millhaven. Their blood has cried out to God Almighty, and I am come on their behalf, as well as for my friends who died in Nottingham this day, and for every citizen you wrongfully imprisoned, banished, or executed. Your time is at an end."

"No one is innocent," he spat with disdain.

"Least of all you!" The series of blows knocked Godfrey back, but he parried them nonetheless.

"Do not imagine yourself to be my better," he snarled. "You are nothing! I killed my own deputy for failing to catch you, so do not think you will escape my wrath." He saw the surprise–no the shock–that registered in the outlaw's face and took that opportunity to move in with a backhanded slice. The scoundrel had been taken aback by his declaration, yet still managed to turn away from his strike and counter attack with his own. *How is it that this leggy trifle, known for his bow, can hold his own with a sword like this?*

Amid careful footwork, Hood retorted in a disgusted tone, "You murdered your own deputy?"

"He failed me too many times; no one does that and lives. What is it to you?" Hood shook his head and pinned him with piercing chestnut eyes. *Brown eyes... I've never been near enough to see them before. I shall be the man to close them forever!*

"*You* have failed the people of Nottinghamshire and your King for the last time," came his biting words. Next the young brigand took a bizarre action; he opened the large wardrobe affixed to the wall behind him, stepped in, and closed the doors.

For an instant the Sheriff simply stood in confusion, baffled by the idiocy. Upon abandoning the search for reason, he plunged his blade into the oak paneled doors several times. There was no cry of pain, and on the last thrust his broadsword became wedged in the wood. He had to brace his boot against the wardrobe and use both hands to dislodge it. Just as he was about to open the cabinet and examine the body, he experienced a tingling sensation and the distinct feeling that someone was behind him. Spinning around, his eyes went as round as saucers to see Hood standing there.

He quickly raised his blade, but was too stunned to think of a single strategic play.

The figure before him lowered the hood with his left hand while keeping his sword steady and balanced in front of him. "You still don't know who I am, do you?"

Mystified, Godfrey titled his head and tried to recall where he might have seen this fellow before. "Bollocks! You are the outlaw Robin Hood," he snorted.

"Am I now?" There was a certain lilt in that tenor voice. Had he heard it before? Mayhap, but where? "And if I am the outlaw Robin Hood," he mused as he applied a beat with his sword, a crusader sword? Godfrey noticed the distinctive cross on the hilt for the first time. "It is only because that is who you made me to become, when you callously stole my property out from under me as I grieved my father and brother's deaths."

Godfrey parried Hood's strikes, but was too deep in contemplation to charge forward. He wrinkled his brow. "I have confiscated many properties from those who could not pay their taxes or who otherwise shirked their duties. Why should I remember you?"

Hood toyed with him, belaboring the point. "How do you think I walked into the wardrobe and yet appeared right behind you? How did I find my way to that window? Do I not know every secret passage, every inch of the house I lived in all my life, the house my father built, the house from which *you* ejected me?"

Color drained from his face as he stared wide-eyed in disbelief at the person before him.

In that moment he froze, and Robyn pressed her advantage with several powerful blows which backed him up against the heavy oak wardrobe and a stone wall.

"No, that can't be," he stammered, panic rising up from his belly into his chest. "That is impossible!"

"Why?" She drove her blade against his pinning him as she closed in near enough for him to smell her, to feel her breath on his face. "Because you could never be bested by a woman?"

At first there was a sharp pain, but it was immediately overshadowed by an immense pressure against his chest. The sensation was unbearable and he couldn't breathe. His wide eyes lowered to see the hilt of a dagger protruding from his rib cage. *Just like Blanchard*, was his first thought. *Is this what he felt?*

Godfrey was overwhelmed by a terrible dread, a horror he could not escape. He had sent many a person to their grave without a care, but he had never stopped to consider what that end held for him. *Am I to spend an eternity in hell, or will I simply cease to be?* Truly, he had donated money to the church… when it suited him to do so. And he had been baptized… as an infant. He partook in Holy Communion… on the rare occasion he had attended mass. Was that enough? What would become of him now? He hadn't even produced children to live through. Never in his thirty-two years on this earth had he ever been more terrified!

He lifted his eyes to Robyn's and tried to speak, but there was no air behind any words he may attempt to form. In her eyes he didn't see pleasure, only the steel of grim resolve. Now he was feeling cold, and the pain still burned in his chest, the pressure weighing like a massive stone. His heart seized and his frame shook without his ability to control it. He was sure he felt fingers of fire racing up his body from his feet to his thighs through his girth into his chest and over his head. Then the blade was withdrawn, his lifeblood gushed forth like water through a broken dam, and he dropped to the floor, never to draw breath in this earthly realm again.

* * *

Windsor Castle, *November 23*

Queen Eleanor sat in an elegant cushioned chair by the hearth in her chamber pushing colored threads through cloth with a fine needle. She had never been the kind to sit about engaged in embroidery as a primary pastime; however, something about the repetitive, rhythmic motion calmed her nerves at present. Asides, she was adorning a surcoat for Richard to wear on their voyage home and that fed her hope.

Anticipation flashed through her when she heard the rap at her door. "Pardon me, Your Highness," came George's hesitant voice.

"The door is unlocked," she replied, reluctant to disturb her work should his inquiry prove to be nothing more than mundane castle business.

The neatly dressed delicate man opened the door and peered in. "There are a friar and a nun here to see you. I told them to go away, that you could not be disturbed, but the nun is a most frustrating woman."

Eleanor stopped sewing and gave him her full attention. "What do they want?"

"She says that she is Maid Marian and that you are expecting her. She became infuriatingly insistent when I tried to put her off."

Leaping up from her seat with excitement shining in her eyes, she proclaimed, "Show them into the hall at once! I shall join them straightaway."

"As you wish, Your Highness." George shrugged and proceeded to comply.

Eleanor put her needlepoint aside and tried to push down the butterflies fluttering in her stomach. *She is here! But does she bring the silver?* She took a deep breath and struggled to maintain an ordinary pace as her legs wished her to run to meet them. They all arrived in the Great Hall concurrently. Marian fell into a deep curtsey and the Friar bowed as Eleanor strode briskly towards them.

She grabbed the maiden's hands in hers and probed expectantly, "Do you have it?"

Marian answered with a broad smile, "Yes, Your Grace; we have it all."

Joy flooded her soul and certainly spilled out into the room, enough to drown anyone in their presence. "Oh, child, you make me giddy!" Throwing formality to the wind, Eleanor embraced Marian with the love of a grandmother. "Where is it now? Tell me all."

"Friar Tuck," she said motioning to the rotund clean shaven man beside her, "has it stowed in his mead wagon. Those outside insisted we take it straight to the castle storehouses as that is where supplies ought to go."

"George!" Her voice was loud and strong and her servant soon appeared. "See to it at once that guards are dispatched to the storehouses. No one is to touch that mead wagon until I arrive to inspect it in person. Is that clear?"

Despite the baffled look on his face, he affirmed her command. "Yes, Your Highness. Right away," and he strode off to carry out the order.

Marian recounted the adventure as the three of them walked across castle grounds to the storehouses to inspect the wagon and its valuable contents. The Queen then sent George on another errand to take a carriage to London and bring back the court treasurer, Bishop Richard Fitz-Neal. Then they would began making arrangements for the voyage.

With the doors locked and only a handful of highly trusted aids about, Friar Tuck opened one of the barrels to reveal the treasure inside. Eleanor's face glowed as she brushed a hand over one of the sacks bulging with coins.

"At last," she purred. "I will wish to thank Robin Hood personally once Richard is back safe and sound. I am forever in debt to you all." Her eyes passed from Marian to Tuck.

"Your Highness, if you insist on making this journey yourself, please allow me the privilege of attending you," Marian offered.

Eleanor turned soft eyes to her and placed a hand over the young maid's. "I would be pleased to have your company you know; there are others to wait on me. I need you to do something of much greater import. Seek out all the nobles in the north who are still loyal to the King and secure their oaths to join him on the battlefield should it become necessary. You are well known and well respected; when the King's goddaughter arrives at their door to demand their loyalty, they shall give it."

"Yes, Your Highness," she agreed, bowing her head. "I will gather our supporters so that all will be ready when our beloved King once again steps his foot on English soil."

Eleanor's eyes danced, and the glow continued to shine on an almost youthful appearance. "At last! My baby and your father—they are coming home!"

\* \* \*

S<small>HERWOOD</small> F<small>OREST</small>, *one week later*

C<small>HARLES</small>, Christina and the other youngsters gathered around Alan A Dale.

"Do the Cuckoo Song!" they begged. They sat under a crude open-sided tent near the fire that had been strung up to ward off some of the rain that fell soft on that cold December morning.

Alan strummed a few bars on his mandolin then stopped and passed his gaze over all of them. "You have to sing your parts, like I taught you, remember? Or it won't be right."

They nodded with eager expressions.

"We know our parts," Charles declared with confidence. Christina sat cozily between him and Alan with joy beaming on her face.

Robyn, who sat across from the spectacle, her back pressed up to Grandma Oak, was pleased to see her so happy and carefree. With no word yet from Marian or Tuck, Robyn could not afford that luxury.

"Alright, here we go then," Alan said and repeated his opening chords. "Summer is a comin' in, loud sing cuckoo," and the children joined in the round by repeating the phrases after him.

As the music layered phrase over phrase, something stirred in Robyn's belly. She snapped to high alert and pushed up to her feet. There was a noise in the distance amid the sound of gentle drops on wet leaves, and she caught sight of two figures a far off. The feeling swirling in her stomach leapt into her heart and she ran, holding nothing back, jumping downed branches and dodging trees until she scooped Marian up in her arms and whirled her around. Bursting with excitement, she set her lover on her feet and stepped back to gaze on her.

"Seeing you fills me with joy too!" Marian beamed. "All is well. Queen Eleanor and her escort will be leaving shortly with ransom and hostages to secure the King's release. We did it!"

Robyn tugged her into one more embrace, hugging her as though she would never again let go. There was so much she wanted to say, but no words could she manage through the lump in her throat. When she pulled back once more, she noticed the Friar standing beside them awkwardly observing a woodpecker drilling a hole in a rotting log.

"Friar Tuck, Maid Marian, welcome home," Robyn finally mustered. "Come, dry yourselves by the fire. Alan is entertaining us with cheerful songs."

"Is that onion soup I smell?" Tuck asked and charged forth.

Robyn lingered with Marian who had her cloak's hood up against the cold drizzle. Not certain how Marian would take the news, she decided to go ahead and say it. "I killed the Sheriff." Breathless, she waited for the response, hoping it would not be too damning.

But Marian just shrugged. "Somebody had to," she replied matter-of-factly.

Stunned, Robyn gaped at her wide-eyed.

"He was a vicious little man with visions of grandeur who, among other things, engaged in a plot against King Richard. As I see it, he got what he deserved." Then she took Robyn's arm to be escorted to camp. As they began to walk, she added, "But I'll wager you didn't simply murder him; it is not your style."

"No," Robyn confirmed. "We fought and, though he was likely the better swordsman, I had several distinct advantages."

"You revealed your identity to him," she guessed.

"Indeed I did," Robyn declared emphatically. "I wanted him to know who had beaten him." Then taking on a softer tone, she asked, "Are you familiar with a hamlet near Sherwood called Millhaven?"

"We often send our wheat there to be ground," she said and gave Robyn a curious glance.

"Then I fear you shall need to find a new mill; Giffard destroyed the village and killed everyone in it. That was the last straw," she explained.

Grief clouded Marian's face, and her grip tightened on Robyn's arm to steady herself; but it was fury that flashed behind her eyes. "Your action was just, my sweetling," she stated resolutely, and they were welcomed by a warm fire and a circle of smiling faces.

\* \* \*

LATER THAT NIGHT when the two of them were alone in Robyn's tent, she ventured to ask, "Will you go back to your home on the morrow?"

Marian fussed with the straw pile and blankets attempting to arrange a more comfortable bed. "Yes, but I shan't be there long. Queen Eleanor has sent me on a mission."

"Another one?" Robyn sighed and sat on a crate to pull off her boots.

Marian glanced over at her. "You should have said you were in need of new stockings," she mentioned upon seeing toes and heel poking through the expanse of holes. "I am off to rally the northern nobles who are loyal to the King. She believes, rightly so methinks, that Prince John may yet attempt a rebellion."

"Surely you will not be out alone!" Robyn exclaimed jumping to her feet.

"No, silly goose!" Marian reached to take her hand and guide her down to the bed. "I shall take my little brother, Richard. It will be good for him to prepare for when he is Lord FitzWalter. Do not fear; we shall retain an armed escort. And, while Anna is not fit enough for the rigors of this journey, I'll bring her daughter, Juliana, as my handmaiden. Mother would never allow me to travel with a troop of men without a female attendant."

Robyn thought about her own mother for the first time in a long while. *I wonder what she would think of me now, pretending to be a boy, living in the woods with outlaws, killing the Sheriff... not the refined lady at court she must have dreamed I'd be.*

Marian apparently noticed the faraway look in Robyn's eyes. "What are you pondering?"

Robyn lay beside her and pulled the blankets up. "When I was a little girl, I used to trifle with swords and go on hunts with Thomas, but never in my wildest dreams did I imagine how my life would play out."

"Regrets?"

Robyn held Marian close and kissed her. "Other than being the sole survivor of my family, not a single one. And, by the by, happy birthday." She retrieved a leather-bound volume from a small box by the bed and handed it to Marian. "I picked it up off a merchant a couple of months ago and thought of you. Sorry, to give you stolen merchandise as a gift, but-"

"Oh, Robyn!" she gushed with enthusiasm. "*Chanson d'Antioche*, the epic poem by Richard the Pilgrim, and it looks to be an original edition in French–I love it!" She beamed at Robyn with dreamy eyes. "And, I love you."

\* \* \*

THE NEXT MORNING found the forest blanked in white with a soft snow still wafting through the bare branches. After Marian's departure, Robyn spent a few hours lulling about the campfire acting as if there was nothing to do but wait until King Richard returned. She knew her people needed tending to, but surely Little John and Gilbert do that.

There was an uneasiness in her spirit, and while the others were merry with anticipation of Christmas, the arrival of the King, and the rewards that would follow, she brooded. She also had sense enough to know that was bad for her. So she forced herself to get up and go see Friar Tuck.

She found him clearing snow from the top of his tent so that it would not collapse. "Good morrow," she said.

"Humph!" he barked. "Is it now?" He gave the tie rope a secure tug and turned toward her breathing heavy from his labor. "Asides being past noon, 'tis a might cold and damp for my tastes. I reason a nice, strong ale is in order."

"Gramercy, but none for me. I am here to... I want you to hear my confession."

"Oh." Tuck was a bit surprised as no one had called upon him for that priestly function in quite some time. "Well, now, come inside and take a seat then. Considering the circumstances, we shall make this an informal sacrament; nevertheless, God sees and hears all, so it will count."

Robyn sat beside the Friar on a bench that he, being a bit of a carpenter, had made for himself. After making the sign of the cross, she said, "In the name of the Father, Son and Holy Spirit, it has been..." She stopped to consider. "Eight or nine months since my last confession." She clasped her hands in her lap and looked down at them. "I harbor secrets."

"I expect most people do," Tuck replied benignly.

"Aye, but I am not exactly who I have led you to believe I am."

Tuck smiled and patted her knee. "We know that," he said in a tranquil timbre. Robyn felt a flicker of panic and her heartbeat began to race, but Tuck continued straightforwardly. "Gilbert and I have spoken of it. You are far too skilled, too well educated and too easy with command to be a simple street urchin. But we care not what noble house you ran away or were expelled from, and we care not why. We are simply glad that you found your way to us."

Robyn's nerves relaxed and, satisfied with his explanation, nodded her head. "Thank you, but that is not the main sin that burdens me. I killed the Sheriff."

Tuck's first reaction was of unmasked joy, which he quickly reined in knowing that it did not suit the occasion. "Congratu–uh, I mean, by what manner?" he asked trying to tamp down the exuberance that wanted to burst forth at the news. "Did you put an arrow in him as he slept?"

Robyn's head popped up with a scowl. "Certainly not! I fought him."

"With a sword?" Tuck's eyes widened and he could no longer hide the pride and delight that shone in them.

"Yes, well, a dagger actually, but we crossed swords."

"By God's teeth, Robin! You defeated Godfrey Giffard in a duel? That is amazing!"

Exasperation in her voice, Robyn tried to return Tuck's attention to the sacrament of penance. "I am not bragging, but rather seeking absolution."

Tuck shook his head with a smile. "See here, lad," he explained in a fatherly tone. "The church does not consider killing another in a fair fight to be a sin at all. Trial by combat has long been recognized as a way, in fact, to prove guilt or innocence, for surely God will grant victory to the one whose cause is just."

"You don't understand." She balled her hands into fists of frustration. "It isn't that I killed him that is the sin; it is that I wanted to. I went there with intent."

"If wanting the merciless bastard dead is a sin, then I'm in need of absolution as well." The Friar let his enthusiasm fade. "Have you never killed a man before?"

Robyn's head fell forward again, and she gave it a gentle shake. "I don't know. I've injured men paid to fight in battle, and whether or not they later contracted a fever or succumbed to their wounds, I know not; but I did not see them die, nor did I have any desire to kill them. But it was different with the Sheriff." Her gaze was fixed on the ground as she took a deep breath and continued. "You know by now that Will Scarlet and Roger the farrier were slain at the castle. It was a risk they undertook and a fair fight; I did not blame the Sheriff except for his foul action of throwing Will's mum into the dungeon to force him into an impossible situation. But it didn't end there. In his wrath, he slaughtered an entire village, and murdered his own deputy as well!"

Feeling the ire well up in her again, she raised her gaze to spot the righteous rage in her confessor's eyes at the news.

"He killed them because of me, and Will died because of me, so maybe there was some of that guilt in the mix, but did you know that Deputy Blanchard was actually working with us? Turns out he was Queen Eleanor's spy in Nottingham. He-" She paused thinking back to their meeting in the stable. "He warned me that the lads had been compromised and needed my help. It was he who sent the details about Prince John's plot and the tax money." When Tuck patted her shoulder, she continued. "It was too much, just too much, after everything else. So, I went to Loxley manor, where I knew he would be packing to flee the country. I could have waited and let the Prince's assassins catch up to him, but no. I planned to engage him in a duel and kill him."

"Still, it was a fight, and he is an excellent swordsman. He could have just as easily killed you instead. Intent or not, 'twas not murder. And Robin, get that self-blame out of your heart right this instant; any horrible crime Giffard committed was his own doing, not yours. You cannot take responsibility for everything that happens in this world."

She nodded, lowering her head once more. "I know. But I did bear a secret weapon to use against him."

Tuck declared, "And do you think he didn't keep several knives stowed away in his boot, up his sleeve, on his belt? I have never known the Sheriff to fight fair. But if your conscience is not clear over this, I will prescribe a penance for you to perform so that you can get past it."

"Not a dozen Hail Mary's and Our Fathers," she spouted back as she straightened and pinned him with commanding scrutiny. "He may have been an evil man who deserved to die, but I took it upon myself to become that instrument. I set out to kill him, knowing beyond any shadow of doubt that I would succeed. It may not be murder in the eyes of the law or the church, but my heart is heavy. Strip it all away, and I killed him because I wanted to, because I somehow thought I had a right to. But in truth, I am no killer, and it weighs on me."

Tuck nodded. "The Lord knows your heart, Robin, better than you do yourself. What you need is time spent with God to sort things through. While you have been wallowing in your melancholy, your people have had no meat."

His words struck a chord that tore at her; she had not even considered that!

"Therefore, here is your penance: proceed into the forest and fast for the rest of the day and night. Pray and seek God's face, that He may give you the answers you seek. Then, with the first light of morning, go on a hunt and bring back a large buck that the camp can eat heartily." Then he raised both hands and proclaimed, "May our Lord Jesus Christ absolve you; and by His authority I absolve you from every bond and interdict, so far as my power allows and your needs require." Making the sign of the cross he concluded, "Thereupon, I absolve you from your sins in the name of the Father, and of the Son, and of the Holy Spirit. Amen."

"Amen," she repeated. "Thank you." She rose and started for the flap over the opening, then turned back to him. "Do you honestly believe my action was just?"

Tuck rose and wobbled over to her. "Child, what I believe doesn't really matter, does it? It is what you believe that counts. Do as I have prescribed and you shall receive your absolution."

\* \* \*

WEARING gloves and with a blanket wrapped around her for extra warmth, Robyn walked through the forest over new-fallen snow searching her heart and asking God for guidance. Every once in a while, a cold gust would chill her to the bone, but she only welcomed it as punishment for her sins. Somewhere in the night, huddled in a small thicket near the stream, she fell asleep with hunger churning in her belly.

She woke as light began to emerge amid the shadows. Freezing rain fell, the little droplets of ice plopping from twigs to create tiny divots in the carpet of snow. Robyn was so cold that she didn't want to move, but this was the time of the morning best for a hunt, when she knew the deer would go to the brook for a drink. She was discouraged at having experienced no revelations, no profound discoveries, and no lifting of her burden. In fact, as she readied her bow and arrows, she felt an added layer of guilt. *I was so focused on myself that I failed to care properly for those under my charge. That is simply unacceptable!*

After rubbing her clothing in musk oil to hide her scent, she checked the wind. The air was completely still, save from the slow, steady drip of ice. Her footsteps were silent in the snow and the dawn was as quiet as she could remember. Her eyes scanned the banks of the stream as she crept slowly toward a crossing point where she often observed deer tracks. There she stopped and pressed herself against a tall ash in a spot with a clear view; she did not need to wait long. Awe and wonder overwhelmed Robyn when she saw the majestic smoky stag stride out of the grove. She counted 16 points crowning his regal head as he scoped out his surroundings before bowing to take a drink. Great in stature, with gray and mist markings, she concluded he was the most beautiful animal she had ever seen.

She started to raise her weapon, but hesitated. *How can I kill this magnificent stag? Is he not God's creation, too? But the camp hungers; they need meat. Surely another deer not so grand as this one will come along.* Conflicting emotions began to war within her over what to do. She aimed her bow determinately, but stayed the arrow a moment longer. A voice coming from deep within prodded her thoughts. *You show more compassion for this deer than you did for the Sheriff.*

She stiffened her jaw and rebuked that notion. *The stag has no guile or evil in it; it has done no wrong, harmed no one, while Giffard killed, stole, lied, and conspired of treason. It does not deserve to die, but he did.*

A strong feeling emerged from deep in her core as another voice whispered to her mind. *Was not my son beautiful and had he done any wrong? And yet, it was necessary for him to be sacrificed so that many may live.*

Two words branded her heart in that instant: duty and sacrifice. She thought she had known what they meant. Hadn't she done her duty to manage the manor and oversee the well-being of the serfs while her father and brother were away in the Holy Land? Hadn't she known sacrifice to have lost every member of her family? And yet, in that very moment those words became real to her as if for the very first time.

Duty and sacrifice. Christ's duty had been to fulfill the will of the Father, and He had been sacrificed to that end. To uphold justice was her duty, and the sacrifice had been her own innocence. Those under her authority, under her care were hungry and depended on her even more now that Will was no longer with them. She was the group's best hunter, and the task was more difficult in winter. But to kill this exquisite creature...

The imperial stag lifted his head from the brook licking the drops that rolled from his chin. Then he stared right at her. Perhaps it was Robyn's imagination, but she felt such a deep connection to him. She was sure he saw her; yet he did not bolt away. It was as if he knew his place in the circle of life, the purpose for which he had been born, and now that he had lived many years and fathered many fawns, he did not shy from it. Duty and sacrifice.

With tears streaming down her face, Robyn let loose the shaft and it flew true. In that moment the burden of guilt she carried fell aside like a discarded garment, and she wept.

* * *

A SHORT WHILE LATER, Robyn struggled to drag the tremendous deer weighing more than herself up the bank. She had tried to lift it onto her shoulders, but simply did not possess the strength. Now, having fought cold, hunger and a mighty inner battle, she contended against her own physical limitations. She slipped on an icy patch in the snow and hit the ground beside the body of the stag wishing she could return to her childhood, back to a time before she knew anything of death.

And then she heard a voice–a real voice, booming toward her.

"Robyn, do you need a hand?" Little John reached down and plucked her up like one would a child, a warm smile on his broad face. It was a most welcome sight! "What a giant you have bagged!" He roared. "And while it would be entertaining to watch you push, pull, and crawl your way back to camp with it, why don't I just do what I do best?" He winked at her and tossed the deer over his shoulders.

"Praise all the saints, the Holy Mother and Christ Jesus himself!" she declared. Her friend had lifted her spirits as well as her body. She didn't have to go it alone, and that was another blessing. "Your best is not in the strength of your arm, but in the strength of your heart. Gramercy, my friend."

Little John smiled as they headed through the crystalline forest. "You are a wonderful hunter, Robyn, so I figured if Tuck said shoot us a buck at dawn, you'd have done so. I also figured, being the wee, slight thing that you are, you'd need help to carry it."

Her eyes lit as she returned his smile. "I am glad you are so good at figuring!"

## CHAPTER 23

*Where the English Channel meets the North Sea, December 25, 1193*

The indomitable seventy-one-year old Queen Eleanor, wrapped in a pristine white woolen cloak and hood, stepped outside the aft cabin of the cog to greet the day. The storm had subsided as suddenly as it had arisen and the sea that churned and roared just moments before was now at peace. Shining fingers of sunlight pierced the clouds to touch wet droplets that clung to the ship's rigging, causing them to sparkle like diamonds.

*The angels have given us lights for Christmas,* she thought with an appreciative smile.

Eleanor had departed England with an impressive retinue and large escort after appointing Archbishop Hubert Walter Chief Justiciar as per Richard's instructions, making him the indisputable ruler of the country in her absence or until the King should return. They joined with ships from the ports of Dunwich, Ipswich and Orford which carried the assembled noble hostages, and now the substantial flotilla sailed for the heart of the Holy Roman Empire, to a city where her heart waited to be released. Having made all the preparations, they had set forth only days ago as soon as word returned from Henry agreeing to release her son on January seventh, once he had inspected and approved the ransom.

Naturally, she insisted upon riding on board the ship carrying the 100,000 marks of silver in its hold. It was a sturdy vessel, she had determined: a flat bottomed cog with its oak construction of lapstrake planking and single mast high against the sky. She watched as deckhands unfurled the big square sail adorned in four segments of red and yellow stripes, rampant lions, and crusader crosses. She had been impressed by the innovative rear-mounted rudder and its superior ability to steer the vessel. The larger castle-like tower built into the stern (which usually served as the captain's quarters) and the smaller one in the bow added secure spaces topside while the crew berths and cargo below were accessible through a deck hatch.

Upon seeing her, the captain rushed over with concern etched on his leathery, bearded face. "Have a care, Your Highness," he warned as he extended an arm for her to take. "The wood is slippery still."

She raised her chin and breathed deep of the clean, salty air. "Gramercy, Captain," she replied with a pleasant nod acknowledging his gallantry. Two young maids-in-waiting spilled out of the cabin to assume their flanking positions on either side of the Queen. "But I think we have it covered. How much farther to Cologne?"

"We should reach the Rhine in a few days and proceed up river," he explained with a humble bow. "Perhaps a week more, depending on the weather."

"Bishop Adolf von Berg will be joining us there," she mentioned. "Please arrange suitable quarters for His Grace."

"Yes, Your Highness." After another bow, the captain went back about his business, calling to a crewman, "See that the rigging is tight there, lad!"

Escorted by her attendants who fussed over her far too much, the Queen set out for a much needed walk to get her blood pumping. She had always promoted the notion of morning exercise. Beyond that, her mind raced. *Why did that damned Frederick Barbarossa have to go and get himself killed in the first place?* she pondered. *This is really all his fault!*

As she gazed out over the expanse of sea, Eleanor thought about the powerful German warrior king who'd set out together with Richard and Phillip II of France, answering the Pope's call for a third crusade to recapture the Holy Land from the Saracens led by Saladin. Apart from failing to secure Jerusalem itself, the venture had been generally successful, liberating large portions of the region and reducing Saladin's power. Perhaps if Frederick had not been so impetuous and actually lived to reach Jerusalem, the outcome would have been different... and Richard would never have ended up in his current predicament.

She had heard various versions of the story, each with a different slant, as to how and why he drowned crossing the Saleph River when there was a perfectly good bridge. Frederick's massive army, under his bold and cunning leadership, had just won a major victory over the Turks in the Battle of Iconium and pushed into Armenia.

Saladin must have been worried with three kings' armies converging on him from diverse directions, but alas. Some said he was too impatient to wait while the army crossed the bridge and forged ahead on horseback through the deep. Others said he was so hot and tired from battle and the journey that he simply wanted to cool off in the water while a few claimed he failed to forge the waterway successfully because he suffered a heart attack.

Eleanor shook her head and lowered her gaze. In truth it didn't matter. *Only a fool plunges into a river wearing a hundred pounds of armor!* For that caused him to drown. *Mayhap he was swept from his steed by the rushing current or fell when his heart seized; but regardless, if he had either waited to traverse the bridge or had the sense God gave a goose and removed his armor before attempting the river cross, then his throne would not have been handed to a mere child.*

Henry had been twenty and five when the mighty Barbarossa died, and only twenty-six when he was crowned Emperor of the Romans–a title Eleanor found ridiculous considering no actual Romans lived there. The youngster had grand ambitions and required money to fund his incursions aimed at expanding the empire Frederick had built. Maybe he was also a little jealous and incensed that Phillip and Richard came out of war safely while his father had not. And she shouldn't be too angry with him since it was actually his vassal Duke Leopold who had captured her boy in the first place.

At least Henry did treat him well, even though the monetary demand had been unfathomable! Yet, with the help of her capable ministers, loyal subjects, and a certain enigmatic outlaw, the sum had been raised, and they were on course to bring her favored son home.

* * *

*M*AINZ, *in the Holy Roman Empire, Feb 2, 1194*

. . .

ELEANOR and her entourage were given the most luxurious accommodations within the walled city on the Rhine. All the money and hostages had been counted and approved. Eleanor's excitement and anticipation at finally being reunited with her son after a three and a half year separation was greater than any she could recall. She took Archbishop Walter de Coutances of Rouen's arm as they were escorted into the Romanesque hall. Thick, stone walls rose to a high ceiling and their footsteps echoed throughout the chamber. Across the room, she spied Justiciar William Longchamp, attired in white silk ecclesiastical robes embroidered in gold. He was as impeccably groomed as ever, but the color had faded from his wavy locks, leaving them gray. Where he had once been robust, his physique now waned, but his bright eyes were as lively as in his youth. Upon noting her entrance, he immediately snapped to attention.

"Your Highness," William greeted, crossing one foot in front of the other and granting her a deep bow. His voice was jovial and light. He traversed the floor to meet her and Walter in the midst of the large room with its hodge-podge of furnishings, rugs, and tapestries. "And Archbishop, so very glad we will at last see our Richard a free man!" He bowed over Eleanor's hand, brushing his lips to it, before turning to Walter and repeating the gesture. "I am glad to see you and Walter both looking so fit."

"What of Richard?" Eleanor asked anxiously. "Have you seen him? Is he well?"

The old bishop smiled broadly and with a wave of his hand replied with a wink, "As sturdy a killbuck as ever!"

Before Eleanor had a chance to grill him further, a large door opened at the far end of the hall. A silk-clad, royal herald with a brunet page-boy cut strode through and announced the arrival of his highness Henry IV, Emperor of the Romans. He was followed by the lean young king of modest stature and curly acorn hair upon which sat a gold crown, a red mantle draped over his blue tunic. His brown eyes brightened the moment they rested on Eleanor.

She fell into a deep curtsey as her two aides bowed low in respect.

Henry walked to her and took her hand as she straightened. He inclined his head to her and smiled. "Queen Eleanor, I am so glad to meet you at last. I have heard kings and courtiers speak of you all my life; the most remarkable woman in all the world, they would say. But now, in your presence, I perceive that their accolades fell short."

"I am honored, my Lord Emperor," she replied with a bow of her head.

"But I fear it is not me you came to see this day," he added with humor in his tone. "Where is that most articulate knight?" Henry turned and motioned to a guard at the door from which he had entered and he opened it again.

Eleanor's heart leapt into her throat and she forgot to breathe as time froze. And then there he stood, the joy of her life! Tall and muscular, with broad shoulders, narrow hips, and powerful limbs, he was a man in his prime. His hair was a wavy rust-brown matching a manly beard and mustache, which covered a strong chin and brushed ruddy cheeks. Delight lit his hazel eyes as they met hers. Unable to contain her emotions any longer, Eleanor tossed dignity to the wind and ran to throw her arms around him. Tears of elation streaked her face as she was enveloped in his comforting embrace.

"Dear Mother," Richard hummed. "If you are here, then England has lost her beauty."

Eleanor laughed through her emotion and released him long enough to use her handkerchief, but had yet been able to speak.

"Come, now." He took her arm and motioned to the noble company. "Let us be done with this business so that we may return home, for spring dare not awaken without you to greet it."

"Oh, Richard, my son, the consummate warrior-poet, how I have missed you!"

"And I, you." His strength and his smile soothed her; at last all was well with the world, almost.

"If you would all join me," Henry invited, "we have a few details to discuss." An attendant arrived with a bottle and goblets, and he continued. "Mainz lies in the heart of our finest wine country, so please refresh yourselves."

The royals and their noble ministers took seats around a small rectangular table with Henry and Richard occupying the head and foot positions. After the drinks were poured, Henry began.

"Queen Eleanor, you have achieved what many wagered was impossible–though 'twas I who won the bet. The dowry is complete as agreed upon and all two hundred hostages are in good health, with their peerages verified." Henry, not wanting it to appear he was demanding a ransom for a kidnapped king, referred to the required sum as a dowry to accompany Richard's niece who was to marry Duke Leopold's son, Fredrick. "However, I am compelled to show you this."

The young monarch placed a letter into Eleanor's hands. Her mouth fell agape as she read it. "Prince John and King Philip have now upped their offer to 150,000 marks."

"They claim they can pay the entire amount at once, and as I have to wait on your remaining 50,000…" Henry shrugged and looked as though he was entertaining the bid.

It was Longchamp who came to the fore, speaking as one who was old and wise. "Your Highness is far too clever for that," he stated knowingly. "I can tell you for a fact their claim is false. Mayhap Philip has the 100,000 he claims to be contributing to the bribe, but verily Prince John does not. As it happens, the money he raised in England is right here in the sum Queen Eleanor has set before you. A wily thief loyal to King Richard—what's his name again?"

"Robin Hood," Richard replied jovially. "Minstrel songs of his heroics have even reached Emperor Henry's court."

"Yes, yes, Robin Hood stole the cache out from under John's nose and shuttled it off to the Queen. The Prince hasn't any silver at all—he is bluffing!"

Eleanor confirmed Longchamp's story. "Indeed, Richard's goddaughter, Marian, transported the sum to London herself. I am sorry to say that my treacherous youngest son is as adept at lying as he is at breathing. When Richard at first did not come home, he went about proclaiming the King was dead and tried to procure the throne even though he had not been named heir. Then, once word was out that Duke Leopold had captured Richard, he started more rumors and set about to turn wealthy nobles to his side. The fact is, he will not face his brother on the field of honor, and he will not honor pledges to you, Highness. If you agree to what is in this letter, he shall plague you with excuses for many months. You have counted the silver I delivered in good faith and have inspected the hostages. Would you accept the word of John and Philip over what you have seen with your own eyes?"

Glancing from Henry to her son, Eleanor was puzzled by his tranquility. He must have already known about this underhanded bribe and didn't seem the least bit troubled by it. She frowned as Richard sat back comfortably in his chair and sipped his wine.

While Henry appeared to contemplate her words, Longchamp

continued in her stead. "Then there is King Philip and the 100,000 he promises, but how do we know he has that sum? After all," he said with a gesture, "He had armies in the field all season last year and is preparing them again. How could he sustain these wars of expansion after spending a small fortune on the crusade and still double the amount he previously offered Your Highness? Do the Franks have money trees? Does gold and silver fall from the sky like rain in Paris? Nay, it did not when last I visited there."

Henry appeared to nod ever so slightly at Richard before returning his attention to Eleanor. "Your chancellor makes a good argument, Your Grace, but there are other matters to consider as well. My own Duke Leopold still claims Richard assassinated his kinsman."

"Rubbish," Richard declared as he sat forward with a sudden frown. "I have already produced witnesses and evidence that the accusation is false. Asides, the whole world knows I love honor too much for such a thing. If I wished the man dead, I would challenge him to a duel face to face."

"I find it odd if the Duke truly believed the Lionheart guilty of murder, that he should still wish Richard's niece Eleanor to marry his son," she noted. "No, he just needed an excuse for capturing Richard, and the death of his kinsman was convenient."

"Mayhap," Henry conceded with a nod. "But if I am to follow through with our agreement in favor of King Philip's offer, I risk much. I will lose French favor while at the same time gaining none from England. England will resent the large sum of money brought forth and Philip will be angry with me, so which is worse?"

Walter of Rouen shook his head and steepled his fingers with elbows on the table before him. "These are anxious and difficult decisions. But Your Highness is a shrewd ruler. By honoring our agreement, you gain England's favor, not the opposite. And what can Philip do to you? He is like a small dog barking at a mighty bear."

"As I have considered it, there is one solution that shall satisfy." All eyes and ears harkened to the young emperor as he proclaimed his decision. "All will be well if King Richard were to pledge his oath of fealty to me. In turn, I would return all of his holdings on both sides of the channel– including those John promised to Philip–as his fief. I only ask 5,000 pounds a year tribute and the right to call upon Richard and his army if ever they are needed."

Richard pushed up from the table abruptly, his calm demeanor consumed by his trademark temper. "I am the King of England, son of Fredrick Barbarossa," he bellowed pointing a finger at Henry, "and I bow to none but God alone! You cannot demand that a monarch of my station demote himself to your vassal!"

Henry tilted his head with a smug expression. "Then I take it you wish to remain with me another year? The guards do enjoy your songs and pranks and find you quite entertaining."

"Bollocks!" Red-faced, Richard stomped off to a corner to brood.

Walter and Longchamp both appeared mortified, but it was Longchamp who spoke first. Presenting himself in exaggerated humility, he began, "Great Lord Emperor, assuredly there is a compromise to which we can agree. Mayhap England can pay the tribute without humiliating our King before the courts of Europe."

"Do you consider it humiliation for a king to bow to an emperor?" Henry asked with a raised brow. "I think not."

"But Your Highness," Walter added, "England is a sovereign nation. Perchance the King's holdings through the Queen on the continent could be held as fiefs."

"You are missing the point," the Emperor stated bluntly. "I need absolute assurance that England is my ally if I am to insult France. That is the fact of it."

Eleanor patted Walter's hands and turned an understanding gaze to Henry. "Let me speak with him. I can persuade the King to make a wise choice that will benefit you both."

"You may take your leave, Your Grace." Henry stood in respect as did her two ministers when she rose to her feet. "I have confidence in your influence."

Eleanor could feel the heat radiating from Richard as she approached. He offered her a sideways scowl. "Insufferable boy," he muttered in hushed rage balling his hands into fists.

She stepped up to him and gently laid a hand on his shoulder, siphoning off some of his tension. "I know."

"It isn't fair, it isn't proper, it simply isn't done!" Exasperation and frustration permeated his voice. Richard rubbed the back of his neck and shook his head.

"My best beloved, root of my heart," Eleanor began soothingly.

His gaze shot over his shoulder to her in anticipation. "You are going to tell me to agree to this travesty."

She took a step around so they stood eye to eye, let her hand trail off his arm, and commenced her entreat. "Words, Richard; they are only words, and you get to come home to a kingdom that desperately needs you."

"Nay, Mother, they are not merely words." His brows knit together as he wiped a hand down his beard. "My oath, my pledge, my word–that cannot be broken. Moreover, I already have an arrangement with Philip. To do as Henry demands would require me to break it."

"Who could blame you, seeing Philip's betrayal?" Then she mused foxily. "A marriage vow is deemed unbreakable and yet I managed to divorce my first husband. Under the right circumstances, one can get around a pledge or devise a reason for annulment. As I see it, shifting your allegiance from a king to an emperor is trading up, just as I traded up to marry your father. Once you are home safe and sound, how can he force you to send ships and armies to his aid?"

"So, no one will fault me for breaking fealty with Philip in favor of Henry, that is clear," he reasoned aloud. "But if I give my word to Henry, honor demands that I come if he calls."

"He just wants to assure England as an ally, 'tis all. The tribute will not be a burden, and it is unlikely that an emperor with so many princes and dukes, not to mention lesser nobles pledged to him who are right here where he needs soldiers, need ever call on England at all. Let him have his moment to look important–it does nothing to diminish the man *you* are."

Richard unclenched his fists and shifted his weight to one leg. "Bugger it all," he sighed. Then his eyes shot to hers with renewed fire. "That miscreant brother of mine has caused much of this trouble. I could easily enough sit here another year if he weren't actively trying to steal my throne. Treason is punishable by death and I have a mind to strangle him with my own hands!"

Eleanor held his gaze with one of confident wisdom. "But you won't. A great offence requires even greater mercy."

"You would have me forgive him, after all he has done?" Refusal carved itself into a stone face.

"My son, history records not only your victories in battle, but your every word and deed. For centuries to come, rulers will look to your example for guidance. What legacy would you leave?"

"It is not enough that I be the greatest king of my own time, but you would have me be a king for the ages!" he exclaimed with a humorless laugh.

"It is not what I would have, Richard," she explained stepping closer and bringing her hand to his ruggedly handsome face. "It is who you are. Furthermore, you demonstrate your power by treating John's treason as a mere trifle, declaring to the world that he never presented any real danger to you."

"But we both know he came very close to taking my crown, if not my life as well," he answered, wrapping Eleanor's hand in his. "Had it not been for that random outlaw..." He kissed her hand before lowering it along with his head in contemplation.

"I do not believe there is anything random about Robin Hood," commented Eleanor. "Come now, let us waste no more time. England eagerly awaits her King."

When she took his arm, Richard's foul mood evaporated, his usual good humor taking its place. He smiled at her warmly and made an observation. "You are already the most extraordinary woman in the whole world, Mother. I shudder to think about the power you would wield if you had been born a man!"

CHAPTER 24

*Sherwood Forest, March 24, 1194*

Richard's loyal barons in the north, rallied by Maid Marian's visits, lay in siege around the lone hold-out of Nottingham, but the castle retained command of the bridge over the River Trent. Therefore, King Richard and his escort, now returned to England, took a different route that passed by Clipstone Castle, a hunting lodge on the northern edge of Sherwood Forest.

The King had never hunted in the celebrated wood and planned to return once the rebels had been dealt with. But after a good night's rest, he decided on one small detour before taking charge of the forces besieging John's allies. As he and Sir Robert sat with their squires and a couple of knights who traveled with them, Richard proposed an idea.

"Friends, while I wish to make haste to Nottingham to end this rebellion, curiosity compels me to see for myself what this outlaw Robin Hood is about. But I want to do so in a way to discern his true intentions; therefore, I have a plan. We can still arrive at Nottingham on the morrow, mayhap with reinforcements, if things go as I suppose."

"But Sire," Robert protested sitting forward with concern etched on his face. "Purposely setting out to find a gang of outlaws in the forest would put your royal head in danger."

Richard smiled with confidence at his companion. "I think not, but should peril arise, I feel secure with you at my side. Now, here is what I have in mind…"

* * *

VIRGIN CHARTREUSE LEAVES bathed in morning dewdrops unfurled themselves beneath the springtime sun. Robyn gently brushed her fingertips along soft yellow and pink blossoms as she and her companions strode through the forest toward the road they had chosen to stake out that day. She breathed in fragrant pine and honeysuckle while the songs of finches and robins filled the trees. *Spring is nature's evidence of the resurrection, mother always said,* she recollected. Although there was no new sheriff, her camp of displaced persons feared to return home while Prince John's barons held Nottingham, and they still needed to be fed. Therefore, they continued the practice of accosting wealthy passersby through Sherwood requiring a donation from them for the poor.

They chose one of their favorite ambush sites and assumed hiding places to wait. After a few hours a vicar and his attendants came riding along at a lazy walk. The lads all snapped to attention awaiting Robyn's signal. As the small party of clergymen reached a precise spot, Robyn dropped from a tree branch overhead landing right beside the vicar's horse. The startled animal shied and reared, but Robyn grabbed hold of its bridle to steady the steed. At the same time Little John and Alan popped out onto the road at her flanks while Much, David, and Arthur closed in behind the six men.

"Good morrow, generous Vicar! I am sure your purse will prove heavy enough to bestow an offering to the poor," she proclaimed in good humor.

"And if I should refuse?" inquired the priest.

"Ah, now, you don't want to do that," Little John assured him as he took a threatening step forward. "If so, my staff would have words with you."

"Certs you would not harm a humble servant of God," the clergyman answered raising his palms innocently.

All at once Robyn was overcome by an inexplicable feeling. While something indeed struck her as familiar about the vicar, she retained no doubt regarding the identity of the man seated on the bay to his right. He wore a serious expression with silver brushed temples, a clean-shaven square jaw, thick lips, a crooked nose from where it had been broken long ago, and *Marian's eyes.*

No sooner than she realized her mouth had fallen open, she shut it. *And that means this is... King Richard!* She swallowed the exclamations of joy that formed in her heart and tried her best to pretend she had not identified them. *If he comes through the forest wearing the guise of a cleric, it is for a reason. I only hope Sir Robert doesn't recognize me.*

Utilizing great restraint, Robyn composed herself and replied, "Certainly not, Father. But no humble servant of God would refuse to give alms to the poor."

Richard scanned about spotting the others, accessing their strength Robyn guessed. "And where are these poor of which you speak? I only see bandits and highwaymen. Perchance is one of you Robin Hood?" he asked looking at Little John.

"Aye," Robyn replied. Richard's eyes held surprise as he moved his gaze to her. "If I show you those whom I protect, would you readily give of your coins?"

"Well, now, lad, that is a real possibility. Lead us to your camp."

"Not so fast," Robyn said holding tight to the horse's bridle. "Tell me the truth; are you loyal to Prince John or to King Richard?"

A twinkle shone in his eye at the question while a subtle grin tugged at FitzWalter's lips. "Verily, you could find no man more loyal to the King than I," he pronounced with authority.

"I am glad to hear it, Your Grace, as the territory is crawling with traitors of late. Any friend of King Richard is a friend of mine," she avowed. "But, I am afraid I cannot lead you and your party to our camp without first blindfolding you. It is imperative that our hide-out remain secret, even from a good vicar and his attendants."

Richard shifted in his saddle and FitzWalter shot him a wary gaze. "I am not comfortable placing myself in the hands of strangers. How do I know you do not intend to lead us to our deaths?"

"Reverend Father," Robyn said motioning to her armed cadre. "If we wanted to do you harm, we would not need to coax you farther into the forest to do so. I'm afraid if you want to see those who have been abused, condemned and cast out by Prince John's agents, you will simply have to trust me. Otherwise, please hand over your purse."

Despite FitzWalter's disapproving glower, the King nodded in agreement. "Very well," he acquiesced and slid out of his saddle, his companions following his lead. Once they all had cloths over their eyes, the men remounted their horses, and Robyn and her crew led them through the forest.

As they traveled, Richard made inquiries. "So, Hood, I heard it from a certain abbot that you and your band stole a huge treasure from Prince John not long ago."

"That's right," Alan concurred, beaming with pride. "'twas the most brilliant theft of all time, I say!"

"No doubt," he agreed with a nod in Alan's direction. "But the part I found hard to believe was when he claimed you turned the entire sum over to the Queen to help buy King Richard's freedom."

"As surely as you live, milord," boomed Little John's voice.

"But wouldn't a thief such as yourself keep a portion if not the lot of it?"

"Robyn don't keep nothing for himself," Little John snapped, "and you'll be witness to that soon enough."

"Truly?" he asked with raised brows tugging at his blindfold.

Then Robyn, who led the King's horse, answered suavely, "Not everyone is who they appear to be, milord."

At that, she heard him chuckle. "How right you are, lad."

\* \* \*

UPON REACHING HOOD'S CAMP, the six men in clergy robes became the immediate focus of attention. Robyn told them to remove their blindfolds and the visitors dismounted. She watched Richard's look of astonishment at the multitude of women and children, the crippled and maimed, those with nowhere else to turn. "What happened to all these people's homes? Why are they here in the forest with you?" he asked.

Robyn responded with a storyteller's flare. "My dear Vicar, these honest, loyal English men and women are in a round-about way the victims of our good King Richard." At that his eyes rounded and he puffed out his chest, but she continued. "You see, being a good Christian king, he answered the Pope's call to Crusade and left his kingdom behind to be administered by regents and, while they did the best they could, staving off the worst that could happen, Prince John did all he could to undermine the absent King. He rallied barons to his cause with promises of great reward. Local sheriffs became corrupt and lords abusive toward their serfs because there was no one watching out for the people's welfare. These men," she said motioning to her gang, "are not thieves by choice, but out of necessity. In Nottingham, one cannot even raise his glass to King Richard without being falsely accused of a crime, evicted from his home or sacked. I was more than happy to steal the Prince's treasure and give it straightway to the Queen in order to hasten the King's return to his land, for I am confident that when he sees what the rebellious barons of Nottingham have done, he will make things right for these before you."

While Richard stood mesmerized, soaking in the tale, Friar Tuck and Maid Marian made their way forward to offer greeting. Marian had been dividing her time between her manor and the outlaws' camp while anxiously awaiting her father's return. "Greetings Reverend Father," Tuck exclaimed in a loud sanguine voice. "Always glad to meet a fellow man of the cloth." Then he scrutinized the tall gentleman. "Do I know you? Whence do you hail?"

But he had no time to answer Tuck. Marian's eyes lit with recognition, and in her exuberance ran to Sir Robert, wrapping her arms around his neck with tears of joy.

"Papa!" She kissed both his cheeks, pulled back to look into his worn but joyful face, then hugged him tightly once more. "Papa, you are home at last!"

"Marian, my heart!" He enveloped her in his strong embrace, elation lighting his eyes. "But what are you doing out here in the forest in an outlaw camp?"

Robyn felt the power of Marian's emotion and her own heart swelled with joy. She was beaming affectionately at Marian when Richard sighed and gave a nod to the others. They all threw off their robes—except Sir Robert who was entangled with his loving daughter—to reveal the light armor and crusader's surcoats beneath.

Robyn's attention snapped back to Richard and, seeing that was the proper cue, she fell to one knee at his feet and declared, "My lord and my King!"

The others, most of whom had never seen the monarch and would have no idea what he looked like, followed their leader and proceeded to bow before the Lionheart.

But Gilbert, who had fought at the King's side, recognized him at once and echoed Robyn's words. "Our King has returned!" he shouted excitedly before making his bow.

"Sir Gilbert?" Richard tilted his head. "Is that you, my man?"

"Aye, Sire."

"Arise, loyal citizens of England, for at last I have come home. A friar, a lord, a thief and my own sweet goddaughter! Have you no hugs for me?" Richard turned a doting eye toward the lovely girl. "Why, you have become a grown woman whilst I was away!"

Marian released her father and embraced Richard with jubilance, kissing his cheeks as well. "Your Highness, welcome home!"

"Listen to you, 'Your Highness'! No more 'God-papa' for me?" With a broad smile, he kissed her cheeks in return.

Blushing, Marian stepped back, gave a little curtsey and gushed, "This is the happiest day! I do so love you both!"

Then a querying look appeared on the King's face. "Come to think of it, why are you here?"

"Well, you see," she stammered and backed up beside Robyn who rose to her feet at her side. "Robyn and I..."

Richard held up a hand and smiled at her. "And speaking of Robin," he said turning his attention to her. "I believe I owe a great deal to you and your brave men. Tell me, lad, what reward can I offer for your service to England?"

Robyn's eyes lit. "Pardons for my men, Sire. They have risked all and gained little. Indeed, they were never real criminals after all."

"It is done!" he declared jovially. "Just give a list of their names to my scribe here," he said motioning to the man on his left, "and he will have the papers drawn up. But mayhap something for you?"

"I..." Robyn hesitated, shooting a questioning glance at Marian.

"I have it!" Richard announced. "Take a knee, son. I shall knight you here and now and bequeath to you the land and title of one of those treasonous barons holed up in the castle. Then you will have the proper rank to court my fair goddaughter, if her father approves," he added with a wink to FitzWalter.

But Robyn's expression was shadowed with uncertainty. "Your Highness," she said in a hush so those beyond their immediate circle could not hear. "I am honored, truly, but I fear the matter is a bit more complicated. If you could allow me one indulgence—that after my men and I help you secure Nottingham, you may grant me a more private audience in which to make my petition." Then she bowed, her head low in humble supplication.

Richard rubbed his beard, puzzled by the request. "I suppose that is not too much to ask after the tremendous service you have done me. Very well, now," he waved. "My escort and I must withdraw to Nottingham to command the siege. I plan an attack in the morning and your archers would be most welcome." Robyn straightened and nodded appreciatively. "I must say, the songs and tales about you are indeed true, but I wanted to see for myself. I am most glad to have done so. And by the by, I hear Nottingham is devoid of a sheriff, as they tell you dispatched the former one."

Robyn lowered her gaze and nodded again.

"Good riddance!" he pronounced, further absolving her. "Sir Gilbert," he said raising his gaze to the thin older man whose head lifted at the mention of his name. "I believe you have the rank and experience to fit the position."

Engulfed by astonishment, life suddenly rushed into the old man like one who had been reborn. "Thank you, My Lord King! You are too kind!"

"Nonsense! I tire of hearing about corruption and misuse of power and know that shan't be the case with you overseeing Nottingham. Robert, you will have plenty of time to enjoy your beautiful daughter once the castle has fallen. Oh, and I almost forgot!" Richard reached inside his surcoat and produced a small pouch. "For the poor," he said tossing it to Robyn. "Now, if someone could kindly point us in the direction of Nottingham."

\* \* \*

THAT NIGHT as all gathered around the campfire celebrating the King's return, Robyn sat on a smooth log with Marian resting her head on her shoulder. Joy radiated like sunbeams from every soul and Robyn could feel Marian's delight. Her own anxious thoughts wandered to their private meeting with the King and how–and if–a way would be found for her to remain with the woman she loved. Then a thought struck her: regardless, she would have to leave her band of merry men and no longer live in Sherwood. This chapter of her life was at a close.

In a moment of emotion, Robyn pushed to her feet and stepped into the midst of the gathering. The others quieted to hear what their leader had to say.

"Friends," she began, trying to strike an optimistic tone. "Tomorrow we join our beloved King on the field of battle to drive the rebels from Nottingham and put England back to rights. Then you will all receive your pardons, returning to your homes and families. After the castle is won, you shall see me no more."

Abruptly glad faces turned sad and murmurs of "Why?" "When?" and "Where will you go?" arose from the congregation.

Robyn lifted a hand to calm them. "You shall have your lives back, and there is a home to which I must return as well. But have no fear: if ever injustice raises its ugly head, if the poor are oppressed and freedoms threatened, Robin Hood will be there to defend the weak and thwart the plans of the wicked."

She raised her eyes to the stars and spurred on with inspiration continued. "I love you all, each and every one, and will not forget you. You shine, like the evening and morning star, the brightest in all the heavens."

She looked back out across the crowd, her eyes touching each of theirs for a twinkling: Alan A Dale, whose music and laughter brightened her days; Arthur Bland, who longed to return home; Much the Miller's son, who never complained; David Doncaster, with his youthful exuberance; Friar Tuck, whose knowledge and wisdom guided her; Gilbert Whitehand, her tortured mentor; young Charles and Christina, who had their whole lives ahead of them; and Little John, her strong right arm and substitute father. She thought of Will Scarlet and Roger the farrier who would forever live in her memories.

"Whenever I look into the sky and see this star, I will think of you, and the love that shines in my heart for you all. And mark this truth—as long as our nation is made of such as you, who love what is right and fight courageously against tyranny, then England will stand for a thousand years as a beacon of freedom and justice before all the world."

Amid tears and cheers, and with Marian at her side, Robyn slipped away for the privacy of her tent.

* * *

Nottingham Castle, *the next day*

. . .

KING RICHARD, wearing only light armor and helmpiece, along with his escort marched out onto the field ahead of the army to a fanfare of trumpets and great cheers. He was joined by such noteworthy names as Sir William Marshall, 1st Earl of Pembroke, Ranulph de Blondeville, 4th Earl of Chester, David of Scotland, 8th Earl of Huntingdon, Sir Alfred of Ivanhoe, and the venerable Archbishop of Canterbury, Herbert Walter, as well as scores of lesser nobles and hundreds of knights, footmen, archers, and engineers. But despite the display, the defenders of Nottingham opened fire on them. Richard wondered if perhaps they didn't recognize him, so he commandeered the nearest cottage for his personal lodging to always be in their sights.

Sir Guy and the other barons came to Nonant, Prince John's propagandist who had joined them at the castle, upon witnessing the spectacle without to discuss their options. "That is King Richard, I tell you!" Sir Guy exclaimed, sweat pouring from this troubled brow. "He will have us all hanged if we persist."

"Nonsense," Nonant proclaimed serenely. "'Tis but a ruse. Prince John promised he would return with the French army before Richard could reach Nottingham, did he not?"

"Yes, milord, but—" began a nervous Raoul le Clerc.

"And do you not believe the word of our honorable Prince? Has he not been true to his pledges in the past?"

"But Your Grace," Sir Guy continued. "You were not on the wall. You did not see him standing at the front of the army, arrows raining down at his feet, yet he did not even so much as step aside. He stood confident and firm, like, like," his frantic mind searching an adequate term. "A lion!"

The younger bishop waved him off akin to an annoying fly. "A show meant to frighten us into submission. That alone should convince you I am right, for what king would stand in front of an army unprotected?"

Sir Hugh Diggory contradicted John's spokesman. "With all due respect, Bishop, but I have heard Richard declare out of his own mouth that any man who is unwilling to stand at the front of his army is not fit to lead it. I must agree with Gisborne."

But Lambelin sided with Nonant. "This castle is strong, and we have gathered much meat and grain. We should hold out until Prince John arrives."

Gisborne gave Nonant a hard stare. "For all our sakes, I hope you are right."

Tensions were high in Nottingham castle the next morning. "What if it is the King? Last night's battle did not go well for us," Gisborne insisted. "What if Prince John never comes?"

"Nonsense," Nonant chided.

Raoul le Clerc offered a suggestion. "Let us find out for certs; then we can make an informed decision as to our next course of action."

"And how do you propose that?" the propagandist retorted with a dismissive sneer.

Hugh Diggory's eyes lit with inspiration. "I have a brave and loyal knight, Sir Fouchier de Grendon. We can send him and his squire, Henry Russell, under a white flag of truce to ascertain the true identity of he who leads the attack against us. Sir Fouchier accompanied the King to the Holy Land and will surely recognize his features if it is indeed he."

The other nobles looked eagerly to Nonant, pleased with the suggestion. "It is a brilliant idea," Gisborne exclaimed. "Only good can come of knowing the truth."

Nonant snorted and turned away from the weak-willed barons. "Do as you like," he said with a wave of his hand. "What do I care if you get your knight killed?"

*  *  *

Diggory called for his cavaliers and sent the two out carrying a flag of truce. Young David of Doncaster's sharp youthful eye was the first to spot them.

"Let them pass," Robyn directed, "but keep watch on them."

Two camp guards rode out to meet Sir Fouchier and his squire and escorted them into the fire-lit camp where King Richard and his officers were taking their dinner. "My Liege," addressed one of the guards with a sharp bow. "These two came from the castle to see if it is truly you."

Richard stood, a goose leg in his hand, and twisted from side to side so they could get a good look at him. "Well, what can you see?" he asked in a cheerful tone, seeming completely at ease and unconcerned. "Am I here?"

Sir William Marshall and Sir Robert FitzWalter both laughed while the knight and his squire turned pale and fell to their knees. "Your Highness!" they exclaimed and removed their head pieces at once.

Richard sat back at his table and said to them, "You may return to the castle and tell the others what you have seen. I suggest you see to yourselves as you decide on your next steps."

With that, the two men raced back to inform the barons that it truly was King Richard.

"I knew it!" Gisborne declared slamming a fist into his open palm.

Nonant took a step back from the panicking lords. "How were we to know? It could have easily been an impostor."

The nobles looked about their circle and proceeded to discuss their options and how best to save their necks.

In the meantime, a certain knight and his youthful squire returned to the King's camp and surrendered, throwing themselves on the Lionheart's mercy.

Deep into the night, when almost everyone was asleep, Sir Guy of Gisborne along with his knights and retainers slunk out of Nottingham under the cover of a moonless sky to return to his own estate and pretend he had not been there at all.

On the morrow, the rebellious barons surrendered, swore they were acting under Prince John's orders, that they had no idea they had raised a bow or sword against the true King, and prostrated themselves to declare their allegiance to Richard, and him alone.

\* \* \*

NOTTINGHAM CASTLE, *March 30, 1194*

ROBYN AND MARIAN stood in formal attire before King Richard, who was flanked on his right by Sir Robert FitzWalter and on his left by the Queen Mother, in a private alcove off the great hall. Richard was dressed to impress with his white crusader surcoat emblazoned with its big, red cross, a crimson cloak adorned with a snowy fur mantle draped about his shoulders, and a sturdy gold crown bejeweled with rubies and emeralds. He had just dealt with the disloyal barons, choosing to make them pay financially rather than with their lives. The entire nation's treasury being exhausted, he needed funds to oppose Phillip of France who was advancing against his borders in Normandy. He declared all titles and lands of the traitors forfeit; however, they could buy them back at a premium price. Most agreed after much groveling and apologizing for being foolish enough to follow Prince John.

Both ladies acknowledged the royal family with deep curtsies.

"This is my friend, Maid Robyn of Loxley," Marian gave introduction.

Richard bore a puzzled expression on his stately face. His brows drew together as he raised a hand to rub his burnished beard.

"But where is Hood?" He inquired. "I thought this meeting was for his benefit."

Hesitantly, Robyn removed her wimple along with the thin braided gold fillet that encircled her head holding the linen in place to reveal her short hair. "Your Highness." She swallowed the lump that had risen to her throat. "Robyn of Loxley and Robin Hood are one and the same."

The three sucked in air simultaneously as visages of astonishment swept over them.

Robyn continued meekly. "This is what I meant when I said it was complicated."

She watched in nervous anticipation as realization washed over the King. His expression of disbelief softened into amusement. "Well, I'll kiss the hare's foot!" he laughed, light dancing in his eyes. "Mother, Robert," he said catching their gazes and motioning toward them and then to Robyn. "Do you see this? Do you know what this means?" Marian's father still seemed confused but a sly, clever air of perception shone on Eleanor's face. "The finest archer in all of England is a woman! I'll be buggered!"

Marian's gaze passed from Eleanor to Richard then to her father, who was beginning to comprehend. She moved her hand a few inches to brush Robyn's ever so tenderly in reassurance. "But Maid Robyn," he asked with a curious tilt of his head. "How? Why?"

Robyn recounted the story of the Sheriff's ultimatum and her banishment, meeting the outlaws, and all that followed. Then Richard, who seemed thoroughly charmed by the revelation declared in a deep, jovial tone. "It would appear as though I owe my throne and my life a good deal to you and your men. The rest of them *are* men, are they not?"

Robyn's cheeks turned a bright crimson. "Yes, Your Highness." She lowered her head, not sure if he was laughing at her or the simple absurdity of it all. "But don't forget Marian," she added, raising her chin with bright eyes. "She was very instrumental in gaining information and helping with the planning, not to mention transporting the treasure to the Queen. All in all, it was a group effort."

Marian's face lit as Robyn raced to add her to the credits.

Richard smiled warmly. "Milady, I would knight you if I could. But alas," he said with a sigh and resigned shake of his head. "Neither the law nor society allows for such. It goes without question that your family lands and title shall be returned to you at once to do with as you wish and you are not required to marry anyone to keep them. That much I can do for you. But isn't there something more? I feel like there should be something more."

Robyn bit her lip anxiously and shot a glance to Marian who nodded in return. Stepping forward, Marian raised up on tiptoe to whisper into the King's ear.

"Hmmm," he vocalized at first. Then his expression fell flat. "Oh," he uttered, then lifting the timber of his voice added a stretched out, "Ooooooh! I see, well," he stammered. "I am uncertain I can do anything about that for you." Richard made awkward glances at his mother and Sir Robert before turning a tentative gaze back to his goddaughter. "I understand your dilemma, my child," he began in a fatherly tone.

Marian peered up at him with admiration and an affectionate smile. "I know," she stated. She leaned in and kissed him on the cheek, then settled back to confirm her revelation. "After all, I am my father's daughter." With that said, all color faded from Richard's face and Robyn thought for just an instant that she saw the mighty Lionheart quiver. Marian's eyes full of love and innocence then danced to her father. "Why did you never tell me?"

Sir Robert stepped to her uncertainly with tears straining to burst forth. "No wonder the Queen employed you as a spy," he said with an embarrassed shake of his head. "Can anyone hide a thing from you?" Standing shoulder to shoulder with Richard, he took her delicate hands in his and confessed. "I was afraid that the light of my life and joy of my heart would be ashamed of me."

"Oh, Papa!" Marian threw her arms around him and pressed her cheek to his. After a moment, she kissed that damp cheek as he could no longer hold back the swell of emotion. Standing once more before him, she gazed adoringly into his rugged face. "You are a loving father and a brave, honorable man. In what world could I ever be ashamed of you? I love you, Papa, and my King, both of you." She raised a hand to caress his face and ended up wiping away a tear.

"Sweet Marian, my pride and joy," he uttered. "You are a vision of grace." Then he stepped back, brushing his hand to hers as he did.

Color having returned to Richard's face, he stroked his beard and looked at Marian with pensive eyes. "I can think of no scenario in which society or the Church would ever approve. What say you, Robyn?"

Her reply was steady and sincere. "Honestly Sire, I do not care what anyone thinks nor what society deems proper. But I do care about Marian." Pausing, Robyn cast her gaze to the woman she loved. "As much as it is my heart's desire to remain always at her side, I would not, could not ever do anything that would bring shame to her."

Marian sighed and took Robyn's hand. She felt the warmth and devotion flow through that simple touch. "Neither do I care about those things, my sweetling."

"But you do care about your family," Robyn said to her, "and what touches you touches them. I know your heart and I speak true."

Then Marian turned her face toward Richard and in her gentle and charismatic way captured the King's attention. "The sum of all my life's experience and the education to which I have been made privy, has led me to conclude that love is never wrong," she said thoughtfully.

"Your Highness, it was no easy thing to bring this petition to you, but our future now rests in your wisdom and power. Is there anything you can do for us?" The sound in Robyn's voice was that of a desperate plea, a longing so deep and compelling, so unabashedly passionate that it visibly moved the King.

Richard rested a hand on his hip and rubbed the back of his neck with the other, struggling to grant them an answer. "Ah, bugger it all," he sighed. "There are some rules even a king cannot break." Then he looked back to Sir Robert. "Or I would have done so myself."

"My Liege," he replied with an inclined head. "You are God's anointed to rule England, a heavy burden wrought with responsibilities. We knew that from the start, before you ever took the crown. Nothing outweighs the magnitude of that charge."

Richard nodded and lowered his head, turning back to the young maidens. "Alas, you have done so much for me and there is nothing I can do for you in this matter."

It was at that moment that Queen Eleanor stepped forward, her finger raised and an inspired glow on her alabaster countenance. "I think I may have the solution to your dilemma." All eyes turned to her in hopeful anticipation. Then she gave Richard an impatient glower. "Not you, son. Your solemn duty as king is to return to France to Berengaria, *your wife* and produce an heir... better two or three." Richard's cheeks blushed, and he shuffled his feet, diverting his gaze from her.

"As I remind him frequently," Robert interjected. "It is indeed a matter of great import," he added to Richard.

"I know, I will," he replied, raising his palms in surrender. Then he repeated with more earnestness, "I know." Their eyes met once more before Eleanor returned her attention to the eager young pair.

"Maid Robyn," she addressed with poise, chin held high. "Would you be willing to donate your manor house to the church?"

"Your Grace," she answered eagerly with a delicate curtsey. "Not only the house, but the lands, the crops, the cattle, the serfs, every last farthing I possess..."

With an amused smile and clearly holding in a laugh, Eleanor broke in, "That will not be necessary, my dear. The lodge alone shall be sufficient. And Marian, would you be willing to dedicate your life to the Church in service as a lay person, for the upbringing and care of orphans and unfortunates?"

Her eyes shone wild with excitement. "Why yes, Your Grace, I would love to!"

Robyn recalled their recent conversation about the possibility of adopting children and as the Queen spoke, hope drove her spirit soaring.

"As it happens, Prioress Margery Dourant of Wallingwells has been petitioning me to assist in the establishment of an alms or orphan house in Nottinghamshire for some while now. Of course I was unable to do so as every pence and most of my time was dedicated to getting my son home." She paused long enough to beam lovingly at Richard. "Something the two of you were rather instrumental in accomplishing. But I believe this endeavor would satisfy all parties involved. As it is Robyn's estate, and she has proven herself quite capable of management, it is imperative that she stay on and continue to do so. Loxley profits shall be required to pay for the food, clothing, education, and additions that will be necessary to house the waifs. Furthermore, the children will need a caregiver," she continued, shifting her gaze to Marian. "If Marian were to volunteer her considerable talents to that charitable calling, she would have to be in residence as well to be a mother, as it were, to the children. As it is too much for one person to perform alone, I do not see how the institution could be run properly without the both of you. And with your virtuous generosity, giving up your lives of privilege for those of service to God and the Church, none would dare question your respectability."

Robyn erupted with excitement. "That is bloody brilliant! Uh, I mean, thank you, Your Highness; please tell the Prioress that she has her wish." She and Marian gleamed at each other and clasped hands enthusiastically, both completely giddy.

Eleanor's smile touched her eyes, but she added a serious note. "I must tell you, though; it will unfortunately be necessary for any mention of Robin Hood to be stricken from the official chronicles along with the roles either of you played in obtaining the ransom. It would indeed be too difficult to explain."

"Highness," Robyn replied, "it was never about reward or recognition, none of it. I was just trying to make the best of my unfortunate situation and help as many others as I could in the process."

The king then spoke. "Both of you could marry the most highly placed of nobles, thereby securing your own wealth and influence for a lifetime. Are you sure you want to give that up?"

Marian shrugged and waved her hand dismissively. "Eh, wealth, power... they don't guarantee happiness."

Richard shook his head. "Aye, the sum of my life's experiences agrees with you. However, there is no turning back for me; I must simply persevere. Robyn," he addressed her as he took a step closer. "It would have pleased me to dub you a knight."

"My bow and sword stand ready for your call, My Liege," she replied with a courtier's bow.

The king let out a hearty laugh and shook his head. "Nay, I have hundreds of knights, but only one goddaughter. Take good care of her."

"Aye, Highness," Robyn vowed. "I have dedicated myself to that end with all my heart."

With a broad smile, Richard concluded by placing a hand on each of their shoulders. "As for you two extraordinary ladies, go, care for orphans and be happy. You have my blessing."

Robyn turned to Marian who beamed at her so brightly that she literally saw stars while her own soul radiated with gratitude. Permeating as it was, that emotion was no match for the flood of unspeakable joy that swept through her, spilling out until it filled the entire chamber and encompassed all who stood within. With hands joined, the feeling that passed between them was undeniable. In an instant, Robyn's life seemed to flash before her eyes—the good, the bad, those moments you never forget—and this was the most glorious of them all. *We will be together!*

* * *

AND SO IT was that Robyn's role was omitted from the written record; however, oral histories persisted, the story being handed down from generation to generation until it became legend, woven into the very fabric of England itself: the tale of Robin Hood who robbed from the rich to give to the poor, outwitted the evil Sheriff of Nottingham, won the love of the fair Maid Marian, and thwarted Prince John's plot to steal his brother's crown.

But the one thing the bards, minstrels, and poets never knew was that Robin Hood, perhaps the most celebrated of all Englishmen, had in fact been a woman.

Fin

# AUTHOR'S NOTES

In *Heart of Sherwood* I have endeavored to create as historically accurate a telling of the efforts to secure the release of King Richard the Lionheart from his captivity in Germany by Holy Emperor Henry IV while at the same time remaining true to the enduring legend of Robin Hood (with the notable exception of the protagonist's gender). However, conflict often arose between key fixtures in the lore and actual historical fact. In those cases, more often than not, I acquiesced in favor of the treasured tale. Here I will inform the reader of those details of this story which I know are not factually correct but have included anyway, along with events which using author's license I condensed for brevity.

Let us begin with the most obvious—the very existence of Robin Hood. The first literary reference to Robin Hood dates to 1377 and the various early tales place him in different centuries and hailing from varying locals. The British Museum preserves several antique manuscripts each claiming to chronicle the famous outlaw's life. Most versions agree that Sherwood Forest was his hang-out and he robbed the rich to give to the poor. The latter made him a folk hero whether or not he ever lived. So if there was a Robin Hood, would the character necessarily be a man? Some of the earliest Robin Hood stories describe him as a beardless youth, only 14 or 15 years of age. While he became older and more sophisticated with later accounts, historians often put more trust in the oldest manuscripts. In the Medieval Period being male was a prerequisite to becoming a knight or skilled fighter (a few exceptions such as Joan of Arc not with-

## AUTHOR'S NOTES

standing); however, throughout the ages there have been times when females disguised themselves as males in order to engage in unconventional behavior. We know this was true both in the American Revolution and the Civil War as various women cut their hair and donned men's clothing to fight. So I suppose, since we have no concrete evidence of the existence of a benevolent outlaw known as Robin Hood, the concept that it could have been a woman is no more far-fetched than that of being a man. Besides, in my retelling of the story the circumstance of her femininity constitutes the very reason the name of Robin Hood was omitted from all official records.

The Sloan Manuscript (anonymous) written towards the end the sixteenth century states that "Robin Hood was born in Locksley in Yorkshire or after other in Nottinghamshire, in ye days of Henry II about ye yeare 1160, but lived tyll ye latter end of Richard Ye Fyrst". He is also referred to as "Robin of Locksley" by Sir Walter Scott in "Ivanhoe," (1819), and has been known by that title ever since. While there is a village of Loxley in Yorkshire, too far away from Sherwood and Nottingham to be my Robyn's home, there was not then, nor has there ever been, an Earl of Loxley (nor Locksley). Anthony Munday depicted the enigmatic outlaw as the Earl of Huntington in his 1589 plays, but I have chosen to forgo historical facts to stay true to the most familiar version of Hood as the Earl of Loxley (or in my case, daughter of the Earl).

According to lore, Robin Hood's arch-nemesis was the evil Sheriff of Nottingham. Historically, this presents a sticky point as the city of Nottingham did not acquire its first sheriff until 1449. However, there was a position High Sheriff of Nottinghamshire that dates back to 1068. In the various tales the Sheriff was simply called by his title or had different names depending upon who told the story. Godfrey Giffard is not the name of any real High Sheriff of Nottinghamshire. During the period 1193-1194 there were two high sheriffs and because that did not fit my narrative and I did not want to disparage one of their reputations, I chose to create a fictional sheriff to fill the role of villain.

Friar Tuck is a beloved character and central to Robin Hood's gang, therefore I determined to include him. Friars are Catholic clergymen who make vows of poverty, chastity and obedience, and live and work among the people as traveling evangelists. Unfortunately, the first friars, which were Franciscans, did not arrive on English shores until the year 1224. Since tossing out the connections with King Richard and Prince John were out of the question, I opted to fudge on accuracy and include the good friar a few decades early.

Maid Marian was not in the earliest Robin Hood ballads, but first mentioned around 1500. There was a "Marian of the May Games" from French tradition who was a shepherdess with a lover called Robin, and it has been suggested that the two tales merged at some point. From the late 1500s both Robin and Marian began to be portrayed as nobles who had a relationship ranging from friendship to marriage. In an Elizabethan play, Anthony Munday identified Maid Marian with the historical Matilda, daughter of Robert FitzWalter, a real-life supporter of King Richard who was forced to flee England after a failed attempt to assassinate the then King John. This representation of Maid Marian has held for centuries of lore so I chose to keep it.

I decided upon the identities and personalities of the various merry men after researching dozens of Robin Hood accounts, but focusing on more recent ones. I omitted Will Stutely who appears in two ballads, "Robin Hood and Little John" and "Robin Hood Rescuing Will Stutely," primarily because I did not want to confuse the readers with two "Wills". Will Scarlet's death and burial is in keeping with tradition, and tourists can even visit his gravesite at the churchyard of the Church of St. Mary of the Purification, Blidworth in Nottinghamshire. The master archer Gilbert Whitehand only appears in a few literary tales. One version casts him as Will Scarlet's nephew while another portrays him as an older man. I chose the elder Whitehand so that my Robyn would have a teacher.

One character, Deputy Edward Blanchard, is entirely my creation. I figured, what sheriff doesn't have a deputy? I hope you will enjoy getting to know him as you read.

Most of the royals and nobles in "Heart of Sherwood" were real people who actually did and said things I have attributed to them. If I could not come upon a physical description, I created one. There are a few exceptions. Sir Guy of Gisborne is a traditional Robin Hood fixture, but there is no evidence he was a real person. Sir Wilfred of Ivanhoe is a knight created by Sir Walter Scott and I named dropped him in the battle for Nottingham as a touché to the noteworthy author who also included Robin Hood in Ivanhoe's story.

I had a most difficult time trying to ascertain actual names of Prince John's loyal supporters; therefore I invented the three barons: Sir Hugh Diggory, Sir Raoul le Clerc, and Sir Lambelin Bondeville. The propagan-

## AUTHOR'S NOTES

dist, Hugh of Nonant, the Bishop of Coventry, was a real person. And while other clergymen mentioned truly lived in England at the time, the corpulent, licentious Bishop Albrec of Kirkstall is fictional.

For times' sake, I condensed the action of three days of meetings with Emperor Henry IV down to one scene; likewise King Richard actually spent three days dealing with the disloyal barons after the fall of Nottingham Castle. According to some legends, Richard and Robin Hood did not meet in Sherwood Forest until after the battle of Nottingham, but I chose to include an earlier visit to Clipstone Castle than is historically recorded so that Robyn and her gang could be present for the final military climax.

Queen Eleanor of Aquitaine was indeed the most remarkable woman of her time, and I endeavored to portray her indomitable fortitude and powerful personality in this tale. She did patron Sir William Marshall, probably the greatest knight in English history, and many of her precise words and actions, as well as those of Richard the Lionheart, are incorporated. Eleanor engaged in countless exploits beyond those recounted here and I recommend further reading for anyone whose interest has been piqued.

Historians are divided over the issue of King Richard's sexuality as there exist conflicting accounts and a lack of personal information. It is likely that he engaged in sex with both men and women at one time or another, as one illegitimate son is attributed to him, but he spent very little time with his wife and never produced an heir. However, there is no doubt as to the preference of Chancellor and Justiciar William Longchamp; it is a well-known historical fact that the court minister was gay, and yet Richard not only kept him in his post, but placed great trust in him. There is no evidence to prove Richard and his supporter Robert FitzWalter were involved in a sexual relationship; there is also no evidence to deny that possibility, and if nothing else, *Heart of Sherwood* brims with possibilities!

## ABOUT THE AUTHOR

Edale Lane is the pen name used by Melodie Romeo for her LGBTQ literature to differentiate from her more mainstream stories. Melodie is a native of Vicksburg, Mississippi. She earned a bachelor's degree in Music Education from the University of Southern Mississippi and a master's degree in History from the University of West Florida. Ms Romeo is a retired school teacher who currently travels the country as an over the road truck driver with Prime, Inc. Her first book, Vlad, a Novel, (https://www.facebook.com/VladANovel) an historical thriller, was published in 2002. She has short stories published in anthologies by Seventh Star Press, Charon Coin Press, Alban Lake Press, and Less Than Three Press. She has a son, Peter and daughter, Michele who both serve in the US Army, a daughter-in-law, Jessica and two grandsons, Mark and Asher. Melodie resides in Utica, MS with her longtime partner, Johanna. Some of her works can be found at http://www.amazon.com/-/e/B00WFFFEA4.

Melodie is also a musician who plays the French horn, composes, and has spent many years as a choral and instrumental director. She aspires to be a successful enough author to quit driving and devote herself to writing full-time.

http://www.amazon.com/author/edalelane
http://www.amazon.com/author/melodieromeo

Printed in Great Britain
by Amazon